I0824171

That's WHAT Friends are FOR

Also by Wade Rouse

Magic Season

Writing as Viola Shipman

The Page Turner

The Wishing Bridge

Famous in a Small Town

A Wish for Winter

The Edge of Summer

The Secret of Snow

The Clover Girls

The Heirloom Garden

The Summer Cottage

That's WHAT Friends are FOR

WADE ROUSE

MIRA

MIRA™

Recycling programs for this product may not exist in your area.

ISBN-13: 978-1-525-80005-4

That's What Friends Are For

Illustrations: © Monique Aimee (cacti); © the-flying-hellfish/stock.adobe.com (stars)

For questions and comments about the quality of this book, please contact us at CustomerService@Harlequin.com.

MIRA
22 Adelaide St. West, 41st Floor
Toronto, Ontario M5H 4E3, Canada
MIRABooks.com

HarperCollins Publishers
Macken House, 39/40 Mayor Street Upper,
Dublin 1, D01 C9W8, Ireland
www.HarperCollins.com

Printed in U.S.A.

To Doris: Our eternal ray of sunshine.

"I don't know what I would have done in my life if I hadn't had my girlfriends. They have literally gotten me up out of bed, taken my clothes off, put me in the shower, dressed me, said, 'Hey, you can do this,' put my high heels on and pushed me out the door!"

—Reese Witherspoon

Cold Open

"Picture it! Palm Springs, 2026!"

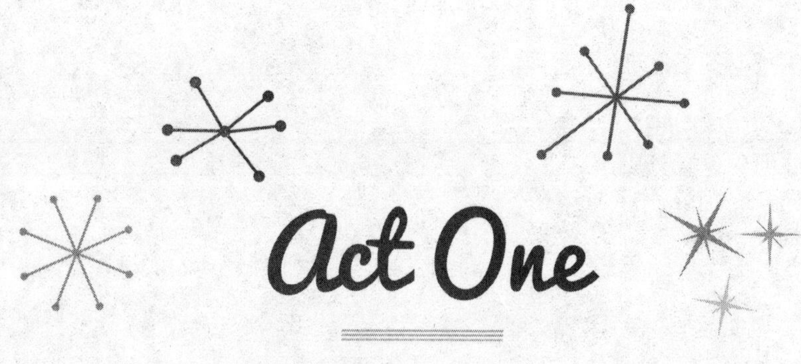

Act One

"Cher was playing, and, of course, I had to sing along because when the queen croons in her signature vibrato, you must join in as a sign of respect . . ."

"What song was she singing?"

I cock my head like the raven eyeing our brunch from atop a palm tree.

If looks could kill, Ron would be face down in the corn soufflé he just whipped up for The Golden Gays.

"It doesn't *matter*, Ron," I say in my deadpan Dorothy Zbornak tone.

"It *does* matter, Teddy," Ron says to me.

Ugh.

Ron has that look in his eyes, the one that—despite all he's been through—still reflects an innocence as beautiful as the cloudless blue sky overhead on this stunning February morning in Palm Springs.

"Was it 'Gypsies, Tramps and Thieves'? 'Dark Lady'? 'If I Could Turn Back Time'? 'The Shoop Shoop Song'?" he continues, face serious. "Each version of Cher is a time capsule of our souls. Each song represents a chapter of our lives."

"He's right, Teddy," Barry says.

Barry leans back and flexes his biceps. I plop another spoonful of soufflé on my plate.

"For once," Sid quips. He is the oldest in our group at eighty-one. Sid is still a cute thing, always dapper like the attorney he once was in crisp slacks and tailored jackets.

I look around the table, one brow raised, giving each of them a withering glance. I pull the brim of my bonnet down over my eyes. It is not to shield my face from the harsh desert sun but a reprimand for their interruption of my story.

"I can't with any of you today," I say.

Ron, Sid and Barry roll their eyes.

"So?" Ron presses. "What Cher song was it, Teddy?"

"It was 'Believe,' okay?"

"Her comeback!" Ron crows, pleased and clapping. He takes a sip of his mimosa. "Continue!"

I take a breath and do so.

"Well, as I was singing, our very young, very pretty server walked over carrying my drink and asked who the artist was. He didn't know Cher!"

I lift my bonnet and look at each of my friends, making sure they are as shocked as I was. Their faces express horror.

"I know! Can you believe it?" I continue. "He didn't recognize that iconic voice! Cher, for God's sake! Well, I was absolutely apoplectic with rage, and it took every ounce of strength I had not to toss my Rose Kennedy in his face!"

"What did you do?" Ron asks, chin in the palm of his hand, riveted.

"I asked him if he were Kimmy Schmidt and had been living in a bunker his whole life," I say. "I told him that I needed to revoke his gay card immediately and send him back to twink school."

The table roars.

The response I was waiting for and deserve.

Finally!

"So?" Barry asks, sipping his protein shake. "What did she do?"

"Well, Mary put her hands on her bony hips, cocked her body at a ninety-degree angle and asked me if I knew Chappell Roan?" I manage to take my first small sip of champagne of the day with a shaky hand. It was a very long night, and I need it to steel myself for the conclusion of this story. "I looked at her and said, 'Of course I do! It's a church in Barcelona.'"

Everyone stares at me, not understanding.

We are old.

Too old to get the joke anymore.

But old enough to be the punch line.

"Chappell Roan is a pop superstar," I explain. "The Cher of 2026. I didn't know just like all of you don't know. The server made sure to school me in front of the entire restaurant. And then he laughed at me—*Me! Teddy!*—and said my drink was on the house as if I were some sort of *fossil*, some poor *pariah*."

"Well, she got one thing right," Barry says. "You are a fossil, you are poor and you are a pariah."

He says "thing" as "thang." Barry's Southern accent comes and goes as quickly as a rainstorm in the desert. He tries so hard to forget his past, but every now and then, the guitar twangs and molasses show up even after decades on the West Coast.

"Shut up and flex, Barry," I say.

He does.

I take a breath and continue. "The only thing I wanted to do was turn back time when I was the young one turning heads, but the only thing I could do was order three more cocktails and leave the restaurant with as much dignity as I could muster." I stare at each of them. "We are old."

"We are mature," Ron amends. "Blessedly late middle-age."

"You expect to live to a hundred and forty?" I ask.

"Speak for yourself," Barry says. "I'm not old."

"You're wearing a Nehru jacket in your Grindr profile picture," I reply.

"I'm at an age when my back goes out more than I do," Barry says, trying to be funny.

"And you're quoting Phyllis Diller, so point proven."

I take another sip of champagne with a trembling hand.

"So that's why you're so shaky this morning," Ron says, ever the mother. "I'll make you my special hangover tonic later."

"And to think I thought you were detoxing for once by the look of your hands," Barry says. He stretches toward the sun. His skin does not crepe. I always look like I'm wearing chiffon.

"I'm still shaking from simmering rage," I say, my head high. "Which is directed at all of you right now for being so disrespectful."

"You know you love us," Barry says with a wink. "You really do care somewhere underneath that cold, dead exterior."

I tip my bonnet adorned with bouncing hearts in agreement with his assessment.

Welcome, dear parishioners, to "The Church of Mary."

For the last decade, God and gays have gathered around the pool at our mid-century marvel—the former, and still very pink, home of Zsa Zsa Gabor—to take communion and build community by breaking bread, drinking wine and spilling tea after a weekend of debauchery in the desert.

It's our way of seeking forgiveness.

Which we rarely receive from one another.

The name of our church is a sincere but sarcastic nod to Mary, the only virgin we know—besides maybe Sid—as well as all the "Marys" in our lives. It's also an homage to the conflict of growing up gay and Christian. If you do not know, gay men often call one another "Mary" when we see each other. Historically, it was a slur that we reclaimed as a term of affection. Believe me, Marys have always had their doubters.

(It should be stated for the record that the vote to name our gathering "The Church of Mary" was 2–1–1. Ron and I voted yes, and Sid—who is Jewish—voted no, arguing, "She's just another nice Jewish mother of a nice Jewish son!", while Barry—our agnostic—abstained. To me, this serves as a microcosm of

American politics, where the slimmest of majorities hold on to power, usually as a result of voter apathy.)

We are four gay men of a certain age who years ago became the unlikeliest of friends. We started out as acquaintances before joining forces to stage a monthly performance at the local community theater entitled *The Golden Gays*, a spoof of the still-popular 1980s TV comedy, *The Golden Girls*, in which we play the different characters: I am Dorothy, Ron plays Rose, Barry is Blanche and Sid is Sophia. Each of us is essentially the real-life version of the TV character.

Ironically, over time, the show became more catharsis than spoof for us.

And then an idea hit us one night after a show like an earthquake.

Okay, it really was an earthquake: a 5.2 reality rattler that not only damaged my business but also revealed that I was living in a historic building in the Uptown Design District that had never been deemed mixed-use, would cost a fortune to repair and was filled with as many painful memories of my husband, John, as it was with vintage clothing. I had sketchy insurance, no savings and nowhere to go. I finally realized in my late fifties that rooms filled with coiffed wigs, costume jewelry and fabulous caftans did not a retirement portfolio make.

I needed a home, Sid needed companionship, Barry needed to grow up and Ron needed a family to dote on.

That is why every Sunday—despite my histrionics—I truly thank God for my friends.

I glance at our home, Zsa Zsa.

If not for these boys, I would likely be renting an apartment with a drunken drag queen and working the night shift at Ralphs.

So we pooled our resources—some more than others, thank you very much—and Ron found us this pink palace we now call home.

Historically, the gay community has flocked together in order to protect ourselves from a world that has tried to harm us. We have done it in certain cities, neighborhoods, bars, beaches. We watch out for one another. We have each other's backs. It is communal. It is safe. It is a tribe unlike any other. The Golden Gays have made that a reality in our home.

We four lost souls made a pact after a lifetime of loss, pain, humiliation and heartbreak—after losing our parents and most of our relatives to death or disownment—to live together and care for one another, just like the women we watched in our youth and now play in our golden years, in a fabulous midcentury modern home in Palm Springs that we could never afford on our own.

The faces of my friends glow as pink as our painted house in the morning sun.

We're approaching Valentine's Day and Modernism Week in Palm Springs, the two times of year in the desert that aging, single gays dread more than (1) Coachella, with its Kardashian wannabes swarming our town in daisy headbands, and (2) an eternal summer that's like living in an air fryer.

"I love your bonnet," Barry says to me. I nod my head to bounce the hearts dangling from it.

"Oh, I could write a sonnet about my Valentine's Day bonnet," I sing, changing the lyrics of the famed Easter song.

"Do you like my hat?" Barry asks when I finish.

"To be accurate," Sid—ever the attorney—interrupts, "that's not a hat. It's a fascinator."

"And Lord knows you need it to be fascinating," I add.

"Touché," Barry says, standing, striking a pose to show off his cropped sweater that features a bear on the front and shows off his too-tan six-pack. "Less is more, ladies."

"I do love that sweater," I say. "Does it come in men's?"

Barry bows at my quick wit.

Barry is an actor who appreciates a great line. He actually has a more impressive body than body of work. He is infamous for a starring role that no one ever saw. Barry's career has seen a resurgence of late, thanks to our little show. And by resurgence, I mean he does gigs for local restaurants and hearing aid companies.

"Everything *old* is new again," I always tell him to keep him grounded. "Just give it time. You'll eventually come back in style like women with Farrah hair and men with moustaches."

Barry is sixty-five and goes to the gym seven days a week. His muscles have muscles. His hair is cropped short and dyed black to match his ever-present five-o'clock shadow. He is what gays my age call a "bear" and what the young gays call a "daddy." I just call him an old queen.

Barry is the living, breathing embodiment of the name of the vintage clothing store I own, Dorian Gay. Fashion, like Barry, will remain eternally young, even if both of them are beginning to show a little wear.

"Someone obviously brushed his teeth and sharpened his tongue this morning," Sid says to me.

I laugh and tip my glass of champagne.

"You know how much this Dorothy adores Dorothy Parker."

Sid takes off his pink bonnet—the same shade as our house—and fans himself.

"You're welcome," he says.

"Can we start our brunch now?" I ask. "I have to eat an hour after I take my meds."

I begin to reach for the sausage-and-egg casserole Ron made. It's fabulous, like biscuits and gravy in a baking dish. You'd think the fancy Le Creuset Sauteuse it was made in would reject the spicy Jimmy Dean sausage and cans of condensed soup like a bad kidney. It's a recipe from Ron's mom. We all loved and respected our mothers—more than most of them ever loved and respected their boys—and still do to this day. It's like making their favorite dishes is a way to understand and forgive.

Recipe repentance.

Ron slaps my hand. Our routine never changes.

"Ouch!" I say.

"We haven't prayed yet."

Ron is wearing a proper, respectful church bonnet—in black, without showy flowers.

Yes, we wear bonnets to the Church of Mary every Sunday, based on theme, season or holiday.

I mean, who do you think we are? We were raised right. Mostly Midwestern and Southern boys who went to church and Sunday school every week with our mamas and grandmas.

Plus, it doesn't hurt that Dorian Gay is one of the most popular vintage mid-century resale clothing stores in the desert. I can pluck the best bonnets for my family.

"Let us pray," Ron says. "Dear Lord, thank you for having us gather here on this glorious Sunday. We thank you for the sustenance of this food and this friendship. As I was hiking the other day, I realized that we all seek a way to be better people. We all seek to ascend."

I open my eyes and take in the breathtaking San Jacinto Mountains that surround us.

"Which is why the four of us go to church every Sunday," Ron continues. "We strive to live at a higher level . . ."

Barry titters.

"Ssssh!" Ron reprimands before continuing. "We strive to be worthy of you."

Ron has faith as high and majestic as these mountains. I glance at him as he prays. My mother told me before she died that it's easy for those who have never been tested to have faith.

"When you feel like you've lost everything and have nowhere to turn, that's when true faith comes to call."

Ron has true faith. I think my telephone has been ringing my whole life, and I just don't want to answer.

"Close your eyes please, Teddy," Ron says, catching me staring at him.

Ron is now an esteemed interior designer who grew up on a farm in a town of five hundred people. He wasn't allowed to watch TV or listen to music, so he watched thunderstorms roll in from the horizon for entertainment and listened to the purple martins sing at night. His father was a pastor at the country church. He preached fire and brimstone, and he tried to beat the sin out of his little boy, but the holy spirit still burns in sweet little Ronny, a pint-sized man with a mass of coiffed white hair that looks like cotton candy. You can actually see the sun through it. It looks just like his mama's hairdo in old Polaroids.

"Dear Lord, thank you for our blessings and for allowing us to join together again in your outdoor church." Ron takes a breath. "As I was shucking the corn today to make mama's casserole . . ."

We release a collective groan at the meandering prayer of our Rose Nylund.

"Forgive them, Lord," Ron continues undeterred. "Anyway, I was reminded of what she taught me growing up: that each strand of silk on an ear of sweet corn represents a single kernel of corn on the cob. One silk for every kernel. Lord, we all know the world tries to rip those special strands from our souls until we appear nekked, but let us remember today that you gave us those strands, and even if just one silk remains, it holds on to remind us of the person that you created, the unique soul that still remains. This tiny, soft thread ties us to our pasts and our futures. In God's name we pray, amen!"

"Amen."

Ron squeezes my hand hard.

"Ouch," I say. "Amen."

Ron looks at me and nods his head because he knows I need this affirmation more than anyone else.

He squeezes again, even harder, and I finally squeeze back. Ron smiles, pleased, and releases.

"Now we can eat," he says. "Bon appétit!"

We dig in, going around the table sharing stories of our weekend and talking over the next show.

"I have an announcement," Barry says.

Ron has made Barry his own special Sunday brunch: no fatty, salty casseroles but rather a protein shake, plate of fresh fruit and three grilled chicken breasts with steamed broccoli.

I should hate Barry, but he's the only man left who can still score us free drinks.

Barry pulls out his cell and holds up a photo of a young man about the age of my rude server who resembles Patrick Schwarzenegger.

"Don't you already eat enough chicken?" I ask.

"His name is Colton . . ."

We again groan collectively.

". . . and he's very sweet."

I act as if I'm gagging.

"He's pursuing *me*, if you must know," Barry continues undaunted.

I roll my eyes. I actually didn't realize they could go that far back in my head.

"Spare me," I say.

Barry taps on his cell for a second and then holds it up again for us to see. A stream of texts—accompanied by a number of photos that would make the lemons in our trees turn red—goes on forever.

"Where did you meet Colton?" Sid asks.

"Oh, let me guess?" I add. "A dating app? How original."

"No, it was very old-fashioned," Barry says. "A real meet-cute. It was my chest day at the gym, and he asked if he could work in."

"You're right. That is so old-fashioned," I say. "In fact, I think I saw that same scene in a movie at a bathhouse once."

"Stop it!" Barry says, his voice rising suddenly. "He really is nice. Sweet as a date shake. He has his degree in theater . . ."

We all groan even louder.

". . . and," Barry continues unthwarted, "he wants to be an actor."

This time, we pull off our bonnets and sling them at his face.

"He saw our show," Barry says. "He loved it. He says he has some ideas. Oh, he's calling! I'll be right back!"

Barry leaps from his chair and walks to a chaise by the pool, where he takes a seat under a yellow-and-white-striped umbrella with fringe.

"Is he *giggling*?" Sid asks.

"Maybe it is love," Ron says with his forever-sunny demeanor.

"Right," I say. "You know what Dorothy would say right now? 'When a twenty-two-year-old girl marries a man who's eighty, chances are she is not after his body,'" I say, before adding, "'Even his.'"

"Eat, eat," Ron says. "It's getting cold, and I cooked all morning."

I watch Barry as I eat. He's sitting cross-legged like a schoolgirl on the chaise, leaning forward, holding the phone so tightly it looks as if it might break, his free hand drawing a heart on the orange Sunbrella fabric.

Am I jealous? A little.

Am I worried? A lot.

This is my family. The one I chose. The one who chose me.

A chosen unit so we wouldn't be alone.

But how much time do we all have left? Not just on this earth but with one another?

We made a pact. We went through hell to get here. All it takes is the smallest quake in the desert to tear it all apart.

The table vibrates.

I jump.

"It's not an earthquake, Teddy, it's your phone," Ron says.

I look down at my cell humming on the table.

Caller ID reads: She Who Has No Name

My sister, Trudy.

Whom I haven't spoken to in decades. She's left messages for me over the years—*I had a grandchild! I had heart surgery! My husband retired!*—that I have never returned. She wants me to forgive and forget. I want to make her pay forever.

"Who is it?" Sid asks. "And pass the corn casserole, please."

"Chappell Roan," I say.

Why would Trudy be calling me this time? Hasn't she already blamed me for everything wrong in her life? Everything wrong I did to make our parents miserable? Everything wrong in the world? What hateful words are possibly left in her vocabulary?

Cher may be queen, but my sister proudly suffers wearing her crown of thorns.

My cell vibrates again.

I turn my phone upside down on the table.

When it stops, I pick up the cell and hold it to my ear.

The mere sound of her voicemail makes me knock back my glass of champagne and grab the bottle for round two.

"Theodore? It's Trudy. Your sister. Remember me? We need to talk. It's an emergency. Call me."

In the background, I hear names being called over an intercom. She must be eating somewhere fancy after church, like Applebee's or Olive Garden.

I set my phone down and take a bite of corn casserole.

Trudy is the last silk on my dried-out cob of a soul. And I ripped her out of my life a long time ago and boiled myself until I could no longer feel any pain.

You see, when you've been not simply hurt but gutted like a fish, when you've lost everything and everyone you believed would keep you safe, when you forged a life without family, when you have been to hell and back and realized the devil does not reside there but sits in your kitchen, living room, church and school, when you have put a knife to your wrist and were found by your sister, who bandaged you up and said, "Just wear long sleeves for a while," when you have called home at Christmas praying for a miracle only to hear your father and sister say in the background, "Hang up, Mom! Teddy's dead!" well, honey, you are not only forced to take chances you never would have taken, but—somewhere along the way—you die and are reborn as the person you dreamed of becoming even when you didn't think it was possible.

"Is everything okay?" Ron asks.

He has the instinctual empathy of your favorite dog.

I sip my champagne and nod as Barry returns to the table.

"I'm good," I say.

I am lying.

Bad things are happening.

Really bad things.

I, my dears, am dying.

My starring role is soon to be over. My sitcom is being canceled.

But I'm the only who knows. There's no reason to reveal the finale to the cast yet. It would only spoil our last season together.

I will not burden my friends with my health issues during what are supposed to be the carefree years of their lives. I'm a year away from Medicare, and my wonky insurance wouldn't cover all my costs. I do not have an IRA to cash in to help with medical bills. I have bonnets and baubles.

What if they had to sell this house because of me?

I cannot—*no, I will not!*—burden them with my struggles.

And that's okay. Truly it is.

To be honest, I died a long time ago. When John passed away. We were one soul, and that rarely happens in this life. I was given the greatest gift, and I will leave this world forever grateful for that.

My friends laugh.

I wish they understood that happy endings only take place on old sitcoms where a snappy one-liner, a laugh track, a glass of Bartles & Jaymes and a platter of pizza rolls could erase all your troubles, if for only a half hour. As my waiter made abundantly clear, we are old. Our calendars are stamped with an end date. I just happen to know mine will come a little sooner than theirs.

Ron eyes me closely. He is suspicious. I must lie again.

"To the Church of Mary!" I suddenly say, holding up my glass.

"To family!" The Golden Gays yell.

"Alexa!" I command our outdoor speaker. "Play Cher!"

I cannot help but smile at Alexa's choice. That AI vixen is an even bigger bitch than I am.

"Do you believe in life after love?" Cher asks, singing "Believe."

I have not watched a sitcom on TV in over forty years.

Not a single *Seinfeld*, *Cheers*, *The Office*, *Big Bang Theory*. Not one episode of *Friends*, my friends.

That's because I bet you never knew that in the pilot episode of *The Golden Girls*, there was a gay character named Coco, the ladies' housekeeper and cook.

He was supposed to be one of the leads, alongside Dorothy, Rose and Blanche.

Estelle Getty, who famously played Dorothy's mother, Sophia, was originally just a guest star. She was to appear on occasion but never be a series regular.

That role was Coco's.

But everything changed when the pilot was shown to test audiences. Sophia was such a hit with viewers that she was promoted to a full-time cast member. The audience adored Sophia's mix of withering one-liners, honesty and maternal tenderness.

But perhaps, in retrospect, they were a bit too scared to say they did not like the out gay character, who—at the time—was a rarity on TV save for, say, Jodie Dallas on *Soap*, played by Billy Crystal.

Instead, producers blamed the kitchen.

If you ever watched the show, you know that the kitchen was the center of the women's universe in Florida.

It was pure '80s grandmotherly glory with its laminate countertops, builder-grade cabinets, peel-and-stick tile, neutral tones, copper molds *everywhere*, vintage Italian ceramic vegetables on a jute rope, a rolling island (probably from Pier 1), café curtains and the famed faux bamboo dinette set that included . . .

. . . only *three* chairs.

If you don't know anything about television, set design or blocking, here's a short lesson: Blocking is a collaborative but carefully choreographed plan between a director and actors for the physical movement that occurs during a performance. *The Golden Girls* was taped before a live studio audience. This means—as with the live theater I produce with my friends—that an actor cannot be seated with his or her back to the audience. Thus, there can only be three chairs so those seated can be seen by the audience. Bea Arthur—the tallest and the one whose facial reactions to her castmates' conversations were TV gold—was always seated in the middle. The others rotated, with the fourth member always standing nearby or entering/exiting the kitchen.

All of which meant that a fifth cast member clogged the kitchen.

Coco was cut.

And no one ever knew he was missing.

Except the young actor who portrayed him.

He went on to audition for hundreds of roles, big and small, for TV and film. He auditioned for thousands of commercials. He auditioned for infomercials. He auditioned for walk-on roles and spots as corpses on crime shows, but his career ended before it even started.

As an out gay actor during a time in Hollywood that didn't embrace such honesty, either he was considered a bad omen for being cast out of a successful sitcom, or he would open his mouth to utter a few words and immediately be typecast in the minds of casting agents as a gay man in an industry where gay roles didn't yet exist.

His entire life became an endless reel of, "Thank you! NEXT!"

As a result, Coco went loco.

He—quite literally—turned the tables on all those who turned him down.

Professionally, that is.

Hollywood's rich "straight" men—producers, directors, actors, screenwriters—who always said "No!" to Coco during an audition in the light of day were the ones who always said "Yes!" to Coco at night.

So Coco took names.

And pictures. Along with some grainy video.

He was paid quite nicely, ironically, as an actor to not say a word but rather to keep his mouth shut and disappear.

Then Coco—like so many stars before him—slinked into the desert, where he could live behind a hedge and sunglasses in a cloak of anonymity, warm days and cold cocktails merging into one, a place where young men were looking for older men to take care of them, and where Coco could continue to see himself as he once was—young, unlined, innocent, filled with hope—in the faces of the men he devoured at night like a vampire.

And then one summer day many years later—quite by accident—Coco got a second chance to start over with (ah, the irony!) two new men "of a certain age": his therapist, Dr. Doolan, and one of Dr. Doolan's clients.

Hold your horses here: It might have been hot (temperature wise), but it wasn't *hot*.

On a sweltering Tuesday, Coco arrived on time for his appointment, but the door to Dr. Doolan's office—a bougainvillea-drenched casita overlooking a pool and a low-slung 1930s

Spanish home with a terra-cotta roof—remained closed. Coco took refuge in the shade. While he waited, he heard a deep, dramatic, sarcastic voice booming inside the casita—a voice that sounded so familiar and yet so triggering—and he sneaked to the door and put his ear to it.

Is that, Coco thought, the voice of my former costar, Bea Arthur?

Did the cosmos conspire to bring us together again?

Was the nasty Hollywood gossip true? Was Bea a lesbian who found her way here to the scorching heat of the desert to melt away her facade and find her truth like me? I mean, she had taken up the cause of LGBTQ+ youth homelessness of late and been an outspoken advocate.

The door suddenly opened, and Coco stumbled inside. He had not made such a hammy pratfall entrance since he was cast as a Cylon robot on *Battlestar Galactica* and was killed in the show's opening, falling through the entrance of a spaceship.

A very tall figure simply stepped over his body and—as the shadow exited the casita—turned and said, "You're one chromosome away from being a potato. Grow up! I'm not that interesting!" The figure stopped. "Actually, I am."

Coco looked up. It was a man who looked and sounded much like Dorothy Zbornak.

As he walked away, he said, "I'm Teddy, and, yes, *Coco*, I've seen every episode of *The Golden Girls*. And if you were that bad an actor, I can see why they cut you."

At our meeting that day, after I talked about Teddy's resemblance to Bea, Dr. Doolan told me I suffered from Peter Pan syndrome.

"You are an adult who—like so many gay men—are trapped in childhood," he said. "You have difficulty growing up and taking on adult responsibilities because you never got the childhood acceptance or experienced firsts—first date, first kiss, first love—that everyone else did. Now you want it back, and you become trapped in a fantasy world—even for a few moments—that is not real."

Dr. Doolan offered an idea: "What if you staged a performance of the show that ruined your life as a way to deal with your long-term anger and depression over losing a career-defining role? A way to, essentially, grow the hell up once and for all and perhaps meet some nice men your age who could become the friends and role models you desperately need?"

Coco held auditions, and the three men he finally selected—Ron, Teddy and Sid—were ones he had met over the years. No one he had ever slept with—or wanted to, for that matter—so it seemed like the start of a perfect career and life remake.

But the show—like his career—didn't get much attention or make much money. They staged it once a month at a local community theater, the men kicking in the money to keep it going.

And then, at the height of COVID, *The Golden Girls* was reborn. The show was streamed for some eleven million hours, making it as popular today as it was when it originally aired. It became a way for younger people to connect with their grandparents and a way for the LGBTQ+ community to connect with their aging parents and start a discussion about who they really were and are.

People started coming to the show.

As the only surviving member of the show, Coco began to work again.

It took only forty years.

Coco began to travel to 1980s sitcom fan festivals across the country and tour assisted living facilities, signing—for ten bucks a pop—the one and only cast photo he ever appeared in with Bea Arthur, Betty White, Rue McClanahan and Estelle Getty before being excised from it forever.

If you want to know one thing about gay men, they're survivors.

The screenwriter of *The Golden Girls* did an interview with

People not long ago stating that it was "smart" to axe Coco, but he wished they'd had a concluding arc for his character at some point.

"I wish they had dealt with Coco, or had him back for a special episode," he said. "Maybe he fell in love . . . Maybe he opened a B&B in Key West."

But I don't need a screenwriter to tell you how it turned out for Coco.

Coco never fell in love, but he did become best friends with the men from their show, *The Golden Gays*—including Teddy from Dr. Doolan's office who would become Dorothy—and they all moved into a fabulous mid-century modern house together just like the gals they portrayed.

How do I know?

I am Coco.

And I still hate being in a kitchen with a bunch of old queens.

"On your left!"

"Hot Jew alert!" Esther says as a very fit man in shorts and a tank top overtakes us on the track.

"Where did he come from?" I ask. "It's like we're standing still."

"He's fast," Esther says. "And he's new! Oh! And look at that tight tuchus!"

"You're yelling!"

"You're single!"

"You're meshuga!"

"Proudly!" Esther says, lifting her tiny arms over her tinier body.

Every Monday, Wednesday and Friday during the winter, I walk exactly two miles on the outdoor track with Esther Himmelbaum at the Wasserman Senior Center. When it gets too hot come May, we move to the inside track. Every Tuesday and Thursday, Esther and I do a seated workout class.

Yes, we're older than Methuselah.

Besides The Golden Gays, Esther is my BFF, my wing woman. It only makes sense I would befriend a woman who embodies the unbridled honesty and sarcasm of Sophia, the character I play in our show. I, on the other hand, embody Sophia's feebleness and inability to edit anything that leaves my mouth, especially when I'm nervous.

"Fresh meat!" Esther says in what she thinks is a whisper but sounds like a garbage truck at five in the morning. "You should talk to him when he laps us again. Or trip him. That might be the only way you can catch him."

"Especially when he sees my face."

"Sha!" Esther scolds me. "You are a handsome man. Regal. Do you want me to fix you up with him?"

I stop on the track and grab my friend's arm. She is the size of a footstool. She jerks to a halt.

"No!" I say. "Do you hear me? I cannot be humiliated again in this life."

"And yet you chose to wear that eggplant-colored blouse today," Esther says, staring at me.

"You told me to buy this!" I say. "And it's a workout shirt."

"You've been lost style-wise ever since Stein Mart closed," she says. "And give me a break: I'm eighty-seven. I can have an off day. Or year."

Esther fancies herself a shadchanit. She said she came from a long line of Jewish matchmakers in New York City. She didn't. Her father owned dry cleaning stores all over Manhattan, and her success rate in fixing me up has always been more Mets than Yankees.

I met Esther at Temple Isaiah when I retired to Palm Springs. I was depressed and lonely at Passover after moving from Chicago, mourning a faith and family that would no longer have me, and Esther parked herself next to me at synagogue services and asked, "Single? Gay? You must come to Seder at my house!"

Passover commemorates the Hebrews' liberation from slavery in Egypt and the "passing over" of the forces of destruction and the sparing of the firstborn of the Israelites.

That Passover, I felt as if had been passed over by everyone I loved.

I had not been spared.

Esther stuffed me with gefilte fish, matzo ball soup, brisket, potato kugel and tzimmes. More importantly, she filled me with what I needed most: acceptance.

I came out at the age of sixty after thirty-five years of marriage and three children. It was just as the gay marriage ban was gaining momentum across the United States. My sexuality was categorically forbidden by the Torah.

I divorced my wife, Rebecca, who promptly played the victim in our community and temple, though she was not without sin herself.

My kids hated me for hurting her and ruining our happy family.

But we weren't ever happy. We only played happy on TV.

We were "don't ask, don't tell" before Bill Clinton ever uttered the words.

Rebecca knew the truth and kept her mouth shut just as much as I did.

She found the phone numbers from Tim R. and Steve J. in my suit pockets before cell phones existed.

I found all the hotel receipts on her credit card for her girls' weekends *without* the girls.

We lay in silence beside each other in bed without ever uttering our truths.

Yes, I was a coward. Yes, I was to blame for fooling her when I knew I was gay even as I was courting her. Yes, I robbed her of having a man who wanted her. But I also gave her everything she wanted: a beautiful home. A beautiful family. A beautiful life.

And I was not solely to blame.

Rebecca cheated before I did. Sadly, my discovery of that emboldened me.

From the outside, we seemed the perfect family, but there is no perfect family. There is only a photo of smiling faces perched on a mantel or office desk that people see, never the imperfect outtakes that came before that solitary image.

The law firm I had been with since the start of my career, the one in which I had become a partner, offered to buy me out. I was suddenly bad for business.

So I ran to the only place I knew where old gay men retired: Palm Springs, California.

Heaven's Waiting Room.

At Esther's Seder, I met Teddy, Ron and Barry, none of whom was Jewish but all of whom were as kooky as Esther. But welcome to Palm Springs where, I quickly learned, any event—religious or otherwise—is viewed as one of three things: a party, a business meeting or a pickup joint.

Teddy was there with his sweet husband, John, who looked like a human version of a basset hound, big ears, brown hair and eyes that could melt you with their puppy dog cuteness. They owned a vintage clothing shop together. Teddy saw Seder as a party and was holding court in the living room of Esther's stunning home in The Movie Colony, spilling tea (and occasionally his cocktail), a huge throng of people gathered around him laughing at his stories and cutting wit.

Ron was a designer who had done work on Esther's 1930s home. He had studied under the disciples of Palm Springs legends like Arthur Elrod, Hal Broderick and William Raiser—a trio he would teach me was responsible for designing the interiors of most of the iconic mid-century homes in the desert built by famed architects like Albert Frey, Donald Wexler and Hugh Kaptur.

"Esther originally wanted an iconic mid-century home," Ron told me, "but when she showed me this, I saw its beauty, the nod to mid-century design and to Spanish architecture. I told her the same thing my grandma used to tell my mama: 'A little powder, a little paint, makes a lady what she ain't.' All this grande dame needed was a touch-up, not a facelift."

Ron was smart, talented and goofily sweet, and he sparked my love of design that day discussing Spanish Revival and mid-century architecture, slump stone, clerestory windows, breeze block, and post and beam.

Ron loved an open house, it turns out, because he considered it a business meeting. He could charm guests with his knowledge of all things Palm Springs, which might lead to a new client.

"Turns out Esther's storied neighborhood is filled with Hollywood ghosts," he told a group of potential clients, "including Jack Benny, Cary Grant and Dinah Shore, many of whom left openings in their garden walls so they could carry their cocktails to the next house during parties and occasionally, you know, have a little fun."

"Have we met?"

Which is why Barry was there.

Before I could turn, a muscled arm had slipped around my back, and a hand holding a mid-century coupe filled with amber liquid appeared before my face.

"I'm Barry. And you are?"

When I turned, Barry recoiled.

"You're . . ."

He didn't have to finish the sentence. Barry might as well have just screamed "OLD!" and tossed the drink in my face.

"Barry," Ron said, his tone a warning. "This is Sid. He's new in town."

Barry, I quickly learned, was a "chicken hawk": a gay man of a certain age who liked (much) younger men. Barry wasn't old by any means at that time, but he saw himself twenty years younger and preferred men twenty years younger than that. He was at Esther's Seder to feed on new meat at the buffet table. He was, of course, an actor.

It seemed every other person I met—waiter, bartender, roofer—was a wannabe actor who had come to LA seeking fame but just wasn't quite as pretty or talented as the next guy. So they disappeared to the desert seeking a second chance and maybe a man with money.

The fact that so many had purposely chosen Palm Springs as their home made me feel at home. People were here for a reason. That made this town special.

There was no Google at the time, so I couldn't dash into the kitchen to search for Barry on IMDb, but I did hear from others at that surreptitious Seder about Barry's infamous career.

As I watched Barry stalk the room, I recalled a short story I had just read, a piece by F. Scott Fitzgerald called "The Curious Case of Benjamin Button" about a man who ages in reverse. Should there ever be a movie made from this, I thought, Barry would be perfectly cast.

I actually walked out of that Seder not thinking I would ever be friends with Barry, Ron and Teddy. They were outspoken, confident and wholly comfortable being gay. They had experienced the thrill of kissing a guy they liked under a starry sky. They had gotten butterflies before going out on a date. They had lived their lives on their own terms.

I thought they had the perfect lives until I actually got to know them.

No one does, I realized. We are all passed over in some way. We must face a lifetime of plagues until we are freed.

The only thing I had done was hide, like I used to do with the afikomen at Passover Seder.

Who knew I would be the missing rya rug needed to pull their mid-century room together?

The man with the tight tuchus begins to lap us again, and Esther sticks out her leg.

"Damn it," Esther says. "I missed him."

"Your leg is shorter than a ruler," I say. "Look at him go. I feel like we aren't even moving."

"We're moving as best we can for two old Jews with three new hips between us," she says. Esther slaps me on my behind. "And we need to keep moving if you don't want him to lap us again. That would be so embarrassing for you."

We finish, out of breath, and take a seat on the stands that ring the track.

Esther and I pretend not to ogle the man as he exercises, but her decibel level is the equivalent of blowing an air horn.

When the Hot Jew finishes, he walks over to the water fountain near us and takes a long drink. He suddenly rips off his tank top, tucks it into the back of his shorts and proceeds to splash himself with water.

"I think I'm going to pass out," I whisper to Esther.

"I haven't seen anything this hot since I threw my panties at Tom Jones in Vegas." Esther grabs my leg. "Give me your panties, Barry. I can't throw my Depends."

We cover our mouths and laugh.

When we look up again, the man walks toward us and begins to stretch.

He is tan and fit. A fountain of thick hair falls in his face as he bends.

"He doesn't even schvitz," I whisper. "He shimmers."

"Go talk to him," Esther says. "Ask him out."

"Do you have eyes?" I ask, hand covering my mouth, as if the man might be able to lip-read. "He's out of my league. I mean, there isn't even a league." I glance quickly at him and lower my voice even more. "I mean, he can touch the ground and get back up without a medevac."

Esther giggles in her throaty way, as if she's just smoked a pack of Pall Malls.

"Stop it!" she says. "You know nothing about him."

"He may not even be gay," I add.

"No man that pretty is straight in Palm Springs."

"He may not even be Jewish."

"Really, Sid?" Esther says. "You're going to be picky at eighty-one? You need to get laid before you die. You already have three husbands at home."

"And what exactly is my pickup line to a man who looks like that?" I ask. "'I see we have so much in common! You have plantar fasciitis, too?'"

"Stop it," she says, taking a big drink from her water bottle.

"Or what about, 'Didn't I see you at PT?'" I ask. "Oh, and this always turns the boys on: 'New knee?'"

Esther spits like a geyser, her water spraying onto the man's leg.

"Consider it a mikvah," she yells.

The man laughs.

"This is Sid," Esther continues. "He's nice. He's Jewish. Attorney. Single. Very successful. Very lonely." Esther stands and claps her hands together. "My work here is done."

I feel my eyes grow absurdly large and my face turn the color of borscht. I look at the man and smile as if to say, *I don't know her.*

Esther heads toward the parking lot just beyond the track. "I'm meeting Talia Goldfarb at Sherman's for lunch. I've earned a pastrami on rye. Go get laid, Sid!"

I want to crawl under the bleachers.

The man watches all five feet of Esther crawl into her mammoth Mercedes SUV, pull on a pair of sunglasses that engulfs her head and pull onto busy Sunrise Way without slowing to look for oncoming traffic.

"She reminds me of my bubbe," the man finally says. He walks over and extends his hand. "I'm Leo. Leo Levy."

"How alliterative."

Why did I say that? I'm an idiot.

Leo laughs.

I shake his hand. "Sid," I say.

"I gathered that from your friend. Do you have a last name, Sid?"

"Silverstein. Sid Silverstein."

"How alliterative."

Is he making fun of me? Flirting? Why am I staring at his chest? Why does he have that sexy little trail of hair? And that cute cluster of freckles off to the side of his six-pack that looks like the Milky Way?

Stop it, Sid. You're an eighty-one-year-old man.

"Are you new to Palm Springs?" I ask. "I haven't seen you around here."

"I'm staying with friends," Leo says. "And looking at houses in the area." He stops. "Actually, I'm interviewing for a job in the area. Don't know if I'll get it, but . . ."

"What is it you do?"

"I'd rather not say. Don't want to jinx it."

He hates me.

And he's still working. Not even close to using the words IRA or Medicare Part B in every other sentence.

"And you?" Leo asks.

"I was a lawyer." I stop to correct myself. "Am a lawyer. I still practice." I stop again. "And Esther already told you that, so I'm just repeating myself now."

"How long have you lived in Palm Springs?"

"A very long time now," I say.

Leo looks at me, waiting for more.

Say something else, Sid.

I try to open my mouth, but it's rusted shut.

For a moment, there is that uncomfortable silence that has always filled me with guilt, made me feel unworthy, wholly transparent. I fidget with the sleeve of my ridiculous workout shirt, which, by the way, Esther said looked good with my hair.

I resemble an aged aubergine.

"You should definitely look in south Palm Springs," I finally add, my voice tinged with nerves as if I'm speaking into a box fan. "No wind. Twin Palms is centrally located and filled with mid-century beauties. Oh! And there's The Movie Colony, Old Las Palmas, Deepwell Estates . . ."

I realize I am babbling, but I cannot stop now. My mouth, like Sophia's, is a runaway train.

"And make sure to eat at Copley's or Eight4Nine. Copley's is a must. It is Cary Grant's former guesthouse. So romantic. I mean, I don't know if you're seeing someone . . ."

A resounding honk pierces the humidity-free air. In the parking lot, a hand motions.

"I gotta go," Leo says apologetically. "Jack dropped me off here while he ran errands."

Of course, there's a Jack.

"It was nice to meet you, Sid," Leo continues, extending his hand once more. "Maybe I'll see you around."

"I'm here every Monday, Wednesday and Friday. Oh, and a seated workout class every Tuesday and Thursday. But I stand for much of the class. I mean, I can stand. You saw me walk!"

Oy vey! I sound like a complete idiot.

Leo takes off jogging, his perfect torso glistening in the sun.

"And wear sunscreen!" I yell. "I think you might have a suspicious mole!"

He doesn't turn back and still I stand there, smiling and waving, as if my grandchildren were pulling out of the driveway. It's better than weeping into my hideously colored cover-up.

As the car leaves, I hear the popular Palm Springs radio station K-Gay blast from the windows.

I stand motionless, watching Leo fade into the mountain. My cell hums.

How did it go with Hot Jew? Did you blow it?

Esther has wasted no time.

What I want to text is:

I'm an old man, and nothing has changed.

My wife has remarried. My kids have children. Yes, I have dear friends, but I also still have my old BFFs, Guilt and Shame. I can dish out advice and pearls of wisdom like your favorite bubbe, but what gay Jewish man wants to date his grandmother? I am exactly the same as that day long ago when I went to Seder at your house. Utterly, completely alone.

Instead, I reply to Esther:

Yes, I blew it. I told him he had a suspicious mole.

I watch the bubbles dance on my cell. I brace myself. I know this is going to be good.

You just made me spit out my decaf. I can't leave you alone with a man. Every time I do, you turn into Albert Brooks from Broadcast News. Come to Sherman's. I'm ordering you a slice of cheesecake the size of Talia's new ring to bury the pain.

More bubbles. Esther sums up my thoughts exactly:

I miss Hot Jew already.

When you're alone and life is making you lonely . . .

I wake up every morning at 6:00 a.m. sharp to my favorite song, "Downtown" by Petula Clark.

I lie in bed, listening to the lyrics, coming awake along with the desert.

Everything at dawn is but a soft silhouette right now: my body under the covers, the slumbering mountain, resting boulders, dreaming palms.

The silhouette of the San Jacintos is sporting a purple shrug.

Zsa Zsa, as we call our dream home, is tucked directly into a canyon.

The former estate of infamous Hungarian actress and socialite Zsa Zsa Gabor sits upon a hill in the Little Tuscany neighborhood, with a three-hundred-sixty-degree view of the mountains and the city of Palm Springs.

It is a rare jewel, as breathtaking as any of the real Zsa Zsa's diamonds.

I sit up in bed.

"Good morning, *dahlink*!" I whisper.

This is the home I not only manifested as a child but also made possible as an adult through blood, sweat and a whole bunch of Tammy Faye tears.

"And good morning to all of you, too!"

Silhouettes of what look like human heads—a chorus of singers to back up Ms. Clark—begin to take shape in the burgeoning light.

My bedroom also serves as the wig room for our show, and I am, as a designer, the main hair stylist. It takes one man—me—a dozen hours to style four women's wigs each month. We put them on so carefully, but we rip them off as girls might do a Barbie head.

You must know one thing about a mid-century home: There is no room to spare. There is no basement to store your junk, no attic to hide holiday décor, no root cellar to keep food cool in the summer heat, no massive closets to store a dozen wigs.

These homes were built when we had less, when things were tinier.

Now, every square foot—at roughly a thousand dollars a square foot—is precious real estate.

Just like an older gay man's head of hair.

I have brought more homes—and wigs—back to life than any other designer in the desert. That is my calling. Teddy does our costuming. Barry is writer, director and producer, while Sid—with a very unsteady hand from Esther—does our makeup. Sid used to do his wife's makeup when they were married.

Your husband does your makeup? Wake up and the smell the Maybelline, honey!

I have rescued as many Wexler, Cody, Lautner, and Palmer and Krisel homes from peel-and-stick linoleum, Z-Brick walls, floor-to-ceiling floral drapes and La-Z-Boy recliners as Teddy and I have rescued estate sale wigs that have been fried by curling irons, drowned by little girls, and discarded by performers and women trying do a walk of shame at three in the morning with a broken heel and one false eyelash.

"A little powder, a little paint . . ."

The sun begins to illuminate the mountains, and my own head casts a shadow on the terrazzo tile in my bedroom. I touch the peak of my hair as Petula croons.

My fascination with home and hair all started in downtown Raymore, Alabama.

My best friend growing up was Jolene Perkins. My parents hated not only that my best friend was a girl—I was a pariah among the BB gun, football playin', catfish catchin' crew of boys who made my life a living hell—but also that she was named for a Dolly Parton song about a loose, cheating woman.

It also didn't help matters that her mother, Dotty, was a divorcée (you must, by the way, draw that word out slowly and with disgust as we did in the South—*day-vor-sée!*) who owned a beauty parlor named The Curl Up & Dye in downtown Raymore.

All the women in town went there to get their hair did, even my mama, a secret my daddy never knew. They went despite Dotty's history, because no one could back-comb a head of hair like Dotty Perkins.

"Higher the hair, closer to God," she'd always say. "And most of us need all the help—and height—we can get."

One day, my daddy caught me playing makeup with a Barbie doll Jolene had given me. I was applying a coat of Bonne Bell Root Beer Lip Smacker I'd stolen from Jolene's purse to both of our lips. My daddy, a pastor, whooped me until his hand and my head went numb, before praying over my body and begging the Lord to take my sin.

I never cried when my daddy hit me. I just stared past him, searching the heavens, trying to understand why God would make me like this if he didn't want me to be like this.

That day, after my daddy left, I took off running, ready to hightail it out of town. In came a thunderstorm as I ran—a colossal boomer as loud and angry as his preaching voice—and I took cover in The Curl Up & Dye.

Not a customer was in there that day.

When Dotty saw me, she fell to the black-and-white-checkered floor and opened her arms. I ran into them, and she held me forever.

"You didn't cry when he hit you, did you, angel?" she whispered.

"No, ma'am."

"Good boy. I never did either. Strength in the face of hate. That's what'll help us survive." She kissed my cheek. It hurt.

Dotty helped me into her big styling chair, angling me away from the mirror.

"You sit, my sweet, little boy, and I'll make you as pretty as sunshine again."

She had an old stereo console in The Curl Up & Dye that played albums and 45s.

That day, she put on "Downtown" by Petula Clark, and she sang to me as she styled my hair and dabbed foundation under my eyes.

And you may find somebody kind to help and understand you . . . Someone who is just like you . . . So go downtown . . .

Dotty never let me see my own face until she was done.

My bruises were gone. My bouffant looked like a white cloud of cotton candy.

"It's reaching heaven!" I said, touching her wondrous work.

"'Cause you're an angel, and don't you ever forget that."

When I left, the sun had done come out, and I walked back home with my head held high.

Today I get out of bed and stare at a new day of a new life in a different time brightened by the exact same sun.

Candy-colored rays splay toward heaven.

I have retained my faith and sunny optimism despite the thunderstorms in my life.

What option do we have? Curl up and die?

I still cannot experience a sunrise without hearing my father's voice from the pulpit.

"And God promises that with each morning sunrise, He offers mercies anew and love unfailing."

I grab my robe from the footboard bench at the end of my

bed. I pull it tightly around my body to ward off the cool desert morning and the memories.

I stare at the colors in the distance, which mirror my own life.

The black and blue of the desert floor and bruises of my youth.

The gold of the cross over my father's head and color of Barbie's hair.

The Technicolor light through the stained glass windows of the church and the old Hollywood movies I watched to experience a world that was not endlessly gray and drab but gloriously bright.

And then I see it, peeking over the mountains, the color that still takes my breath away.

Pink!

The color of the Barbie Dreamhouse I wanted more than the BB guns and fishing poles I was given every birthday and Christmas to make me normal like the other boys. The color of the Polo shirt I saved up to buy that my father ripped off my back and whipped me with to teach me about weakness and sin. The color of the welts that remained on my skin for weeks, the pink of his hand striking me over and over even as I prayed for forgiveness under the beating hand of God.

But more than anything, pink was the color of the Golden Girls' house in Florida, the place that—for thirty minutes every Saturday—not only let me escape to a home filled with love, acceptance and friendship but also let me know there might one day be a home like that for me, one in which I would feel safe, one I could happily enter instead of flinching every time I opened the door.

If there were one thing that I prayed to God for, it was a pink home like that.

And that prayer came true.

Thanks to me.

So many people have wishes, but few have dreams. What's the difference?

Dolly Parton taught me that a wish is just something you hope might happen one day, but you never put any blood, sweat and tears into making it a reality. A dream is something you work toward every single day of your life with great intention until, one day, it has become a reality.

Everyone else may wish, but I always dream.

Big!

I tiptoe to the kitchen from the principal suite—yes, I earned one big perk for finding us Zsa Zsa and putting down the lion's share of the down payment—careful not to turn on lights. I do not wish to wake the Sleeping Beauties on this magical Monday morning. Believe me, they need their beauty sleep—and aspirin—considering the three of them went out to Hunters' happy hour after Church of Mary. They may range in age from their mid-sixties to early eighties, but they still act like college boys.

I step on a pair of still-wet swim trunks in the middle of the narrow hallway and stifle a scream.

Barry's briefs glow on the white tile, a tiny mankini decorated with bright yellow bananas.

He's so predictable.

I pick them up as if they were radioactive—which they might be, considering they're Barry's—and start to set them on his doorknob, but there is already a ball cap with an Arizona State University Sun Devils logo hanging from it.

Let me repeat: Barry is *so* predictable.

I place his suit atop the hat and can't help but wonder how Mr. ASU College Kid will react waking up next to his dream daddy attached to a sleep apnea machine.

I stifle a laugh and pad through our living room. Glorious views greet me in every direction.

I click on the lights and groan when I see the nightmare in my dream kitchen.

Pizza boxes and wineglasses line the countertops. Chips are ground into the floor. Every cabinet door is wide open.

I refuse to clean up their mess this time, I say to myself.

I have my hands full already being the mother of this group. Hell, I'm mother, father, babysitter, cook, mailman, and lawn and pool company. My Golden Gays see any task that requires a little manual labor as beneath them.

I head to an open cabinet and pull out my espresso roast whole coffee beans. I place them in the coffee grinder and silently smile at the cacophony it creates. I grab a filter and make my coffee before reaching for my favorite Monday morning mug. A fan gave this to me after a performance of *The Golden Gays*. The mug features a picture of a smiling Rose on one side, and on the other it reads, "It's like you people don't pay any attention to me whatsoever."

I tap a finger on the counter as I wait for the coffee to brew, trying to distract myself from the urge to clean up everyone's mess yet again.

I am the busiest one in this household. Yes, Teddy owns his business, but the shop is truly only slammed in the winter, and he has help. Sid still works part time with select clients—I mean, maybe ten hours a month—while Barry spends most of his days tweaking our monthly show, staring at his cell waiting for his agent to call and auditioning for Miracle Ear commercials he somehow believes will resuscitate an acting career that has been on life support since MC Hammer was popular.

But I still have a full roster of clients. I am on the board of Modernism Week in Palm Springs. I still love what I do. I look out the window.

I have no desire to melt into the horizon.

I survey the mess surrounding me.

No, I just don't have a desire to live a never-ending replay of *Groundhog Day*, where every day is the same: a late-morning juice glass turns into an early afternoon cocktail glass, a statin turns into a gummy, the warm days fade into cool nights, and the world becomes as beautifully hazy as the morning light over the mountains.

Out of nowhere, a bighorn sheep leaps onto a boulder and stands motionless. I hold my breath and reach for my cell to take a photo.

I snap a photo of this majestic beast.

Without warning, it turns and takes aim at a barrel cactus, ramming it with its massive, curled horns. It strikes it over and over and over, until the cactus bends like the Leaning Tower of Pisa before finally collapsing.

The sheep totters over the cactus, looking momentarily dazed. Then it nods its head as if pleased with its work and begins to eat the moist interior, satisfied that the payoff has been worth the effort.

And with that, I begin to clean the kitchen in a flurry and do not stop until it is gleaming like the morning sun.

When I am done, I froth some coconut milk, add it to my coffee with a dash of cinnamon, and eat my morning yogurt and fresh fruit.

I head back to the bedroom and get ready for my day, working on my hair—blowing and back-combing—until it reaches a height that pleases me. I slip into a pair of Mr Turk slacks and matching jacket—lime green with a velveteen mid-century pattern that resembles a flower garden on acid (my new clients and the out-of-town visitors who come to Modernism Week for my tours and talks about design love that I dress like this—*He must be great if he has style like that!*)—and I finish my outfit with a simple crisp white shirt.

I grab my keys and as I head out the door, I say, "Alexa, please play Anita Bryant's greatest hits! Louder!"

If there's anything that will get my boys to wake up, it will be hearing the sound of her voice in their home.

I smile and lock the front door. And then I stop, as usual, feeling guilty.

I reopen the door. "Alexa," I say, as if it's a dog who's gotten on the sofa. "Off!"

I stop to touch a small plaque outside the door that I had made for our home that simply reads *Zsa Zsa*.

I am the only who truly knows what her name means in Hungarian:

God is my oath.

I head to my BMW convertible, which is parked in the driveway.

Our immaculate driveway looks like a used car lot.

Barry's and Teddy's cars are parked at forty-five-degree angles as if they are cops who stopped a carjacker in the middle of the highway. Behind them, parked partially on our perfect grass, is a car I don't recognize—a jacked-up black pickup truck on tires so high I would need a stepladder and oxygen mask to enter—but instantly realize belongs to Barry's boy toy from Arizona.

I stand in the driveway, shaking my head.

This should never happen.

Every week, I create an elaborate assignment grid that I not only email to each Golden Gay but also laminate and hang in the pantry. It details whose turn it is to park in the garage, who can have the turnaround area and who must park on the street. It lists whose turn it is to go to the grocery, who picks up the dry cleaning, who is home for the pool and spa cleaning, who places the ads for our show. This is ignored each and every week just like . . .

Me.

And yet, like the bighorn I just saw, I operate out of instinct. I must make everything right.

I head back inside and gather up the key rings scattered around the house as if I'm a squirrel collecting autumn acorns. I rotate the cars like a valet, return the keys and lock the door once again.

I again glance at the Zsa Zsa sign on the house, but this time, I touch my heart.

"Ron, you need to wear a sign that reads Disease to Please," I say to myself.

I get in my beloved vintage Mercedes, wrap a scarf around my head à la Audrey Hepburn so the wind won't ruin my coif and turn on Petula Clark.

Finally—*finally!*—I head downtown.

"Excuse me? How much is that?"

I jump at the customer's voice. I had been deep in thought wondering why the spawn of Satan has continued to call me multiple times out of the blue. Perhaps she had just butt-dialed me. Lord knows her butt is ample enough to have its own area code.

"I beg your pardon?"

I follow the woman's manicured finger.

My mother's Bakelite bracelet lives in a shadow box on the wall behind the front counter.

"Oh, that's not for sale," I say. "But all of the jewelry in the counter display is. Let me know if I can show you anything."

I smile at the woman and return to styling a mannequin in the front window of Dorian Gay. In honor of Valentine's Day and Modernism Week, my front window is a tribute to TV legend, gay icon and former Palm Springs resident Lucille Ball and her famed *I Love Lucy* chocolate factory episode.

Lucy and Ethel mannequins are standing before an assembly line of chocolates. Behind them, a big red heart fills the window, like the logo from the TV show. Instead of being dressed in pink uniforms like in the famous episode, the two are dressed head-to-toe in fabulous red frocks, heels and jewelry, vintage scarves tied in their hair.

Have a Ball this Month in Palm Springs! my sign reads.

"Name your price," the woman presses. "My mom had a bracelet just like it. I don't know what happened to it."

I stop mid-motion.

"My mama did, too," I say. "And I'm sorry, but it's NFS."

"I'll pay any price you ask," she answers with great confidence. "And you know what I always say? NFS simply means Not For Sure."

The woman stares at me, head held high.

Suddenly, I remember her face and her voice. I eye her carefully. I sold her the brightly colored geometric pattern caftan and orange fruit salad earrings she is currently wearing. She spent a fortune here last year. So much, in fact, that I popped a bottle of champagne.

Be kind, Teddy, though I know that's a big ask.

I glance again at the Bakelite bracelet. It hovers like a UFO in an acrylic orange box against a backdrop of *Brady Bunch* wallpaper.

"See?" The woman laughs. "I can see the wheels turning. You're not for sure, are you?"

Why am I holding on to this bracelet? What hold does it have on me?

I do not have amber-colored memories of my childhood like most kids. In fact, I try not to have any memories of my past at all. I have locked them away, airtight, just like that bracelet.

Long before political division and social media and light-years before familial estrangement and the new normal of no contact, the Copelands were the poster children for finger-pointing and hateful derision.

I *should* sell the bracelet.

The hands on the mid-century atomic starburst clock near the shadow box click.

My doctor's appointment is in three hours.

I need the money more than I need this bracelet.

The woman continues to stare at me, smiling. I can almost hear her hiss like a cobra.

I open my mouth to spit out an exorbitant amount, but then my cell trills, and it is a selfie of Ron standing before Frank Sinatra's Twin Palms home. He is waving and smiling, happy to be a Modernism Week board member and docent, even though I know he is still seething for having to clean up our mess this morning.

Ron is forgiving.

I think of his Church of Mary prayer.

This bracelet is my last connection.

My only remaining silk.

And when that is gone, what do I have left?

The woman moves toward the counter as if I have already decided.

Isn't that why we watch reruns even though there is so much original content streaming today? Isn't that why a show like *The Golden Girls* remains eternally popular?

We don't watch an old TV show to return to a time that was perfect, but rather to return to a time that marked a turning point in our lives.

The woman pulls the wallet from her bag.

What would it say about me if I sold the past—as I do in my business—but I did not believe in it? Wouldn't I be just as big a hypocrite as a family that waltzed into church every Sabbath in their Sunday best pretending to be perfect when they were the epitome of the darkness and evil our pastor warned us about?

"I'm so sorry," I finally say. "It's really not for sale."

The woman's face falls. She's not used to being told no.

I must make her laugh or risk losing even more money.

"You know, my mother was a farm girl," I continue, taking Lucy's wig and placing it on my own head. "Sturdy stock. From a distance, her wrists looked like her calves. I used to joke that my mother didn't ever buy new heels, she just got re-shoed every few years. Her bracelet wouldn't fit your petite wrist anyway."

The woman roars.

I know how to turn the tables with wit and sarcasm.

"Follow me," I say, stepping down from the window and grabbing her hand. "Be my Ethel for the day. Pretty please! Let me give you a private trunk show so you can see the baubles I've been holding back for Modernism Week. I can sell those to you before I 'ten X' the hell out of them."

We head into the back room, where I keep my stock. I serve her champagne and one-liners, and she walks out an hour later, tipsy, happy and a thousand dollars lighter.

If there's one silk I retained from my mother, it's her sense of humor.

My mother was damn funny.

We had to learn to laugh, or we would not have survived. Humor is the great connector *and* deflector. It has both saved my ass and kept people at a safe distance many times over my life.

If there's one thing I know for certain about the world today versus when I was growing up, it's that we're too damn serious. Was the world cruel to me? You're damn right it was. Did I survive? You're damn right I did.

I learned to be a fighter. I learned to be self-sufficient. I learned you can get spit on and have your head smashed into a locker every single day and still hold your head high.

Should it be that way?

No.

But I learned if you don't have a sense of self-deprecating humor, then you have no coping mechanisms. You take yourself too seriously. You cannot laugh when the going gets tough. And it always gets tough, my dears.

Did I—and my Golden Gays—pave the way for so many today?

You bet your sweet asses we did.

With our bodies, blood and lives, so maybe say thank you on occasion instead of gagging when you see an older person at a bar for your gift of being able to walk around in the world today without being ashamed of who you are and identifying as you please.

Sadly, our society has the attention spans of gnats, so we forget our history, fooling ourselves into thinking the world has become more accepting.

But we must always remember that when we take two steps forward, we take a mighty one back, and we must never be fooled: We must always be ready to fight.

I check my watch.

I have an appointment with destiny.

Where is Patty?

I pick up my cell to call when she saunters in with her Starbucks.

"You're late!"

Patty stops and touches her belly.

"How did you know?" she cries dramatically. "And, yes, the baby is yours! I know because it's marked with the sign of the beast."

I shake my head. This is our routine.

"I'm having a late lunch with Barry to go over this month's show," I lie to Patty, my assistant and second mother who—by the way—is not a woman but an eighty-five-year-old man named Hank who warms up the crowd before our show by performing as a drag queen named Patty O'Furniture. "Can you watch the shop until I get back?"

Patty lifts one narrow, overly plucked Pamela Anderson brow to survey me with great skepticism.

"You never trust me even though you hired me," she says.

"You steal my clothes and stuff dollar bills down your bra when customers pay in cash." I point. "I have cameras."

"I thought I was auditioning for *RuPaul's Drag Race*." Patty eyes me closely. "And I thought you had already planned this month's show."

Patty's voice sounds as if she's just smoked a carton of unfiltered Marlboro cigarettes and chased that with a gallon of gasoline. If Harvey Fierstein and Brenda Vaccaro had a child, Patty would have been it.

"Last-minute changes," I say.

"Well, I have to be out of here by six," Patty says. "I have my own show to get ready for tomorrow, remember?"

Patty has been doing the same exact act for the last six decades: song, joke, insult bachelorette parties, do a shot, repeat.

She used to open as Tina Turner performing "Proud Mary," but two decades ago her knee snapped, last decade she got two hips and three stents, and Patty had to switch to ballads. She is still pissed off about it.

But she can sing "Fancy" just like Reba. No lip-syncing either. Patty is old-school. She doesn't make an entrance, sing a couple of lines and immediately exit the stage to stuff dollars down her bra, no. Patty performs an entire number, start to finish.

The dollars come to her.

"Where is this gig?" I ask.

"Vegas-adjacent," she says with a wink of her butterfly lash.

Every gig outside Palm Springs that Patty does is Vegas-adjacent. Which means Reno.

Which means her audience will consist of inebriated cowboys who just lost their last dime at the blackjack table and women sporting breast implants and oxygen machines.

"Just be back—*and sober!*—by next Saturday night for *our* gig," I say. "I have enough to worry about without adding 'find old, drunk drag queen' to my list."

Patty puts a hand over her mouth and feigns indignation at my insult.

"I'll give you drunk, but old?" she gasps. "And drag queen? I'm a professional."

"A professional what?" I quip.

She laughs and then hacks.

I stride toward the door.

"You're still wearing a wig, by the way," Patty calls.

"I feel like being Lucy today," I say.

"Red doesn't suit you," Patty says. "That color turns your skin pink and makes you look like an alcoholic." She stops. "Which you are, by the way."

"No," I say. "I'm a professional, too." I look at Patty before I exit. "Professional drinker."

I march toward my car—not a soul in Palm Springs giving me a second glance for wearing a wig in the middle of the afternoon—and see my own reflection in the window of my store. I survey my appearance and take stock of the situation I'm in.

"How would Lucy get herself out of this mess?" I ask myself, smoothing the loose ends of the wig. "There's not a chocolate anywhere in sight to shove in my mouth nor a grape to stomp in Palm Springs."

My doctor looks like Doogie Howser, MD.

If you don't know who that is, google it.

We didn't have Google when I was young. We researched subjects using things called dictionaries and microfiche. We carted heavy books around and had to turn pages and scour lines to discover truths.

We found locations—like the hospital I'm currently seated in wearing a paper robe with my flabby behind hanging out for Doogie to probe—using folded maps, directions written on napkins and our own internal compasses.

We didn't even have a hint Doogie might be gay—much less Boy George—until years later because no one even uttered that word out loud. I mean, my father thought Liberace was just a showman. Paul Lynde was simply the hilarious "center square" on *Hollywood Squares*.

What I'm trying to say is, if you don't know Doogie, it means I'm too damn old.

I watch Doogie's mouth move.

To me right now, his voice sounds like Charlie Brown's teacher from the *Peanuts* holiday specials.

Wah-wah.

Again, google it, my dears.

I'm being "staged," and not in the glamorous Broadway, Tony Award–winning way.

I have cancer.

Stage T3a to be exact, meaning my tumor has extended outside the prostate on one side but has not spread to my lymph nodes or distant organs, my PSA is under 20, and I have a Gleason score of 7.

I should play the lotto today with those numbers.

So many numbers, so little time.

"In other words," my doctor says to me, "after all our tests, this is the best possible outcome of a bad situation."

My head snaps up.

"I thought I was dying," I say. "You said at my last visit, and I quote, 'This doesn't look good.'"

"I've been told my bedside manner could use some work."

My doctor is trying to make a joke to lessen the tension.

"Some work?" I ask. "I've spent the last few weeks digging a hole in my backyard for my own funeral. So, cut to the chase. How long do I have to live?"

The doctor shakes his head and pulls his chair toward me. I guess he believes this gesture equates sympathy.

"I don't look at your situation that way," he says, voice calm as the desert air in the morning. "We have a number of treatment options available, including external beam radiation therapy in conjunction with long-term androgen deprivation therapy."

My doctor pauses.

"It sounds like—to make an obvious pun—there's a big 'but' in there," I say.

I pivot on the exam table and give my rear a little slap.

He doesn't laugh.

"My suggestion would be to deal with this aggressively," he says. "And as soon as possible."

"Meaning?"

"A radical prostatectomy."

"Is that a new pop group?"

"It involves the surgical removal of the prostate gland and a small amount of normal tissue surrounding it to—in the simplest of terms—make sure we got it all," he explains. "You're fortunate that the cancer has not yet reached the seminal vesicles or lymph nodes. *Yet!* Nearly eighty-five percent of patients who have this surgery are alive and doing well five years after surgery. Most of those patients—like you—who die do so of causes *other* than prostate cancer."

"And this is good news?" I ask.

"It actually is."

"Give it to me straight, Doc," I say. "And I rarely utter those words."

"I have to be honest with you. The surgery is quite invasive, which makes it less popular than any other treatment options," he says. "It poses distinct complications, including risk of death following surgery, long-term sexual dysfunction and urinary incontinence."

"Is there at least a gift with purchase with this option?" I ask.

No laughter.

"However, this procedure would—I firmly believe—be the best option for your long-term health and survival."

"You have just described the ultimate living nightmare for a gay man," I say. I look my doctor in the eye. "Little chance of sex again combined with an ever-present aroma of tinkle rather than a Tom Ford cologne. No, thank you. I think I'd rather die."

"Mr. Copeland, many women today who have the BRCA1 or BRCA2 mutation opt to have a bilateral mastectomy in order to survive," he says. "It reduces the risk of breast cancer by at least ninety-five percent for those who have this harmful variant. Most patients would be grateful to have a surgical option that would allow them to live."

I think of John.

I think of the havoc, stress, and financial and emotional

burden his death placed on me. I think of the havoc my surgery and recovery would cause my family.

My mind turns to my mother. How quickly she went.

Wouldn't that be for the best?

For me? For everyone?

I don't even have any family left.

"I'd like to get you scheduled for surgery as soon as possible," the doctor presses. He rolls back to his laptop and begins to tap on it. "I can get you in for surgery in two weeks."

"I need some time to think," I say.

"You don't have time to think."

I plop into an uncomfortable chair by the exam table and pull on my socks and shoes. I glance up at my doctor.

"Then I think I want to die."

"No one wants to die."

"No one wants to live like this either."

"But you'll be alive."

"But not living."

He shakes his head at me.

"I'll give you a chance to think for a second while you change."

He leaves, but I can hear him standing outside the door. I stand, wiggle out of my paper robe and dress.

"I'm done changing!" I call.

He comes in.

"But still not changing my mind," I finish.

"Mr. Copeland . . ." he starts.

"Listen, I'm an expert at this type of conversation," I say, cutting him off. "We can go round and round all day long like a merry-go-round." I stop. "And to think I could survive playgrounds and bullies in the 1970s, but not old age."

I pull on my wig.

Humor is my coping mechanism. It has always been my coping mechanism.

"Thank you, Doctor," I say. "I'll be in touch about what I decide."

"Mr. Copeland?"

I stop at the door.

"My wife and I went to see your show a few years ago."

I turn, my face etched in surprise. I have misjudged this man. Badly.

"You buried the lede," I say.

"You have friends who will support you," he continues. "On stage and in real life. You have a big family that loves you."

"But they shouldn't have to deal with this."

"That's why we have friends," the doctor says.

"Thank you," I say. "I'll think about what you've said. Oh, and, Doctor?"

"Yes?"

"What did you think of the show?"

"We loved it," he says. "You know, my grandmother in Kansas died of COVID in her assisted living facility. She was all alone. My grandfather had passed, and her children and grandchildren weren't nearby. Her favorite TV show was *The Golden Girls.* I'd never seen it before, but I started Zooming her every weekend during COVID, and we watched it together as a way to not be all alone. Even when she was dying—when she wasn't conscious—I'd call, have the nurses turn on the show and we'd still watch it together. And for a half hour, everything was okay."

The doctor stands and takes a step toward me.

"You keep living, Mr. Copeland, to have moments just like that," he continues. "You keep fighting to live, Mr. Copeland, not just for yourself but for those who love and need you."

I inhale sharply.

"Are you a sports fan?" he asks.

"Do I look like a sports fan?"

Finally, my doctor laughs.

"There's an old saying in sports: The longer you stay in the game, the more chance you have to win."

"Meaning?"

"You give up, and the game is over before it's even been decided."

He gives me a handful of pamphlets and a printout of his suggested next steps.

I nod and open the door.

"You will need to stop drinking if you decide to have the surgery," he says. "Your blood work could be better."

"You mean, my blood work could be a martini."

I exit and walk down the long corridor toward the exit sign.

Behind me, the doctor calls, "I don't think red is your color."

"*Now* you're funny?" I yell without turning back.

"Welcome to Palm Springs!" I say to a woman boarding the double-decker bus. She is sporting a sun visor, her face slathered in zinc.

"Ah!" Teddy screams when he turns and sees her. "An apparition!"

Teddy tentatively pokes the woman's shoulder.

"Ah!" he screams again. "You're real! That's even scarier."

"The heat is bothering him, ma'am," I say quickly to cover. "Please have a seat and enjoy the tour.

"Can't you be nice for one day?" I hiss into Teddy's ear. "I can't believe you!"

"And I can't believe you talked us into doing this," Teddy says. "I'm not under court-ordered community service to be kind to the locusts who swarm our town for Mid-Century Modern Week."

I glare at him, but he continues unbridled.

"I swore I would kill myself before I stepped foot onto this . . . this . . ." Teddy glances around the top of the double-decker bus ". . . *this* Hindenburg equivalent of a pedal pub party bike for old people. At least bachelorette parties have the dignity to get drunk while everyone ridicules the spectacle of them riding all over town looking like idiots."

"Lest I need to remind you, dear Teddy, *we* are old people."

"Not *this* kind of old people," he says, eyes wide, aghast. "The four of us are the only ones to have the self-worth to put on under-eye concealer this morning before going out in public."

Barry sidles up next to us.

"They don't need it," he says. "They have BluBlocker sunglasses to cover their entire faces."

Teddy laughs.

"Just be nice," I say. "I mean, look at Sid."

Sid is assisting an elderly couple with canes up the steps.

"You and Sid have this yearning desire to be liked by people you don't even know," I say. "It's sadder than listening to 'Alone Again (Naturally)' on repeat."

I feel a pang in my gut. That verbal spear hit an emotional organ.

"That was really hurtful, Teddy," I say.

"No, Ron, *this* is really painful," Teddy counters, gesturing dramatically around the bus.

"Just so we're clear, I thought this would be a wonderful bonding experience with my three best friends," I say, trying not to sound like a child who got his feelings wounded by a bully. "As a board member for Modernism Week, I thought we could see through fresh eyes what we all take for granted every day." I gesture around the bus at the tourists and then at the palm trees glistening before the mountains. "We chose to live here for a reason. Look at all of these people wanting just a piece—a moment—of what we have. I thought it would be good for us to spend some time together other than two hours—hungover, mind you—on Sundays. We're barely together anymore except for the shows. And this is good for my business, too. Believe me, we still need the money."

Teddy and Barry look at their feet. This spear struck an organ, too.

"And I kind of wanted you all to see me in my element," I continue. "I see your talent on display, Barry, in our shows. I see your talent on display, Teddy, in your shop. I watch Sid bring financial clarity and security to older couple's lives through the work he does as well as the joy he brings to children through his volunteer work at the library. But you never get to see my design work. You never get to experience my expertise on what makes this city so special." I wait until they look into my eyes. "You only see me in the kitchen, or cleaning the house, or complaining about the tasks you refuse to do." My breath hitches in my throat, but I push on. "You don't see me much of the time."

"Like that woman with the zinc oxide?" Teddy asks.

"See what I mean?"

Teddy puts his arm around my shoulders. "I'll try." I raise a brow at him. "I promise."

A younger gay couple appears wearing matching eyelet shirts showing off perfect bodies.

"I got them!" Barry says, rushing the couple. He slides between them. "Right this way, gents."

A cacophony echoes up the stairs of the bus. Teddy and I glance down, and a *very* large bachelorette party—all wearing crowns and sashes—are boarding. They sound like grackles.

"Good morning, ladies!" I call. "This kind man will assist you to your seats."

"Ah, hell no," Teddy says.

"You were just asking for a bachelorette party," I say. "Your wish came true."

I push Teddy toward the stairs. The women screech when they see him and surround Teddy. When they part, he is sporting a penis crown.

"How sweet," Barry says. "They know a real dick when they see one."

Teddy touches his crown. "One of the sweeter gifts I've ever received, actually," he says.

"Picture!" the bride screams. "We gotta get a picture!"

She doesn't add *with the gay guy!*, but that is abundantly implied. She will likely show this photo to the gals in marketing on Monday when she's back in the office, probably at lunch, with her voice husky and low as if posing with Teddy was the craziest thing in the world she might ever do.

And it just might be.

She is cute in a "I was just named Corn Queen!" sort of way, but I can tell she believes she is light-years ahead of her bridal party in terms of looks.

"Gretchen, you take the photo!" the bride continues. "You're always so good."

My heart drops for the chubby girl who is already carrying most of the bags for the group. I smile warmly at her.

Have you ever noticed there's always a Gretchen in a bridal party or group of friends? The pleaser? The one who will do anything and everything—even sacrifice her dignity—to make the group not only happy but functional?

I glance at Teddy, laughing and posing.

I am the Gretchen.

"I'll take the photo," I say.

And there is nothing wrong with that as long as you're shown a little damn respect.

Gretchen melds into the group, uneasily at first, but I wait until she finally smiles.

"Got it!" I say.

When everyone on the bus is seated, I ask them to put in their earbuds, and I turn on my mic.

"Welcome to Modernism Week!"

Those on the bus—young and old—applaud.

"You may proceed, Donna," I say.

"You got it, Boss Man," Donna says into my mic as the bus pulls out of the parking lot of the Hyatt and onto a backstreet. Donna has been driving the double-decker bus for my tours during Modernism Week since the '90s.

"What a shocking surprise!" Teddy said when I introduced him to Donna this morning. "A lesbian bus driver!"

I begin my spiel.

"Mid-century modern architecture is about stripping away unnecessary ornament. The spaces reflect the optimistic post-war era and focus on clean, straight lines . . ." I pause as Teddy laughs and mouths "straight, my ass!" but push on after shooting him a death stare ". . . as I was saying, clean, straight lines, simple forms and—most importantly—the seamless integration of indoor and outdoor spaces. It's about being at one with nature. When you look at homes and buildings today, focus on the unifying characteristics including flat roofs, large windows, and the use of materials like wood, glass and metal."

The bus edges close to the mountains. The streets begin to narrow and wind in all different directions.

"Welcome to Old Hollywood!" I say. "The neighborhoods we are about to drive through embody the Golden Era of Hollywood Homes: Old Las Palmas, The Movie Colony, Little Tuscany, Vista Las Palmas. Throughout the decades, these were the homes or second homes of stars like Elizabeth Taylor, Kirk Douglas, Cary Grant, Judy Garland, Goldie Hawn and Kurt Russell, Liberace, the Reagans, Elvis and Priscilla, and . . . Zsa Zsa Gabor."

I see Teddy's, Barry's and Sid's heads pop up.

"Yes," I say, as if only to them, "we are blessed to be in the midst of history and elegance."

They smile. I continue, still looking in their eyes.

"As we make our way through these magnificent estates, imagine yourself living here. What would that be like?" I pause to let that question sink in. "The beauty of a double-decker bus tour is that you get a glimpse over the hedges and into the homes of those who came before us and those who seek to preserve such beauty."

The bus ends up in front of Frank Sinatra's original Twin Palms home in the Movie Colony neighborhood.

"Ol' Blue Eyes," I say.

Most on the bus—i.e., those of a "certain age" (read: older than dirt)—sit up like kids, showing more excitement for this stop than any other on the tour. If you are of this *certain* age, then when I utter "Frank Sinatra and the Rat Pack," you instantly think of Palm Springs. Not only did their music define the era of old Hollywood glamour, Sinatra and his friends defined the desert.

However, if you are of a certain age—read: younger than thirty—you likely think of Coachella and all the stars from the Kardashians to Leonardo DiCaprio who have made Palm Springs hip again.

The gay couple and bridal party on the bus have no idea whose house this is when I say "Ol' Blue Eyes." I might as well be saying "typewriter," "rotary phone," "dial-up."

Or Cher.

"Frank Sinatra," I say. "The iconic singer and actor."

Finally, they nod.

"The two palm trees that stand next to the Sinatra house are the reasons for it its name," I say. "This house epitomizes a style that would become known as desert modernism, but the playboy crooner didn't want this type of house at first. *No, no.* Brash Ol' Blue Eyes, whom MGM had made a millionaire with a brand-new contract, came to Palm Springs looking to escape the snooping eyes of the studio and the press following a series of romantic scandals. Palm Springs became the hot spot for Hollywood royalty in the 1940s and 1950s largely because of new clauses that were built into actors' contracts."

I take a breath and continue.

"After surviving the Great Depression, Hollywood studios made sweeping changes. They agreed to avert a showdown with the Roman Catholic Church by adding a morality clause to workers' agreements, and they sneaked in the so-called 'two-hour rule' that mandated that talent—when in production—had to stay within a hundred miles, or a two-hour drive, of Los Angeles in case they needed them for reshoots. Where could celebrities go to avoid snooping studio eyes and paparazzi? Palm Springs! The weather was consistently nicer than Laguna or

Santa Barbara, and a celebrity could slide behind a 'Hollywood hedge' and into a pool and keep their private lives private. Studios had such control over actors' personal lives, public image and relationships that many gay actors started flocking to Palm Springs to be themselves. During the AIDS crisis, gay men battling pneumonia flocked here as well for the humidity-free weather and endless days of sunshine."

Murmurs now. Always murmurs.

"The Sinatra story goes that the singer marched into E. Stewart Williams's office wearing a white sailor cap and eating an ice cream cone and asked the architect to design a Georgian-style mansion with brick and columns—heresy in the desert. Williams, thankfully, didn't listen. Instead, he ignored Sinatra and created renderings of a house composed of long, horizontal lines and built from nontraditional materials, a style more 'desert-appropriate.' It also included an owner's suite that occupied a private wing of the house. Sinatra loved it and immediately handed over one hundred fifty thousand dollars to build it. When it was completed, the home and desert setting set the standard for postwar Hollywood glamour and resort living, including cocktail hour. Twin Palms became not only home to Sinatra's family but also the setting for his off-screen drama: His marriage to Nancy ended in 1948 while the couple lived in Palm Springs. Ava Gardner replaced Nancy as Frank's second wife, but the drama continued. In fact, one of the original bathroom sinks retains the crack in the basin from a champagne bottle Sinatra hurled at Gardner. He then tossed all of Gardner's possessions onto the driveway and kicked her and Lana Turner out of the house."

I stare at the two palms towering over the low-slung linear masterwork like two parents watching over their sleeping child.

My eyes drift to my three best friends listening to me.

How many fights have we been in? How many losses have we endured?

I think of Teddy losing John and finding him face down

floating in the pool—three bottles of champagne and an empty bottle of pills on the edge—me fighting to breathe life and hope back into Teddy again.

I can still see Sid after his family disowned him for many years, his wife remarrying, and how he would sit on the patio and stare at the mountains for weeks at a time as if they were speaking only to him in silence.

And the men that Barry has kicked out and discarded onto our driveway like Frank discarded Ava and Lana.

A house can be filled with historical significance and unparalleled beauty, but it is simply walls and a roof without love, family, struggles and stories to fill it.

My Golden Gays sense that I am staring at them—*BFFs have that instinct, don't we?*—and when they look me in the eye and smile, I know that I am seen. Even if just for a moment.

"Hey!"

Someone on the bus yells, and I look up to see a man in Sinatra's backyard giving us the finger. This house is now, sadly, a VRBO—like too much of Palm Springs—and clearly this renter paid a pretty penny for privacy, likely not realizing his home is on tour every hour of every day.

I weigh how to react, but Teddy beats me to the punch.

"Fuck you, locust!" Teddy yells, flipping him off.

Then Teddy winks at me and says, "I got your back, buddy."

"Uncle Sid!"

"Aunt Sophia!"

Esther's great-grandchildren rush me as I enter the Palm Springs Public Library, calling me by both my given name and my stage name.

I bend down and wrap Jack and June in my arms.

"Did you bring them?" they yell.

"Don't I always bring some?"

I open my pocketbook and retrieve two pieces of butterscotch candy.

The kids squeal in delight—earning a *sssssh!* from Mrs. Marquez at the circulation desk—and then hug me again before bolting toward the library's reading room.

"Sorry about the sugar," I say to Esther.

"Their parents tell me sugar is forbidden when they visit me and then send me pictures of them sucking down Unicorn Frappuccinos when they get home," Esther says. She stops and eyes me dressed as Sophia. "You really are a grandma. You make me look bad. All I ever give them are reasons to see a therapist in the future."

She eyes my pocketbook and holds out her hand. I place a

hard candy in her open palm. She unwraps the candy and pops it in her mouth.

"My bubbe used to keep these in a candy jar," Esther says. "They'd melt and congeal together into one giant piece. No wonder I have issues."

"I bet her couch was covered in plastic, too."

"We owned dry cleaners," Esther says with a chuckle. "No bare skin could touch fabric."

I start to walk, but she grabs my arm. "Have you heard from Hot Jew?"

I laugh. "After what I said?"

"Why don't you text him and recommend a dermatologist?" she asks. "I mean, can't love blossom over a suspicious mole?"

"Stop it," I say. "That ship has sailed."

"You mean you drove that ship right into an iceberg."

Esther takes my arm and escorts me to the library's reading room. Every Wednesday at 10:00 a.m., I host Drag Queen Reading Hour, a program for children aged three to eight that is meant to raise awareness of diversity, promote self-acceptance, build empathy and foster an early love of reading.

When I enter, I am greeted by familiar faces.

"Grandma Golden!"

"Mr. Sid!"

"Mrs. P!"

I read to the children dressed as my character, Sophia Petrillo. They have no idea who she is, but their parents and grandparents do. To the kids—dressed in my floral print dress, brooch, dusty-rose sweater with a lace collar, reading glasses dangling from a chain, short silver-white curls and ever-present pocketbook in the crook of my arm—I am their grandmother, great-aunt, babysitter, neighbor, reading buddy, but most of all, friend.

The reading room is decorated like a living room. I take a seat in a rocking chair.

"Who's ready for a story?" I ask.

The kids yell and, just as quickly, quiet.

I pick up one of my favorite books, *The Very Hungry Caterpillar* by Eric Carle. I read it to my own children when they were young. It is a book that has aged beautifully, and whose message seems even more necessary today in our society. The book, as Carle once said, is a "literary cocoon" for children as they approach kindergarten and for all little kids preparing to leave the warmth and safety of home for school.

I look out at the families gathered today. I nod at Esther, who has my phone, and she FaceTimes Rebecca and our great-grandchildren, Noah, Naomi and Aviva. Every Wednesday, they join us from Chicago.

I wave at them, and the four of them wave back.

Rebecca smiles. She is an old woman now, but in her eyes I still see the young girl I knew so long ago. The eyes of my great-grands are filled with nothing but innocence and love. When I look at them, I see what they see: hope and love.

That is why I am here, to build a connection to a future that will not physically include me but one I pray includes my history. Because it is in the eyes of our elders—me, Rebecca, my friends, the ones we rarely look deeply into because we are frightened by what we see reflected in the dim pupils—where the stories lie.

A few years after Rebecca and I divorced, she remarried a mutual friend named David who was also an attorney from my firm. I let that go, and am glad I did, because I was able to see her experience true love for the first time in her life, a love with no secrets. Slowly, her anger began to soften. In return, my children's wrath diminished as well.

I sacrificed everything for years so my family would feel "normal." I traveled back to Chicago for every big birthday, ball game, every moment of my children's and grandchildren's lives. For years, I was in Chicago nearly as much as I was in Palm Springs. I traveled so much and purchased so many gifts to buy my family's love, I had to un-retire and handle estate planning for my and Esther's friends.

When I finally looked up, I was well into my seventies, and my children were grown and married with growing children.

And me?

Still single.

Not only had I missed out on love and romance in my youth, I had missed my window of opportunity in the gay dating world, that sliver of time when widowers were looking to recouple, younger men sought stability with a successful, older man, and being gray was considered hot.

Now?

I look into the eyes of my great-grands.

Would I do the same thing all over again? Of course I would. I love my blood family as much as I do my chosen one. But I also must be brutally honest: I sacrificed my own happiness for theirs. I felt I was not worthy of loving a man because it was wrong. I felt—and still do—*overwhelming* guilt.

The trysts, the one-night stands, the things I did when I was married, I still feel guilt about because I did not have the strength to be honest with myself, my wife, my family, my friends, my religion, my community, this world.

But I learned I am not a one-night stand type of guy either. I am a romantic. I want what I never had, what I see in books and movies, the flutter of the heart, the dizziness of a first kiss, being held so tightly at night that the world and all its ugliness disappear.

I want *that.*

But I do not believe I *deserve* that.

And so I fill my days with distractions.

I begin to read:

"In the light of the moon, a little egg lay on a leaf."

When I finish, I ask the children what they think the story of the hungry caterpillar is all about. Their answers are as beautiful as the story.

When they finish, I say, "I once took my own children to

hear from the man who wrote and drew this beautiful book. He explained what it was about. Do you know what he said?"

"No!" the kids yell.

"He said that this is a book of hope. That children like you need hope. That we *all* need hope. The author said, 'You, little insignificant caterpillar, can grow up into a beautiful butterfly and fly into the world with your talent. You'll think, "Will I ever be able to do that?" Yes, you will.'"

Parents and grandparents lead the children in applause.

I say this little message every time because kids need to hear it.

I need to hear it.

I pick up my next book off the floor and read it before I give hugs and candy and pose for pictures with all the kids who have gathered.

Esther and her grandkids escort me out after the Reading Hour. She takes a photo of us with my phone and then hands it back to me. I say goodbye in the parking lot, watching them drive away. I drop my cell into my pocketbook and then fish my keys out of it.

The temperature has soared since I entered the library, and I open my door, pull off my wig and toss it on the passenger seat.

"Groomer!"

In the reflection of my car window, I see a woman charging toward me. I turn. The woman spits. I lift my pocketbook in front of my face just in time, and her saliva slides off my patent leather clutch and onto my shoe.

I recognize her face. She was just inside listening to me. She looks to be in her sixties, plump, dyed black hair, her arms out to the sides protecting her two grandchildren as if I were the one who just prompted this attack.

"Ma'am?" I ask in a sweet voice, trying to de-escalate the situation. "Are you okay?"

"No, I'm not okay, you disgusting pedophile!"

Her words ricochet off my body. I take a step back, mind and heart racing.

This is Palm Springs. Roughly half of the residents are part of the LGBTQ+ community. *We* are the majority here.

She edges closer.

I take another step back until I'm pressed up against my car. The hot steel burns my legs.

"You show up here and try to make children believe that all of this is okay?" She waves her hands at my body. "What is wrong with you? What is wrong with our society?"

The woman is red-faced, simultaneously weeping and laughing. The little ones behind her are whimpering in terror.

"I'm scared, Grandma," a little girl with curly red hair says.

"You should be," she says, leaning toward me. "Everyone should be scared of this sick, twisted . . . *thing*."

"Ma'am," I say. "Please."

"A man in makeup," she sneers. "Acting like a woman. You are going to burn in hell."

I press my body even tighter against the car. My skin singes.

I wince. I certainly know what that will feel like.

Suddenly, the woman reaches into her purse.

The world becomes a slow blur.

I shove my hand inside my still-open pocketbook. I pull out a handful of candy and throw it as hard as I can at the woman. Hard butterscotch ricochets off her soft face. As she lifts her hands to cover it, I pull open the car door, jump inside and lock the doors. By the time she has recovered, I have started my car.

The woman reaches back into her purse and pulls out a Bible. She thumps it on my car, screaming, "I will ban you and your kind from this library, so help me God!"

I screech out of the parking lot. I do not even check traffic as I pull onto Baristo and then yank my car onto Sunrise.

When I finally slam on my brakes at a stoplight, I see myself in the rearview mirror.

My mascara is running. My lipstick is smeared. My hair is matted. My lace collar is askew.

I am an old man in a dress.

I glance over at the car next to me. A group of kids—shoving french fries down their throats—obviously on lunch break from the local high school barely react to my appearance.

So much has changed.

So much hasn't.

My legs are shaking. My right foot is pressed so tightly on the brake pedal I feel my ankle might shatter. I look down. That's when I realize I am barefoot. I literally ran out of my shoes.

I lean on the steering wheel and stare at my foot.

One step forward.

Two steps back.

I suddenly picture my grandfather's foot. He lost toes to diabetes and yet he could still feel them, would swear he was wiggling them.

"The pain is excruciating," he'd tell me when I would visit him.

My grandmother would sit on a footstool and pretend to massage them, even though they were not there.

"Ghost pain," she would say.

For the first time, I begin to cry, my old wounds reopened.

No matter how much time has passed and scar tissue has built, it only takes a word, a look, a confrontation, hate to tear it wide open again.

The ghost pain never goes away.

Cars honk.

I head my car toward Dorian Gay to tell Teddy about what happened. I need a protector. As I drive, my cell begins to buzz.

Why didn't I think to call the police?

I retrieve my phone from the pocket of my sweater.

Texts from Rebecca and my daughter, Leah.

Esther said you met someone.

Mom said you met a man.

Esther's gossip travels faster than a migrating hummingbird.

I laugh suddenly. And then, just as quickly, I veer into the left lane and do a U-turn.

I drive back to the library.

The digital sign and calendar of events out front of the mid-century building flashes the message:

BANNED BOOKS TO READ THIS WEEK!

I will not be banned.

I park my car and scan the lot for the woman. She is gone.

But my shoes are right where I left them, lined up in the parking lot as if they were by my bedside and I'd just slipped out of them for the night.

I step out of my car and put them back on.

"This old lady is fucking tired of running," I say.

"Teddy, I think I'm dying."

I am sitting on the end of a weight bench at the gym, talking to Teddy on the phone. The gym overlooks the Palm Springs Airport. Let's just say I've helped a lot of men empty their pockets before they ever reach TSA.

The airport is spread out before me. As I work out, I can see the planes coming and going, a never-ending stream of visitors from across the world arriving in and exiting from our winter oasis.

I think of the guy I was with last night . . . Levi? Liam? Lonnie?

I know it had an *L* in it.

"But you can still work out even on your deathbed?" Teddy asks.

"I have to work out," I say. "I have Nostalgia Con tonight at the convention center. That '80s convention, remember? My agent's assistant says it could big for me. I need to look good for producers and pictures."

"You still have an agent?" Teddy sounds surprised.

"Oh, my head. I'm dying, Teddy. Help me."

I hear Teddy sigh over the phone.

"What are your symptoms, Barry?" he asks. "Besides bad eye work that will always make you look perpetually surprised."

"I have a horrible headache. When I blink, I see spots. I think it's a brain tumor."

"Were you on WebMD again?" he asks. "Everything ends with a brain tumor. Even a splinter."

I don't answer.

"I take that as a yes," Teddy continues. "Sweetheart, you have a migraine because you're hungover. You see spots because you're dehydrated. I mean, I have a hangover just hearing that dreadful music at the gym and those loud planes taking off, and I only had two Rose Kennedys. If you're really worried about your health, I'd do a spot check down south. Logan did not look like he was a poster child for abstinence."

Logan! That was it!

"He was nice."

"He was a senior in college, and he stole twenty dollars from my wallet."

"That was me. I needed a venti Starbucks and oatmeal before I worked out. I'll pay you back, I promise. I plan to sell a million headshots tonight."

He doesn't say anything, but his exasperated sigh speaks volumes: *Yeah, sure, you'll pay me back. With what? The three dollars in residuals from your last commercial for no-rinse bathing wipes? I know how you make money: The down-low straight college boys toss you some cash to keep them happy and to keep your mouth shut. The money pipeline may have shut down from the Hollywood types you used to blackmail since everyone is gay now, but nothing has changed for men in the closet.*

"My big break is coming soon," I continue. "I promise."

"Your big break is going to be a shoulder considering those weights you sling around at your age," Teddy says.

"Can I work in?"

I look up. A man as beautifully dark and chiseled as the Chocolate Mountains outside the windows is staring at me.

"Speaking of dumbbells," Teddy says, overhearing.

"I have to go."

"Barry . . . don't! Have some dignity for once in your life!"

I hang up on him.

"I'm Cole."

Cole is holding an eighty-pound dumbbell in each hand.

"Barry," I say, lowering my voice. I stand. "Have a seat, brah."

"Spot me?"

I move behind the bench as he lies down on his back.

This man is perfect.

He lifts the set of dumbbells into the air. I count.

"Just one more rep," I say. "C'mon! You got it!"

The strain turns Cole's muscled arms jiggly, as if they're made of Jell-O, but he releases a grunt that would stop a charging elephant in its tracks and finishes his set strong.

"Nice work, man," I say.

"Thanks, Daddy."

Anyone over thirty today is a *daddy*.

"You're welcome."

"I'm mixing in legs today," Cole says.

"Your legs don't look like they need any work," I remark.

"More my ass," he says, giving it a slap. "It always needs work."

My headache begins to fade.

"Back in a sec."

I watch him walk away. I catch my reflection in the wall of mirrors.

I do not look my age, but no one's mistaking me for thirty either.

Fifties? Perhaps.

In a dimly lit room, I can hear Teddy add. *After cataract surgery. And three martinis.*

I look over at Cole doing squats.

What does he see? I wonder. A father figure fantasy? A meal ticket?

I look at myself again.

What do I see? My lost youth? Another momentary distraction?

Shall I be honest, or continue to write a screenplay and present it as a documentary?

My life as a gay man runs parallel to my life as an actor: It is constant, relentless rejection based on appearance.

I wrap this rejection in a false belief that the next man—or gig—will complete me.

I lost the *Golden Girls* gig at the same time I lost my first real boyfriend, Kyle Moses. We were both actors, of course. I worked at the Sherman Oaks Galleria at night, and Kyle delivered Domino's so we could keep our days free to audition. We met as extras on *Dynasty.* Joan Collins could sniff out a gay man more quickly than cubic zirconium, and she introduced me to Kyle at Craft Services.

I felt like Cupid shot an arrow through my heart that day. I fell head over heels. We were like lesbians and moved in together after three months of dating.

Kyle was from the Ozarks, a sweet boy with an all-American face, dimples you could plant tomato seeds in and a voice that sounded like a creek of running molasses. I had what casting directors called "gay face." In my youth, my appearance was fragile, pretty almost, and that alone was certain death in Hollywood in the 1980s. Couple it with a voice that sounded distinctly unmanly, and roles for me were, back then, as rare as an out actor. I have worked to change my face and voice over the years.

Kyle and I auditioned for everything. We would work for free. We just wanted to build our credentials.

We were contestants on *The Price Is Right* and *Let's Make a Deal*, played corpses on *Hill Street Blues* (we held hands between takes underneath our shrouds) and servers at The Regal Beagle on *Three's Company.*

And then Kyle and I both booked auditions to play Coco, neither of us believing we had a shot in the world at securing the role with such established actresses. When I got the call from my agent that I'd won the part, I ran out to buy a bottle of champagne I couldn't afford. When Kyle came home and I told him the news, he threw the bottle of champagne at me from across the room, and our world—quite literally—exploded.

Kyle blamed me for the breakup. He said I was selfish for taking a role I didn't deserve. When I left to start filming, Kyle accused me of abandoning him.

"You will regret this, you piece of shit!" he yelled. "I hate you! And so will the world! I hope you fail!"

I did.

And when I was cut from the show, I believed I deserved that, too.

Barry Goggins, I told myself, was not a nice guy. I hurt men. So why not just make being a villain my starring role for life?

Just a few months later, I was out of work, and Kyle was starring in the hit movie *Billy the Hillbilly* about a country boy who avenges his family's death. It spawned five sequels and made Kyle famous and richer than God.

I ended up on the cutting room floor, in life and love.

And so I slinked to the desert.

But that unquenchable desire to be wanted is never sated. It only grows stronger the older you get and the less time you have. You want to leave a mark before it's too late.

Sex and fame are drugs, and I can never get enough.

I even tried SCA for a while. Sexual Compulsives Anonymous is a twelve-step recovery program, like AA, for sexual addiction and romantic obsession, inclusive of all sexual orientations.

The few times I went to meetings, I thought, *No wonder these guys are here. They're butt-ugly. They couldn't get laid by a carpet installer.*

Hollywood isn't original. How many *Batman* reboots and teen romances can you make?

Some might say the same thing about me: trying to make

a living off of a show no one even remembers I got cut out of and then performing it in drag for old queens who want to relive the past. How original.

But we were among the first. Long before RuPaul and *Drag Race*, The Golden Gays were bringing humor and heart back to people who desperately needed to be reminded that they were loved and accepted, and that—despite the world telling them that we weren't equal, didn't deserve to have equal rights, couldn't marry, weren't accepted by God—we still had more in common than what separated us.

That's the show I wanted to bring to life.

I wanted to heal souls.

But somewhere along the way, that message got lost.

"Spot me again, Daddy?"

Cole is back, this time with hundred-pound dumbbells.

Gay men have turned themselves into walking stereotypes. I have done nothing to dispel those myths. I've turned myself into the exact opposite of what Hollywood hated when I began acting.

As Cole lifts, I suddenly see this same gym as it was in the 1980s, a time when we did not stare at our phones, when we had to look someone in the eye. There was an art to cruising: a look, a smile, a head nod.

We did not immediately ask—or dismiss—someone by asking if they were a bear or otter, twink or top, side, vers, pansexual, asexual, bisexual, androsexual.

We once built a tight community here, inclusive for all, but over time we have turned that into a gay *Hunger Games*, in which we hunt one another and tear each other apart. Our community belittles and ridicules—*Too fat! Too fem! Too poor! Too old! Not A-list!*—quickly depositing one another into categorical silos in order to make ourselves feel more worthy. But this only isolates us. We no longer meet those who are different from us, those who have battled similar wars. Now we view each other's differences not as a single stripe on a flag that makes us whole but as a scarlet letter.

As Cole does chest presses, he releases an ear-shattering grunt that sounds like an elephant.

I shake my head. There are even more categories for gay men who work out.

Grunting Gays—like me and Cole—are weightlifters and body builders; Cardio Queens monopolize the treadmills, elliptical machines, stair climbers and bikes to stay thin; the Yoga Queens come seeking calm and a lithe body only to emerge from class, get in their cars and cuss you out if you back out before them; Dancing Queens listen to music so loud it blasts from their earbuds, dancing around the gym as if they're at a circuit party; Quiet Queens go about their routines silently and with a sense of purpose as if they're cleaning house; the Silver Sneakers are seniors—like Sid—who do chair classes and walk the track, often six wide, blocking the path; the Professional Gays rush into the gym for a forty-five-minute exercise sprint and then disappear like ghosts; and the Selfie and Social Butterfly Queens don't really work out. They walk around the gym, often shirtless, taking selfie after selfie, giggling, FaceTiming with friends about who they're dating.

"Thanks, Daddy," Cole says, finishing his set. "Do you need a . . . hand?"

He jerks his head toward the gym bathroom and showers.

I hesitate just a moment, hearing Teddy's voice in my head.

"If you're really worried about your health, I'd do a spot check down south."

I look into Cole's amber eyes, seeking some sort of connection, anything.

I hesitate just long enough for Cole's phone to buzz, telling him someone else—someone better, hotter, richer, ready now!—is waiting. He begins to tap on his cell and walks away without another glance.

Next.

Just like Hollywood.

I check my watch. I have to finish and get ready for my date with destiny.

Or rather, infamy.

"You're out of paper towels."

I am standing at a card table at the end of a long hallway somewhere in the labyrinth of the Palm Springs Conference Center. I am not simply far removed from the Nostalgia Con stars speaking in conference rooms, I am parked directly in front of the men's and women's bathrooms.

"I'm not a restroom attendant," I say. I grab a headshot and hold it next to my face. "I'm Coco from *The Golden Girls*."

"Who?" the woman asks, giving me a once-over so severe that even God Himself would second guess His choices. "I thought they were all dead. And there wasn't a man on the show."

"There was! Me!"

I hold up a cast photo. I jab a finger at the man in the middle of the four women. "See?"

"You're charging twenty bucks for a creased picture autographed by an actor who wasn't even on the show?"

"I was in the premiere!" I insist. "And a question on *Jeopardy!*"

"Just let somebody know the women's room needs paper towels," she says.

Over the PA system, I hear, "The stars of *Saved by the Bell* and *ALF* will be appearing in Conference Room A in one minute!"

"Mario Lopez!" the woman screams. She begins to run. "I'm going to faint!"

The woman at the table next to me looks over and smiles. She is selling *Mr. Belvedere* T-shirts.

"First time at this convention?" she asks.

I nod.

"I'm Heather," she says. "This is actually good placement."

"You mean, as in next in line to clean the toilets?" I ask.

She smiles. "I'm serious. After this session, everyone will be lined up to use the bathroom. People get desperate when they have to tinkle, and they'll buy stuff like crazy just to keep their minds occupied. Better yet, most of the attendees usually don't buy tickets for the whole weekend, so they get desperate for merch at the end of the day."

She picks up a cast photo from her table and points at a young girl.

"That's me," she says. "I was the daughter on *Mr. Belvedere.* People only remember the butler and Bob Uecker. TV fans tend to only remember kids on their favorite shows as they were when they were young. It's too painful to realize we've gotten old just like they did."

"Like Thindy Brady?" I ask with a lisp.

Heather laughs.

"At least your show ran a long time," I continue. "I was cut before I could even get canceled."

"Just gives you a chance to reinvent yourself," she says. "I'll forever be Heather to those who watched our show. My acting career is over. You can still be anything."

In the distance, a small roar grows.

"I think Conference Room B with the former MTV veejays just released," she says. "Brace yourself."

A rush of Nostalgia Con attendees swarms the bathroom after ingesting a gallon of Coke Zero.

But Heather is right. People are ready to reminisce and buy merch while they wait.

"Oh, my God, I read about you," a gay couple says to me. "You would never be cut from the show today."

"Didn't I see you in a commercial out here for that new Indian restaurant?"

"You're Blanche in *The Golden Gays*, aren't you?" an older man asks. "I saw it with my family when they visited. You were so good. What are you doing now?"

Nothing.

"Still doing the show," I say with a big smile. "Come see it again. We reenact different episodes every month and give them our own unique spin."

"There's so much streaming content now," he says. "You'd think you might get a part in *something*."

And, punch to the gut. Barry nearly goes down but remains standing and smiling like the loser he is.

"I'm up for a few parts. Fingers crossed."

I sell about twenty headshots during the break, enough to keep me from locking myself in a bathroom stall and weeping, enough to shut Teddy up for another week or two, but not enough to keep me here to endure this new-school/old-school humiliation.

After everyone disappears, I'm packing up my wares when I hear, "Barry?" My heart stops. I would know that twang anywhere.

"Kyle?"

Kyle looks around, concerned I've said his name too loudly. He puts a finger over his lips and winks.

Everyone in the world knows the famous face of Kyle Moses. It's featured in *People* and the trades nearly every month. I also—between us—might have been stalking him online for decades out of jealousy.

"What are you doing *here*?" he asks.

I deserve to be punished for being so . . .

Kyle glances back at the men's room.

. . . shitty.

"Doesn't every A-lister get the table just outside the bathroom?" I quip.

He laughs.

I know he likes funny men because he's said his perfect husband (Brent, but of course, right?) makes him laugh harder than anyone. I also know that he has two Labs (named Pride and Joy, of course) and that his favorite paint color is Elephant's Breath by Farrow & Ball (*Architectural Digest* said this was a "very bold color" when he chose it for both his library *and* bedroom in his Malibu home).

"What are *you* doing here?" I ask.

He leans over the table until his face—which, for God's sake, still looks the same—and his mouth—which, kill me now, looks even better—are inches from mine.

Kyle stage-whispers, "I'm a surprise guest tomorrow. They sneaked me in the back to show me where I'll be going tomorrow. We're announcing a new *Billy the Hillbilly* sequel: *Billy's Back*. The TV show *Ozark* made the whole genre popular again."

"Congratulations," I say, my heart sinking into the gray carpet. "That's amazing."

"You should come," Kyle says. "I'll put your name on the list."

"Sure," I lie. "That's very sweet of you."

"So?" Kyle shakes his head and stares at me for the longest time. "Barry freaking Goggins? How have you been? It's been way too long."

"Forty years," I say. "Give or take a few."

"Jesus," Kyle says. "That long?"

It feels even longer. Years in Hollywood are measured like dog years: Every year is like seven you age on screen. I nod.

"I can't believe our paths haven't crossed," Kyle continues.

"I've been red carpet–adjacent these last few decades," I say. "And by that, I mean men's room–adjacent. And all the friends we used to know gave up the dream and moved back home to start families. They're grandparents now."

"What are you up to? Are you married?"

I want to tell Kyle there's this thing called social media now, which is how I know so much about him. Obviously, I've never crossed his mind. Not even one time where he might have thought, *God, what happened to the man I used to love?* But isn't that just like rich, famous people: They simply erase their pasts under a mantra of positivity that says *I am constantly evolving. I embrace change with an open mind and heart.* But what if you can't let go?

Kyle puts his hands on the table, and I suddenly remember when I would hold them as we ran dialogue together. They were smooth and strong. I glance down. They still are.

I open my mouth to answer, to say I'm sorry for hurting him, to ask why he was never happy for me, to tell him I'm still running and lonely and hanging on to the last rung of hope with my increasingly arthritic knuckles when a woman yells, "Billy the Hillbilly!"

From every corner of the Palm Springs Conference Center, people run, swarming Kyle until he's in the eye of a hurricane.

I grab my stack of headshots and disappear into the darkness of the desert, walking—faster and faster—until the pandemonium becomes a dull din.

When I reach my car, I place the headshots into the passenger seat, lock the doors, turn on the engine, turn up the radio and finally allow myself to scream.

"Ma, how would you react if one of your kids was gay?"

"I'll tell you the truth, Dorothy. If one of my kids was gay, I wouldn't love him one bit less. I would wish him all the happiness in the world!"

"That's because you're the greatest mother in the world, and I love you."

"Fine. Now keep your fat mouth shut so I can get some sleep."

The curtain closes. The crowd erupts.

"Let's hear it for The Golden Gays!" Patty O'Furniture says.

We take our final bows. I rush backstage into the dressing room while everyone remains to sign playbills and headshots, lock the door and will myself not to weep.

"Get a grip, Teddy," I say to myself in the mirror. "You do not cry!"

I dab the corners of my eyes with Kleenex.

I reposition my wig and stare at both Teddy and Dorothy, mother and son, character and real person.

"No one can see us be weak," I whisper to my reflection. "We are the strong, sarcastic, painfully honest glue that keeps everyone together."

I slap my cheek hard to sober myself though I have yet to have a cocktail.

"And yet you cannot be honest with your best friends," I sigh.

The thing most fans never realized about *The Golden Girls* is that they were friends, yes, of course, but first they were outcasts.

Four elderly women without husbands who no longer offered anything "of value" to society.

Who would protect an aging floozy, a dimwit, a stroke victim with no censor and her caustic daughter who wore her humor as a protective layer like her tunics?

Only each other.

They were fiercely funny, yes, but their humor masked their pain.

Especially Dorothy's.

I look in the mirror again.

Make others laugh so you won't get hurt.

Laugh, so you can't feel the stinging pain as sharply.

I think of my mother and all the years that have passed since her death. Would I—would all of my tribe—have turned out to be entirely different people had our mothers reacted the way Sophia did?

The doorknob rattles.

Or would we never have met?

I must make a decision—and quickly—about what to do and what to say.

"This is not a sitcom, Teddy," I whisper to my reflection. "This is life."

"Hello?" Barry calls in his Southern Blanche voice, now knocking on the door. "Teddy? I can hear you in there! Yoo-hoo!"

I stand and open the door.

"Sorry, I had to tinkle," I say. "Old bladder."

Barry looks at me and sweeps a hand dramatically across my body.

"Old man."

I give him my and Dorothy's signature withering glance.

Barry looks me over. "Well, I'm glad you didn't get any pee-pee on that tunic. We need you outside. Everyone wants to talk to Dorothy. You're like truth serum to fans."

A pain strikes me out of nowhere in the groin, and I wonder if it's an ironic phantom pain of guilt or a symptom of my cancer.

I turn to check my appearance one last time, and Barry catches me.

He eyes me even more closely.

"Oh, honey," Barry says. "Have you been crying?"

"No!" I protest. "Why would you ask that? I never cry."

"I can always tell when someone has been crying. It's instinct. Like when a man tells me he's thirty, but I see the truth in his hands."

"I wasn't crying." I pat Barry's cheek. "It just might be time for another eye job."

Barry places a hand on my shoulder. He tilts his head, and I see him become Blanche again.

"Crying is for plain women. Pretty women go shopping," he says, reciting a line from another *Golden Girls* episode.

"Well, this pretty woman wants to go drinking."

"Streetbar after, as always," Barry says.

I walk out, and Teddy turns into Dorothy again, releasing zingers and casting withering looks as photos are taken.

We finish and return to the dressing room. Ever the stage mother, Ron helps the other Golden Gays change. I remain in costume—sometimes Dorothy is my armor—and watch the routine. Ron removes their silicone breastplates, which adhere to the skin when we sweat, and then gently rubs lotion onto their backs to help soothe the red welts they have created. He takes off the wigs and gently places each atop its personal mannequin head for transport home.

I watch Ron buzz around, caring for each of us.

"You know what my great-uncle Sven, from St. Olaf always used to tell me, don't you, Dorothy?"

"No, Rose," I say, as if we're still on stage. "Illuminate me."

"Helgenbargen flergenflurfennerfen!"

I smile.

"You seem like you need a laugh tonight."

"You do seem off tonight, Teddy," Sid remarks.

"What is wrong with the three of you? I'm right as rain."

"But it never rains in the desert," Sid says with a knowing wink.

Be honest, Teddy. For once in your life.

"Tonight's episode always brings up memories of my mom and my family," I say.

Points for partial honesty.

Ron pins a wig to the mannequin form and walks over to me.

"Did you ever call your sister back?" he asks.

The man never misses a thing. He must have seen my cell ringing at Church of Mary. He knows how I refer to Trudy. He must know she's been on my mind. He knows . . . *everything.*

I shake my head.

Ron smiles sadly and touches my arm. Sid meets my eyes.

"Look, you didn't ask for my advice, but I'm going to give it to you anyway because I'm the oldest around here," he says, using a makeup wipe to scrub the dark lines off his forehead that make him look even older on stage.

"By far," I add.

"Don't look back," Sid continues. "All you'll see is your tuchus, and you can't change that either."

The room explodes into laughter.

"Feel better?" Ron asks.

I nod. "What should I wear to Streetbar?" I ask.

Barry looks at me, considering.

"No knits. Bad tits."

"Nothing sleeveless!" the rest of the girls yell in unison.

They head out the side door of the theater.

"Coming?" they call back to me.

"Meet you there!"

When the door slams, I walk back into the theater, still dressed as Dorothy.

I stand on stage all alone.

"You come into this world alone, and you leave this world alone. Always remember that."

This was one of my father's favorite lines.

"But you sent me into the world alone as a kid, Dad," I say.

There is a world of difference between being lonely and alone, and there is a yawning void between the family we are born into and the one we choose.

I square my shoulders, lift my head and say one of my favorite Dorothy lines ever, the one that sums her up best, reveals she isn't actually a pessimist but a realistic optimist.

"The bottom line is, in life, sometimes good things happen, sometimes bad things happen. But honey, if you don't take a chance, nothing happens."

I take a bow to no one.

Like millions of people, I watched *The Golden Girls* every Saturday night at 8:00 p.m. sharp with my mom. The only difference was that—for many years—my mom and I watched it separately but together across the country from one another.

My mother would sneak upstairs after Daddy had fallen asleep on the couch downstairs watching sports and downing a six-pack of Stroh's and call me from her red rotary phone. I could always picture the handset held to her ear, the cord snaking as far as it would uncoil from the hallway to her bedroom, a pretend umbilical cord stretching from Michigan to California.

John would always tease me about the dinners I'd make when I'd watch the show long-distance with my mom: appetizers that ranged from Funyuns with French onion dip to Jeno's Pizza Rolls, a dinner of Cheeseburger Macaroni Hamburger Helper, Manwiches or TV dinners, a dessert of Hostess Fruit Pies (I loved all things lemon now that I lived in Palm Springs), and a couple of watermelon Bartles & Jaymes wine coolers to wash it all down. You can take the boy out of the country, I always told John, but you can't take the country out of the boy.

"What about the cholesterol?" he would joke.

For the first couple of years, my mama and I would chat at commercial breaks about the show, but *never* about our lives.

Then, one Saturday, after the show had ended, she said casually, "Your Daddy died last night. Stroke."

"Good riddance," was all I could manage to say at first, before finally asking, "Are you okay?"

"Best night of sleep I've ever had," she said.

I went home alone for Christmas that year to see her. John had to work, and we didn't have much money. I was finally allowed back now that Trudy had moved out and Daddy was gone. First night home, I went searching for some comfort (Southern Comfort, that is), and I was shocked to discover the liquor cabinet—and Windex bottles—were empty. See, Mama used to pretend to clean the windows and bathrooms every single day. But I knew those Windex bottles were filled with vodka, and Mama was just trying to erase her life.

"How'd you finally give up drinking, Mama?" I asked.

"Just listen," she said, cocking her head.

The old windows creaked in the wind. Birds chirped outside in the snow.

"I don't need to silence your father's demons anymore," she continued. "His pain is no longer mine."

"What do you do with all your spare time now that you used to spend washing the windows?"

"Why, you little sumbitch," she said. "You always knew!"

She laughed so hard she spit up blood.

That's when we knew the end of her show was near. I came home to stay with her the next fall 'til her finale.

First Saturday I was home, my Mama looked over at me and said, "We can finally watch the show *together.*"

My God, my mama was strong. Gave up drinking. Fought cancer. Refused to leave her home. I got all that fire, too, deep inside. I just wish she'd used an ounce of that strength to protect me when I needed it most.

One Saturday when we sat down to watch *The Golden Girls*, Mama finally asked what my life had been like after I'd been kicked out of the house after being discovered taking a literal roll in the hay in the barn with a local farm boy who'd been hired to bale. I didn't pull any punches. I told her I hitchhiked my way across the country to a place I'd heard of called Palm Springs. I told her what I had to do to survive. I told her I'd nearly died many times because of her. Told her I wanted to die many times because of her. Slept in a shelter. Slept around. Sneaked into bars. Finally met an old queen everyone called Madame Q who told me I'd be dead in a year if I continued living the way I was.

"Murder or AIDS, you pick," he'd told me, sipping a Rose Kennedy.

He let me stay in his casita for free, helped me get my GED and a job. I thought he wanted to sleep with me. One day, I walked into his bedroom shirtless and asked how I could pay him back.

"Oh, my dear, I don't eat chicken," he said with a laugh. "I was just like you when I was young. Too many of us have the same sad story. Kicked out. Unwanted. Unloved. It's not fair, but life never is, straight or gay. Want to pay me back? Love yourself. Be good to yourself. Be proud of who you are. Don't walk around in shame. Find your community. And give back to your community when they need it most, and—believe me—they will always need it. When you go to a bar, seek out a friend, not a fuck buddy. Now, shoo. And eat a burger and some fries."

My mother didn't cry or apologize. She just listened.

"Palm Springs," she finally said. "Your father called it the land of fruits and nuts."

"That's not funny, Mama. No child should ever endure what I did," I said, looking her right in the eye. "You had the power to stop it, and you didn't do a thing about it. And you will face God with that decision. And if He tells you that you did the right thing, well, then, I'll be on a different cloud watching *The Golden Girls.*"

"Your Great-Aunt Dizzy sent me a bracelet from Palm Springs years ago when she vacationed there." That was her response to me. Didn't protest or deny a thing. "Prettiest thing I ever saw. She told me it was the color of their sunsets over the mountain."

When she looked at me, I saw one tear.

One tear.

I got my Mama's one and only tear in life. God, I'm just like her.

"Ssshh!" she then said when the theme music started. "It's on!"

My mother's death rattle reared up every time Dorothy landed a zinger.

"You're just like her," my mom would say without looking over, jamming a bent finger toward the television. "Damn spitfire."

When that episode ended, my mother grabbed my face between her hands as I cleared the plates. "We've always been a lot alike, the two of us. In fact, you got both Dorothys in you, Theodore. Me and Bea. And don't you live your whole life alone like I have. Die surrounded by friends like them Golden Girls. Surrounded by love. Real love, not pretend love."

"What do you mean?"

"There's a big difference between pretend love and real love. I pretended to love your daddy, but I never did. Grew up in a time when I didn't have a chance to do anything else but survive: I wasn't rich, I wasn't smart, I wasn't pretty, but, my God, I did love you, Teddy. I'm sorry I grew up in a time when we didn't know how to show it."

"And Trudy?" I asked.

"Don't know if she's capable of being loved."

"I am loved, Mama," I finally said. "Even though I've never felt like I deserved it."

Every week when *The Golden Girls* would end, my mama would always say, "Now I gotta wait another week. What if I'm not around to see a new episode?"

"They got TVs in heaven, Mama," I'd say, "although I'm not sure that's exactly where you're headed. Elevator goes both ways. But just in case," I'd add, "I'd better work my magic. You don't want to wear those ratty old pajamas and nasty housecoat forever in the afterlife."

"Do your magic," she'd say to me.

Before I came home to look after Mama, I had been working the Lancôme counter at the mall in Rancho Mirage, down valley from Palm Springs, trying to make corpses look like MTV stars. But I was getting really good with makeup and hair. So good a fine-boned man asked me one afternoon if I did drag. I didn't really know what that was at the time.

I learned fast and started doing the wigs and makeup of drag queens all over the desert. Then I started dressing them. I had a real eye for glamour, it turned out. You can make a black eye go away with concealer and fake lashes. You can become a different person with the right hair and makeup.

"A little hair, a little paint, makes a lady what she ain't."

I just hope God thought Mama was someone else when He greeted her. My handiwork might have been the only thing that gave her a shot with the Big Guy.

John always told me before we went out on a date that I had to put on something extra nice just in case we got in an accident and died. He was serious, too.

"If you die today, that's going to be your ghost outfit," John said. "You'll wear it forever in the afterlife. So plan accordingly."

So, the last night of Mama's life, I dressed her up real pretty like the ladies she loved on TV and made her some Jeno's Pizza Rolls. I worked my magic on Mama while she just watched me: Despite her pain, I got Mama out of her ratty old gown and into a fabulous caftan, a bold cat eye, fake eyelashes, red lipstick and a red wig I teased within an inch of its life. A sweet hospice nurse had been bringing me wigs from the American Cancer Society.

"You can die in peace now, knowing you look like an angel," I told Mama when I was done, not expecting it to be a premonition.

"Or a whore," she said when I held up a mirror.

An hour later, Mama went to heaven or hell looking like Ann-Margret.

Bye Bye Birdie.

Man, Mama hated to miss an episode, so I curled up next to her in that bed, put my head on her shoulder, and we watched it together, like we'd done every Saturday the past few months.

This was our finale.

And if you don't think God has a sense of humor, the last episode of *The Golden Girls* we watched was about a funeral. The show was entitled "It's a Miserable Life." How's that for irony?

In the show, Sophia attends a funeral service for a woman she never liked.

"Pay your respects?" Dorothy asks her mother, stunned by her attendance. "You hated her."

"I did," Sophia says. "But when a person dies, you go to their funeral to show the man above you have respect for human life, no matter how wretched it was. Any idiot knows that."

God, Mama's life was wretched.

Why did I go home again? To pay my damn respects.

I quit my job and moved home to take care of a woman who didn't take care of me. I even left John and all my friends. I left a man who was too good for me. Too good for this world. Good people are like butterflies: beautiful, fragile, but short-lived. But John reminded me what was possible when you believe in the good in life and others. And you want to know the strangest thing? When someone believes in you, loves you so much, fills you with so much warmth that you can actually hear your heart crack like the frozen earth on the first spring day in Michigan, it changes how you see the world and yourself.

You see light, not dark.

And that light led me home to the early winter darkness of Michigan to give Mama what she could never give me: a sliver of forgiveness. A molecule of understanding. One damn moment of peace.

Unconditional love.

Maybe I did it because she didn't have anyone or any money. A lifetime of living isolated in rural America and outliving her friends meant she had no one. You sure weren't coming back now that Daddy was gone. Sure, Mama had Medicaid, but that didn't mean the only hospital within a hundred miles accepted it. And how could she even get there on her own for her treatments, scans and doctor visits?

Maybe I came home because I wasn't allowed at Daddy's funeral. No one wanted a scene, but let me clear the air: I wasn't planning on causing one. I was simply planning to take a piss on the old man's grave in front of the whole town just as he'd done to me my whole life.

Or—let's be completely honest here, okay?—maybe I came home again to prove to Trudy, Mama and Daddy that I was a better person than any of them. Maybe I took care of her to prove to myself I was a good person, like the one John saw. Or maybe I did it to show her I was the same person I'd always been.

Or maybe I did it because I knew that, for the first time in her life, Mama just needed a friend.

Then I called the funeral home to pick up Mama and make the arrangements, and I told them to call my sister and tell her our mama had died happy, after watching her last episode of *The Golden Girls*. I couldn't afford a funeral, I didn't want to stick around long enough for one, but, mostly, I did it to piss off Daddy: My God, he loved a funeral. He loved forcing the entire town to come out and pay tribute to a monster they saw as a hero. As I said, I think God has a sense of humor.

By the time the funeral home called Trudy, I had written a letter to her telling her everything I felt, put the flag up on Mama's mailbox for the last time, turned around and took the letter back out, and was already back on the road headed west.

The only thing I took from my mama's house was the beautiful Bakelite bracelet of orange and gold that Dizzy gave her, the one I used to sneak out of her jewelry box. It was the one I was wearing and waving in the air when I dressed up in Mama's finest the first time. I was pretending to be Cher, and Trudy caught me. She called for Daddy to beat the devil out of me.

Inside Dizzy's bracelet was a stamp that read VINTAGE JEWELRY OF PALM SPRINGS.

This was the reason I had gone to the desert in the first place so many moons ago.

I didn't stop driving until I arrived home to a sunset over the mountains that was as orange and gold as the bracelet I had slipped around my wrist.

Dizzy was right. This bracelet was magical.

I never heard from Trudy again.

Even after my friends reached out to let her know John had died.

Unlike my bracelet, family and guilt would never be ligatures that strangled Trudy.

A Rose Kennedy is already waiting for me at Streetbar.

"Why didn't you change, Teddy?" Ron asks.

"Nobody fucks with an old lesbian in a gay bar."

He laughs. I survey the crowd.

The bar is packed to the gills inside and out, not an inch to move. A line snakes down Arenas.

"How's your drink?" the bartender asks me as soon as I take my first sip. He knows the regulars.

"All vodka," I say to him. "Just the way I like it. Just the way you like it so you'll get a big tip at the end of the night."

Mario winks. He has been hermetically sealed into a tank top, and his biceps could form their own government.

"I would never let Dorothy go thirsty."

"Thank you, baby. You want a real tip, Mario?" I ask. "Don't sleep with Barry. Ever."

"Too late," Barry says, leaning down the bar to salute me with his martini.

"Whatever happened to the art of conversation?" Ron asks us, shaking his head.

"Exactly!" Sid concurs. "Getting to know one another is still the hottest part of dating."

"Says a man who hasn't been on one since *MacGyver* was on TV," Barry yells.

I can see Sid's face fall.

"There's no need to talk anymore," Barry continues, not realizing he's embarrassed Sid. "All it takes is a text and the right photo. Bada bing bada boom."

I listen to my friends verbally spar as they eye the hundreds of sweating men packed into the place like sardines.

There is nothing like a gay bar. It is our community's Church of Mary.

This is the thing you need to know about a gay bar: It is our safe space.

It is communal, almost spiritual, a place where we can unashamedly, unabashedly be ourselves.

I hear even louder verbal sparring and turn my attention toward the door.

A group of gay men is barring the entrance of a bachelorette party.

The fact that bachelorette parties have overrun our gay bars is a huge bone of contention. Palm Springs has become one of the most popular destinations for bachelorette parties; women arrive in droves, dressed in sashes and crowns, taking over our drag shows, gay bars, restaurants. I get it: They like our music.

They want to dance. They want to be complimented on their too-short dresses. They love our company. They desire our advice. But the reality is, they can go anywhere and be welcomed. We cannot. And so we have taken our community back.

Many gay bar owners in the area have let bachelorette parties know in not-so-subtle terms that they are no longer welcome. Does that sound wrong to you? Discriminatory? Judgmental? I don't care. Go to Tommy Bahama.

What would happen—may I ask you—if my gay bachelor party showed up at your local sports bar? Would the fellas there buy us drinks and dance with us and treat us like we were the most special human beings in the entire world for doing something we weren't allowed to do until only a decade ago because we were denied the most basic of rights? If anyone would have the right to celebrate our marriages, it would be us, right?

Uh-huh.

But there is a deeper reason: Gay bars have saved the lives of many a gay man seeking inclusion in a world that told him he didn't belong. Gay bars saved my life when I moved to Palm Springs. When you are exhausted from running from hatred, you need a spot to rest and be accepted without any judgment.

I know that the four D's usually come to mind when we think of gay bars (and I'm not even including the "Big D" in this analogy): drinking, drugs, disease and debauchery. And, yes, it can be all of that. I've witnessed some bad scenes along Arenas, many of which included movies from my own life, but there is something more that is found here: a common, united history.

I glance around the bar.

We fought to be here.

I look around this bar and suddenly think of Stonewall in Greenwich Village on a summer's night in 1969. Some fifty years later, these bars, you must understand, are still the places we gather as society continues to demonize us and take away our rights.

Where can we go to forget the hate that surrounds us?

Here. And few other places.

Our beloved Streetbar was the first gay bar in Palm Springs, long before Arenas Road became the epicenter of gay culture and fun in the city. It was originally called A Streetbar Named Desire.

I mean, c'mon. The gays are always the cleverest creatures, my dear.

I look out the windows that face the street. Arenas is packed. Every bar.

Today, Arenas is home to a block filled with every type of gay bar imaginable, from dance tunes and show tunes to strippers, leather and lesbian. It is even filled with shopping, from upscale clothing to GayMart, a sort of Walmart for the gays.

Over the years, Streetbar and Arenas have become an oasis during our fight for equality, and today are a welcoming spot for the LGBTQ+ community and their allies.

"Are you supposed to be Hillary Clinton?"

I turn my head as a very drunk man elbows his way to the bar.

"Yes," I say. "And I was supposed to be president."

He looks at me like I have two heads and orders a vodka Red Bull, the drink of choice for a generation that also likes espresso martinis. By all means, let's get hypercaffeinated *and* drunk.

I finally take a sip of my pink drink.

A Rose Kennedy is always the same: vodka, club soda and a splash of cran with a lemon wedge. Simple, refreshing, does the trick, and even a moron could make it right in a busy bar. The cocktail got its name many moons ago in a DC gay bar called Trumpets, and the drink contained only enough cranberry to make it subtly pink. We wanted to get drunker faster back in the day.

PS: When a lime is used as garnish, it becomes an Ethel Kennedy.

I told you the gays are the cleverest creatures.

The man grabs his drink and, as he turns, attempts to focus on my appearance again.

"Who are you, then?"

"I told you," I say. "Hilary Duff. I've aged a bit since *Lizzie McGuire*."

He stumbles away.

I glance down the bar, wondering why my friends didn't laugh. That's when I see: One of the hottest men in the bar is standing next to Barry, chatting him up.

"Are you kidding me?" I ask Ron, nudging him with my elbow. "What is it with Barry? I mean, every gay man gets a couple of drinks in him and thinks he's Hugh Jackman."

Ron glances down the bar.

"That guy is actually talking to Sid."

I do a spit take with my drink.

"What? Is he seeking legal counsel in Streetbar?"

"I have no idea, but just look at Barry," Ron says with a laugh. "He's apoplectic."

I lean onto the bar and glance at Barry, who has puffed his chest like a rebuffed turkey. Ron is absolutely filled with delight. The man talking to Sid is quite attractive, even by weekend bar standards, but there is something that makes him stand out in the crowd: an old-school Hollywood look—a sort of modern-day Gregory Peck—squared shoulders, a look of ease and confidence, as if he could care less what the world thought about him in a world like Streetbar where we only cared what everyone thought. I glance at Barry and revel in his being overlooked for once.

"He's coming unglued! Barry hasn't received this little attention from a good-looking man since he got his facelift. Remember how long that took to settle? He looked like Tootsie for a year."

I laugh and glance down the bar again. I nudge Ron to look.

Barry slowly unbuttons his shirt, takes it off and tucks it into the back of his too-tight jeans. He presses closer to the man talking to Barry and is essentially eye-fucking the back of the guy's head. The man continues to remain fully focused on Sid.

"Barry is going to lose it," Ron says, giggling.

I lift my glass to take a sip when someone crashes directly into my back, causing me to spill my cocktail.

"Excuse you," I say, turning.

A twink wearing a bridal crown and a sash reading SAME PENIS FOREVER elbows his way to the bar as if he owns it.

He ignores me and motions for Mario.

When Mario finally makes his way over, the kid deigns to look at me. "I'm getting married. You're supposed to buy me a drink." He looks at Mario. "Cosmo. And you can put it on this lady's tab."

Mario holds his hands in the air. He already knows what is about to go down.

"I'm not buying you a drink," I say.

"Why?" he pouts.

"Because you're a disrespectful little shit. You don't even know who I am, do you?"

"I know you're old and ugly."

"Touché, thou with the concave back and hideous highlights. May I suggest you google a TV show called *The Golden Girls*, sweetheart? It aired long before you were a mistake in your white trash mother's beer-bloated womb and long before any of us sitting at the bar had the right to marry."

"The golden what?"

"*The Golden Girls*," I say. "Just so you know, the show was so popular that most gay bars on a Saturday night just like this would dim the lights, pause the music and dancing, and put the show on their screens so patrons could watch it together. The show and these bars were about found family, community, respect and safety." I shake my head at him. "We've gained so many rights but lost so much of our history. It's sad."

"What's sad is you," he says. "You're just angry because no one ever wanted to marry a nasty old drag queen. And now you're going to die all alone."

My rage builds.

And then he pivots on his toes, reaches out and tweaks my nose. "Are we angry because no one ever wanted to marry a nasty, old drag queen? And now you're going to die all alone?"

I can hear my heart thump loudly in my ears, louder than the music playing in here. My thump is a soundtrack to our collective history—the history of my marriage, of Stonewall, of Streetbar, of every gay man who went to war so this entitled twink could get married—and it is now playing in sync with the disco music in the background.

Mario places a Cosmo on the bar.

I pick it up before the young man can and toss it into his face.

"You're welcome," I say. "For everything. And, yes, you can put that drink on my tab!"

I feel Ron's hand on mine, squeezing firmly, urging me to calm down just as he does when he asks me to shut my eyes and pray.

The twink howls and storms away.

"That wasn't nice, Teddy," Ron says. He leans over and puts his head on my shoulder. "But it was necessary," he whispers.

I kiss him on top of the head and slam my cocktail. "I must go be with my people."

I walk out of Streetbar and cross the street, past a dance club and directly into a show tunes bar.

"Hi, Dorothy!"

Bob, the bouncer out front, gives me a kiss on the cheek when I arrive.

"Finally, the respect I deserve!"

I head inside. The first thing I hear is the crowd screaming, "*No wire hangers!*" A clip from *Mommy Dearest* is playing on the big screen TVs, the patrons roaring in laughter. In the blink of an eye, *Oklahoma!* begins to play, and the crowd roars again, changing the lyrics ever so slightly to fit the mood.

The bar is full, nearly everyone is over sixty. Televisions play the same songs from the same old musicals over and over: *Hello, Dolly!*, *Seven Brides for Seven Brothers*, *The Best Little Whorehouse in Texas*, *Mame*, *Wicked*. It never changes. And that routine is comforting.

Keith, the head bartender, holds up a Rose Kennedy as soon as he sees me. When he hands it to me, I hear the crowd roar again.

"Oklahomo! So gay!"

I scan the bar for a seat.

A line of small tables sits against the back wall, a long banquette running the length of the wall before the windows, and I lift my tunic to prevent it from being stomped on as I slink toward the only open spot. As soon as I get settled and take a sip, I hear my name.

"Teddy?"

Larry and Phil are seated next to me.

I stare at them, unable—for once—to find any words.

Their faces look as surprised as mine must.

I haven't seen either of them since John died. The two of them used to be constants in our lives: euchre nights, Church of Mary, Bill's Pizza once a month. They were John's friends when we met, but I believed they became mine, too, over time. In fact, I was the social conduit for the four of us, the one who scheduled our meetups.

"How have you been?" Larry asks.

How do I answer?

People always talk about which friends you lose after a breakup, when people eventually end up taking sides, but few talk about the friends you lose when a spouse dies. It's a double death. I tried a few times to reach out to Larry and Phil in the weeks and months after John's funeral. At first they offered weak excuses for not being able to get together. Then they stopped responding altogether. I was pissed, but figured that some people simply couldn't revisit the sadness and grief that lingers like a fog when they see me, now a third wheel without my other half. Then I heard firsthand that Larry had been suggesting to our mutual friends that I had somehow contributed to John's depression and suicide.

Ron coaxed me out of the house to grocery shop with him at Ralphs a few weeks after John died. It was one of my first public appearances, which I agreed to solely because I had been promised pints of Ben & Jerry's Cherry Garcia ice cream and gallons of vodka. I was moping behind Ron, who actually shopped with glee.

I was standing behind a fogged and frosty freezer door, headfirst into the ice cream, when I heard Larry and Phil talking to Ron.

"How is Teddy doing?" Larry asked.

"He's . . ."

Before Ron could say, "right here," Larry continued.

"I mean, knowing how his behavior must have influenced John's mental health."

"What do you mean?" Ron asked.

"Teddy's antics," Phil added. "His drinking. He was never very sensitive to John's ups and downs. I mean, a joke and a gin and tonic don't make someone better."

"Teddy loved John," Ron said, his voice trembling. "He was the one who got John help. This was a tragedy. He will live without his husband the rest of his life, questioning what he could have done. But love and emotional support are not a substitute for professional treatment, and John had been lying to all of us about the help he had been receiving."

"Teddy should have known," Larry argued.

"This conversation—and alleged friendship—is over right now!" Ron said furiously.

By the time they had finished, I was standing in the freezer, door closed, entombed in mint chocolate chip. Ron played nursemaid to me for another month before I could venture out again.

And here they were acting like nothing ever happened, not the conversation at the grocery or the ones behind my back, as if we just saw each other last week for drinks and a card game.

"Wonderful!" I lie. "Show's going great, as you know." I bow dramatically and give my tunic a dramatic flick. "The Golden Gays are all still golden."

Phil and Larry exchange a glance. It is not subtle. They are reading one another's faces to gauge whether to believe my levity.

"I'm so relieved," Larry finally says. "We've missed you."

I look at both of them, my head nodding even as bile sears my stomach.

And that's when I see it: Larry is wearing one of John's old watches. A gold Timex I'd given to John when we first opened Dorian Gay.

"This will forever be a symbol of time," I told John. "Of how much it took for us to find each other, and of how much we should celebrate every minute we have left together in this world."

Why did I let Larry have it when he told me it would just be too painful for me to keep?

In the background, I hear Keith announce, "Karaoke is starting in the next room!"

I stand.

"Well, they're calling my name," I say. "It's been too long."

"Yes," they both say, fidgeting, smiling a smile that lets me know I will never, ever hear from them again. Larry looks at John's watch. "Well, look at the time. We never stay out this late."

I nod at the Timex. "Time sure flies," I say. "Bye."

I move through the crowd and head into karaoke, where I patiently wait my turn while a middle-aged gay who fancies himself Britney Spears croons off-key, "Hit me, baby, one more time."

"I'd like to," I tell a couple next to me.

When it's my turn, I pick a song few will know. Even fewer

will understand its personal history. Dorothy performed this on an episode of *The Golden Girls*, and when I first heard her sing it, I wept—for one of the few times in my life—like a baby. I was all alone at the time, and it struck a chord deep inside. I now sing it only when we perform that episode, and its lyrics touch me like no other.

The music to "What'll I Do" begins to play. I sing in a deep, dramatic mezzo-soprano.

As I do, my eyes scan the crowd. Slowly, patrons began to sway.

A man walks through the spotlight, and—for one moment—his face is highlighted. My heart leaps. He looks just like John when we first met. The man's eyes briefly catch mine. He nods, and then he's gone, moving through the dark like a ghost.

What'll I do with just a photograph to tell my troubles to?
When I'm alone with only dreams of you that won't come true, what'll I do?

What will I do without you, John?

When the song is over, I take a bow and then head into the darkness of the desert.

I think of Larry and Phil as I walk down the street, texting for an Uber.

So many people believed that John lived in my shadow, but he was my light. The moon, you realize, my dears, is only illuminated by the reflection of the sun.

I stop, feeling something unfamiliar, and look up.

It is raining in the desert.

Alone at a bar yet again.

The second half of the movie of my life has frequently been filled with such memorable lines as "Table for one?", "Will someone be joining you?" (as the extra settings are swept from the table), "So, why are you still single?" and "Don't you get lonely?"

I have never gotten used to going to a movie alone or having a drink by myself at a bar. I already feel so self-conscious sitting alone, and it doesn't help that everyone stares as if I have two heads and whispers behind their hands, trying to figure out my story, before giving me that sad smile that reads, *Widower, Loser,* or *Too uptight for a relationship.*

Esther tells me that it is a sign of strength to navigate the world alone. I tell her she can barely navigate her SUV out of a Ralphs parking lot without orange cones and a traffic cop.

Over the din in Streetbar, I hear the song "Alone Again (Naturally)" by Gilbert O' Sullivan in my head.

Could I be sadder on a Saturday night?

I need a laugh. I turn to ask Teddy if Gilbert O'Sullivan is Irish, or perhaps is related to Patty O'Furniture, but he looks sad tonight, too. Is it his sister that's on his mind? Ron had told me she had called during Church of Mary and that Teddy had ignored her.

I understand what it's like to be ignored.

I feel a hand on my shoulder.

Don't turn around, Sid.

No one ever talks to an old man in a gay bar unless they've mistaken him for Harrison Ford or are blind drunk and want an easy target for a free drink.

I swivel on my barstool. A beautiful man is smiling at me.

I pivot my head around the bar, wondering who is lucky enough to be at the receiving end of this man's radiance.

"Sid Silverstein?" he asks.

It finally hits me.

"Hot Jew?" I exclaim.

I slap a hand over my mouth.

"Oh, my God! I am so sorry," I continue. "I am not a big drinker. My lips have little synchronicity with my brain but—after half a martini—there is zero control."

"I take that as a compliment." He laughs. "Don't worry. I heard you and your friend the other day. She's quite the fireplug."

"In stature and volume."

He laughs again.

"Leo Levy," he says, extending his hand.

"How could I forget?" I blurt. "I'm just flattered you remembered me."

I stare at this man's perfect face. I had a dream about him the other day that was not G-rated. I think we were making out in the back of an Edsel, which pretty much sums up the time frame in which I was last intimate with a man.

"Better a slap from a sage than a kiss from a fool," Esther said about the dream. "And I know you've kissed some fools. That dream means something!"

I realize I am staring at Leo.

Speak, Sid, speak!

My mouth is wired shut. What do I say to him?

You . . . so . . . pretty. Me want.

Say something, stupid!

"What on earth are you doing here?" I finally ask.

"Well, I saw your show tonight," Leo says.

"You saw our show?"

"I did."

"You did?"

"Are you mirroring me?" Leo asks.

"What?"

"It's an old journalist's technique. You repeat what the person you're interviewing just said to trick them into losing track of what they're saying and eventually give up some good information," Leo says.

"I'm not doing that," I say. "You're just so good-looking I don't know what to say. I'm all tongue-tied."

Leo smiles. "That's very sweet, Sid."

Sweet. Ugh.

I hold up my cocktail.

"This martini sure has a big mouth," I add.

He chuckles.

"So?" I continue. "What did you think of *The Golden Gays*?"

"I absolutely loved it," Leo says. "Although *The Golden Girls* was never my thing, considering I was still in high school when it first aired."

Kill me.

"But I recently started doing research on a subject I plan to interview, and I started watching the reruns. It's still very funny, timely and relevant. And each of you was a mirror image of the characters. I enjoyed it more than I can say."

"Thank you," I say. "So? Who are you interviewing?"

Mario brings Leo a gin and tonic.

"You."

He lifts his cocktail in salute to me.

I again cannot form any words as he smiles at me. His dark eyes are locked on mine, and I finally notice he has the cutest little dimple in the chin of his strong jaw, as if a small sliver of granite was chiseled away to make him look a little bit more vulnerable.

I set down my martini glass and try to act casual. I place my chin in my hand and pull up the loose skin on my face with my fingertips.

"Are you okay?" Leo asks. "I hope that didn't come as too much of a shock."

I release my head from my hand. I can feel my face fall.

"It is a little," I say. "You're a reporter? You kept that a secret."

Leo laughs. "I'm superstitious like my Ima."

And I have confirmation: Leo Levy, as his name implied, is Jewish.

Hot Jew in the house.

"I'm a TV reporter," Leo explains. "Earlier this year I was let go from a station in the Bay Area after working there for nearly thirty years, and I was planning on retiring until I came to Palm Springs to lick my wounds. I fell in love with the desert, which I didn't expect. I ended up having lunch with an old friend who is the GM at a local TV station. He told me he was hiring for a morning anchor, and I told him I was too old to get up at four in the morning." Leo pauses. "And goodness knows I'll be hitting the early bird specials and going to bed at seven p.m. before too long."

I laugh and take a sip of my martini. Leo continues.

"But I started watching the local news in the desert, and I discovered there was a vital piece of reporting missing. Nearly half of Palm Springs is gay, and a quarter of the Coachella Valley is over sixty. Very little news was being reported specifically for those populations. On a lark, I created a segment called 'Gray and Gay.'"

"Very clever."

"Thank you," Leo says. "I thought about 'You Bet Your Sweet Bippy,' but that seemed too much."

"True."

"I ended up recording a few segments about issues that directly impact those communities," he continues, "from affordable housing and health care to elder abuse and elder care. And the GM offered me a job. I'm moving to Palm Springs full-time. I didn't want to jinx it when I was talking to you at the track. I'm a little superstitious."

His announcement makes me feel as giddy as a schoolgirl. I choose my words carefully, so I don't blurt *I love you, Leo!* or *Suspicious mole!*

"That's so fascinating and so needed," I say instead. "But why do you want to interview me?" I smile at him. "I'm not that interesting. You really should talk to Barry or Teddy about the show. They're the masterminds behind it. They have all the talent."

Leo surveys my face.

"A source at the library told me what happened to you in the parking lot after your Reading Hour."

My heart stops. I glance around to see if Ron or Barry heard what Leo just uttered. I motion him to come closer.

"I haven't said a word about this to anyone. How did you find out?"

"A good reporter has his sources," he says.

"Tell me. Please."

"The incident was recorded on the security cameras at the library," Leo says. "It was reported to the police by the administration. No one could identify the woman—her face was blurry, she parked out of sight so they couldn't ID her license plate, but they suspect it was likely her first time coming to the library, obviously with the intent to harass you. But someone from the Palm Springs Police Department is planning to take a report from you. They will probably be monitoring your next reading at the library."

I shake my head. "If I ever go back."

Leo puts his hand on my arm. It is strong and warm.

"You have to go back," he says.

"No, I don't," I say firmly. "That woman's attack brought up so much forgotten deep-seated self-hatred. It revived so many memories I thought I had buried but are still living underneath the surface. I'm eighty-one years old, and she made me feel as weak and vulnerable and disgusting as I did growing up in the closet."

Leo tightens his grip on my arm.

"Do you know how many hate crimes go unreported even in a community like Palm Springs?" he asks. "It doesn't just happen to those on the margins. It happens to people like you, every single day, and it has to stop. That woman's hatred flamed because it has been given oxygen in our country, and her sole goal is to silencc your voice. It's the same thing happening around the country with book banning, and the only way to extinguish that hate is by speaking out." Leo gives me a pleading look. "Speak out, Sid. And don't just do it for yourself but for every person this is happening to right now that you can't see and will never know. Do it for all those who fought for you to be right here, right now. Believe me, if it's happening to you, it's happening to a little boy or girl this moment—a kid feeling as much shame and self-hatred as you once did and still do, a kid who is out there somewhere fighting to survive. When we're silent . . ."

"I know," I interrupt. "We give up."

"No," Leo says, shaking his head. "We're complicit."

He releases his hand, and my forearm pulsates, missing his touch.

"I told my GM about this, and he'd like you to be my first feature for 'Gray and Gay,'" Leo continues.

"Me?"

"I actually think it could make for an amazing launch. We could cover so many issues all via a lifestyle segment on you," he says. "Your friends here filled me in a bit on your communal living and health care situation, your show that mirrors your life, and—despite all of this—how none of us are immune to hate. Say yes."

I look at Leo.

Yes, I think. *I will marry you.*

"Did you come here to ask me all this?"

"I did. I'm a tireless reporter."

Mario leans across the bar and whispers to me, "Say yes. You'll get to see more of him."

I look down the bar at Teddy. I think of what happened to John.

What happened to him and what happened to me will happen again and again and again if I—*we*—don't take a stand.

I turn back to Leo to say yes, but Barry now has him cornered. He is handing him yet another drink and has him pinned against the bar. In the blink of an eye, Barry removes his shirt and tucks it into the back of his jeans.

"Well, aren't you a tall drink of iced tea," Barry says. "And I am parched."

Barry's six-pack hardens with every word out of his mouth.

I can't watch. I turn away and see Teddy leaving. And then I see my reflection in the windows of Streetbar.

I'm wearing a sport coat.

At a gay bar.

I look like I should be leading a tour of bird watchers. I'm about as sexy as Bernie Sanders.

God, I'm delusional.

And what the hell is a sport coat anyway? It's neither sporty nor a coat, and yet I'm wearing one, just like I was wearing an eggplant blouse when I met Leo.

Barry laughs at something Leo has said.

"Well, I do declare, you make me happy as a clam at high tide," he says, running a finger down Leo's chest.

"God, you're a bad actor," I say to Barry as I stand. "And I'm getting diabetes from your terrible accent."

"Sid?" Leo calls after me as I part the crowd with my elbows to leave.

I rush onto the street to catch my breath. I see Teddy through the window of the show tunes bar across the street, talking to Larry and Phil.

God, what an awful night for both of us.

I linger at the entrance and then follow him into the other room when karaoke is announced.

I stand in the back, hidden behind a pole, and listen to Teddy sing.

My heart cracks.

The hardest thing about growing old isn't the aches and pains, or the short amount of time you have left.

No, it's the fucking loneliness.

And that will be the thing that kills you before anything else even has a chance.

A red carpet leads into the Palm Springs Convention Center.

On this perfect evening in the desert—temperature in the seventies, sun peeking over the San Jacinto Mountains like one of the paparazzi lined up along the carpet—the red carpet for Kyle's event has turned gold.

Flashbulbs pop.

Why did I come?

I mean, do I still carry a torch for Kyle? Am I hoping he will take me back? Or I am hoping that he will throw this pathetic old dog a bone?

I narrow my eyes behind my sunglasses and study the cult of celebrity before me.

Celebrities line the carpet, entertainment reporters and fans calling their names.

For a moment, these stars make eye contact, notice the invisible, and our collective hearts stop.

And then it hits me: *That's* why I'm here: to be seen again.

This is all a game: Money begets money. Fame begets fame. These events not only pull ratings and readers, putting ad money in the coffers of the networks and newspapers, but they also put rears in seats. If a movie doesn't sell tickets, the game is over.

A reporter pushes me, a microphone is extended before my

face. For a moment, I think it is for me, but Ida Red—one of the stars of *Billy's Back*—moves onto the carpet.

I am invisible. I am on the outside looking in. And having fame and losing it begets a hole in your soul created by a green-eyed monster called envy that only money and fame could possibly fill again.

I missed my red carpet. I missed my yellow brick road. Hollywood pulled the rug from beneath my feet forty years ago, and I'm still navigating a path that has only been filled with roadblocks and rejection.

I smooth my hair and my suit, watching the actors wave and pose, and begin to move down the red carpet when I hear, "Where the hell do you think you're going?"

A security guard—hand already on his holster—is blocking my path.

"I was invited by Kyle Moses," I say.

"Who wasn't?" the guard says. He lifts a meaty hand and points to a snaking line under the colonnade. "The Nobody Line is over there."

"But I'm on the list."

"Jesus Christ, buddy, the entire world is on a list."

The world shifts underneath my feet.

Ego earthquake.

This happens nearly every week, when I'm rejected professionally, or dismissed as an untalented nobody.

For some reason, I am transfixed watching Ida Red walk the red carpet. She made her mark just as I was being erased, and she never looked back.

Ida Red is not her real name of course. Very few people's names—or souls—are real in Hollywood. It's all invented. Every actor was born and then named twice: once as a baby by their mama, and once again by their agent.

Ida Red grew up Emma Jean Simmons in Fort Smith, Arkansas. No one is born in LA, they are drawn to it, like gays to the desert. Emma Jean moved to Hollywood at the age of eighteen and was discovered working at the ticket counter by a famous producer who wanted to gauge the crowd reaction to his latest horror movie in a real movie theater. At the time, he was casting for his latest low-budget movie. It was a new take on the horror genre in which the producer intended to take the mechanics of a scary movie and incorporate them into a thriller where the hero and villain were equally matched. When he saw Emma Jean's flame-red hair, emerald eyes and porcelain skin and heard an accent that needed no work, he brought her in for an audition, and the rest, as they say, is Hollywood history. She was cast as Kyle's girlfriend, Loretta, in the *Billy the Hillbilly* movies, an innocent country girl whose brothers and father kill Billy's family for simply being darn good people.

And which character took the last shot that killed her brother and uttered a line that became legend?

"You was right," Loretta said to her brother, holding a gun over him as she watched him die, a swimming pool of red at her feet. "We *is* blood relatives."

Ida Red is wearing an emerald gown that matches her eyes and my envy. Her hair is still dyed flame-red, but now it's *too* red, as if her head has burst into flame. Ida has undergone more work than a mid-century home. With makeup and extensions, she looks like a wax figure melting under the sun on the red carpet. Ida has been married more times than Elizabeth Taylor and—for the past few years—has been "working" as a Real Housewife of Hollywood, where her drunken behavior has made her a fan favorite. I'm sure that helped fuel this remake, too.

"You high, man?" the security guard asks. "I told you to move away from the carpet."

He puffs his chest and again places his hand on his holster.

I turn and retreat on the carpet. I cut between a camera for *Entertainment Tonight* and a woman wearing a media badge that screams *People*. I am about to step into the shadows and hightail it to my car when I hear, "Barry?"

I turn. Kyle is standing on the red carpet—surrounded by a

team of handlers—in a too-tight suit and a crisp white shirt that is open a dangerous number of buttons. He waves and motions for me to come closer. I near the red carpet again when the same security guard blocks my path.

"It's okay," Kyle says. "He's with me."

I shoot the security guard a look that walks the line between *I told you so* and *fuck you, asshole.*

For a moment, the fault line underneath my feet stabilizes again.

"Where were you going?" Kyle asks.

"Getting in line with the other guests," I lie, gesturing toward the colonnade.

"Bullshit," Kyle says. "Sherry, this is a dear friend of mine from long ago. Would you have someone escort him inside and put him in one of the reserved seats up front?"

She nods and speaks into a headset. Seconds later, a girl who looks like she should be home babysitting puts her arm around my back and guides me through the crowd.

"See you after the event!" Kyle yells.

When people hear his voice, they rush the red carpet.

"Billy the Hillbilly!"

I glance back.

Fans are weeping, snapping photos, trying to be a part of his aura for even a split second.

This should have been my life.

Instead, another gay Moses is parting the Red Sea.

"That was quite a spectacle," I say.

"Just part of the game," Kyle says as if red carpet galas are as normal a part of one's day as pumping gas.

We are seated at the intimate curved bar in Counter Reformation.

Counter Reformation is a "secret" restaurant, hidden in the gardens behind the famed Parker Palm Springs hotel, which was once owned by Merv Griffin and recently redesigned by Jonathan Adler, the place where celebrities, Coachella acts and hipster wannabes can linger in mid-century luxe without being ogled. Counter Reformation serves decadent small plates paired with an eclectic selection of exclusive wines and champagne.

"I've never been here before," I say.

"You haven't?"

Again, a two-hundred-dollar bottle of champagne is as normal to Kyle as a stop at In-N-Out is for most folks. His reality is a little different.

The team behind *Billy the Hillbilly: Billy's Back!* reserved the entire space at Counter Reformation for the after-party. Counter Reformation is a sort of Paris tabac hidden behind massive jewel-toned doors and sculptures of potted golden palm trees. I gained access from yet another security guard solely because my name was on a list.

Your name must *always* be on a list in Hollywood or you are invisible.

A tower of canapés, almost too pretty to eat, arrives before us. I raise a glass.

"Thank you so much for inviting me. It's been such a wonderful night, I still can't believe we ran into each other after all this time," I say. "Congrats on all your success, Kyle."

"Thanks, Barry."

Kyle clinks my glass.

I take a sip of champagne.

"Was that a convincing monologue?" I ask with a smile, letting my facade drop. "I wanted it to sound sincere, but I'd be lying if I said I weren't a tad jealous and a little bit bitter that this never happened for me." I take another sip. "And I'm still confused by our breakup. We were so young, but we were so in love."

The end comes out like more of a begging question: *Weren't we so in love?*

"I'd also be lying if I said I hadn't followed your career and personal life," I press on. "God, therapy has turned me into a loquacious oversharer. I should be performing Shakespeare."

"Therapy, huh?" Kyle asks, sipping his champagne. "Over me?"

His burly hands hold the fragile flute tenderly, and I think of when he used to hold my face that way.

Stop it, Barry. You're just pathetic.

"To think we both started out living in that tiny apartment over the Blockbuster," he continues. "You worked at the mall, right?"

I nod at the memory. "And you delivered Domino's," I add. "Free pizza, remember?"

Kyle nods. "Do you know how hard it was to deliver a pizza in LA in under thirty minutes, man? That was a *much* more stressful job than I have now."

I laugh. "Those were the days."

Tribal music thumps quietly in the background like a heartbeat.

"You know you fucked up when you broke up with me, right?"

"But I didn't break up with you," I say softly. "You told me I was selfish for taking a role I didn't deserve and threw a champagne bottle at me." I nod at the one before us. "You told me you hated me and hoped that I would fail. Am I remembering that correctly?"

"Perspective is the architect of fate, Barry," Kyle says with a smile. "From my point of view, you essentially not only broke up with me when you accepted the role of Coco, but your life changed for the worse almost immediately because of it. If you look at it from my perspective, I was right, Barry, and you should have listened to me from the beginning. I always know best. I always take care of those I love."

My years of therapy with Dr. Doolan set off alarm bells in my head that chime, *Control freak!* and *Run for your life, Barry!*

But then Kyle's arm brushes mine, and my skin immediately

ignites like a match at his touch. I half expect a fire to start in the soft fur of his forearm.

Kyle reaches out and slowly grazes my fingers holding the flute.

The beast inside is now controlling me once again.

"I forgive you, Barry," Kyle finally says, his fingers remaining on mine. "I forgive you."

The thrumming in my head grows louder.

For what?

Kyle leans closer and whispers, "Now I know you'll never leave me again."

He sits back and reaches for the champagne bottle, and I flinch.

"Kyle?"

One of his PR people approaches.

"We have a table of reporters over here from *Deadline*, *Variety* and *The Hollywood Reporter* who want to ask you a few questions. Do you have a moment?"

"It that okay?" Kyle asks me. "I promise I'll be back in a few."

"Okay? This is your night," I say. "I'm just stargazing."

He laughs and moves toward the reporters.

I try to quell my growing anxiety from my interaction with Kyle and feeling so out of place here that I down my glass of champagne and head to the bathroom.

I lock myself in the men's room, lean against the sink and shut my eyes. Over and over, I see Kyle throwing a champagne bottle at me. I can hear him yelling.

"You will regret this, you piece of shit! I hope you fail! I hate you! And so will the world!"

I turn on the faucet and splash water on my face. I shut my eyes and count breaths until my heart slows. I open my eyes and look in the mirror.

What the fuck are you doing, Barry? Get out of here now.

I unlock the door, ready to leave this mistake of a night.

As I open it, Kyle appears. He puts his hand on my chest and pushes me back into the bathroom. He attempts to lock the door behind us when it pops open again and a man enters, drunkenly stumbling toward a urinal.

"Knock much, asshole?" Kyle mutters.

We walk out, and my instinct is to run like hell and never look back, but Kyle has his arm around my back and is holding on to me closely. People are watching. I feel as if I need his attention, their attention, his eternal forgiveness, his . . .

Power.

We take a seat again at the bar. Kyle looks at me for the longest time as if we're in a movie together, and—even for one moment—I know I am in control. I have regained a little bit of power.

Perhaps I just want my power back.

I take a sip of champagne and ask, "So, where is Brent? Home watching Pride and Joy?"

"Talk about a buzzkill," Kyle says, finishing his glass and pouring another. "Please don't mention my bore of a husband again in my presence."

Kyle turns from me and begins to scan the crowd.

"Sorry," I say. "You're known in paparazzi as one name: Bryle. I thought you were the perfect couple."

Kyle turns to me again, smiling that megawatt smile.

"Bryle?" He laughs. "You want to know about beautiful Brent?" Kyle spits his name. "Brent absolutely hates this shit. He likes his alone time. He's fucking boring. He's like talking to a candle, but at the least the candle has some light to it. Brent is an idiot, and we've gotten used to leading separate lives." Kyle stares not at me but through me. "Want me to be completely honest?"

"That wasn't completely honest?" I say.

He laughs. "See, you have a spark, Barry. Damn, I need a spark. And I really needed this new movie, man. I can't be a fucking character actor playing the bad cop in a two-series arc on a shitty TV drama or some teenage brat's unhip grandfather on a multi-camera sitcom anymore. It's like being a trained gorilla performing before a live audience of applauding baboons." Kyle shakes his head. "Not to mention, the paparazzi is all over me right now. Lots of stories about how much time Brent and I spend apart. *Is Bryle headed for a breakup?*" he asks in an announcer's voice. "And there's a lot of money at stake on this new project—*my money!*—and so much pressure on me. I haven't had a major movie role since I came out. The studio is banking on the fact that an audience will turn out to see a gay leading man who is seen as the grandson every grandmother wants and the son every mother adores. Brent and I are like Neil Patrick Harris and David Burtka. America doesn't think of us as gay, they think of us as sexual spores, as nice boys. But what if we broke up? What if they found out we play separately? What if they found out we're not into each other anymore? Gay don't sell tickets, my man. Family does. Brent and I have grown apart, but we're golden-handcuffed together."

"So, there are strings?" I ask.

"There are always strings, Barry. And maybe some ropes, clamps and gags, too, if you want." Kyle leers at me and then shakes his head. "It's fucking Hollywood. You gotta learn to play the game again."

"I'm not in the game," I say. "You know that."

Kyle puts his hand on my arm.

"And you know acting is all about luck and timing," he says. "You've always had bad results with both of those."

"So why does losing that role and losing you still feel like it was yesterday?" I ask.

"I'm sure it still stings. Let me put some salve on it." He winks and raises his glass. "A toast: to old times and old friends."

Did I judge him too harshly at first? Has he changed? He seems to be going through so much.

"Old?" I wink, sipping my champagne, which, by the way, is damn good, smoother than Veuve. "And friends? We haven't spoken in decades."

"It's just like in the movies," Kyle protests. "I think we were meant to meet-cute again."

I take another hit of champagne, and as the bubbles begin to obliterate my brain, I ask questions I might not otherwise venture to ask.

"Have you ever thought about me?"

"All the time," he says. "What could have been, what *should* have been . . ."

His voice trails off.

"Why didn't you ever reach out?"

"Life got crazy." Kyle sighs. "Everything blew up. It took me a decade to come back to earth again. But I credit you for helping me get here. Nobody believed in my dream until you did."

"But . . ." I start. I have no idea what to say because I don't know if I believe him, or if I just want to believe him.

"I was such an asshole," he says. "Young and in love. I'm sorry."

He just apologized? Is it sincere? Or does he just want to sleep with me?

But I do see an opening. And those have been few and far between in my life the last few decades.

"I was an asshole, too," I say.

"Maybe that long, winding road finally led us back here."

"Meaning?"

"Meaning, maybe we can help each other." Kyle pops a canapé in his mouth. "We're actually going to be shooting in the desert. Some of the areas in Joshua Tree and Idyllwild resemble the Ozarks, and we're close to LA." Kyle turns his gaze upon me. "Let me help you."

"How?"

"So I googled you, too, after last night," Kyle admits. "Searched you on IMDb. Nothing much there except a few cameos on shitty shows. Then I did a deep dive. What's the deal, Barry? You do some sort of *Golden Girls* drag show with a bunch of old queens? That's kind of . . ." he pauses ". . . fucked up, don't you think? That's gotta be like rubbing salt in an old wound every day. I just don't get it."

His words sober me for a split second.

"It actually started as a way to cope," I explain. "Like I said, I've been in therapy for the longest time. When I got cut from the show," I begin cautiously, "everyone looked at me like I was contagious. I couldn't get a gig, not even one line on *Saved by the Bell*. I starved myself. I thought if I were thinner or more attractive, I would get the call. I tried to change my voice. I tried to change *me*. But it never came. But all those closeted producers still called. So I made a little cash off camera and got the hell out of LA. I came to the desert, where I was surrounded by gay men dying of AIDS, who came here for the community of support. I actually got a little bit of perspective and the help I needed. I began to work out and eat well. I took care of myself. My friends and this stupid little community theater act saved my life. Now I'm the only one still alive from *The Golden Girls*, and—as you know—everything old is new again. I've fought to stay in the game. I had to learn to overcome all the rejection. I finally feel . . ." I stop, searching for just the right word ". . . safe."

"But not successful."

"I've tried to come to terms with the fact that maybe safety is what I need most in my life."

"Bullshit," Kyle says. "Safe is sad. Safe is for losers. You gotta be scared out of your wits to be a success. You have to want it again, and there is nothing safe about that. Everyone wants to be rich and famous. I know you, Barry. You want that, too."

Kyle rubs his knees against mine.

"Is that why you never married?" he continues. "Still hung up on me after all these years?"

"I have a lot of companionship," I deflect.

"I'm sure you do," he says.

"I'm the one who does all the rejecting now," I say. "Makes me feel powerful."

"But you want more, don't you?" he presses. "Don't you want what you should have had from the very beginning? Tell me the truth, Barry. You want real power."

"I do. Yes."

Kyle leans in close and whispers in my ear.

"Then let me help you."

His tongue lingers on my earlobe.

"It's time for a second act," he continues.

I lean into his hot breath.

"How would that work?" I ask.

"I was about to show you earlier, but let's take a walk."

Kyle stands and heads toward the door, high-fiving and air-kissing one beautiful man and woman after another. He stops abruptly.

"Mitch, my man!" he calls to a rugged-looking fellow in the center of a circle of onlookers that I recognize as Kyle's director. "I wanted you to meet Barry Goggins. Crazy story, dude: Barry was originally cast in that '80s sitcom, *The Golden Girls*, as one of the main characters, but he got cut after the pilot."

"No shit?" Mitch says, running a tan hand through his long, silver hair.

"He's a helluva actor, Mitch," Kyle says. "I think he'd make a great Levi in the new movie. I know all this early publicity was to attract some big-name stars to the project and supporting roles, but do we really need anything other than a great actor for the part of Loretta's long-lost older brother—the only one who got away—who shows up seeking forgiveness, but we don't know if he's good or bad? Can't you see him as that guy?"

Mitch swivels on his stool, scrutinizing my face and body for much too long, as if I'm prized cattle. I shift on my feet, uncomfortable.

"I can," he finally agrees. "You've got a look . . . hard but vulnerable. I see it, Kyle." He hesitates. "But Billy Bob Thornton has this pretty much sealed up already. His audition tape was perfection. And he'll bring the buzz. Sorry, man."

The earth shifts underneath me again.

I start to walk away, but Kyle grabs my arm and stops me.

"Power," he mouths. "He's the right actor for the role, Mitch," Kyle says, leaning in to talk to the director, his voice suddenly threatening. "Remember, it's my fucking money that's making this fucking movie."

Mitch's smile is tight as he extends his hand. Finally, he nods, and Kyle releases his grip.

"Let's talk, Barry. If Kyle says you're the man, then you're the man." He holds out his cell. "Give me your agent's number."

I tap in his number. He puts his into my cell.

"Have your agent call me."

The world stops.

"Thank you," I finally manage to say. "It was a pleasure meeting you."

I follow Kyle into the dark. He knows I would follow him anywhere now.

Kyle nods at a guard, who disappears behind a thick ficus hedge. He obviously knows this game well.

Kyle moves next to me until our bodies are touching. The silhouette of the mountains hovers in the distance as if we are on a movie set standing before a green screen.

"Thank you," I say, my heart racing. "I can't believe you just did that for me."

"Now it's your turn to do something for me."

Kyle grabs me and kisses me, his tongue going deeper and deeper.

"But you're married," I finally gasp when we come up for air.

"You're the one who dumped me, remember?" Kyle whispers. "You used to want to conquer this world. What happened?"

"I got old."

"No one ever gets old in Hollywood. They just get forgotten." Kyle's hands slide to my hips, and he keeps moving them lower. "Let me help them remember you again. Let me remember you again."

"How would this work exactly?"

Kyle laughs softly. "Ah," he says. "We always have to negotiate a contract in Hollywood, don't we?"

He stares into my eyes.

"Let's just say, I get what I want, and then you get what you want," he whispers huskily. "*Whenever* I want."

He kisses me again, slowly at first, and then harder. I stumble backward. The hedge catches me.

I kiss back. I lose myself in Kyle, who we were, what I could still become.

The power.

"Yeah," he murmurs. "That's the Barry I remember."

Kyle is rubbing against me. His breath is hot. He smells like too much Tom Ford cologne.

Everything feels right.

And so wrong.

My body may be fully into this, but my head is not.

I may be a whore, but I have never been *this*.

I may break men's hearts, but I don't break up their marriages.

Fuuuuuuck! What has therapy done to me? And why do I hear Ron's voice in my head saying a prayer for me?

But if I push Barry away, I lose a second chance at everything I ever wanted.

"Barry."

A movie star whispers my name. I've dreamed of his voice saying my name again for so long. I press against him, panting. *Control your own destiny, Barry. You will never get another shot. You'll be signing headshots by men's rooms and doing denture commercials for the rest of your life.*

He starts to push me to my knees.

I'm not doing anything anybody else wouldn't do right now . . .

"Kyle? Kyle, where are you, handsome?"

Ida Red stumbles out of Counter Reformation.

Kyle quickly pushes away from me.

"There you are," she slurs. "Why are you hiding from me? And who's this fine piece of man meat?"

"This is Barry," Kyle says, "and he just may be your long-lost brother."

Ida puts her arms around me and gives me a sloppy kiss on the cheek.

"My big brother is back," she says. "I missed you."

As Ida is draped on me, I catch Kyle's eye.

Me, too, he mouths.

"You need some water," Kyle says to Ida. "Press day tomorrow, remember?"

"Boooo!" she yells. "No fun!"

Kyle puts his arm around Ida and begins to escort her back inside.

"It was nice to meet you, Larry!" she yells.

"Barry," I say.

The security guard moves back into place.

"Let me show you to your car, sir," he says to me.

Something tells me he's seen this movie before.

When I get home and crawl into bed, I cannot sleep.

A mockingbird calls outside my window.

It is a single, lonely male—probably very old—seeking a mate in a world that is already coupled. It only wants its voice to be heard.

Its song is loud, desperate, and I pull the pillow over my head, knowing it will not stop calling.

I start preparing for Church of Mary days before the Sunday event, much like my father would prepare and practice his sermon in the days leading up to the Sabbath.

For many years, I have chosen themes for our Sunday services: In the summer, for instance, considering it is hotter than Hades, I might channel the classic movie *Some Like It Hot*, with each of us dressing as a character from the film, or perhaps *The Towering Inferno*, with flambé as a featured course. One Christmas, we all dressed as versions of Dolly Parton throughout the years while her Christmas album played, and I served delicate pastries called Minne di Sant'Agata that, fittingly, look just like boobs.

Last week we celebrated Valentine's, and this week is a tribute to the Rat Pack and the kickoff to Modernism Week in Palm Springs. For fashion, I've decided on fedoras, and for food?

My mother's recipe box sits rather unironically in a Zsa Zsa–designed cabinet in the kitchen. When I pull the worn, wooden box free and set it on the fancy countertops by the Wolf stove, the juxtaposition is jarring, a bit like finding a La-Z-Boy recliner in the middle of the Frey House, a desert modernism masterpiece perched in the mountains, where I will be a docent this afternoon.

I open the lid and scan the handwritten tabs—*Appetizers! Sal-*

ads! Sides! Entrees! Desserts! I pull cards I placed Post-its on and took photos of earlier this week from the box.

I trace my finger over my mother's cursive, tilted letters that look as if they are being blown off their foundations by a tornado like the ones that seemed to pop up out of nowhere every spring.

What is it about food and family? A favorite recipe? A beloved dessert?

Once you taste it, you are home, and the memories—no matter how bad—are, for a fleeting moment, tinged with sweetness and nostalgia despite all the horrific storms.

In honor of bygone Rat Pack days, I already have the menu planned. For appetizers, I have decided upon stuffed celery and pepperoni pinwheels. Brunch will be beef stroganoff with scalloped potatoes along with creamed peas and onions. Of course, I will serve a salad: a Jell-O salad chock-full of carrots and marshmallows. When my mother used to ask if we wanted a salad, she did not mean a healthy one—say, spinach or kale—but rather dessert before dessert. For dessert? A pineapple upside-down cake.

Barry won't eat a bite, of course, but he will critique my menu. He's what I call "pretend Southern." Barry is like a woman from Charleston who leaves the South behind for good but then goes back for the holidays and starts saying things like "I'm as happy as a clam at high tide," although she didn't even know clams lived in the water.

I sip some water and think of recent nights: My gays have not been so golden. Teddy, who has seemed off for weeks, tossed a drink in a bachelor-to-be's face (he did deserve it) and then left Streetbar without any warning; Sid followed suit; Barry dressed in a tuxedo last night—a real one, mind you, not a tearaway tux—and left without any explanation, returning home and heading straight to his room like a sullen teenager.

Me, you ask?

Not a single friend asked if I was okay being left alone at Streetbar. They just vanished. They still haven't asked about it.

I am sick and tired of being the tonic water in a cocktail, the one thing nobody notices is there but is essential to making the drink cohesive.

After being dumped at Streetbar, I ended up taking an Uber to Ralphs before it closed for the night. I shopped for this week's meal at midnight alongside drunks, crazies and lonely people with carts full of Ben & Jerry's ice cream and boxed wine.

Lord, I am a broken record playing the same Petula Clark song.

As I shopped, I grew so angry at being the responsible, overlooked one yet again that I went through the self-checkout and shoved the most expensive items into a bag when the single cashier on duty wasn't looking. My final receipt for today's meal was only twenty-one dollars.

On the way home, the pit of my stomach filled with remorse, so I tried to fill it with a bag of cherry Red Vines, part of my illegal contraband.

I woke at dawn, showered and dressed. While everyone continues to get their beauty sleep, I am now cooking to keep the family together and our traditions alive.

I open the fridge to begin pulling ingredients and see a bottle of tonic water.

Would anyone even notice if I was missing from our communal cocktail?

I sigh. The fridge is a mess again.

I cannot find the pepperoni I placed in the cheese drawer, so I begin to search for the carrots and celery, which I finally realize were moved from the crisper at some point and wedged under a bowl of . . .

Something congealed and deeply disturbing.

I remove the cling wrap to find a yellow clot of cold cheese flecked with red. I pull my glasses down to the end of my nose for a closer inspection.

My pepperoni.

I open the built-in cabinet that hides our trash. It is overflowing. On top are egg shells along with an empty package of pepperoni and containers that once held the Gruyère and Swiss I was planning to use in my scalloped potatoes. Beside that is a half-empty jar of maraschino cherries I was planning to use for my pineapple upside-down cake. They were used for late-night cocktails—the glasses are still in the sink—and obviously to top the empty container of Häagen-Dazs I was planning to serve with my cake.

I take a deep breath.

Re-center, Ron. It's all going to be okay.

I remove the trash—because it's pissing me off so much to look at it—and take it to the garage. I add a new bag to the bin and then begin to load the dishwasher. It is full. It has never been unloaded. I walk over to look at the laminated sheet I posted for the week: Barry did not run and empty the dishwasher, and Teddy did not empty the garbage.

I place my hands on the counter and stare into the majestic mountains surrounding us. I say a prayer I remember from childhood.

"Almighty Father, in this moment, when it feels like the whole world is against me, I turn to You, my rock and my refuge."

When I finish, I unload the dishwasher, then reload it, place a pod in the dishwasher, start it anew and hand-wash the glasses in the sink. When I finally finish, I decide to start over. I open the fridge to retrieve the sirloin.

I open the wrapper. Half the meat is gone.

Steak and eggs. They made steak and eggs when they were drunk.

The world around me turns to static, and I do not realize I am screaming until Teddy, Sid, Barry—along with a very hot shirtless young man who came over at some point last night to see Barry—are standing before me.

"Are you okay?" Sid asks, eye mask atop his head.

"What is going on?" Teddy asks. "You scared the hell out of me."

"You scared the hell out of us, too," Barry says. He puts his arm around the shirtless guy, who looks to be about a third of his age. "Are you okay . . . um . . ."

Barry hesitates uncomfortably.

"Vince," the young man says. "My name is Vince." His face droops, and his mountain-y shoulders slump. "You told me you loved me last night."

"I know what you'd love," Barry deflects. "A big breakfast."

"Yeah!" Vince rubs his taut stomach and then stretches. Eyeballs hit the floor.

"We worked up an appetite, didn't we . . . um . . ."

"Vince!" he says.

Teddy releases a resounding laugh.

Barry looks at me expectantly.

"Have at it," I say, wiping my hands on a kitchen towel. "I'm not your short-order cook." I toss the towel at Barry. "This whole routine is getting old." I look at Vince while nodding at Barry. "Older than he is."

Vince finally looks at Barry in this harsh morning light as if he is seeing him for the first time.

"You told me you were forty."

Teddy laughs again.

"In dog years," he says. "You just couldn't tell in the dark that he has mange."

"So why did you yell, Ron?" Sid asks. He sees the beef on the island, a knife beside it. "Did you cut yourself?"

"No," I say. "You're the ones who put the knife in my back."

"What did we do?" Sid asks.

"Nothing!" I yell. "That's the whole point. None of you ever do a damn thing around this house!"

"Dramatic much, Ron?" Teddy says, turning to walk away. "I'm going back to bed."

"No, you are fucking not, Teddy!"

He stops in his tracks. I look each of my friends in the eye.

"I do everything around here. *Everything.* I cook. I clean. I grocery shop. I pay the bills. I balance our collective budget. I take out the garbage and wash the dishes. I print a list of chores for each of you that goes unnoticed each and every week, and has gone unnoticed *for years*. I keep up our traditions, from Church of Mary to the holidays." I take a breath. "Did any of you realize—or care—that you left me alone at Streetbar the other night?"

Teddy, Sid and Barry glance at each other and then the floor.

"I'm sick and tired of doing everything in this house, which, by the way, I helped buy and redecorate on my own dime." I try to control my rage. "And I'm the one doing all of this while still working full-time . . ."

"I work!" Teddy interrupts. "I have my shop!"

"And I still work," Sid says. "Occasionally."

"I am very busy," Barry adds.

"Yes, you are, Barry," Teddy says, eyeing Vince. "You stay *very* active."

I shake my head at their childishness.

"Let's be honest for once, boys. I bring in the money. The repairs on this house are not cheap, and the monthly maintenance on the pool, spa and lawn are outrageous, and you all act as if you live in a hotel."

"We all put money into the budget to care for this house," Sid says. "It is equitable."

"It *was* equitable," I say. "A decade ago. We agreed to put in an amount to cover our main expenses that was equitable given our individual circumstances *years* ago, but, boys, everything is more expensive now, and that lid doesn't cover the pot anymore."

"Why didn't you say something, Ron?" Sid asks. "You know I can and will help."

I shake my head.

"I shouldn't have to," I say. "I don't want to sound like a martyr."

"Too late," Teddy stage-whispers.

"You're always so funny, Teddy," I say, glaring at him. "But that act is getting old, too. Some things in life are serious, like friendship. I didn't want to bother any of you because I'm a nice guy, but I'm sick of being nice, and, if I'm being completely honest . . ."

"Please," Teddy says.

". . . I feel overlooked around here and need just a little bit of help."

Teddy and Barry glance quickly at one another, and I know them so well that I can tell their residual hangovers from last night have not faded and that they think I'm just being ditzy and overdramatic this morning because they hurt my feelings.

Just appease our little Rose. She goes all St. Olaf on us every now and then.

"I'll help you," Vince finally says in the sweetest voice. "I like to help my mom around the house."

"He still lives at home," Teddy says. "We have a winner!"

Vince looks wounded.

Teddy doesn't stop. He grabs the sirloin off the counter, walks over and holds it in front of Barry's crotch. "And you look like you know how to handle an old piece of meat."

Vince recoils.

"What is wrong with you lately, Teddy?" I ask. "You're even more vicious than usual. You're more like a Mean Girl than a Golden Girl. Something is up."

"Yeah, *I'm* up," Teddy says. "And I shouldn't be at this hour."

"I'm sorry," Barry says to Vince. "Teddy doesn't know what he's saying."

"Yes, I do. What's your friend's name, Barry?" Teddy asks, his tone becoming even more belligerent. "Do you remember? He just said it. Venture a guess since you two are destined to marry and be together forever."

"Stop it, Teddy," I say.

"Say it, Barry!" Teddy prods.

Barry looks at the young man.

"Vince," the young man says. "My name is Vince."

"I'm con-VINCE-d Barry will never call you again," Teddy says.

"Shut up, Teddy."

"Fuck off, Barry."

"Yeah, fuck off, Barry," Sid adds.

"What did I do to you?" Barry says, turning to Sid.

"You hit on my friend at Streetbar and acted as if I wasn't even there," Sid says.

"Like you had a shot," Barry scoffs.

In the awkward silence that follows, Sid's chin quivers, and a sad tear springs free.

"I'm sorry, Sid," Barry says quickly. "I didn't mean it."

"Yes, you did."

"Is that why you hit on me last night on Grindr?" Vince asks Barry. "Because the guy you wanted wasn't interested?"

"No," Barry says. "I mean, last night was a different guy. I mean . . . We had fun, didn't we . . ." Barry falters.

"Vince!" the young man yells. "My name is Vince! I'm outta here!"

"Not before I take a picture," Teddy says, lifting his phone to snap a photo of Vince's perfect body clad only in a pair of skimpy Andrew Christian briefs.

Vince storms out of the kitchen and down the hallway. He reappears seconds later, carrying his clothes from last night.

"Now that's a real walk of shame," Teddy mutters.

The door slams.

"Stop it!" I say. "All of you. It's always about *you*. I'm always taking care of you. And I'm tired of it."

I lean against the counter and sigh. "I signed up for all of this because I love you. I thought we were a team, friends who would always help and support one another no matter what, but we've become total narcissists who only care about our own place in this house and this world, and I'm sick of it."

I open the fridge and place the sirloin inside.

"To celebrate Modernism Week, I was going to make beef

stroganoff with scalloped potatoes and creamed peas and onions along with a pineapple upside-down cake," I continue. "Manhattans and champagne, just like the Rat Pack used to have."

"The Rat Pack fought sometimes, too, Ron," Sid says.

"So did the Golden Girls," Barry adds.

"They did," I say with a small smile. "All friends do sometimes. But they don't take each other for granted. They value one another's strengths and faults." I look at Teddy. "They don't put you down, and they don't lie." I look at Barry. "They don't leave you alone." I look at Sid. "And they know when you need them most."

I walk out of the kitchen.

"Come back, Ron," Sid says. "Where are you going?"

"I'm going to Spencer's for brunch, where someone will finally wait on me for once," I say, continuing to walk toward the door. "And then I'm going to be a docent at the Frey House, where people will appreciate the effort it takes to make a home beautiful."

I stop at the door and turn off my cell. "Don't call me," I add. "Right now, I feel like crawling under the covers and eating a box of Velveeta."

It's a Rose Nylund quote from *The Golden Girls*. I've said it a million times, but I have never understood its deeper meaning until this very moment.

I open the door to leave.

Two women, one old, one young, are standing in the doorway. The older one, sporting the worst wash-and-set I've ever seen—and believe me, I saw some bad hair growing up—has her hand in mid-air about to ring the doorbell. The girl is yawning.

"Does Teddy Copeland live here?" she asks.

"He does," I say. "May I ask your name?"

"Trudy," she says. "I'm his sister."

Could this morning get any more *Dynasty*?

How did she find us? How many calls and texts did Trudy make that Teddy avoided? I saw his phone light up more these last few days than Barry's Grindr account. Why would she suddenly show up on our doorstep? I mean, she could be selling Avon based on the amount of makeup she's wearing, but she'd certainly look a bit more polished, right? Who does she remind me of? Oh, yes: Mimi from *The Drew Carey Show.*

Or, could it be revenge—served cold, unlike my pineapple upside-down cake—for Teddy's dismissal of her existence all these years. Who knows? But it feels fabulous to turn the tables on the others for once and make them do some dirty work.

I rub my hands together in delight and happily escort them into the kitchen.

Teddy's eyes pop from his head when he sees his sister.

"I've changed my mind," I say with a big smile. "I think I'm staying for brunch."

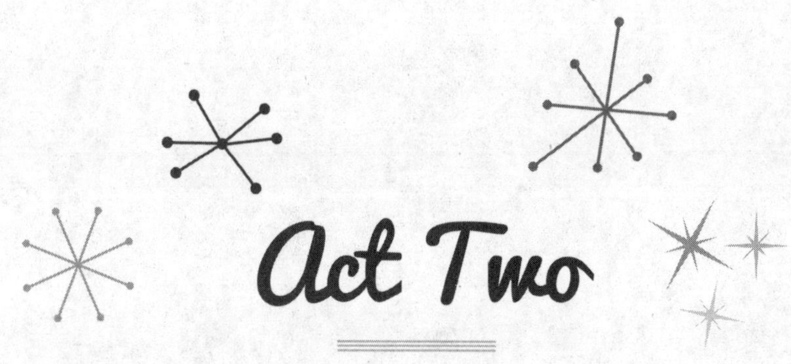

Act Two

Even after washing down a Lexapro with one of the airline-sized bottles of vodka I always keep hidden, well, everywhere, I sweep down the hall and into the living room, my silk caftan billowing around me.

I texted the other Golden Gays and told them to go outside to avoid any blood splatter. The queens are now holding court on the patio overlooking the pool and the city, trying hard not to stare, though they are pressed against the glass like old cheese in a deli window. God help a gay man: We love to witness a spectacle.

"Now that's an entrance," the girl says.

"How lovely," I say. "My sister and her teenage streetwalker are still here. Uninvited. I guess I wasn't hallucinating."

"Me either," the girl says. "You're still old."

"And you still have an STD, by the looks of you." I glance at Trudy. "*This* is your granddaughter?"

She nods.

"Great job." I applaud and bow. "You've always had great nurturing instincts. God does have a wicked sense of humor after all, doesn't He?"

The girl laughs. "I'm Ava."

"I'm Teddy."

"Yeah, I know."

"My sister doth speak of me? Without fear of being struck by lightning?"

Ava laughs again. "She didn't tell me you were so fucking hilarious, though."

"Language, Ava!"

"I bet you say that a lot around her."

"She does." Ava nods.

"Unfortunately, I've never heard of you," I say, smiling at my sister. "Trudy has always been a secret keeper. We haven't spoken since stamps were fifteen cents." I look at Ava. "Stamps were like dial-up but slower." I take in her blank look. "Nothing? I'll explain what both of those are later."

"Hello, Teddy," my sister finally says. "You look very Liberace in that caftan."

"Remember when Daddy thought he was just a showman?" I laugh and look down at what I'm wearing. "The gays and the Golden Girls have always loved a caftan." I smile at my sister. "And an RSVP if a guest is coming."

"Where does an old queen buy something like that?" Ava asks.

"She knows her homophobic slang at such an early age! Well done, sis." I turn back to Ava. "One can buy such a fabulous piece at my shop, Dorian Gay." I eye her. "I could teach you a thing or two about fashion. Right now, you look as if you raided a Five Below and got everything for *way* below that dollar amount. First impressions are everything." I look my sister up and down. "To wit."

Trudy is wearing some sort of nonflammable sweater with a giant glittery cross on the front that states *I Will Not Be Shaken! Psalm 16:8.*

"For instance, I have a similar sweatshirt," I say. "Except mine has a giant martini on the front standing defiantly with its hands on its stem, which makes it so much more ironic. Oh, and mine is not made of aluminum."

"This is quite the place you have."

Trudy is not taking the bait.

"Isn't it?" I say with an even bigger, faker smile. "Found a home even after getting kicked out of mine. This one is big, though, and filled with love. Oh, and I don't get the shit kicked out of me when I put on a dress or kiss a boy."

Ava's face contorts in confusion, and she looks back and forth between me and her grandmother as if she's watching a tennis match.

"The hardest thing about living in the desert," I continue, "is that sometimes filthy rats manage to find their way inside despite all of the hard work we do to keep them from finding us." I take a step toward Trudy. "Because once they do, they will eat you alive." I take another step. "Now, shoo, rats. Shoo!"

Trudy doesn't budge. Her face doesn't flinch.

"It's good to see you, Teddy. And it's good to see you haven't changed. You're still funny."

"Funny, ha-ha, or funny weird?" I ask.

"Give me a hug, Tedster."

That nickname gives the icks, more so than kissing a woman.

Trudy moves toward me in the living room. She opens her arms strangely, like a marionette being manipulated by a puppeteer.

I take a big step back.

"Good God, woman. You look like a creepy doll from a horror movie," I say. "Just cut to the chase, Trudy. What are you doing here?"

"I came to see you." Her voice is too chipper, like a costumed character. "We haven't seen each other in ages."

"Your choice."

She stops in her tracks.

"You didn't answer my calls," she says.

"And you never acknowledged the death of my husband!" I suddenly yell, tired of our repartee. "Nor did you take my calls after our father kicked me out of our house. I was a child, you monster!"

My voice echoes through the house.

Trudy drops her arms. Her round head follows, doughy chin drooping into the folds of her neck. She shuts her eyes and mouths a prayer.

"You're my brother," Trudy says. "I just missed you."

"You don't have a brother. You lost that privilege a long time ago when you sided with our devil of a father." I stare at Trudy's sweater and shake my head. "You want an appropriate Bible verse? How about what God says about rats? 'You are allowed by God to kill it—not for the pleasure of killing—but for the protection of your household.'"

Trudy's eyes grow as wide as the inflatable round rainbow floaty spinning in the pool beyond.

"Yeah, I can preach some shit, too, sis. I learned from a PK. The gays got some faith, too, believe it or not."

The patio door slides open, and Ron sticks his head inside. "Everything okay?"

"Peachy!" I yell. "Our guests were just leaving."

Ron actually looks displeased at my pronouncement, but he shuts the slider.

"Just tell him why we're here, Grandma, so we can get the hell out of assisted living. God, I hate old people. They give me the fucking creeps."

"Watch your fucking language, Ava!" Trudy yells. "I will not warn you again."

I lean my head back and roar with laughter. I look at my sister.

"Perhaps you have changed," I say. "Cursing. Yelling. It's like I'm having a séance with Dad."

"I'm sorry, God," Trudy whispers, eyes raised to the ceiling. Then she looks at me. "I'm exhausted and stressed from the trip . . ." She stops herself from finishing.

I follow Ava's eyes as they pivot to Zsa Zsa's wide windows facing the pool and mountains. Ron, Sid and Barry are watching the scene as if they are on safari and just waiting for the lion to kill the adorable Ohioan antelopes.

"Are you okay, Grandma?" Ava asks.

She is able to express genuine emotion?

Trudy nods. "Vintage Teddy."

"Ah, hell to the no! Liza and I call bullshit!"

"Who's Liza?" Ava asks, looking around, confused.

"Liza Minnelli, you sad child. I have so much to teach you! We have both endured hard lives, and we do not play games. She's always with a gay man when he needs her most!"

I jab a finger in Trudy's direction. "You don't get to turn this around on me, Trudy, and rewrite our entire history simply because it suits your narrative," I continue. "You and Daddy made my life a living hell, remember? You told me to buck up and wear long sleeves after I tried to cut my wrists, remember? You ratted me out to Dad every time I tried to be myself, remember? You refused to allow me to come home, remember? You never returned *my* calls, remember? You cut me out of your entire existence, remember? You didn't come home when Mom was dying, remember? You didn't reach out when my husband died, remember? And now that you're in *my* home, you conveniently choose not to remember any of this, and *I'm* vintage Teddy? Hell to the no, honey, *you* are vintage Trudy, and that will never change. I may wear a caftan and a touch of concealer, but I'm not the one living in drag, sis. You are."

Ava stares at her grandmother as if seeing her for the first time. Her face is scrunched in confusion and pain. She is a tiny thing, more Olivia Rodrigo than Taylor Swift, with a mass of luminous raven hair, dark eyes and huge lips. She is a raven.

"Is this true?" Ava asks.

Ravens are fierce fighters.

Trudy nods.

Ava turns and looks me in the eye, and—for one moment—I see . . . *me.* My heart cracks because I was once this young girl: fiery, funny, fabulous, trapped.

Trudy tries to grab Ava's hand.

"Don't touch me." She jerks away.

"I'm sorry," I say to Ava. "Truly, I am. My anger isn't with you, child. You shouldn't even be witnessing this. This is our past. It has nothing to do with you."

Ava turns back to me, head still high.

"Oh, it does," she says, finally looking me in the eye. "Just tell him why you're here, Grandma. Please."

"You remember that Mama and Daddy's house was left to me according to the will."

"Daddy's wishes," I sing like a child.

"Well, as executor, I also ended up with Mama's credit card and medical debt. The real estate agent in Michigan thought once I sold the house, I'd probably break even." Trudy attempts a conciliatory smile. "Turns out a family farm down the road ended up buying our acreage—and all those around us—for a bit more than we had imagined. My husband invested the remaining money into a stock account, and it grew over time, and . . ."

"And, what?" I ask, cutting her off. "You came to rub it in my face? Congratulations for kicking me out of my childhood home and then cashing in on my pain."

"Just tell him, Grandma!"

Ava's shout makes me stop and turn. Trudy stares at me, her plump cheeks quivering. She looks at the ground. A tear plops onto the terrazzo.

For some reason, the song "It Never Rains in Southern California" pops into my head. We could use a soundtrack right now. Something dramatic and cheesy to make Trudy's emotions actually seem real.

"My husband . . . Ralph . . . died," she whimpers. "Unexpectedly. Widow-maker."

"Well, that makes sense," I say. "Lucky man."

"You are horrible," Trudy says, her voice a hiss. "Still so vicious."

"Now, that's the girl I remember," I say.

"We're leaving," Trudy says. "I knew this was a mistake."

"Time out!"

I turn. Ron rushes inside, along with Barry and Sid.

Ron, ever the peacekeeper, even after his own emotional exit has been postponed by my sister, of all people, settles between me and Trudy. "Let's all just take a deep breath."

Trudy wipes her eyes, collecting herself.

"Go on, Trudy," Ron says.

"My son, Ted, and daughter-in-law, Laura, are in England with my grandson this semester. Ted is a professor at Ohio State . . ."

"They have professors there?" I ask.

Ava chuckles. Trudy ignores me.

". . . and he's teaching a study abroad semester. My grandson is a sophomore at OSU, and he went with them. Ava was staying with me and Ralph, and we were planning to see them in London over this winter break. Ava came home from school last week and found Ralph dead in his favorite chair." The tears begin anew. "My kids couldn't make it home, and I just couldn't take the trip without Ralph, so we had a small funeral, and I didn't know where else to turn. I just had to get out of that empty house. I saw him everywhere."

Trudy collapses into a real *Real Housewives* weep fest. Ron puts his arm around her, and I try not to roll my eyes. Ava watches the scene without emotion as if she's behind a wall of glass. I'm not buying any of this bad acting.

"So you came to Palm Springs on winter break to see a brother you haven't spoken to in decades and despise more than Obama, because your husband died and you were sad to be home alone?" I ask. "Oh, and you wanted to tell me about some money you invested fifty years ago? I'm sorry for your loss. Truly, I am, but I am still not buying a word of it."

"He did die," Ava says, voice low. "That's all true."

Ava glances at me, and I try to read her eyes behind all that dark eyeliner and attitude.

"Ralph's estate requires that I divide the money I inherited from Mama and Daddy's house," Trudy says. "The money was placed into a joint account with both of our names."

My eyes grow wide. "Why would Ralph do that?" I ask.

"He didn't do that, Teddy. I did. It just happened to be in his name, like everything else." She continues. "But our attorney—like us—is on winter break right now with his grandchildren."

"Who's your attorney?" I ask. "Matlock? Do we have to show up at a courthouse in Savannah and sign papers under a magnolia tree? There's a thing called Docusign."

"He's out of the office until the end of the week," Trudy says.

"Of course he is," I say. "And I'm Timothée Chalamet."

"Maybe Timothée Shallow-gay," Ava says.

Barry laughs, hard. "I like you."

"She bites," I say with a wink.

"And, remember, I've always loved you, Teddy," Barry adds.

"You're not getting a cent, Barry. You still owe me twenty dollars. With interest." I turn to Trudy. "Get a hotel, and we can talk in a week, okay?"

"Hold on. This is my house, too, Teddy," Ron says. "I'm putting my foot down! They can stay. As my guests. I insist. Sometimes a person should be given grace when they're trying to make amends. At least Trudy is trying." Ron shoots each of us a calculated look. "Trudy and Ava can have my room. I can move onto the sleeper sofa out here."

"Ron—"

"Teddy," he warns. "And I have another suggestion, Trudy. Why don't you stay for church?"

He is simply trying to agitate me now.

"*You* go to church?" Trudy gasps.

"We do," Ron adds sweetly. "And after we eat and all feel better, maybe Teddy will come around and agree with me that you should stay the week to rest a bit." Ron eyes me as he does when he prays, urging me to be calm and present. "I'm sure you're exhausted from your loss and the travel."

"I will never forgive you," I say to Ron.

"Yes, you will."

"Can I get in the pool?" Ava asks.

"If you wash your face and take an antibiotic," I say with a smile.

She laughs a fake laugh and shoots me a fuck-you smile.

"You are so kind, Ron," Trudy says. "Where do you go to church?"

"Right here," Ron says.

Trudy looks out, scanning the yard and the mountains.

"I don't see a church," she says.

"Would you care for a cocktail, Trudy?" Ron asks, not answering her question. "I think you could use one."

"Oh, she doesn't drink," I say. "Do you, Trudy? Tell him. Drinking is evil."

"Oh, I do now," she says. "Even Jesus drank wine."

I lift a brow at her.

Ron heads to the kitchen, Trudy following like the baby quail that run through our yard.

"Could you be a dear and retrieve our luggage, Ava?" Trudy calls in a now happy tone, wiping her brow with a Kleenex she pulled from the sleeve of her hideous sweater. "The Uber driver just dumped it out in your driveway."

"How did you find me anyway?" I ask, teeth clenched.

"It's called Google, Grandpa," Ava says.

"Call me Grandpa again and I will kill you in your sleep," I say. "I am not joking."

Ava quickly heads toward the door.

How *did* Trudy find me, though?

Has Ron secretly been conversing with her? Did he confiscate my cell and give her our address after listening to her sobbing voicemails? And why is she really here? My sister is a riddle wrapped in an enigma swaddled in a blue-tinted old lady perm, polyester sweater and a shade of eye shadow not found on a color wheel.

But most importantly, how the hell do I get rid of them? They're the last people I want to be around before I die. Or they kill me like Ralph.

"Wanna help me with the luggage?" Ava asks me at the door.

I glance at her. "Do I look like the help?"

"You look like you *need* help."

Ava glares at me. I roll my eyes at her.

I finally realize that I, too, am but a teenage girl.

Ava flips her hair, and I watch my mini-me walk out the front door.

"You must feel like you are back home in Michigan with this beef stroganoff, scalloped potatoes and creamed peas and onions," I say to Trudy, who has seemingly not lost her appetite even after her fight with Teddy.

"Our mother didn't cook," Teddy says. "Did she, dear sister?"

Teddy is on his second Manhattan. It's 11:00 a.m.

Trudy nervously shoves heaping forkfuls of food into her mouth.

I am seated between Ava and Trudy. Teddy positioned himself at the far end of the Pink Lady dinette set as far away from his family as he could possibly be without being seated in Idyllwild.

"Well, it must at least feel like you two just sat down for Sunday dinner again together, right?" I continue undeterred.

"No, Ron," Teddy says, taking too big a sip and rattling the ice in his glass. "What do you not understand? It feels nothing like that because our mama isn't hiding in the kitchen drinking vodka from a Windex bottle, Trudy isn't humiliating me and Daddy isn't beating the shit out of me. We acted like the Waltons, but we were more like the Mansons." He lifts his cocktail glass. "To family!"

Teddy leans back in his chair, waiting for a reaction from Trudy. She continues to eat, not looking up.

"Did your grandma ever share stories about growing up with me?" Teddy shifts in his chair and looks at the girl.

Ava refuses to open her mouth, either to eat or speak.

"I didn't think so, but they went a little something like this," Teddy continues. "I made dinner every Sunday while your grandma and our father were sitting in the living room belittling me and my mother. Eventually, your sweet, little grandma—the woman who, I'm sure, is the pillar of your community, deacon in the church and beacon of light for so many upstanding folk—would rile up our old man so much that he'd turn on me and beat the shit out of me. Finally, when he was full from dinner, satiated by a twelve-pack of Stroh's and exhausted from beating the living daylights out of me, I'd run away crying. No one ever came looking for me. No one ever tried to help."

Teddy stares at Ava. "Oh, and this is one of my favorite family stories! Once, I tried to kill myself after Daddy beat me up. Your grandmother came into the bathroom and found me. Seems I'd cut my wrists the wrong way and didn't bleed out. Rookie mistake. So she bandaged me up and told me in the sweetest tone, 'Wear long sleeves from now on, Teddy.'"

Ava's jaw trembles. She looks at her grandma—horror etched on her face—as if a rabid coyote is racing toward her.

"Grandma?" Ava asks, her voice no longer that of a rebellious teen but of a scared girl. "That's not true, is it?"

The table remains silent.

"Oh, it's all true, sweetheart," Teddy says to her.

"Teddy," I say. "This isn't the time or place."

"It's *never* the time or place, is it, Ron, to discuss something painful?" Teddy yells. "You know what I endured! I know what you endured! I'd think church on a Sunday would be the perfect time to exorcise our demons." Teddy glares at me. "You act out this church fantasy every Sunday to pretend that you didn't have the same exact childhood I did, as if you were the one who needed to pray for forgiveness and not the father who beat the crap out of you every week after pretending to be the voice of God. We moved as far away from our childhood homes as possible to escape that hell, and now we're old men who are still running, and I'm exhausted. God, I'm just so tired, Ron. Aren't you? And you still say this isn't the right time or place?" Teddy sets his glare on his sister. "This is *my* home, Trudy, and I want you and this white trash Barbie doll out of here after that jaw of yours finally gets tired of eating *our* food."

Teddy stands suddenly, pushing his chair back so violently it flips backward onto the lawn, pink pirouetting across green.

"Now, if you'll excuse me," he says in a polite tone, storming toward the house.

"Teddy," I call, my tone somewhere between hostage negotiator and parent. "Where are you going?"

Teddy stops and turns.

"To book a hotel room and then get a few Tupperware containers so our guests can take their dessert to go."

A light breeze skitters through the palm trees as Dean Martin croons "That's Amore."

Teddy disappears inside.

Barry actually looks up from his cell, and Sid keeps picking up his fork over and over again without taking a bite. He looks as if he's been kidnapped and forced to appear on tape acting as if everything is normal.

Teddy warned me not to do this, even as payback for his earlier behavior. Perhaps he was right. Perhaps I overstepped.

"I know you, Ron," Teddy said to me earlier when I was making dessert. "You just have to be the savior. You couldn't save your family, so you think you can save mine. Well, you're going to be sorely disappointed. You'll think Trudy is sweet until she turns on you. My sister acts like Tammy Faye from the Church of Goodness and Light, but she's really in disguise for the Westboro Baptist Church. She will destroy you, Ron. I'm sorry for not chipping in more. I'm sorry for not being more appreciative of you. I've just had a lot on my mind lately. But I am *not* sorry when I tell you that you are wrong for letting her stay in our home after all she's done to me."

I could tell he was about to say something more when Trudy came into the kitchen, and Teddy scurried to the patio.

"Well, we're having pineapple upside-down cake," I say in a too-high voice, pulling the top off the pan in the middle of the table. "Ooh, it's still warm! Hopefully, this dessert will turn everyone's mood upside down."

Barry and Sid stare at me as if I've been possessed by the spirit of Dolly Parton.

I smile at them. Ava looks around the table, her eyes begging for help. She puts AirPods into her ears to silence the commotion. My heart breaks.

Teddy is wrong: If I can win a war against all the demons in my life, I can win this war, too.

I motion for Ava to remove her AirPods. "Aren't you hungry?"

Ava sighs dramatically, holding the pod in mid-air.

"Not for this," she says, looking at the table. "I feel like I'm in a nursing home."

"Language, Ava!" Trudy scolds.

"What's your favorite food?" I ask.

"Starbucks and pizza."

"I have some coffee brewing in the kitchen, and there's some leftover pizza in the freezer if you'd like it," I say. "Why don't you change into your swimsuit and enjoy the pool."

You don't need to be a part of this, I don't say.

"Finally," she says, pushing her plate away and standing to leave.

Barry and Sid look at me.

"You don't have to stay either," I say.

They grab their plates and flee.

Trudy and I carry on eating without saying a word, the clatter of silverware filling the silence.

"So?" Trudy finally asks, scooping a slice of pineapple upside-down cake onto her dessert plate. "When do we go to church? It's getting awfully late. I'm guessing you go to church later on the West Coast?"

"I told you earlier, we are at church."

Trudy carefully places her knife and fork on her plate, folds her arms into her body and looks me directly in the eye.

"What do you mean?"

"This is our church," I say, spreading my arms to encompass the sun, sky, mountains, trees, all of nature.

"This is not a church," Trudy says. "This is a backyard."

"No," I say. "This is our church. We call it Church of Mary."

"To honor the mother of Jesus?"

"Sort of," I say. "We created this tradition decades ago as a way to celebrate our friendship as well as our special relationship with God. My father was a pastor."

"Then he should have taught you that you need to go to a proper church, right?" Trudy asks.

"We have faith, Trudy, but we do not participate in organized religion. There is a big difference between faith and religion. Organized religion has caused irreparable harm to me and my community. But I do believe that one does not need to attend church to have faith. Have you ever read *Walden*?"

"No, I only read the Bible, and I'm sorry to inform you that you will go to hell."

My mouth drops open, and I stare at Trudy, who simply nods emphatically at my disbelief.

I jump at applause behind me. Teddy is back. With a new cocktail. And Tupperware.

He has placed them on the bar behind us and is clapping his hands loudly.

"Told ya, Ron. My sister will never change. She speaks with a forked tongue."

"The Bible never changes."

"You are the greatest actress to walk this earth since Meryl Streep," Teddy says. "I'm shocked you haven't won an Oscar."

"Hollywood," she says dismissively and with disgust.

"And yet they make all those Tom Cruise movies I'm sure you still love to watch."

Trudy's face beads with sweat. I cannot tell if it's the heated debate or escalating temperature, but she tugs at her sweater and dabs her dewy face with a cocktail napkin that was hidden under a basket of rolls. My eyes bulge, and I look at Teddy.

Damn it, Teddy! You picked these napkins on purpose.

He smiles at his sister as she dabs her forehead again.

Please, I pray. *Don't look at the napkin. Crumple it up and toss it on the table.*

"Would you like to go change, Trudy?" I ask. "It warms up quickly here. Cool mornings, hot afternoons."

"She's leaving, Ron, remember?" Teddy admonishes. "Believe me, she's not changing either her clothes or her way of thinking. And we need to get used to this heat, Ron, since we'll both be burning in hell, right, sis?"

Trudy shifts in her chair. She looks light-years older than Teddy with her red cheeks, wash-and-set, pursed lips and figure that is more SpongeBob than SilverSneakers. When I look at Trudy, I do—*God, forgive me*—picture Shelley Winters in the movie *The Poseidon Adventure* trying to make it off the ship alive.

Trudy leans over to grab another napkin. This time, she dabs the corner of her eyes.

"Save your crocodile tears, Trudy," Teddy scoffs. "The only time I've seen you really cry is when you caught me wearing Mama's wedding dress and realized it not only fit me better but that I looked better in it than you ever would." Teddy takes a step toward her. "As I told you, I'm not the one living in drag, sis. You are. And you will never fully know yourself until you remove that mask you wear to please the world."

"You've always tried to wound me, Teddy. We used to be so close."

For a long moment, there is only the dead calm silence of the desert, a whisper of a breeze through the palms.

Trudy stops dabbing her eyes. She places the napkin on her lap and smooths it nervously.

Then her eyes narrow. She picks up the napkin as if it is a snake and tosses it onto the table, where it lands face up.

The napkin features an image of Jesus before a rainbow-colored world. His cloak is emblazoned with a big heart. Above His head, it reads: Ah, Men!

"Do you believe in Jesus, Teddy?" Trudy asks, her voice clear, high and steady as if she has begun to sing a hymn.

I am in hell already.

"I'm not doing this, Trudy. I played this game for too long." Teddy stops. "Actually, do you want to know what I really believe?"

"Please, enlighten me," she says.

"I believe a wonderful man walked this earth and was probably killed by haters who didn't understand his purpose in life, and, sadly, that has not changed much over time. But I do not believe that you or I are any more righteous or right than Jews, Muslims, Catholics, Methodists, Unitarians . . ."

Trudy laughs. "Unitarians believe in nothing."

"I'm done," Teddy says. "You think your faith is the only appropriate way to believe. That shows you have no ability to change, much less think for yourself."

He turns to leave once more but stops again.

"I believe you weaponize your faith against people like me. I believe you live your life out of fear instead of joy. I believe you hate yourself. I believe you don't believe half of what you say you do. And I believe you're the reason your husband probably died. He couldn't take living with you anymore."

My breath hitches in my chest.

Trudy squares her shoulders. Her face morphs into steel. She raises one eyebrow at Teddy.

"And I believe your husband killed himself because he was sick, inside and out," she says without an ounce of emotion in her voice. "The difference between them is that my Ralph is living in eternity in the Holy Kingdom, and your John is burning in eternal damnation."

My breath catches again. My chest aches. Angina.

Teddy stands as still as the Marilyn Monroe statue in downtown Palm Springs. I wait for him to toss his drink into her face. I wait for him to slap her. Instead, Teddy says very quietly, "Don't you ever utter his name again." Teddy shakes his head pityingly. "Do you even know what love is, Trudy? Real, true, unconditional love for another human being?"

She does not respond. Teddy continues.

"True love is the way John reached for my hand every night before he fell asleep and said, 'Time for beddy, Teddy. I love you to the moon and back.' True love is how I'd smooth his cowlick even after he'd styled his hair. True love is the way he held doors open for people who would likely let them shut in his own face. I know true love because I had never received it in my life before John. I wish I had his capacity to forgive, but I do not and cannot. That's what I mean by true love, Trudy. I loved every single thing about that man, but it wasn't enough to save him, and I will live with that—and without that love—for the rest of my life, so do not talk to me about hell, because I'm already there."

Teddy takes one unsteady step to the left, pulls his spine straight and walks away.

This time, I can feel my heart shatter in my chest, as if a stained glass window has been dropped from the heavens.

"I will not allow you to speak to my family this way, Trudy," I say. "I invited you into our home, and with that invitation comes a requirement to respect those I love most in this world. That was below my family's standard of respect. Do you understand?"

Trudy casts her eyes my way.

"Your family?" she asks.

"*My* family," I say. "That man you call your brother is more mine than yours. All of these men are my family, maybe not in blood, but in blood spilled."

Trudy thrusts a finger at the napkin, the table, the house and, finally, me.

"You are making a mockery of God," she says, "with this . . . this lifestyle, this so-called church, your lack of morals."

"No, *you* are making a mockery of God with your judgment," I say. "And this is not a lifestyle. Our sexuality was never a choice. If you believe in God, why would He create us to be imperfect? Why would He make us this way?"

"To reject it."

I smile.

"Ah, the old playbook and double standard. Why have you not rejected a lifestyle of cruelty? Do you not think you will be judged for your lack of compassion?"

She shakes her head at me.

"Let me explain something to you. Most of my friends, including myself, tried to kill ourselves at one point in our lives because of the shame we felt, the rejection from family, the desire to love and be loved but believing we didn't deserve it. Most importantly, we were secret keepers, Trudy, unable to share our true selves and light with the world. I cannot imagine a world—or a heaven—without these men in it. Not only would it be wrong, it would be horribly boring."

"But—" Trudy interrupts.

"No, I want to finish." I continue. "You believe that we desecrate God by not attending church when we have been the target of hate from organized religion for centuries. Just a blink ago, our own country dehumanized us, refused to give us equal rights, literally made it impossible for a gay man to walk into a church with our heads held high, and you think *we* are making a mockery of our faith? We should be lauded for gathering and believing in not only a higher power but also in each other. That, Trudy, is a real miracle considering all we've been through. That, Trudy, is true faith."

Trudy pushes her chair back.

"Faith by itself, if it is not accompanied by action, is dead,"

I say. "Show me your faith without deeds, and I will show you my faith by my deeds."

"James 2:18?"

"Yes," I say. "I listened to my father, and I listen to my *Father*."

Trudy remains seated.

"One more," I say. I spread my arms like the wings of a raven circling the mountain. "'The righteous will flourish like a palm tree . . . planted in the house of the Lord.' It is easy to have faith when life has not challenged you. But when you have been outcast, when you have nothing and no one, that is when true faith materializes." I reach out and touch Trudy's arm. "Why are you really here, Trudy? I've never seen you. I've never spoken to you. You've never called or sent a holiday card. Even after John's death."

Trudy looks away.

"I know why you're here, Trudy."

She looks back quickly, her face conveying a million emotions.

"It's why we're all here. It's why we created this sanctuary for one another," I say. "You are filled with shame, you have been rejected by family, and you doubt if you've ever been loved in your life and whether you're even worthy of love, including God's. But most importantly, Trudy, I believe your brother is right: You are a secret keeper, unable to share your true self and light with the world."

My voice reverberates in the still of the desert, and in those vibrations I can hear the voice of my father, my mother, my shame, my pride, my faith, my family and God.

I see Trudy's mask finally slide for a moment.

One big fat tear slides down her face. Trudy suddenly gasps. It is a horrible gasp that shatters the silence. It is a shudder so hideous—one that I and so many of my friends have let escape from our bodies when we could no longer contain our shame or pain—and yet it is as familiar as a hymn.

I know immediately: Trudy does have a secret. A very, very big one.

"Is there something else on your mind?" I ask. "Is that why you're here, Trudy? Do you want to talk about it with me?"

She looks at me as if she's been caught stealing, but shakes her head until she must be dizzy.

"No!" she says. "Please. No!"

"Then shall we pray?" I ask, extending my hand.

Trudy grips it and unleashes a torrent of tears.

"Amen," I say.

I hear a splash in the pool.

I look up, and *that* girl is floating on our rainbow unicorn.

She is wearing a red bikini no thicker than a Twizzler. She stretches her lithe, translucent body out like a sheet of paper and sighs as the warm water and sun envelop her.

"So, how old are *you*?" she asks.

I lower my vintage Versace sunglasses—which may or may not be women's and which I may or may not have "borrowed" from one of Teddy's trunk shows when he wasn't looking.

"Questions we don't ask out loud," I say.

"So, old, then?" she asks.

I sit up on my chaise, give her porcelain-colored skin a slow once-over.

"Have you ever seen the sun before?" I ask. "Do they have that in Ohio?"

She opens her mouth, but I wag my finger at her.

"No, ma'am," I continue. "Don't pull any BS with Barry. Girls like you are a dime a dozen in California. I'm an actor and a writer, so I know a good story when I hear one. You packed that swimsuit, so you knew where you were going."

"I thought we were going to a hotel for spring break."

I laugh.

"Your grandma on spring break? Now that's a rom-com waiting to be made! No, no. You knew you were coming here. You went to an airport. You knew we had a pool. How?"

She smiles sheepishly, caught out. "I *may* have helped her find your address out here. The nosy guy with the cotton candy hair . . ."

"Ron."

"Yeah, him. He sent a letter to my mom about Teddy's husband a long time ago. It didn't have a return address, but all I had to do was google his name and Palm Springs, and it brought up your address, your ages . . ."

"Our ages?"

"Well, Ron's age," she says. "All I knew was that my grandma was hell-bent on talking to him. I thought at first she just wanted to get away from the house after my grandpa died, but I think it's more than that. My grandma is the most boring person in the world. She's *never* out of control. I mean, do you see her?"

I laugh.

"Well, just enjoy it before Teddy drags your grandma out by her horns."

She opens her mouth, but the sun is working its magic, and she can't find the strength for another comeback.

Ah, the magic of the desert, an elixir for the young and old.

I look at this girl child who thinks she is so grown up, and then lean back in my chaise, hold up my cell and take a selfie, a man boy who fools himself into believing he is still so young.

I actually see myself in her.

Time isn't fleeting, it's a torture chamber, a fun house mirror that constantly reflects our youth back on us.

Just a blink ago, Hollywood made Palm Springs famous. Then, times changed, and stars could travel anywhere. Palm Springs in the 1970s and 1980s was an isolated place, tumbleweed literally bouncing through downtown, until gay men returned seeking hope and health and—like this child—sun and solace. The gays rehabbed the homes, returned the glamour, and then the straight people—as they always do—flocked here as if they were the first to discover a hidden jewel. They bought up the property and, in turn, that gentrification isolated the group who actually made the town and neighborhood beautiful again.

And then these Coachella kids—all about Ava's age—show up and act as if they brought retro style to our sun-drenched oasis. White Party partiers descend on the desert, desecrating it like a cheap motel room. And those who found it in the first place—all the stars and queens—are either dead, too old or too tired to give them a history lesson.

"So . . . how old are you?"

The girl has closed in on me, a hand with blue-black nails to match her hair gripping the silver railing just below from where I'm seated in a Speedo.

"You can tell me," Ava continues.

"How old do you think I am?" I ask. "I mean, you already know Ron's age."

That's more gay math: Like Zsa Zsa, a gay man of a certain age never discloses his true age. And if pressed, always subtract eight years and add two inches to your South Pole.

It's not lying, and it's not exaggerating.

It's simply gay math.

"I don't know," she says, her eyes hidden behind a pair of plastic gas station sunglasses. She lowers them for a second to study me. "Eighty, but you pass for younger. Am I close?"

"Ah, you are related to Teddy," I say.

She laughs. "God, I hope not."

"I'm not even close to eighty," I say.

"Define close," she says.

This time, I laugh.

She pushes her sunglasses up her nose again and shrugs. "Everyone looks old to me."

"Just wait," I say. "In a few years, everyone will look young to you: your doctor, your children's teacher, your barista."

Water droplets spill from her hands, gleaming in the sun. She floats off into the deep end.

"Why are you wearing a Speedo if you're so old?"

"Why are you wearing dental floss if you're underage?" I ask.

"I forgot your name," she says.

"Barry."

"Now *that's* an old man name."

"Haven't you ever heard of Barry Manilow?"

"Who?"

I think of Teddy's story about Cher.

"Famous singer from my day," I say. "He actually lives in Palm Springs."

She shrugs. I return to texting.

"Are you, like, famous or something?" she asks. "You said you're a writer and an actor."

I glance up, and Ava is back at the railing.

"Damn it. You didn't drown."

She grins. "I'm a survivor."

"Finally, we have something in common."

I take off my sunglasses and consider her question.

"I should be," I finally say.

"So should I."

I nod. "Touché."

What is it with me and young people? I've also sought their approval more than anyone else in my life. And they've always been more honest than my therapist.

For some reason, perhaps the two cocktails I had at Church of Mary to deaden the horror movie I was trapped in, I tell this young stranger my abbreviated life story.

"God, that sucks," she says when I'm done. "And you're *still* trying. Why don't you just get drunk every day and hang out at this ridiculous house with a bunch of hot guys?"

"Um, I already kind of do that," I say.

"I think I love you."

I get up and walk to the edge of the pool. I take a seat, still holding my cell, and dangle my feet into the water. A glorious pattern of blue shimmers beneath the surface.

"I still have this overwhelming need to prove myself," I explain. "I have this desire to be . . ."

"Famous?" Ava asks. "Rich?"

"Immortal."

The word drifts across the pool like the bee that is now dipping its body into the water to cool off, and then it sinks, like the bee.

I jump into the pool, swim to the other end, cup my hands and save the bee. It flies off.

"You want a second chance," Ava says.

"Yes."

"Everyone wants to be rich and famous," she says. "But no one thinks they have to try."

"You are an old soul."

Ava slips off the floaty and swims over to me, resting her arms on the side of the pool, facing the mountains.

"My brother, Sean, is the chosen one," Ava says, using her fingers to emphasize "chosen." "Straight A's, great athlete, I mean, like, he got every good gene in our family and, believe me, there aren't that many. My parents sacrificed everything for him. It's like I don't even exist. I mean, whose parents *both* go off and leave their daughter alone with their grandparents while she's still in high school? They couldn't wait a year or two? It's not normal." Ava looks at me. "Is it?"

"No" I say, "that's not normal."

"Thank you," she says, slapping the pool, hard, with her hand, water flying. "I may not be book smart, but I am street smart."

"I always say I'd rather be street smart than book smart, otherwise you won't know how to survive in this world."

"I love to write music, I play the piano, but none of that is, like, normal to my family."

"Preach, sister," I say. "When I told my parents I wanted to be an actor, my father laughed in my face. And they both died without seeing me make it." I hesitate as the words hit me harder than I imagined. "I still want to make it. I still want to prove to people that I did it. I still want to prove to myself that I'm talented."

"So do I," Ava says.

She holds up her hand, and I high-five it.

"I have a boyfriend, Gabe," she offers. "My parents and grandma know I'm seeing someone, but they would hate him if they ever met him."

"Is he hot?" I ask.

Ava releases a girlish giggle. "Of course! Do I look like a girl who would date a boy who wasn't hot?"

"No. Do I?" I ask. She laughs again. "How old is he?"

"Eighteen. Too young for you."

"Eighteen, high school, or eighteen, college?" I ask. "There's a big difference."

"Eighteen dropout," she clarifies. "He's a musician, and my family thinks the arts are a ticket either to being poor or to hell."

"Well, I'm sure they're just concerned about your future and his influence on you," I say.

"You, too?" she asks, moving away from me. "I thought you'd see it differently."

"As an actor and writer," I say, "I see it from every point of view. But I will give you this: Older people always tend to think poorly of artists. It's easier to take the safe route in this world. It's easier to fit in and just get by. Try being gay and in musical theater. I had a target on my back from elementary school."

"Can't I just be a kid?" Ava asks. "Sean is, like, this robot, programmed for success. No time for fun. I just want to be a teenager, but I feel like if I don't have the next forty years planned out, I'm a failure. It's not fair."

"Ava?"

She stops and rotates in the water until she is facing me. I continue.

"Let me tell you something: I don't know what you believe. Hell, I don't even know what I believe still, but I do believe this: Someone in this universe made each of us to be unique. And we spend our entire lives letting the world deplete us of our gifts one day at a time until we're not even close to being the people we once dreamed of becoming. I've never had my next day figured out, much less the next forty years. I don't plot out every detail of my life. I'm not handcuffed to the norms of the world. I can be who I'm meant to be, and I believe that—just like your Great-Uncle Teddy and all the men in there who are my family—my light changes not only those around us but also the world."

Ava tilts her head back, sun on her face, hair trailing in the water. She looks like a child for a moment, a girl on vacation, a young woman free from the troubles of the world.

"Can I ask you a question?" I ask.

Ava doesn't respond. I take her inertia as confirmation.

"What was it like to find your grandfather?"

Her body spasms in the water as if she's had an electric shock, and she flails her arms in the water until she's upright and has steadied herself. I ready myself to be verbally dismembered by the girl I now remember who walked into the house and not the kinder, gentler intruder who has recently overtaken her body.

"Thank you for asking," she finally says, her voice breaking. "No one has asked me that."

I nod and wait until she is ready to talk.

"Grandpa was the first person in my life who's ever died," she says. "I mean, I had a goldfish named Goldy . . ."

"So clever," I interrupt.

Ava gives me the finger.

". . . who died when I was a kid, but my parents wouldn't even allow us to have, like, a dog or cat. Too much care. Too much emotion. Too much mess. But Grandpa was the first real person I've lost. I came home from school, and he was, like, just sitting in his chair watching ESPN like he always did. I thought he was taking a nap. I got a snack, texted Gabe and my friends, came back out, and it was then I realized his eyes were open. And I knew even though I didn't know. I touched him . . ."

Ava stops.

". . . and his head fell to the side."

She looks toward the house. When she speaks again, her voice is a low hum.

"I feel like such a horrible person saying this, but he was so closed off that it was like he was already dead."

She shakes her head, hard, as if she cannot believe she just uttered this aloud. Ava looks up, almost expecting a lightning bolt to appear on a perfect day in the desert.

"It's okay," I say.

"No, it's not," she says. "I feel awful."

"Ava, it's okay," I repeat, this time with more force.

"I mean, I think Grandpa loved me, but I'm not sure he ever liked me," Ava says. "He never told me he loved me. He never really said anything at all, just sat in that chair every single day and watched sports." She clambers back onto the unicorn and lets her hair dangle into the water. It floats on the surface like an underwater beast stalking her, waiting to pounce and eat her whole. "I'm not sure he liked anything but the Cincinnati Reds. And even that was stretch." She is silent for a moment. "He and Grandma fought all the time, about *everything*. And then they just stopped talking. For, like, years. He'd eat dinner in his chair. He stopped going to church with her. It was like they were strangers in their own home, and so Grandma focused all of her attention and anger on me. You know, they weren't really planning to go see my parents in London. That's all a lie. Grandma just says that to make people think everything was okay. He wouldn't even get in the car to go to Meijer with her to grocery shop. I think he hated her guts." She takes a deep breath. "And I think she hated him."

"Are *you* okay?"

Ava releases a sad, quick laugh.

"You're the first person to ask me that, too." She looks up at me. "I don't know, to be honest."

"And that's okay, too, you know."

My cell trills. I swim to the edge, grab it and tap a message.

"You're on your phone way more than I am," Ava says, raising a brow. "Boy trouble?"

"Are you psychic?"

"I know boys," she says. "You're acting pretty sus. I think you're up to something, and you don't want anyone to know."

I cock my head and smile. "Bingo!" I say with a wink. "Street smart."

"Spill it," she says, pushing through the water to the other side of the pool with me.

"Can you keep a secret?"

Ava mimes locking her lips with a key. "Vault."

I turn my screen towards her.

"This is Kyle. My boy trouble."

"That's *Billy the Hillbilly*!" she gasps.

"Vault! Remember?"

"Sorry, he may be old, but he's hot."

"Which is why I'm in trouble."

For some reason—again, perhaps the two cocktails I've had coupled with the fact I will never see her again—I tell this stranger about breaking up with Kyle and seeing him again recently and his indecent proposal.

"This is like a spicy rom-com," Ava says. "But, like, for old gay people."

"Thank you," I say in a deadpan tone. "And? Do you have any advice, boy wizard?"

"It seems like you and all of your friends have spent your entire lives trying to live openly and honestly without secrets," Ava says very seriously. "Why would you let someone, like, walk into your life again after all these years and completely fuck it up by asking you to be dishonest? Believe me, if Billy the Hillbilly is doing this with you, it's not his first rodeo."

I am stunned by her clarity and wisdom.

"But what if I still have feelings for him? What if I made a mistake? What if he can resurrect my career?"

"TBH? What you just said is the biggest cap I've heard in a minute."

I have no idea what Ava just said but pretend as if I do.

"Go on."

"He's using you, bruh. He wants a little boy toy in the desert. Then, when the movie is over, he'll go back to his life, and you'll be replaced with someone else."

"But he promised me a role in his movie."

"Is he lying? And is it worth it?" Ava asks. "You just preached to me about being unique, and I'm sorry, but cheating is basic as fuck."

Ava suddenly flips over on the floaty. On her lower back is an infinity tattoo, the ink freshly purple, the skin surrounding it still pink.

"Gabe and I got matching tattoos after my grandpa died," she says, catching me looking. "It was a way to bond us together, and a way for me to see my future as having infinite possibilities, not like my grandma and grandpa."

"That's permanent," I say.

"No shit, Sherlock," she says. "My family is gonna find out. And maybe it's a mistake, but it's my mistake."

Ava flips back over to face me.

"Your mistake isn't permanent yet," she continues. "But I guarantee it's a mistake that will leave a bigger mark than my tattoo. It'll leave a forever mark. Inside. One that will never fade. At least I can turn this tattoo into, like, a butterfly or something if Gabe turns out to be a total asshole, but can you turn your scar into something beautiful if your fling with Kyle goes up in smoke? Just know you have to be able to live with the consequences of your decision. You, Barry, and no one else. If not, walk away. Now."

"What if it never happens?" I ask.

"You said you haven't had the next day figured out for the last forty years," she says. "You said you love the unknown. You said my light could change not only those around us but also the world. So could yours. I actually don't think you have boy troubles."

"I don't?" I ask. "What do I have, then?"

"You have Barry troubles," Ava says. "All the boys in your life are just a distraction from your dream because you don't think that you're good enough. And that's really pretty sad, don't you think?"

My cell trills.

Ava glares at me.

I ignore it. She smiles.

"Alexa?" she calls. "Play . . ."

Ava turns to me.

"What's the name of the singer out here who has your name?"

"Barry Manilow."

"What Barry Manilow song would you suggest we listen to?"

"Alexa?" I call. "Play 'I Made It Through the Rain.'"

When the song finishes, Ava says, "That was beautiful."

It's then I notice she has tears in her eyes.

"My turn," she continues. "Alexa, play 'Anti-Hero' by Taylor Swift."

This time, Ava sings along, spitting the lyrics of the chorus into my own face.

"Yeah, you are the problem," she says with a laugh.

My cell trills again.

I ignore it again.

"Good boy," she says, pulling me into the pool.

Sid

I am sitting in my car clutching my clutch.

I scan the parking lot of the Palm Springs library. My car is parked at the curb, right in front of the doors. A security camera stands guard above the entrance. It is a bright, sunny Wednesday for Drag Queen Reading Hour, and yet I see only darkness.

I look to the left, then right, before scanning my mirrors. Patrons walk by, children happily skipping, and I slump further into the driver's seat.

I nervously rub the brooch I wear at the top of my blouse. It was my grandmother's, and I used to sneak it out of her jewelry box and admire it as a boy, mesmerized by its beauty. It looks like a cameo, but it's actually a Star of David embedded into ivory. My grandmother wore it as a necklace, but I removed the chain, saved the pendant and refashioned it for Sophia Petrillo.

And myself.

I would rub it for good luck and protection when I first started performing. Out of all the boys, I am the least theatrical. I mean, Teddy is all drama, Dorothy except with an Adam's apple. Ron is a creative, and Barry is an actor. I fell into place like the last piece of a jigsaw puzzle solely because of my age and the fact I look a little bit like Sophia. All I had to do was learn to say, "Picture it! Sicily . . ."

"You've lied your whole life," Teddy teased me before our first performance years ago. "This is all scripted. It should be so much easier for you."

When I rubbed the brooch the first time before I went on stage, I could feel my grandmother beside me.

As I sit there, I see in the mirror an older woman approaching with two children. I slouch further, until my body is practically underneath the wheel.

I watch her pass.

Is that her?

My heart is racing.

Is she back?

My memory of the incident is blurry at best. I didn't realize how blurry until the police called for a statement.

Another woman passes, and I jump.

Is that her?

I grab my clutch even tighter. I have cleaned and shined it a hundred times to ensure her spit has been removed, but I cannot erase the memory.

"Screw this!" I finally say.

I start the car and begin to put it into Reverse when I hear a knock on the window. I scream bloody murder.

Esther Himmelbaum and Talia Goldfarb are standing at the passenger window. Only their heads are visible.

I roll down the window.

"What the hell are you doing?" Esther says.

"I'm leaving."

"No, you're not," she says, tugging on the door handle. "Open the door!"

I hit Unlock, and Esther and Talia slowly climb inside. They pack their tiny tuchuses against one another in the passenger seat.

"What kind of car is this?" Talia asks, rubbing the leather interior. "Very nice. Is it new?"

"It's a Tesla."

"Ack!" Talia yelps. "That man is meshuga!"

"May all his teeth fall out except one," Esther says, cursing Elon Musk, "so he can have a toothache."

Talia cackles.

"Why are you in my car?" I ask.

"We came here to support you," Esther says. "We love you."

I had told Esther what happened. She told Talia. I'm surprised CNN doesn't know yet. Or Santa Claus. Or my friends. I don't want anyone to know. Which is why I haven't responded to any of Leo's messages yet about being featured on his segment.

"We knew you'd be scared," Esther continues. "We're going to walk you inside."

"My bodyguards are two Jewish women in their late eighties?"

"No one will fuck with us!" Talia adds.

I shake my head. "I can't."

"You can," Talia says. "And you will."

"You have to do this, Sid, not just for you but for everyone who is hated every single day in this country simply for honoring who they are," Esther says. "Look at what our people have endured lately."

"I'm not going to change anything," I say.

Esther puts her hand on my arm.

"Do you remember the story you told me at our first Passover together?"

I stare at the library entrance, racking my brain to remember.

Esther prompts me. "You told me your favorite part of Passover as a child was . . . ?"

"The afikomen." I finish her thought, remembering. "It was."

"Why was that, Sid?"

"It was fun." I shrug. "It was one of the final rituals, and it gave us kids something to look forward to."

"But there is more than that, too, right?"

I manage to look my friend in the eye.

"Seder revolves around a stack of three matzos, correct?" she asks.

I nod.

"We take out the middle one and break it in half," Esther recounts, "but, of course, they never break evenly, so we put the smaller piece back into the stack and wrap the larger piece in a napkin and hide it for the children. When they find it, they deliver it to the table at the end of Seder. This middle matzo represents the human situation: broken and small. This is the bread of affliction, impoverishment and enslavement. Seder begins with the acknowledgment that—like the Israelites in Egypt—our need for redemption is extraordinary, and that the world we live in is broken, too, filled with suffering, injustice and despair. The first bite of the broken matzo is internalizing this truth. We place the salty tears of the enslaved on our tongues. We understand we are in a place of brokenness and about to set out on a journey."

Esther grips my arm even harder as a group of kids head into the library.

"But who delivers this message to us, Sid?" she asks.

"The children."

My voice breaks.

"Yes!" she exclaims. "And that is the secret of the afikomen ritual. Who do we trust to bring us this? The children. The remaining piece, the point of all of this—our future, our redemption—is in the hands of the next generation. We must trust them, again and again, to deliver it."

I place my head on the wheel, and my eyes fill with tears.

"Isn't that why you're here, Sid?" Talia asks. "Why you've been reading to kids for years? Because you trust that the next generation will be different, that our community, the gay community, the world will be different because of them?"

"Yes."

"Then take our hands," Esther says, "and let us lead you to the table where you can trust that maybe, just maybe, the next generation will not experience what we have endured, because they will no longer allow it."

Talia opens the car door.

We slide out.

Talia and Esther flank me, grabbing my hands, and we walk into the library as one, me in the middle—broken, shattered—but our united shadow bigger, stronger together.

"Thank you for agreeing to do the interview, Sid."

"I'm nervous."

"We can sit here as long as you like, okay?"

Leo and I are seated in the midst of a thick grove of palm trees in the Downtown Park, staring up and directly into Marilyn Monroe's panties.

Fittingly, the untrimmed Washingtonia fan palms surrounding us look as if they are wearing hula skirts.

The park is new to downtown Palm Springs and sits across from the Palm Springs Art Museum. It has already been embraced by locals. The controversial sculpture entitled *Forever Marilyn*, however, has been met with significant skepticism.

Towering over the park, the twenty-six-foot-tall *Forever Marilyn* captures the famed image from Billy Wilder's 1955 film *The Seven Year Itch*, the actress's skirt blowing skyward as she stands over a subway grate, baring her backside.

And I am old Marilyn, still dressed as Sophia—per Leo's request—following my Reading Hour at the library.

"Tell me about her," Leo finally says, breaking the silence.

I know it's a way to get me to start talking ahead of the interview as a cameraman stands before us, adjusting his lens and checking light levels.

"The sculpture has been a source of great controversy in Palm Springs over the years," I say to Leo, as tourists of all ages flock to have their photos taken underneath Marilyn. "The sculpture has been moved around to various locations all over town. Many prominent local citizens have tried to sue to have the sculpture moved from its current location."

"She seems so popular, though," he says.

"She is," I say, as each tourist does the same thing: They laugh and hold a finger up to point at her undercarriage.

"What's the issue?" he asks.

"Some worry that museum visitors, particularly schoolchildren, are being flashed on their way to and from the museum," I say. Leo chuckles, but my rote explanation stops me cold. "Others feel the sculpture of her captured in this moment is misogyny disguised as nostalgia. If you remember, Joe DiMaggio allegedly beat up Marilyn after she posed for this photo shoot."

Leo stares at the sculpture as the sounds of water cascading down a brutalist concrete fountain drown out the traffic and voices of visitors just a block away.

"I understand all of that, and that is horrific, but isn't the point of art to make people think? Perhaps the sculptor's mission was not simply to recreate this moment in time but to create a piece that forces us to ask ourselves to consider how women have been viewed throughout history and still are today?" Leo nods toward the tourists. "Is it bad art simply because it appeals to the masses?"

For a moment, I am not lost in Leo's eyes or his deep dimple, but in his sensitivity and intellect. There is nothing sexier than a brain.

"Are you Sophia from *The Golden Girls*?" a young woman says as she approaches. "Can we get our picture with you?"

A group of women wearing sashes reading GIRLS WEEKEND! gather around. Leo is game and takes the photo.

"We loved that show!" they yell as they take off toward Marilyn.

"Then you should go see *The Golden Gays*," Leo says. "He and his friends do a tribute show to them. It's amazing."

"We will!" they yell back.

I watch the tourists and ponder Leo's questions.

"Speaking of controversy . . ." Leo says gingerly as if reading my mind. "Are you ready?"

"Yes," I say.

He nods at the cameraman standing beside us.

"Tell me about what happened at the library," he asks.

I shut my eyes and take a deep breath. I tell my story.

"How did that make you feel?" he asks when I finish.

"Violated. Scared. Worthless. As if I had done something wrong." I pause. "As if *I* were wrong."

My voice breaks.

"Do you need to stop?"

I shake my head. "No."

"Go on."

"If something like this can happen in Palm Springs, it can happen anywhere. And it is happening right now. This very instant. Across the world. Someone, somewhere is experiencing a hate crime. Being victimized for simply being different." I speak in halting sentences. "I am eighty-one years old. I have experienced anti-Semitism, job discrimination based on my sexual orientation. I have been an outcast from my family. I am often an outcast in my own community simply for being old."

I look into the blue sky and continue.

"Eight decades of life, and we are still fighting the same hate in this world. When will this stop? How does it stop? One voice at a time. That's why—even though I am scared—I don't want to remain silent about what happened. Children will be the change. They will be, I hope, what saves us from one another. I am reading the same stories to kids in this community that I read to my own children in Chicago decades ago. I'm just doing it in a dress as Sophia Petrillo because kids connect with her. Kids love costumed characters, be it me or those at Disneyland. They let down their guards. We should be focusing on the fact that kids are going to the library and reading. We should be thankful they do not judge at this age. I have to believe the next generation will simply see that we have more in common with the person standing before us than what divides us."

I look at Leo. A soft smile crosses my lips. He nods at me to keep going.

"I doubt I'll be around to see this change, but if standing up for myself right now allows someone watching this to value their identity and stand up for themselves, or a child, mother or grandmother sees this and has a little more compassion, then this will all have been worth it."

Leo turns to the cameraman.

"We good?" he asks him.

"All good."

"Is that it?" I ask.

"Yep," Leo says. "It should air in a few weeks. The station wants to do a lot of promo in advance of this first segment."

"Very exciting."

Leo stands.

"We will interview your friends at your home in a few days, if that's okay?"

I nod.

I just need to tell them about all of this first.

"And right now, we need to get some B-roll to go along with the footage we got at the library," Leo says.

"B-roll?"

"Just some footage of us walking and talking, no sound, so that we can use it during the introduction and for promotion. Do you mind walking around the park with me for a moment?"

"Not at all."

We stroll through the grove of palms.

"So beautiful," Leo says.

"It is, isn't it?" I say. "Reminds you of what Palm Springs was before it became such a popular tourist destination. Palm trees, sunshine, blue sky and mountains. That's it."

Leo places his hand tenderly on my lower back.

"No," he says. "I mean you."

My knees lock, and I stumble. Leo catches me.

"I don't understand," I say, turning to him.

"*You*," he says. "You're beautiful."

The world around me falls away, one piece at a time—the

palms, the mountains, Marilyn, the cameraman—until it is only me and Leo, alone in the universe.

"I'm an old man dressed as an old woman," I say, confused. "What could you possibly find beautiful about me?"

"Everything."

Am I being mocked?

"Why are you doing this to me?" I ask. "It's cruel."

Leo gently turns my body until I am facing him.

"Oh, Sid," he says. "I want our community to see you as I do. I want *you* to see you as I do. Your beautiful soul." Leo glances back at the cameraman, who is standing a few feet away, unable to hear our conversation. "I've never done this before during an interview. It's quite unprofessional. I just think you are a special man. That's why I've been seeking you out."

"But you're . . . perfect."

"There is no such thing as perfect," he says. "We're all the same, broken people with broken parts we try to piece back together into a beautiful mosaic."

My body begins to shake out of nervousness, panic and excitement.

"Would you like to go out with me?" he asks.

"Why?"

"Those are things you don't utter out loud." He laughs. "Just say yes."

It takes every ounce of strength I have to put aside the feeling I will end up being crushed by this man and to form the word.

"Yes."

My sister is waiting for me in the kitchen Monday morning.

"I knew you'd need coffee," she says. "You drank coffee even as a boy."

"Someone had to get up and take care of the family. I barely slept for years."

I make my way around my sister without touching her, a feat considering her ample behind. She already has a cup by the machine, waiting. It's a favorite mug of mine featuring Dorothy from *The Golden Girls* saying, "No, I will not have a nice day."

"Thank you," I say, nodding at the mug. I fill it with a shaking hand.

"You drink too much, Teddy."

I shake my head.

"And you judge too much." I turn and look at my sister. "I have vodka, you have holy water. Each impairs our judgment. At least my addiction only harms myself. Yours has killed my community."

"Please, I don't want to fight, Teddy. I just want to talk."

"Then talk."

I lean against the island.

"I'm sorry for what I said about John. It wasn't my place."

"No, it wasn't. You don't even know why John killed himself, do you? Why it's so hard for me to forgive you?"

She shakes her head.

I sigh.

"After the last election, we were walking in downtown Palm Springs, me and John, where we've always felt safe, and someone screamed, '*Faggots!*' at us. John collapsed on the street. That single word on a sunny day in a safe haven broke him because he felt he'd never feel safe again. He believed the world was coming after him after all the years of finally feeling protected. Do you know what that is like? To not feel safe?"

"I'm so sorry, Teddy." Trudy is quiet for a moment. "And I do know—whether you believe it or not—what it's like to not feel safe."

"Right."

"Do you remember when we used to wake up early on Saturday morning and eat cereal and watch Saturday morning cartoons?" Trudy asks. "We loved Wile E. Coyote and the Road Runner. We went as them for Halloween."

"I do," I say.

"That was the last time I felt safe, Teddy," she says.

Trudy takes a breath to continue, but her phone trills. "Oh, it's Nina from church," she says. "I'm sure she's worried about me. I didn't tell her I was leaving. I have to take this."

God and image, one, Teddy, zero. That's my sister.

As Trudy slides into the living room, I think of what she just said and the letter I never sent to her when I left Mama's house for the last time. I close my eyes and can still remember every word. They are scorched in my soul, largely because I still read the letter every month.

"Sorry about that," Trudy says, coming back in.

"I found a picture at Mama's of us from Halloween when we were all dressed up," I say. "In those hard masks. I should have kept it."

"I still remember," she says. "I could barely breathe in that thing."

Trudy walks over and refills her mug. She looks out at the mountains through the windows.

"I always imagined the desert would look more apocalyptic," she says as if to herself. "Brown. Dead. But it's so lush . . . so alive . . ." A cloud slides away, and the mountains dance in sunlight and wind. The wildflowers—purple sand verbena, yellow brittlebrush, brown-eyed primrose—glow. "I never dreamed it would be so colorful."

My sister is saying this to me, you understand. She just can't say it *to me.*

This is her version of apologizing without apologizing.

I wait silently for her to rephrase her thoughts in a more personal way. I've waited my whole life for this. Instead, Trudy sips her coffee.

"Why are you really here, sis?" I ask. "You could have waited to wire me the money. Sent me a text to let me know your attorney needed to talk." I look at her. "I'm touched you did this for me. But we haven't been family in decades. You have your family, I have mine. Let's not pick at old wounds, okay?"

I look into my sister's eyes. They are hazel, but—right now—they just look dead to me.

"I didn't know where else to go," she says with a small shrug.

"You have a home. You have friends from church. So why pack up and come to Palm Springs to connect with a brother you haven't spoken to in years and whose existence you've never approved of?"

"My husband just died, Teddy. I couldn't be in my house, my church, my town without seeing my past. I had to get out of there."

She steps back to lean against the kitchen counter. I cannot stop myself around my sister when anger takes control. She was supposed to protect me. I was never safe.

"I'm sorry, but where were you when I got kicked out of

the house?" I ask her. "Where were you when I was sleeping alone at truck stops? When I was shattered, broke, starving and prostituting myself to survive? Where have *you* been, Trudy?" I spread my arms. "Where? Your recent acquaintance with grief, pain and loneliness does not suddenly wash your soul clean and allow you to waltz back into my life and seek the comfort, love and forgiveness you never gave me."

"Teddy . . ."

"Just be honest with me, for one damn time in your life," I say, holding up my hand.

"Well, Ava is interested in studying design. She's even talked about going to college in California. She needs a mentor. She doesn't look up to me or her family."

"She's a stranger, Trudy. I can't be a mentor to a stranger."

"And I needed to see you, too, Teddy. I . . . I . . . Can't that be enough of a reason? A sister wanting to see her brother?"

"No, it can't," I say. "You're a stranger, too. And if you came for sympathy, you will not get it from me, and I certainly don't need your pity, or want your acceptance. I deserve your love and respect. You used to tell me that God makes no mistakes, and yet that's how you've always seen me."

"Teddy, Jesus walked with prostitutes and lepers."

I laugh.

"You will never get it, will you?" I ask. "Still equating me as someone defective, ill, sick, less than. I'm not. I'm *more than*, Trudy. And, believe me, I am not worried about my one-on-one with God. I've changed this world by being me. Who are you, Trudy? Sixty-eight, and you still don't know."

"I don't. But I'm trying. Teddy, look at me. Please." I lift my eyes to meet hers. "I've changed, Teddy. God knows I'm not perfect, but I'm still evolving. Please. Give me the benefit of the doubt. I never understood your lifestyle."

I shake my head.

"It's not a *lifestyle*, Trudy! A lifestyle is when you decide to walk more for your health, cut back on your sugar or give up smoking. I'm gay. I didn't have a choice in the matter from my first breath."

"I keep saying the wrong things. I know I messed up. I know I was a bigot for so long. I don't mean to say the wrong things."

"It's too late, sis. But I've had a great life."

I don't catch myself quickly enough and see those words floating in the air: *had* a great life. Past tense.

"I haven't Teddy. I've had a miserable life." Trudy's voice quivers. She steps forward and leans two shaking arms against the island. Her voice is a whisper.

"Do you want to know why I really came here?" Trudy asks.

She clamps her eyes shut, and her face contorts in agony. She opens her eyes. A tear rolls over her cheek just as Ron saunters into the kitchen.

"Good morning! I didn't mean to break up your coffee talk. But I'm glad to see everyone is playing nicely." Ron nudges me as he walks past.

He fills his mug. I look at Trudy. Her face is flushed, but she wipes her eyes and puts on a smile.

"I came because I was thinking of how Mom and Dad rented that old fishing cabin every summer on Suttons Bay. Remember? We'd take the pontoon over to Gull Lake?"

"What?" I ask. "*That's* why you had to see me?"

"Yes," she continues brightly. "I thought it might be possible to have another vacation like that. As family. Here in Palm Springs."

She will never be honest with me.

I look at Ron. He is giving me that *be nice!* look.

Who am I to judge? I mean, I'm not being honest with him either. I'm no better than my sister when you get down to it.

And I do need the money. For medical bills. Maybe even to pay it forward when I'm gone, help those who have helped me so much. That would be nice, to leave it to my family when I'm gone. I smile at Ron.

"You can stay the week," I say. "Just stay out of my way." I pat Ron's back. "She's your responsibility until Friday."

I take my mug and walk out of the kitchen.

"Teddy—" Trudy calls after me.

"One week!" I yell. "Keep her busy and out of my hair. Maybe get a new 'do, Trudy. You wanted her here, Ron, you got it. You two can be bosom buddies. Read the Bible together. Talk about how to fix me. But leave me out of it. I already have enough problems."

I head down the hallway.

"And don't you dare fuck with my happy hours!" I call. "They're supposed to be happy!"

"Are you okay? I think you were having a nightmare."

I rise slowly, my head throbbing.

There is nothing worse than sobering up the same day you got drunk.

I went for drinks at Streetbar after work. I couldn't have a happy hour—much less a magical minute—with my sister watching me down a martini.

Someone is talking, but I see only darkness, and at first I think I have gone blind. Then I reach a hand to my eyes and pull off my sleeping mask.

As the world fuzzily comes into focus, I see two black ravens perched on the breeze block wall that separates our yard from the surrounding mountains. They are staring, heads cocked, peering into my soul.

My thumping headache makes the birds look as if they are in 3D, chests pumping to the heartbeat in my temples.

I should not have asked Mario for doubles.

I blink.

When I open my eyes again, I realize that there is only one raven on the breeze block. Ava is seated on the white Herman Miller Eames molded chair Ron has placed by the sliding door, her dark hair spilling over her shoulders.

"I *was* having a nightmare," I groan. "And it's real: You and your grandmother are staying all week."

Ava laughs.

"What are you doing in my bedroom?" I ask.

I am too tired to sit up.

"I heard you crying as I was heading to the pool," Ava says, shifting her tiny body to perch on the edge of the tiny chair. "Was it about John?"

Talking about John made me want to drink to forget about him, but it only made me dream of him, miss him, call out for him.

I sit up in bed and comb my hair with my fingers.

Reclaim your attitude, Teddy.

"That is none of your business."

"Want an aspirin?"

She nods toward the Three Wise Men I always have sitting on my bathroom vanity: Advil, Aleve and Lexapro.

I nod.

Ava flutters barefoot across the bedroom in an Olivia Rodrigo "vampire" T-shirt and cutoffs, returning with two Aleve and a glass of water.

"Thank you."

I take the pills, drink the water and dab my mouth with the sleeve of the vintage knit shirt I passed out in. Ava retreats back to the chair.

"Strong shit," she says, nodding toward the bottle of Lexapro.

"Life is shittier without it." I look at her. "Where is everyone?"

"Gone," she says. "Ron took my grandma to some store with a guy's name . . ."

"Ralphs," I say. "It's a grocery store."

"My grandma's stomach was upset from the heat, so Ron took her to get some ginger ale."

"Trudy is quite the actress. Our modern-day Shelley Winters."

"Who?"

"Never mind," I say with a sigh. "Just google *Poseidon Adventure* one day. I only pray Trudy makes it off this ship alive. I can't dig a hole big enough to bury her."

"You scared me," Ava says. "I was worried."

"You were hoping I would die."

"So I could inherit your caftan collection? No, thank you."

Ava does not break eye contact with me. It unnerves me. She nods toward the bathroom.

"You know, I take it, too."

"Advil?"

"The stronger stuff," she says casually. "Grandma takes it, too, but it's a secret."

"Her life is a secret."

"You know, finding a dead man can really fuck a girl up."

Ava means to say this as a joke, but it comes out as heartbreak instead.

The crow outside leaps off the breeze block and hops toward the patio door. It peers inside.

"Tell me about it."

"You first," she says. "My grandma told me about what happened to John."

"What did my sister put you up to?" I ask. "Are you getting something in return for information? You have no right to utter John's name. You never knew him."

Ava lifts her hands in a defensive gesture.

"I'm sorry," she says. "I didn't mean to pry. I just really want to know how you handled it. I can't imagine. Finding my grandpa was bad enough. I mean, if my boyfriend died, and I found him . . ." Ava stops, her face frozen.

"I hope you never do."

"My grandfather never loved me," Ava says. "My whole family really. They say they love me, but only if I act a certain way."

"Any way but yourself?"

She nods.

"Story of my life, sweetheart." I take a sip of water and sit further up in bed. I rub my eyes, my temples. When I look up, there are many floating Avas, many floating ravens.

"Does your grandmother ever talk about me?" I suddenly ask. "Be honest."

"She does."

"Really?"

"At the holidays when she's making your mother's stuffing, or Christmas cookies. She says, 'Teddy always made it better than Mama.'"

"Were you ever curious about me?"

"Who do you think really convinced her to come out here?"

I do a double take.

"Really?"

"I couldn't deal with her anymore. Something's going on with her, something bigger than Grandpa's death."

There *is* something going on. I knew it.

Ava continues. "It was winter break, and I wanted to get out of that house. It was creepy to be there. And she was driving me nuts. You know her. She can be a sanctimonious beyatch."

I raise a brow and then laugh, hard, which turns into a long, painful cough.

I reach for my water. It's empty.

Ava grabs the glass and gets up to refill it. When my coughing eases, I finish it in one big gulp.

"Hungover, and it's not even dinnertime," I say, eyeing her closely. "Why are you being so nice? I had you pegged for a bitch."

"Back at'cha," Ava says, shooting her finger at me as if it were a pistol. "Birds of a feather. That's a Billie Eilish song. Barry told me about what you said to that waiter about Chappell Roan. So cringe!"

My chin rises to turn my mouth into a half-moon smile. "Cringe. I like that. Teach me more pop music and cultural slang," I say. "I'm trying my damnedest to stay young."

"But not alive?"

Ava nods at my nightstand.

The pamphlets and notes from my doctor are jutting from

beneath a stack of books and magazines. I thought I'd hidden them well.

"Snoop much?" I ask.

"I have eyes like a hawk," she says proudly. She looks toward the bathroom. "You have Aleve, Advil and Lexapro, but no other meds for your cancer. Why do you want to die?"

"Why do you want to live?"

She shrugs, stands and moves over to sit on the edge of my bed. The raven watches her closely.

"I don't know yet, but there's gotta be a reason, right?" Ava says. She nods toward the mountain. "Life can be beautiful sometimes." She reaches over and runs a soft hand over my old brow. "But it can be pretty damn lonely, too, huh?"

Ava begins to hum and then sing "Birds of a Feather" in a breathy voice that is surprisingly good.

Birds of a feather we should stick together 'til the day that I die.

Ava runs her fingers through my hair, calming me, as she sings.

"Your friends don't know, do they?" Ava asks when she finishes.

I do not answer.

"I'll teach you music and pop culture if you decide to give living a shot, how's that sound?"

I shut my eyes and feel the soft touch of another soul for the first time in a very long while.

My eyes grow as heavy as wings, and I can already feel myself flying, soaring over Gull Island and Suttons Bay like the birds used to do when I was but a boy, unsure as to whether to return to this world or escape for good.

"Let me get you something to eat," Ava whispers. "I make a mean microwave burrito."

The last thing I see before I fall asleep is the raven behind Ava taking flight.

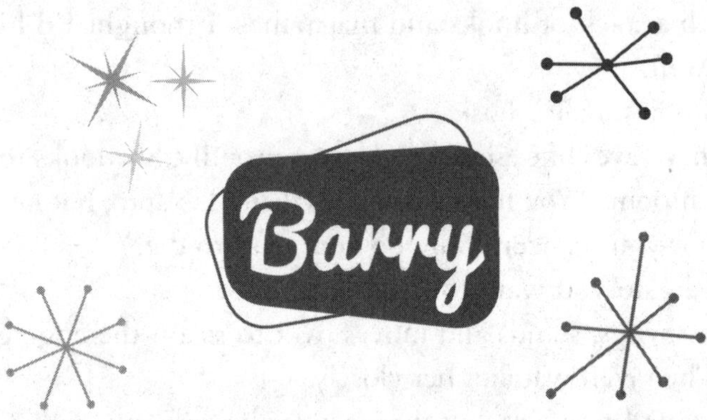

My cell rings.

“Barry Goggins! What’s up, buddy?” My agent’s voice booms down the line.

“I thought you’d deleted my number.”

“Found it in my Rolodex, buddy!”

“Makes sense,” I say. “I don’t think you’ve actually called me since the ’80s. I always talk to your assistant’s assistant. Are you too embarrassed to talk to me in person when offering me all those shitty commercials? Is that beneath your pay grade?”

Stu Matthews has been my agent since he booked me on *The Golden Girls*. Stu represents huge TV clients now, mega stars and legends, and yet he didn’t dump me after my career went into the toilet. He hasn’t actually deigned to talk to me, but I gotta give it to the guy, his connections may have not landed me another huge role, but they have kept me alive and in the game these past few decades. Most agents would have burned my number, but he has funneled those shitty roles to his assistant’s assistant to teach her about the biz and keep me afloat with a steady stream of projects anybody with a semblance of self-respect would turn down: commercials, minor roles on shows that have already been panned or canceled, acting in industrial videos for corporations and human resources training where I say inane things like,

"As an employee of Industrial-ite Manufacturing, your benefits package includes two weeks of paid vacation, five sick days and a health care plan that covers up to ten percent of your hospital stay," or where I get reprimanded for saying sexist things in the break room like, "Have you lost weight, Betty?" and "That sweater sure looks good on you, Tina!"

And I can guarantee Tina—as a card-carrying gay man—that sweater did not look good on her.

I have done anything and everything over the years to stay in the game.

Anything and everything.

"Listen, buddy—" Stu starts.

"Please don't call me buddy," I interrupt. "I'm not the Lab you rent for those creepy family holiday photos you take to make you seem human."

"I forgot how funny you were, buddy!" he roars. "I'm actually calling with good news!"

"Another car commercial for Desert Kia?"

"A script came for you," he says. Dramatic pause. "Paramount, buddy. I've already read it. It's a damn good role. This is what you've waited for the last forty years!"

I know what he's going to say before he says it.

"The new *Billy the Hillbilly* movie!" Stu yells. "Role of Levi, Loretta's long-lost brother who escaped in the first movie. Good guy or bad guy? Nobody knows, buddy! It's the role of a lifetime. And get this: They don't even want you to read. It's yours if you want it. Kyle fucking Moses says you are the perfect actor for it. They're booting Billy Bob Thornton to the curb for you. Director has signed off on it, too."

I cannot open my mouth to speak. Kyle wasn't lying.

"And they sent a contract! It's movie money, buddy, not commercial cash! But, being the great agent I am and since they want Barry and only Barry, I will squeeze every penny I can out of them. This will resurrect your career, buddy! You won't have to do that sad little drag show in the desert anymore. And once the casting news hits the trades, you will be in demand. Everyone in Hollywood loves a comeback story, and I will have you on the cover of every magazine in the country. The Golden Guy!"

"When does shooting start?" I ask.

"Two weeks."

"That's fast."

"That's Hollywood, baby. They're FedExing a script to you today. Want you on set for fittings end of week. Shooting in the desert, so you don't even need to uproot your life." He pauses. "Yet."

Stu releases a resounding *whoop!* that echoes in his all-glass office in Beverly Hills. "I gotta know, though. How'd you pull this off, buddy?"

"Aren't I supposed to be asking you that?"

Stu laughs.

"Let's just say it was all timing," I say vaguely.

"Good enough for me! Timing is everything in Hollywood! Barry Goggins is back! Let me know when you receive the script. I'm calling the director now!"

"I take it I'm being moved from Rolodex to speed dial."

"FaceTime, buddy! FaceTime from now on! It's a new era for you, buddy! We need to celebrate! Ciao, Barry!"

Stu hangs up, and I stand motionless—phone still fixed to my ear—by the pool. I stare at my reflection in the aqua water. How many times have I stood right here praying for this phone call? How many times have I wished for this dream to come true? How many years do I have left to make up for lost time?

I take a step toward the edge of the pool. The wind pulses through the palms, and my reflection breaks into a hundred pieces of aqua. Eventually, they remake a picture of a man standing on the precipice.

But on the edge of what?

Fame? Power? Stardom? Wealth?

Or something as unreliable as the San Andreas fault that runs beneath me?

A figure emerges from Zsa Zsa, a blur of white in the sun and the pool's reflection.

"You look like you're thinking of drowning yourself. Let me get seated first so I can enjoy the show. I've always wanted to know if your face work was water-resistant."

Teddy.

Another figure.

"I'm back."

Ava.

"Are you okay?" she asks, noticing the phone still pressed to my ear, my body as rigid as brittlebush.

"Undecided," I finally say, lowering my cell. "I never dreamed I'd see you two together. This seems like the start of a horror movie."

A raven settles on the yard.

"*The Birds!*" Teddy cries dramatically, covering his face as if he's being attacked. "I always resembled Tippi Hedren."

"After the attack," I say.

"Well," Ava says, "a little bird asked me to teach it to sing again."

I eye Teddy.

"Chirp, chirp," he says, flapping his arms at me with a mischievous smile.

"You're the bird?" I ask.

"I prefer misunderstood velociraptor on Ozempic," Teddy says. "We're living in PC times now, Barry."

"So you did make a decision?" she asks me, raising a dark brow.

"Undecided," I repeat.

I toss her my cell and jump into the pool.

I stop outside the saloon in the middle of the dusty, narrow street in Pioneertown. I skew my eyes on the swinging doors, half expecting a drunken, crooked sheriff in a ten-gallon hat and curled moustache to stumble out and challenge me to a quick-draw duel.

But this morning, Pioneertown is a ghost town.

The once-vibrant real-life movie set—founded in 1946 by a group of Hollywood investors with dreams of creating an 1870s frontier town with facades like saloons and jails for filming movie and TV Westerns—has been nothing but dust since the days Roy Rogers and Gene Autry rode on horses down these same dusty trails. Today, it is a tourist destination for Palm Springs locals heading to Joshua Tree National Park to hike. Soon, however, Pioneertown will serve as the Ozarks setting for *Billy's Back*, where many of the movie's key scenes will be filmed.

I can see signs of life already: Trailers—filled with equipment, soon to be homes to actors, ground zero for the crew and caterers—line the periphery. Cranes sway in the gusts that blow through the mountain pass of the high desert, the wind whistling like a passing train.

A few years back, I was hired to do a commercial in Pioneertown for Desert Kia. My role was that of a rugged cowboy, and I was in a duel to the death with high auto prices. I, of course, came out victorious in the commercial but left feeling as if my long-suffering career had finally taken a shot to the heart.

I did my own makeup for the commercial. The "director" was the car dealer's twenty-year-old daughter who used her cell phone because she said she wanted the commercial to feel "gritty and real" and not because the total budget for the shoot—including my salary and lunch of McNuggets for the "crew" of three—was less than five hundred dollars.

I move into the middle of the street to reenact the scene.

"Now," I say to myself in a low, menacing growl, "it is time for you to die, high prices!"

I drag the toe of my shoe through the dirt to make a line, step on one side of it and take ten paces, counting off as I go:

"One, two, three . . ."

I spin, and when I yell, "Ten!" I turn.

The saloon doors swing open.

Kyle appears in tight jeans and an even tighter T-shirt. He lifts his right hand and makes a gun with his fingers.

"Bang!" he yells.

I act as if I have been shot. I stagger backward, dust billowing around my feet.

Kyle races toward me and grabs me before I collapse to the ground.

"I win," he says. "Again."

He takes me into his arms and leans me back as if I weigh little more than a feather. Kyle looks into my eyes.

"One final kiss before you die."

Kyle's dimples flash, and my legs grow weak. I suddenly feel like every female costar, every fan—gay or straight—who has dreamed Kyle Moses would be staring deep into their eyes, uttering those same words.

His lips are on mine, and I am no longer on this earth, but floating somewhere high above the high desert.

Kyle pulls me to my feet.

"I saved you," he says. "Now you owe me your life."

My life? Is that the price I will pay for selling myself to do this movie?

I search Kyle's eyes.

Is he acting right now? Is he always acting?

"I do owe you my life," I say. "And career. I owe you everything."

Am I acting right now?

He bites. Literally. My lip, hard.

"You're welcome, Barry," he murmurs. "I knew you'd be perfect for this role."

Of Levi? Or as the distraction from being Bryle?

Kyle releases me, running a hand through his hair and then down his perfect chest.

"Thanks for meeting me," he continues. "I have one day off from shooting to get settled up here. They rented me this insane house with a stunning view of Joshua Tree. I thought we could head over there after this to run lines." Kyle smiles that megawatt smile. "Just like we used to."

Or is he trying to recapture something real with me?

It is so quiet out here at dawn, and yet my heartbeat sounds like the Blue Angels are flying overhead.

"Did you get the script?" he continues. "Is your contract okay? I can change anything you want."

"My agent has taken care of everything," I say. "I still don't know what to say."

"Thank you," Kyle says. "Just say, 'Thank you, old friend.'"

"Thank you, old friend."

"This is finally the role that will make you a star, Barry. Doesn't matter if it came forty years later. It's still the chance that every actor dreams of."

"I feel like I'm in a dream," I admit.

"You are! It's karma, babe. The world always comes full circle," Kyle says. He trails a finger down my chest. "Hollywood is quid pro quo. You broke up with me, and now you've come back into my life for a reason. We can give each other what we need and want."

"What do you need and want, Kyle?"

Kyle puts his hands on my shoulders and pushes me to the ground with force. My teeth rattle. He grips the back of my head and presses it against his crotch.

"I want you, big boy. Don't you want me again?" he asks, voice low, breathing hard. "Like old times. Remember?"

I look up at him. His eyes are closed. He is here. He is not here.

I unzip his pants.

Behind Kyle, a cactus rises, green, from the scorched earth. It is flowering, and a hummingbird puts its beak to the bloom. I focus on it and pretend I am that bird, simply doing as nature instructs.

When Kyle finishes, he looks down at me and says, "I guess I was the final shot in the old Western."

He laughs and begins to walk away.

"I have to go," he continues. "I'll see you on set."

"I thought we were going to see your house in Joshua Tree to run lines?" I ask, still kneeling on the ground, wiping my mouth with the back of my hand.

Kyle stops but doesn't turn around.

"Don't be weak and don't fucking embarrass me, Barry," Kyle calls as he walks. "Go study your script. My career, your career, my money and this entire movie are riding on my decision to cast you. Don't let me down, or I will ruin you forever." His voice suddenly turns chipper again as he fades into the desert's golden light. "I'll call you!"

Kyle disappears behind the saloon, and I slump back on my heels. I'm still on my knees when Kyle's red Mercedes convertible comes tearing down the dirt road, covering me in a cloud of dust. He smiles down at me, pleased I have not moved, and I suddenly understand that we both realize I am completely beholden to him. He lifts a hand as he drives away, his car melting into the sun.

I finally stand.

When I look down, the knees of my new jeans are filthy.

I wipe them with my hands, over and over again, but the dirt will not come off.

“I can’t wait to try this coffee place,” Trudy says. “I’m a McDonald’s iced latte girl myself.”

I have lied to Trudy. *Sorry, God.* But I know in my soul she is lying to me.

In fact, I can feel my entire family is hiding something.

We *are* going to get coffee, but after I take Trudy to church.

My heart pounds in my chest as I drive.

Why did I take Trudy in? Maybe Teddy is right. Maybe I’m trying to rewrite my tragic family history with a happy ending. I know this unwavering belief in the good in people will either be my saving grace or my road to hell.

I glance over at Trudy admiring our city like the first-time tourist she is. Palm Springs isn’t just beautiful, it’s breathtaking. The mountains aren’t just magical, they’re mystical. They change us. I only hope their light and shadows can change my passenger as well.

I look down at my lime-green pants. Teddy always asks me if he can squeeze me into his gin and tonic when I wear them.

Or, is taking Trudy in my way of taking revenge on Teddy and the boys for not appreciating my efforts enough?

“The Center?” Trudy reads the name of the building as I enter the parking lot. “Is this the name of the coffee house?”

"Sort of," I say. "They have coffee. It's just bad. We'll get the good stuff after."

Trudy tugs herself out of my convertible and stops cold in the parking lot when she sees a rainbow flag and a sign that proclaims, LGBTQ COMMUNITY CENTER OF THE DESERT.

"Ron?" she asks, not moving.

I walk over to Trudy.

"You wanted to go to church," I explain. "Besides Church of Mary, this is where I go to find meaning in this world. It's where I go to do some good."

She shakes her head.

"Please, Trudy. You're in Palm Springs. You came to see your brother. Maybe it's time you *really* saw him. And all of us."

I tug her arm, and she takes a reluctant step and then another until we're in the lobby.

"Morning, Ron!" employees, volunteers and visitors call as we head down a long hallway to a meeting room in the back of the building.

"What is this?" Trudy asks, stopping at the door.

"The Center provides a safe and welcoming environment for our vibrant LGBTQ+ community," I explain. "I volunteer here. I am a sponsor for those who are struggling. I also provide free design services for the Center and those who receive housing. And on Wednesday mornings, I attend a meeting for victims of abuse—be it sexual, verbal or physical—by their families, spouses, lovers, coworkers or society. It's where we can talk about our experiences. Many of us, including me, have been victimized by abuse at the hands of not only those we love but also by religion, Trudy."

"No," she says. "I won't let you defile my God by subjecting me to this nonsense."

"Your brother and I nearly took our own lives," I say, my hand on her arm. "I think you need to understand what a lifetime of systematic abuse does to us. *All* of us. I think it would help you appreciate your brother better. Just give it ten minutes. You can leave at any time, deal?"

Trudy moves slowly into the room. I pour us two cups of coffee, and we take seats in the back.

We listen to story after story, each gut-punching, heart-wrenching and agonizing, from beautiful souls who have been tortured for simply being beautiful souls. When it ends, we pray, the crowd disperses. Trudy and I remain seated.

"I didn't know that gay men had faith," Trudy finally says.

"Oh, honey, that's *all* we have," I say, my laughter echoing through the room.

She sips her coffee and cocks her head. "Please, go on."

"Well, as you just heard, many of us have experienced nothing in this world but hate, like Jesus," I say. "We often have no family, no love, no respect, no rights, no acceptance, and yet—*yet!*—we find a way through to the other side. In spite all of this hatred, we emerge from our cocoons as these remarkable creatures. And the one thing we have to guide us to this new place is faith, not only in ourselves and our community but in a higher power. Did you hear the power of our people this morning? How else do you think we survive?"

I study Trudy.

"You live in a small town . . ."

"That's not fair," Trudy interrupts.

"I'm not saying that's a bad thing. I grew up in a small town, too, but your view of the world is narrow. I would guess you are largely surrounded by those who, for the most part I'm sure, all think, act and believe much as you do. I understand. We can all start to live in a bubble where we just want to feel safe from change. But that is not the world today. It is big and diverse, filled with many different characters we need to make our story complete. The world today is a rainbow of different races, religions, orientations, beliefs. Not one is right. Not one is wrong. But when you experience that, your worldview changes. You see people who may be different from you not as a category or a group but simply as people."

"But my faith has taught me that how you live is wrong. It is written."

"And everything that is written has been rewritten. Welcome to Hollywood!"

Trudy doesn't laugh. I try again.

"Do you ever watch an old rerun of *Johnny Carson* on social media and cringe at the way he talked to women? What we thought was okay at one time isn't okay later on. We evolve as a society."

"Some things are set in stone," Trudy says firmly.

"I believe that gay men and women have always been the target of hate, but I also believe that we're reading our own cultural bias into a text that is talking about different things. Does that make sense?"

She shakes her head. "Such as?" she asks.

"Such as sexual violence and the Ancient Near East's stigma toward violating male honor, for one. Such as a society that is nervous about retaining its healthy family lineages, and the sexual exploitation of young men by older men," I say. "I know I can't convince you, or anyone else, to believe otherwise, but I am saying we choose to focus on those passages of the Bible that are the easiest to use to discriminate."

I reach over and pull the collar of Trudy's top.

"Excuse me," I say, gently exposing the label. "Just as I thought. You should be killed right now for wearing a cotton blend. According to Leviticus, that is."

She gasps. "You're good."

"I've studied the Bible," I say, "but I've also just studied people. Yes, I am a Christian, but there are many things I hate about Christianity. I am a gay man, and yet there are many things I don't like about our community. I am a Midwesterner, and there are many things that appall me about the Midwest. But I am all of these things, Trudy, and they have made me who I am. We are all flawed in God's eye, but we probably judge ourselves more harshly than He ever will. I cannot hate. So I give. Usually too much of myself, as I am doing with you right now. I give so much of myself to others, in fact, that I'm too much for most men. I get trampled on for being an open book. It's why I'm single. But I have come to terms with that in this life. I have found love in my friends, community and work. I have found love through my faith."

"I'm so worried about my brother," she finally says. "It feels like he's hiding something." Trudy looks at me. "Do you ever pray for Teddy?" she asks. "I pray for him every day."

"I always pray for Teddy. But he doesn't need it," I say. "I think he's good with God."

Her expression changes to bewilderment. "How?" she asks. "He drinks too much. He's so angry and mean. So conflicted and flawed. He always has been."

"How could he be any other way with all he's endured?" I ask. "Just like those stories you heard today. Teddy is brutally honest, not only with himself but also the world. He is fully transparent, whereas most people are not. God knows exactly where Teddy stands, and I think He likes that quite a bit."

"Do you pray for yourself?" Trudy asks. "I pray for myself even more these days."

I shake my head. "Rarely. Perhaps only for guidance. Otherwise, it seems so self-serving. I want my actions to serve as my words. My faith has taught me to always try to be a better person."

"Is that why you went against Teddy and invited us to stay?"

"You just looked like someone who could use a friend right now." I smile at her. "Now, let's go get a decent cup of coffee."

I wipe the fog from the bathroom mirror with my towel and stare at my naked reflection.

I gaze uncomfortably upon the topographic map of my life.

This is the body of an eighty-one-year-old man.

Hello, hernia scar.

Howdy, hip replacement.

Good evening, gall bladder surgery.

I pivot.

Calling 911! Where did my ass go?

I look like a candle that was mistakenly left outside during the summer: melted into an amorphous lump.

I turn and analyze my manhood.

Even my candle wick has disappeared, obviously frightened by its surroundings, a groundhog that does not want to emerge for the winter.

I study my pubic area. I lift my arms. I touch my head.

And where did all of my hair go?

I have become a sphynx cat in my golden years.

And yet there is a shag rug on my lower back.

My hair has simply relocated south like every other retiree.

I take full stock of the image before me—as clear and as unsettling as the sag of soft skin at my belly—and yet my eyes play a trick on me: In the reflection, I can still see the picture of "Center Sid" when I was seventeen years old and playing high school basketball. My dark hair was thick and lush, and it fell across my forehead and onto my lashes as if I'd spent an hour styling it that way. My jaw is set, my dark eyes intensely focused on something. What? The future?

My body is lithe, my biceps pumped, my arms veiny, tufts of black hair popping from my armpits. My legs are muscled and hairy. My cheeks were always pink, as if I'd just completed wind sprints.

Sid Silverstein was a stud.

I remember in high school Rabbi Weiss always telling us, "Time is an invitation."

His deep voice echoes in my head:

"The life of man is like a breath exhaling; his days are like a passing shadow. We drink time, we eat time, we live in the shadow of time, and yet we are oblivious to it, especially what is happening this very moment."

Standing here—over six decades later—staring at my elderly reflection, I finally understand the importance of his message: A thousand years have passed, and yet it feels as if it has only been a single day.

I touch my body, run a hand over my chest and stomach.

It's not that I'm in bad shape.

For eighty-one!

I work out five times a week. I watch what I eat. I don't even take a statin.

But the reality is, existing within an eighty-one-year-old body is like living in a haunted house: It is filled with unexplainable creaks, moans, horrors and—when you least expect it—screaming terror.

A shriek pierces my bathroom.

"Oh, my God!"

"Jesus, Teddy!" I yell, grabbing my towel to cover up.

He slaps his hands over his eyes.

"Oh, God! It's like looking directly into the sun. I will never unsee this!"

Teddy spreads his fingers, and I can see him peer through them.

"And yet I can't stop looking," he says. "It's like a train wreck."

"What are you doing in here?"

"I'm out of painkillers. I've been so distracted, I didn't refill my prescriptions." Teddy looks at me. "Now I need something stronger. Like morphine."

"Get out!"

"I thought you were gone!" he says. "Speaking of which, where did your ass go? Witness protection? Have you tried to iron out those wrinkles?"

"GET OUT!"

He starts to leave but turns on a dime and, without warning, raises his phone and snaps a photo of me standing half naked.

"What the hell are you doing?" I yell.

"Torturing my SIM card! Blackmail, Sid. Now you will owe me when I need it most."

"You'll be dead so it won't matter!"

I pull a large hand towel from the gold stand perched on my bathroom counter and flick Teddy with it, just like I did as a boy in the locker room. It catches him hard on the side, but he doesn't wince. He just stands there, already looking pained.

"Teddy?" I ask. "Are you okay?"

"I honestly don't know," he says. Teddy rubs his temples. "This headache just won't go away."

"Here," I say, reaching into my cabinet. "I have Advil."

Teddy takes the bottle.

"Thanks," he says, forcing a smile. Teddy never forces a smile.

"You want to talk?" I ask.

"We'll talk later. Okay? I don't want to spoil your date."

His demeanor concerns me. My face falls.

"I mean, this is your first date since *Grease*."

I can tell when Teddy is trying to divert attention. He knows it, too.

"Stop it," he continues. "I'm fine. My sister's visit has just thrown me for a loop."

"You sure?"

"I'm sure," Teddy says. "Are you going out with that cute guy who turned down Barry? Is that why he came to Streetbar? To find you?"

I nod. "His name's Leo."

Teddy gives me a once-over. "Remind me again? Is he a blind man?"

"I think you're feeling just fine," I say.

"Told ya so."

"Just keep this our little secret for now, okay? I'm not ready to say anything. Too fragile."

Teddy leans against the doorframe and watches as I put gel in my hair.

"You deserve to be happy, Sid. You know that, right?"

I cannot believe Teddy is being so tender. I stare at him in the mirror.

"You deserve love," he continues. "It's your *time*."

The way he says this fills my eyes with tears.

"Teddy," I say, my voice breaking.

"Now I don't have to be nice again until you're ninety. By then, you won't remember a word I'm saying anyway."

He turns to leave again.

"Wait, Teddy. Can I ask you a question?"

"I'm basically *Jeopardy!*," he says. "I know everything. And I'll answer in the form of a question, too, if you'd like."

"Why would Leo want to go out with me?"

"Sid, don't do that to yourself."

"I'm serious. Why would a man like *that* want to be with *me*?"

I gesture to my reflection in the mirror. "I'm sorry, but as you just clearly saw, I am not what is considered the fantasy of any gay man today. I saw Leo working out. He's in great shape. I mean, thirty-year-olds would jump his bones. Everything that is marketed to us today is the image of masculinity and the perfect body: six-packs, pecs, hairy, muscular. I am anything but. My body is in decline, closer to incontinence than sexual fantasy."

"I thought that was just your cologne," Teddy says. He lifts his hands. "Joking, joking." Teddy leans against the doorframe again—as if he needs it for support.

"I know you haven't been with many men in your life, Sid, and I know you are scared of being judged, but Leo likes you or he wouldn't have asked you out. I'm guessing that he's smart, successful and obviously could have any man, but he likes *you*. So much of attraction, Sid, is not based on physical appearance but how someone makes us feel inside." Teddy touches his heart. "Believe me, I'm not the hottest man to walk this earth. John was much more attractive than I ever was, and I had a lot of insecurity when we first started dating. In fact, I had it most of our relationship: I would get insanely jealous when other men would hit on him. But he loved me. He found me hot for some reason. And part of that was my confidence, my humor, my strength, my ability not to take any shit in life. You are so intelligent, kind, gentle, giving to our community. You are a wonderful father and grandfather. You wear your heart on your sleeve. And it's all of that beauty that he'll see when he undresses you, Sid."

I am about to thank Teddy when he adds:

"Just keep the lights off."

"I am not having sex with him!"

"Then I will! How much younger is he?"

"Google search says over two decades."

"Can you send an AI version of yourself?" Teddy jokes. "Listen to me: Have sex, Sid. Have *lots* of sex . . . *while you still can*. Push all those feelings of guilt, insecurity and unworthiness aside and simply enjoy the moment. Stay out of your big head so your little one can have a nice time. A good dinner, some good wine, a good roll in the hay."

I open my arms and take a step toward Teddy.

"I refuse to hug you after what I just saw," he says. "I'm worried it will rub off."

"You know what Sophia always said? 'After eighty, every year without a headstone is a milestone.' And I'm eighty-one."

Teddy chuckles.

"Are you sure you're okay?" I ask him, studying him closely again.

"Are you?" he counters.

"No," we reply at that same time.

"Jinx, you owe me a Coke," Teddy says. "Thanks for the Advil and the nightmares."

He walks away.

"Teddy?" I call.

"Yeah."

"I love you."

"I know," he says. "Who doesn't?"

Leo is seated by the fountain on the patio of Copley's.

It is a quintessentially Palm Springs restaurant—the former guesthouse of Cary Grant—with a gorgeous outdoor patio hidden from the street that serves wonderful food and has incredible service.

It is also known for its eclectic mix of clientele and celebrations: young and old, locals and visitors, birthdays and anniversaries.

First dates.

"It's great to see you, Sid."

Leo stands as the hostess shows me to our table between the fountain and fire pit.

"You, too!"

I say this excitedly—almost as if I'm a game show host—and the couple at the table next to us starts at my volume.

Leo pulls out my chair for me, and I stand there awkwardly.

Will he hug me? Kiss me? Go for a simple handshake?

Leo gestures at my seat, ever the gentleman.

Nothing. Not even a touch.

The patio is dim, and my next thought is wondering whether he chose this table so no one would see us.

I hear Teddy's voice: *"Get out of your head, Sid."*

I fidget with my napkin. I fold it in my lap and then refold it.

"Origami!" I say, again with too much fervor. I lift my napkin. "Is it a swan? A lotus?"

Leo's smile now seems forced.

He hates me. I continue, my mouth a runaway train, my brain like Sophia's after her stroke.

"Oh, wait, I used to do this great dinner party trick for friends! I have to show you! I learned it from an old friend in Palm Springs."

I grab my napkin and fold it in half and then half again before pinching it into a long tube. As I tighten it, the napkin comes to life, rising into a . . .

"Is that supposed to be a penis?" Leo asks.

I place it my lap.

"Voila!"

Leo nods like a preschool teacher might at a child who just yelled, *I made water!*

The waiter appears with menus. He stops cold and assesses my current situation.

"Looks like someone is excited to be with us this evening."

I can feel my face flush. I am thankful for the darkness.

"I'm Michael, and I'll be your server this evening. Would you like to hear about the specials?"

"Please!" I say, thankful for someone else to talk.

Michael tells us about the specials—not one of which, sadly, contains arsenic to end my agony—and when he is finished, the sommelier appears with a bottle of red wine, extending my humiliation without a chance to apologize to Leo.

"I took the liberty of ordering one of my favorite Napa Cabs," Leo says.

The sommelier uncorks the bottle and pours a small amount for Leo to taste. He swishes and smells, sips, smiles and nods.

"Perfect. Thank you."

The sommelier fills our glasses.

"I'll give you a few moments to enjoy the wine and study the menus," Michael says.

"Cheers!" Leo says.

He clinks my glass, and I sip the deep red. When I put my glass down, Leo gestures to my mouth. I feel red wine dribbling down my chin.

I lift my napkin to dab my face, and realize too late it remains in a turgid state.

I cannot even face Leo anymore. I am an old man who has been reduced to the boy on the playground who picks on the girl he likes because he has no idea what to say to her.

I lift the menu in front of my face to hide my humiliation, but it is so dimly lit that I cannot see a letter, much less a word, that is printed. If I were undertaking an eye test, the optometrist would simply start weeping.

"Sid."

Leo takes my menu. He places it on the table and then reaches over and takes my hand in his.

"I can't even see the menu," I admit. "Not a letter. I don't just need a large-print menu, I need it in Braille."

Leo smiles a sweet smile.

"Why I am here?" I ask him. I don't mean for my voice to shake, but it does. "I mean, look at you. Look at me. Do you have a fetish for old men? Do you cruise nursing homes?"

"Sid—" Leo says again.

"No, let me finish. Please."

"Okay."

"I don't do this," I say. "I mean, I've hooked up—or whatever the kids say these days—a few times when I was younger, but I've never even been out on a date—I mean, a real, actual date—with a man before. *Ever.* You could have your pick of any guy in Palm Springs, or San Francisco . . . I mean, just name a city, and you could have the Matt Bomer in any of them. I like you, Leo, but I am *not* like you. I don't think this old body is what you want, and I don't think this old heart can take hearing you say that."

I start to stand. Leo grabs my hand.

"I don't want Matt Bomer. I like Sid Silverstein."

"Why?"

"The fact you have to ask actually breaks my heart in two," he says. "Please, sit."

I do.

"It's endearing that you have no game."

"Gee, thanks."

"I'm serious," Leo says. "Do you know what it's like to date these days?"

"No," I say with a sarcastic laugh. "I just told you that."

"It's awful. No one wants to go out. No one wants to talk. No one wants to get to know anything about someone else. They simply want to hook up and move on to their next victim."

I think of Barry. Leo continues.

"Gay men are too often stereotyped, but some of the stereotypes are accurate: Too many of us use sex as a way to seek emotional connection. We seek sex to fill the gnawing void in our lives that has been carved out by the lethal claw of a society that has gutted us of self-love and self-acceptance and left a black hole that we believe an anonymous touch can fill. But twenty minutes at a time can never replace an endless calendar of abuse and loathing." Leo stops and takes a sip of his wine. "Yes, I'm attractive. Yes, I'm in good shape."

"So we're in agreement?"

"But," he interrupts, "it's part of my job. I have to stay in shape in order to remain on TV. *But*, Sid, we all get old, and that facade fades. And none of that matters if someone doesn't actually see beyond that surface. I thought you might see beyond my surface, Sid."

"I do," I say. "But it's a pretty damn good surface, Leo."

"Thank you," he says with a laugh. "I see it in my industry

too often. Our society is infatuated with anti-aging. We alter our appearance with cosmetic surgery until we don't even resemble ourselves or our family any longer. We diet and exercise and take shots and pills, when we should really be pro-aging because our lines, wrinkles, faults and foibles all tell a story. We try to erase those until we all look the same. I just try to stay in the moment, Sid."

Leo touches my arm.

"It's okay to be nervous," he says. "It's okay to be vulnerable. That's actually very sexy."

"It is?"

"It is."

Leo scoots his chair over and moves his hand to my thigh. My heart stops. He continues.

"I'm nervous, too."

"You?"

"I am." He looks at me. "Do you know why I chose Copley's for our first date?"

I shake my head.

"Because you told me how romantic it was when we first met on the track," he continues. "I see you, Sid. I hear you, Sid." He leans closer. "I want *you*, Sid."

Leo takes my chin in his big hand. He turns my head toward his and kisses me. He tastes like the wine, black cherry, spice, tobacco, wood.

The sommelier would be proud of my intricate taste buds.

My heart is throbbing in my ears. I feel as if I might faint.

"How was that, Sid Silverstein?" Leo asks.

The world is no longer dim. The lights in the hedge sparkle around us.

Before I can answer, Michael reappears. He glances down at the napkin still in my lap.

"I'd say he thought that kiss was pretty damn good," he says.

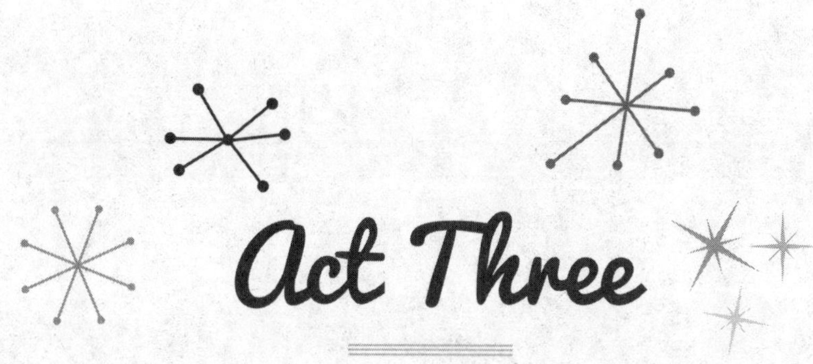

Act Three

"My God! What is this place?"

Ava takes a selfie in front of Dorian Gay and then strides into the shop, arms open, eyes wide, taking in the over-the-top mannequins, the mid-century décor and the vintage fashion.

"We call this Palm Springs, honey!" Patty O'Furniture says, emerging from the back in a giant wig, cowboy hat and rhinestone pantsuit that Dolly Parton would applaud. "Mere mortals call it heaven!"

"This is Patty," I say. "Patty, this is Ava."

Patty extends her hand.

"Enchantée," she says. "You may kiss my ring."

Ava looks back at me, bewildered.

"Kiss the ring," I say. "It's better than kissing her ass."

"Which you will do the rest of your life now that we've met," Patty says, her lips shimmering in a glittery gloss.

Ava obliges, kissing a giant costume ring with a megawatt faux ruby.

"You took that ring from the counter," I say. "Put it back."

"It seems as if someone put a cob back up your ass again," Patty says. "This one's been perimenopausal since JLo and Ben Affleck broke up . . . the *first* time."

"Put it back."

Patty pouts, removes the ring and places it back in the jewelry case.

"You're a drag, and not in the fun way at all," she says. Patty eyes me suspiciously. "Why are hanging around with a girl this young and pretty?" She gasps. "Oh, my God! Did you watch *The Substance*? I knew it was real." Patty walks over to Ava. "Kill her now while you have the chance!"

The bell jingles, and a man and woman enter.

"Get to work while you still have a job," I say.

Patty sashays away.

Ava moves toward the counter and eyes the jewelry.

"When did you open this place?"

"Years ago," I say, "with John. Long before mid-century fashion and design blew up, long before Coachella, when tumbleweed still blew across the streets downtown." I look around the store. "I always loved fashion. And I especially loved taking something beautiful that everyone believed was dead and gone and bringing it back to life again."

"You should take your own advice," Ava says, brow raised.

"Enough about me," I say. "Let's talk about me!"

Ava laughs.

"So," I continue. "Your grandmother tells me you are interested in design. What kind?"

"I'm not sure," Ava says. "I'm just fascinated by bringing some beauty to this world."

"Well, you're in the right place," I say. "Design is personal. It's like home: It should reflect who you are and what you want to say to the world. The one thing you must do is listen to your voice." I walk over to Ava and touch her heart and her temple. "It's the only thing we have as artists and souls. It's the only thing we can trust in this world."

I continue.

"*Everything* comes back into style again. For instance, take a look at the man who just entered the store." I nod his direction. "See his knit shirt?"

She turns to look, and I point up at a mannequin.

"Today, we call it 'eclectic grandpa' or 'grandpa core,' but you can see his outfit draws inspiration from the casual fashion of the late '40s to early '60s."

I nod at the well-dressed woman shopping who has now made her way over to the jewelry counter.

"And just look at her: Chunky jewelry is having a major moment right now," I say. "Large, bold metal necklaces, oversized statement and cocktail rings, bold bracelets are all back in style. That's all mid-century fashion, my dear." I smile. "Everything old is new again. Even me!"

The woman eyes a brutalist bark-textured bracelet, and then I see her eyes drift toward the Bakelite bracelet on the wall.

"How much?" she asks.

"Sorry, not for sale," I say. "It's a family heirloom." I smile at the woman and nod at Ava. "Perhaps it will be a gift for someone special one day."

"Well, you're a very lucky girl if it's you," she says to Ava.

"Thank you!" Patty calls over. "I am!"

When the couple leaves, I walk behind the counter and lift the shadow box off the wall. I remove the envelope—still addressed to Trudy—that is hidden beneath the backing. I hand the letter to Ava.

"I think it's time you read this," I say. "Another family heirloom."

Ava takes the envelope and plops down in a chair on the far side of the shop. She slides the letter free. Ava trains a curious look at me and then the letter. I shut my eyes, and I can still picture myself writing it seated next to my dead mother, I can still feel my fingers penning the opening words:

Dear Trudy,
What is the definition of a friend?

When Ava finishes reading, she just stares at the Polaroid of me and Trudy from the 1970s that I put with the letter, dressed up in our store-bought Road Runner and Wile E. Coyote Halloween costumes and hard masks.

Ava stands, eyes shining with tears, walks over and wraps her arms around me.

And she refuses to let go.

Trudy sits in a shaft of golden light filtering between the intertwined bougainvillea of pink, purple and red. We are seated on the outdoor patio at one of my favorite lunch spots in Palm Springs.

If I had entered this restaurant looking for the Trudy who left the house this morning, I would not have recognized her. A stranger might, at first glance, mistake her for an overworked Orange County real estate agent who had come to the desert for a spa weekend and a few drinks.

As I do every three weeks, I got my hair cut and styled late Thursday morning. I brought Trudy with me to continue keeping her—pardon the pun—out of Teddy's hair. My cotton candy coif, of course, has not changed since I was a boy, and Gaspar knows how to cut and curl, dry and spray without one follicle looking as if it has ever been touched. I pay him an arm and leg to keep me locked in a look that has become my signature of safety.

When Gaspar had asked Trudy if she'd made an appointment—eyeing her wash-and-set while keeping the straightest of faces though there has never been a straight bone in his body—her face flushed, and she hid her head behind a fiddle-leaf fig in the corner of the salon with a copy of *Vogue*, which I'm sure she'd never set eyes on before. And when Gaspar's assistant offered Trudy a glass of champagne, she waved her off, Trudy's face reading, *What heathen drinks at eleven in the morning?*

Then she FaceTimed Ava—who was again lounging by the pool—to show her where she was, and Ava screamed, "Make-over, Grandma! Do it!"

"Oh, I couldn't."

"You could."

"Really?"

"Go for it, Grandma! New you!"

As the salon began to fill with an assortment of clients that made the cast of *The Birdcage* and *Absolutely Fabulous* seem like *The Waltons*, Trudy suddenly nabbed a flute of bubbly, and then another, her unease slowly sloughing away, layer after layer, like the rattlesnakes that sun on the backroads to Whitewater Pre-serve.

Gaspar eventually took a seat beside Trudy, taking her hand in his, and he asked her not about her life but her hair, which—as we know—is the root of all our issues.

I sat in a chair opposite Trudy as she told this stranger about her dead husband and her spur-of-the-moment trip to Palm Springs.

"Palm Springs is old-school glamour," Gaspar said. "Let my work serve as the souvenir of your visit here."

Trudy emerged two hours later with soft layers, a swept bang and an auburn glow, leaving six inches of damaged hair behind on the floor and about thirty years behind in the mirror.

I emerged three hundred fifty dollars lighter in the wallet.

"I feel so . . ."

Trudy stops, touches her hair and then her glass of rosé.

". . . *wicked*," she finally finishes.

I chuckle. "Well, you know, Elphaba and Glinda were both beautiful, even if one was green."

Trudy's brows contort. "Who?"

"*Wicked*?" I ask. "The musical? The movie? The origin story about the witches from *The Wizard of Oz*?"

She shakes her newly coiffed head. "Oh, I've never watched any of those. Witches are evil. My faith didn't allow my children to celebrate Halloween. It's a celebration of darkness."

I hold my neck stiff to keep my head from shaking in disbelief.

Have you met your granddaughter? I want to ask.

"You must have celebrated Halloween as a child?" I say. "And watched *The Wizard of Oz*?"

"We celebrated Halloween when we were very young, because of Mama," Trudy says. "It was one of the few good memories I have with Teddy, but Daddy put an end to that. I had to always be Daddy's little girl. I didn't want to disappoint him like Teddy did."

Trudy takes a sip of her wine and then pulls a compact from her purse. She studies her new reflection.

"I don't even recognize myself," she says. "What will people back home think?" Trudy combs her hair with her fingers, deflating the volume, making the layers less noticeable. She pushes her glass of wine away. "I shouldn't drink."

"Jesus drank."

"Not on a Thursday afternoon in the light of day!"

"My mama used to always say, 'Nothin' good ever happens after midnight.'" I check my watch and smile. "It ain't midnight yet. We got time."

Trudy hesitates.

"No one is watching." I wink. "It's okay to have a little fun."

Trudy's face droops. "No," she says. "It's not. God is watching. God is always watching."

I tilt my head at her. "I have to ask, is this a game you play with yourself? Happiness versus guilt? Because I've played that game for a very long time, too."

Trudy opens her mouth to reply, but the waiter approaches.

"Have you decided?"

We have yet to crack our menus.

"I'll have the chicken tenders and french fries," Trudy answers.

The waiter laughs. *Hard.*

"Oh, honey, this isn't a Cracker Barrel, and we don't have a children's menu," he says. "In fact, we hate children in our restaurant. Sneezing. Sticky fingers. Spilled lemonade. We spend twenty dollars for their six-ninety-nine order. Did you *read* the menu?"

I smile. "We'll both have the Nicoise salad. Thank you."

As the waiter departs, Trudy asks, "Why do you all speak like that?"

"Like what?"

"So . . . sarcastic. So . . . cutting."

"We've learned to use humor as a way to laugh at the cruelty of the world," I explain. "It lessens the pain. It gives us a way to make sense of life. It also brings people in when we want, or keeps them at a distance. It's long been the gay man's secret weapon, sort of like mayonnaise is to straight people when they cook."

"See? You all are just so honest. It's uncomfortable."

"And *you all*," I say, "are just so boring. *That's* uncomfortable."

"Now you sound like Teddy." She sniffs. "Telling me I'm living in drag."

"Are you?"

Trudy shakes her head, utterly confounded by my challenge. She puts her hands on the edge of the table, and I think for a moment she is going to push herself to her feet and flee.

"I'm doing the best I can," she says instead, sounding defeated.

"Are you?" I ask.

"I am!" Trudy suddenly cries. "Stop pushing me!"

Diners turn our way.

Trudy looks away, grabs her wine and takes a healthy sip.

"I'm sorry," she finally continues in a tone between a whisper and a confessional. "I guess I just thought that I'd be different as a grandmother. I'd be better than I was as a parent . . . more giving . . . more forgiving." She searches her hands. "I guess I thought I'd be a better parent than mine were. I wanted to be, but I'm . . ." Trudy pauses ". . . worse. Ava laughs at me. My children avoid me. I'm trying, but I'm incapable of change. I'm trapped."

"You couldn't be any worse than your father was to Teddy," I say.

Trudy lifts a shaking hand and touches her face. It's like she's checking to see if she's wearing a Halloween mask.

"Oh, no," Trudy mutters as the entertainment takes the stage. "Not a drag queen. I hate drag queens."

"You came to the wrong town," I say.

"Good afternoon, Palm Springs! I'm Lulu Lemon!"

A drag queen in a bright yellow dress and matching wig appears. She seems to immediately sniff out Trudy's discomfort.

"Ma'am?" Lulu asks, pointing toward our table. "Did you know that Palm Springs is rumored to have more drag queens per capita than any other city in the US?"

Trudy's face is paralyzed in horror.

"Don't worry, honey, I don't bite," Lulu says. "Hard."

The crowd laughs. Trudy is unmoved.

"You look like you just caught me wearing flats," Lulu continues. "Nothing? Not a laugh? Okay, well, I hope the song I'm going to sing gets some sort of reaction from you. It's an oldie but goodie. As most of you know, Palm Springs is the mid-century capital of the world, and today I'm going to perform some classics from that era. A little mid-mod mood music for lunch and Modernism Week. A little something by Rosemary Clooney. Maestro?"

Music begins to play.

Trudy shakes her head. "I'm leaving. I will never understand why you all have to dress in drag."

"We all don't dress in drag," I counter. "Just like we all don't watch *The Real Housewives* and believe that every straight woman behaves like them. There are as many different types of gay people as there are straight people. But drag is a form of entertainment. It's an elevated art form for us."

"Teddy has always been like . . . *this*," she says, gesturing to Lulu, who's swaying to the opening notes. "So flamboyant. And now you all perform that . . . *that* show. I looked it up online."

"It's a celebration of friendship," I explain. "It's actually saved lives. It saved mine."

Trudy pushes her chair out to leave just as our salads arrive and Lulu begins to sing "My Heart Belongs to Daddy."

Without warning, Trudy bursts into tears and races from the restaurant.

"I've never been a fan of fish either," the waiter says.

I follow Trudy outside. I find her on the ground, collapsed into a heap, leaning on a wall, weeping into the facade of the restaurant.

"Trudy? What's wrong?"

She refuses to look at me. She continues to heave, her body convulsing.

I stand over her awkwardly, cooing, "It's okay, it's okay," massaging her shoulders until her tears and breathing finally slow.

I lean down, grab her chin and force her to look at me. "What's going on?"

She finally meets my gaze, mascara running down her cheeks.

As the lyrics of the song dance in the air, Trudy tells me a story about her daddy that eventually brings me to tears and to my knees as well.

Barry

"What are you doing in here?"

Trudy jumps. She sets the framed picture she's been holding down on the coffee table. It's an old photo of me, Ron, Sid and Teddy—all wearing Santa hats—after a holiday Church of Mary.

"Hiding from Teddy."

"We all do that on occasion," I say with a smile.

"I bet more than occasionally."

Trudy winks.

"Was my granddaughter being nice to you?" Trudy continues, nodding beyond the patio doors toward the pool where Ava is napping under an umbrella. "You two have been talking a lot at the pool."

"She's honest," I say, looking at Ava. "I need some unflinching honesty right now."

"She's a teenage girl," Trudy says. "You'll get that whether you want it or not."

"Teddy's basically a teenage girl, too," I add. "You'll get his opinion, too, whether you want it or not."

I enter the living room, my hair still damp from the pool, wearing a matching bright yellow terry cloth shorts and shirt, which I didn't button. Trudy's eyes float down my body.

"You're in great shape," she says.

"Thank you, although that almost sounded like an accusation."

"No, no, I just don't see many Midwestern men my age so fit."

"It's part of my profession," I say. "It's part of our community. You can't be fat in Hollywood, and you can't be out of shape as a single gay man, especially as you get older."

"Whyever not?"

"We're a very close but judgmental community," I explain. "We end up combining a lot of the judgment that is placed on us by society with our internalized anger and taking that out on our own. It's not right, but it's just the way it is."

"Ralph was so out of shape," Trudy says.

"I'm so sorry for your loss," I say. "I can't imagine."

"Thank you." Trudy picks up another photo of the four of us. "I know this sounds monstrous to utter out loud, but he was already dead. I was, too."

She shakes her head and continues. "We both got so complacent. Well, that's not even the right word. We both simply became invisible to one another. We stopped caring about what we looked like, what the other ate, what the other did . . . we lived in the same house, but we were no longer husband and wife." She touches the framed photo. "I don't even think we were friends." Trudy looks up at me. "Instead of us going for a walk together in the morning, Ralph would make a huge breakfast of bacon and eggs. Instead of working in the yard, he would sleep in his recliner. Instead of us making a healthy dinner together, he would run through the drive-through at McDonald's and bring me back a Big Mac and fries." She looks down at herself. "And suddenly, twenty years are gone, and you look like this."

She puts the photo down. "And then he's gone, and for the first time in decades, I sleep through the night. When I wake up, I'm not even mourning his loss but simply grateful for a do-over."

I stare at her, stunned by her honesty. I cannot find any

words, so I say, "Well, speaking of do-over, your 'do does look great." I gesture to her hair.

She laughs. "Nice segue. Ron took me to see . . . was it Casper?"

I laugh. "Gaspar," I say. "His prices will scare you like a ghost, but he does know how to pull off a glow-up." I wait until she looks at me. "So do you, I think."

"Thank you." She picks up a framed cast photo of me with the Golden Girls. "I think you do, too." Trudy points at Coco. "I did a little online sleuthing while I was in here hiding . . ." Trudy hesitates. "Actually, to be totally transparent, I was just in here hiding from the world. It seems I'm very good at that. I didn't mean to snoop."

I walk over to the modern walnut bookcases that flank the flat-screen TV in the living room.

"Oh, Coco is public knowledge," I say. "It's just that the public doesn't know he existed." I touch the face of a character I'm still running from. But he was really just me all along. "Please, take a seat," I continue, nodding at the low-slung mid-century sofa.

Trudy places the photo back down and sits.

"Speaking of Coco, that's why I came inside," I say. "I was just about to watch an episode of *The Golden Girls*. I have to preview one for our upcoming show."

"If you can believe it, I've never watched an episode of *The Golden Girls*," she says. "In fact, I've never watched a sitcom in my life."

"Well, we have something in common," I say. "Besides an occasional disdain for Teddy. I never watched a sitcom either until we started doing our show."

"My father didn't allow us to watch such nonsense, said it would rot our brains," Trudy says. "We couldn't listen to secular music. We couldn't even shut our bedroom doors. They had to remain open at all times. Teddy and I would sneak downstairs, though, on Saturday mornings when my parents were hungover and watch cartoons."

My heart pings, and I imagine little, fierce, funny Teddy fighting to survive. I watch Trudy hug a pillow. My eyes meet Coco's on the bookshelf.

How the hell do any of us survive?

We fight, or die.

I scroll the TV.

"If you can believe it," I finally say, "I don't think I've ever seen this episode before."

The episode is titled "Mary Has a Little Lamb," and it is about a teenage girl named Mary, who is pregnant and seeks the women's help after failing to get support from her father. Dorothy steps in to offer advice and guidance.

"Is Dorothy always the one who stands up for someone in need?" Trudy asks toward the end of the episode. These are the first words she has spoken since it started. I look over and see she is still holding the Jonathan Adler pillow, clutching it, rocking it like a newborn.

"She is the truth teller," I confirm. "Just like Teddy."

"Our mom's name was Dorothy," Trudy muses. "Did you know that? Teddy was named after her. He was with her when she died. They were watching *The Golden Girls* together."

"He told me about that after we met in therapy," I say.

Trudy turns to me. I pause the show.

"Therapy," she sighs. "So that's something people actually do."

I don't mean to laugh, but I do.

"Not to offend you," she says quickly, "but that is not a staple of Midwestern life that I grew up with, like milk and eggs. Men didn't address their emotions. They drank. And if they drank too much, they didn't get sober, or else they were told they couldn't hold their liquor. Women cried in the bathroom when their husbands were asleep, bathtub faucet running to hide their pain. And children mirror their parents: We become just like them because it's easier to please than become . . ." she stops and meets my gaze ". . . ourselves."

"It took me a very long time and a lot of therapy to realize that running away from my pain wasn't solving anything," I tell her. "I was simply running. To nowhere. I was just masking it all with isolation, anger and bad decisions."

"Masks," Trudy whispers. She looks at me intently. "Are you okay now?"

I shrug. "I don't know. I don't know if I'll ever be, but I'm trying the best I can. Sometimes, you have to face the pain head-on, and I feel like the train is closing in on me. It's closing in on all of us."

"Ron said you see a lot of younger men. Is that a way to cope? Is it about control?"

"You want *me* to discuss my man troubles with a Christian woman from Ohio?" I ask. "Now, *that* is a sitcom."

"I won't judge," she says. "I promise. Ava won't ever talk to me about her boyfriend. I know she has one. I know they sneak around. I'm trying to change. I'm trying to listen. Ron told me the best thing someone can do sometimes is to just shut up and listen."

So I tell her about the young men. I tell her about Kyle. I tell her about what happened, about praying on my knees to a false idol, about what I've had to do to become famous again.

Trudy only listens. Finally, *finally*, she says, "We all do things to survive, Barry. I have to believe God can forgive us when we are pushed into a corner and have no other option but to walk through fire to make it to the other side, even if our souls are scorched. Maybe then we can heal, and we can help others, even if it's our final act."

"Speaking of acts, do you know what makes a sitcom work, Trudy?"

"I have no idea," she says.

"Sitcoms have followed the same basic format throughout the history of television. Every show starts with a cold open that throws you directly into the action, followed by three acts and a finale. That's it. It finally dawned on me while rewatching episodes of *The Golden Girls* that life is just like a sitcom: three acts. We are born, we grow up, we die. And the finale always leaves you in tears because it's so hard to say goodbye to something you love. The biggest surprise of all? A half-hour sitcom isn't even thirty minutes. It comes in around twenty-two minutes without commercials, which isn't a very long time at all to enjoy the show." I look at Trudy. "We all have so little time to enjoy the show."

Tears well in her eyes. "We're all in our third act, aren't we?" she asks.

"The train is coming right for us, Trudy," I say. "The best thing I'm learning we can do is scream in fear and excitement as it approaches, just like I used to do as a kid when I'd stand on a train track with my friends. I'm also learning that being scared again in life can lead to really great things. You just have to walk through that fire."

Trudy yells suddenly, and I jump.

"It feels good to scream," she says. "Can I tell you something, too, Barry?"

"Anything, Trudy."

When she's finished talking, I stand and walk over to the sofa and sit beside her. Trudy puts her head on my shoulder, and I put my arm around her.

She does not cry. She simply asks, "Can we watch another episode?"

I pull the sheet up over my naked body.

Here, in the light of first dawn, my skin is as wrinkled and crumpled as the sheet itself.

Leo is lying face down on the bed, his sculptured back and round rump silhouetted in the pale light of the morning.

I pull at the loose skin on my stomach. It tightens momentarily, but then I release it, and I again am human crepe paper.

A wave of shame and repulsion pulses through me.

"Don't."

Leo opens one eye.

"You are perfect."

I will myself not to cry.

Leo grabs me, spoons me, holds me until I quiet.

"How sexy to wake up to a wrinkled, weepy old man," I whisper into the pillow.

"Stop it," he says. His breath is on my neck. I can feel his heartbeat. "You are perfect," he repeats.

"You are blind."

"No, you are perfect just the way you are," he says.

I want to roll over to face him, kiss him, but I have not brushed my teeth, and I am worried about my breath. No, I am worried about *everything.*

"What do you see?" I ask the pillow.

"Everything you do not."

"Stop being so philosophical."

"Stop hating yourself," Leo says, voice firm. "Don't diminish yourself. Don't diminish me."

For a moment, there is silence, that buzzing sort of silence that grows louder the longer you are quiet, more deafening the longer you remain in your head.

Is he mad now?

Why didn't I just keep my mouth shut?

I almost ruined our first date, and now I've made good on my promise. Why am I so intent on harming happiness?

Leo's hands and arms are wrapped around my body. I should feel safer than I have my whole life, and yet this feels like a ruse.

I don't feel as if I deserve this.

"Sid," Leo whispers. "Sid. It's okay."

The roar in my head diminishes to white noise.

Is this the way my name should be uttered? One single simple syllable suddenly so rich with nuance, emotion, passion that it becomes not just a name but a living, breathing entity.

I think of the very few times I had sex with Rebecca.

I never uttered her name with a quivering shudder.

And she never said my name. Ever. Sex was a job meant to have an outcome: children. Three preferably. To please our parents.

Sex wasn't even quid pro quo for us: You do this for me, I do this for you, and—at the very least—some pleasure is derived. No, sex was perfunctory, pleasure-free, a checklist like the duty chart Ron puts up every week in Zsa Zsa. You are thrilled when it is over, not while you are doing it.

I never yearned for sex with Rebecca, and she never yearned for me. Neither of us was ever present during our most intimate moments.

We eventually turned our fantasies into pathetic, fleeting affairs, finding our pleasure elsewhere, alone with faces and bodies we pretended were lovers. My anonymous encounters were in hotel rooms during the middle of the day, parked cars, restaurant bathrooms. The guilt and panic set in—as they are doing right now for me decades later—when the rush of pleasure was over and I looked into the faces of my anonymous partners and saw—and felt—nothing at all.

"Sid?" Leo asks.

"I'm still here," I whisper.

"Good," he says.

I am still here. Somehow. Just before the hourglass has run out of sand.

I can feel the sun lift higher above the mountain. It shines on me, warms my bare arm, which is wrapped in Leo's.

Leo's closeness makes me uncomfortable. I am not used to it.

He is asking for me to see myself? But what do I see?

I stare at our intertwined arms.

The striations of gold on his tan skin, or the dark spots on mine?

A body that is taut, perfect, without an ounce of fat, or a body pocked by landmines left by a lifetime of war?

And yet I have survived. To be here. Right here. Right now. Have I made it to this point so that finally—for once—I *can* see myself clearly?

The sunlight glimmers.

This same light, this same mountain that watches over us in the near distance will still be here long after I am gone. Shouldn't I view myself—shouldn't we all view ourselves—as eternally majestic?

"Sid?" Leo asks.

"Yes."

"Come here."

I roll over and face this majestic mountain of a man. He smiles and caresses my hair, my cheek, my lips, my chest.

Leo kisses me.

I shut my eyes.

This is the moment writers write about, lovers relish, the

lonely dream of, this moment right here when two bodies become one, and nothing else exists beyond the sound of our heartbeats.

And when it is over . . . Oh! When it is over, the afterglow of being wanted, needed, desired is so overwhelming, I exist in a half state somewhere between alive and dead, this bed and heaven, this bedroom and that mountain, this earth and another realm.

Leo spoons me again, and the stunning simplicity of two becoming one overwhelms me. I have been lonely for so long.

"Don't break my heart. I don't think I can take it."

I intend for these words to be said in silence, only to myself, but I let them come to life because I want this to be real for once. I want Leo to understand the magnitude of this moment to me.

Leo pulls me closer.

"I promise."

We have kicked the sheets off the bed. There is nothing to hide. The sun has now risen over the mountain and is shining unobstructed through the bedroom sliders.

My instinct again is to pull the sheets over my body, run to the bathroom, dress quickly and escape.

"You're not going anywhere," he mumbles, as if he can read my mind. "You are perfect."

Is this what it feels like to be seen for the first time in your life? Utterly, shockingly transparent and naked?

"You are beautiful," he adds, as if he knows his words are as necessary as oxygen.

I am beautiful?

I push my face into the pillow to hide a happy tear.

I am beautiful.

"Blueberry pancakes okay?" Leo calls into the bathroom where I am taking a shower.

"Are you the perfect man?" I call back. "Or I am dating Dexter?"

"We're dating now?"

Why did I say that?

"You'll find out if I'm Dexter if you survive breakfast," he says with a laugh. "I'm also going to cook some chicken sausage, and, oh, I made some lemon curd that pairs perfectly with the pancakes and maple syrup. I'm starving!"

"Sounds amazing."

I hear Leo pad away on the tile, but then footsteps draw closer again.

"You are going to kill me, aren't you?" I ask.

"Not yet. I was going to squeeze some fresh grapefruit juice, too. The Ruby Reds are amazing this year. Is that okay?"

The water suddenly feels as if it's turned ice-cold.

Leo's question is worse than death for men of a certain age. If you don't understand, Leo is asking—in the most polite way possible—*Hey, can you drink grapefruit juice, or are you on a statin?*

I let the water pound my head.

Leo might as well ask if I'd like grab bars installed in the shower.

Suddenly, all the sexy has rushed down the drain.

"Hello?" he asks.

"Grapefruit juice is fine!" I say in a chipper tone.

"Really?" he asks. "Great! I'll see you in a few."

As soon as the bathroom quiets, I get out of the shower, dry off, wrap my towel around my body, find my phone and text Esther.

SOS! Need some help! ASAP!

Text bubbles immediately appear.

Oh! Let me turn down QVC so I can focus. I just ordered a Jaclyn Smith wig. They promised I'd look like one of Charlie's Angels. I'm just hoping it's not Bosley.

I just had sex with the Hot Jew!

You buried the lede! He's a journalist!
Was it good? Did you remember
what to do? Is your back okay?

It was amazing.

Oh! I can die now. Wait. Is that why
you're in distress? Are you having a
heart attack? I'll be right over. Do NOT
tell the Hot Jew to get dressed!

No, I feel fine. Physically. But he just asked me if
I could drink grapefruit juice.

Oy vey. The kiss of death. Wait. Can you?

Yes. That's beside the point. The point is that in
the light of day he realizes I'm an old man.

Honey, I think he realized that in the dark of
night. That glint in your eye was not due to
longing, it was due to your recent cataract
surgery. I mean, when he caressed your skin
and thought he was at a petting zoo . . .

I GOT IT!

I consider flushing my phone down the toilet, but it begins to ring. I roll my eyes, take a deep breath and walk back into the oversized shower with fabulous mid-century tile.

"What, Esther?" I whisper.

"So truly? Was it good sex?" she asks, her voice high with excitement. "I mean, I know you can't compare it to any other encounters because you haven't had any since call waiting was a thing, but was it as good as—say—Sherman's coconut cake?"

"It was like a hundred pieces of Sherman's coconut cake." I smile.

Esther screams. "I have to tell Talia!"

"Thanks for nothing, Esther," I say into the tile.

I start to hit End on the cell, but she says, "Sid! Wait!"

"What?"

"Sometimes fate is tossed directly into your lap purely by accident as if the heavens have experienced an unexpected bout of palsy," Esther says. "Don't take this for granted. Don't let your mind play tricks on you. He likes you, Sid. You like him. You've waited your whole life for this. I beg you: Don't fear the possibility of heartbreak. Instead, be terrified by the possibility of regret."

I place my forehead against the cool, damp geometric tile and gently bump my noggin against it.

"Thank you, my friend."

"I'll save you a piece of coconut cake."

I hear the doorbell ring as I hang up.

I step out of the shower and walk into the bathroom.

Ding-dong.

I lean out into the hallway.

"Leo?" I call.

I move into the living room.

"Leo?"

"I'm out here!"

I follow Leo's voice to the sliding doors, which are wide open on this perfect morning. I see him standing beneath his citrus trees with a fruit picker to pluck the grapefruit.

"Can you get the door?" Leo calls. "Probably Amazon. Still decorating the place."

"Okay!" I call.

As I walk toward the front door, I finally take stock of Leo's stunning MCM house: It is like stepping directly into Slim Aarons's famed photo *Poolside Gossip.*

The man certainly has great taste, if I do say so myself.

His wireless speakers are softly playing classical music, but—as I walk to the door—I realize I have not heard them make the distinct notification sound when an Amazon package is delivered.

I open one side of the massive double doors.

A well-dressed older couple are standing at the door. She is holding a bouquet of fresh flowers. He is holding a bottle of champagne.

The woman tries to be subtle, but I catch her eyes lingering on my near-naked body. I can feel my face flush.

"Oh," I say. "I'm sorry. I thought it was Amazon."

"Oh, my goodness," she says. "No, I'm so terribly sorry. We must have the wrong address. Joseph?"

He lifts his cell.

"Where is 318 Ocotillo Trail?" the man asks.

"This is 318 Ocotillo Trail," I say.

"Joseph," the woman says again, this time his name taking on a more admonishing tone. "You must have entered the address incorrectly." She looks at me. "I'm so sorry. We rarely come to Palm Springs."

Her eyes drift down my towel-clad body.

"Check the address Leo gave you," the woman adds. "I'm so embarrassed."

"Leo?" I ask. "Leo Levy?"

"Yes!" the woman exclaims. "Do you know him? Could you point us in the right direction?"

"Mom? Dad?"

Leo appears at the door holding a basket of grapefruit whose faces are as red as mine is right now.

"What are you doing here?" he asks.

"You told us to stop by and see you," his mother says, brushing past me to kiss her son on the cheek. "We were in the neighborhood."

"Beverly Hills is not *in the neighborhood*, Mother." Leo laughs. "Did you forget how to use a phone?"

"You're our son!" his father says, moving inside and gripping Leo's shoulder in greeting. "We wanted to surprise you!"

"And we wanted to see your house in the desert," his mom adds. "And hear about your new job."

I stand here, motionless, as old and naked as a Roman sculpture.

"I'm so sorry, Sid," Leo says. "This is Sid Silverstein. And, Sid, this is my mom and dad, Miriam and Joseph Levy."

"It's nice to meet you," I say, consciously trying to control any nervous babble I feel coming on. "Usually I'm dressed." I smile. "Which I will go do right now."

I excuse myself and retreat to the bedroom, where I hurriedly dress.

"I'm so sorry," I say when I return.

Miriam is still holding the flowers. She nervously brushes an invisible piece of lint off her blouse and eyes me curiously. Finally, she pantomimes hitting herself in the head, as if she were starring in a V8 commercial, and looks toward the back of the house.

"Silly me!" she says. "Where is the crew? Out back? You should have told us that you were filming a segment for your new 'Gray and Gay' show. We are so sorry to interrupt. Do you mind if we watch?"

Miriam turns to me.

"That explains why you are in such wonderful shape for a man your age," she continues. Miriam smacks Joseph in the arm with the bouquet. "You should look that good!"

"I think I need to open this," Joseph says with a laugh, taking the bottle of champagne. "Now."

Miriam puts her arm around her son and eyes me closely.

"Let me guess: Are you training for the Senior Olympics? Leo, remember Rabbi Katz? He is training for them, too." She smiles at me. "The rabbi is one of the world's best over-seventy power walkers."

"No, Mom," Leo says, exhaling. "This is my friend, Sid, and he is not training for the Senior Olympics."

Friend?

"My mistake," she says. Miriam looks at the grapefruit. "Oh! Now I get it: You're filming a segment on the impact of grapefruit juice on statins! Now, that is an important topic for folks our age, isn't it, Sid?"

Please let there be an earthquake.

"Excuse me," I say. "I should get going. It was nice to meet you both."

I beeline to the bedroom and stand there, frozen. Leo follows me in. He is no longer carrying the grapefruit, only the bottle of champagne.

"I'm so sorry," he says. "I had no idea they were coming."

"How old are they?" I ask.

"My parents? They're in their mid-seventies."

"They're *younger* than me?"

My voice echoes.

"Sid," he says calmly, placing his arm around my back. "It's okay. They will adore you. Stay for brunch. You were going to anyway. At least I can introduce my parents to my new boyfriend."

"You just called me your friend," I say. *Why did I say that?*

"I wasn't thinking. I was just surprised they're standing in my kitchen."

"God, Leo, I could babysit them." I finally look at him. "And you."

"They will be okay, I promise. I once dated a guy in his twenties, and all my mother could say was, 'Does the boychick eat brisket?' as she got blind drunk."

"I can't do family drama again," I say. "I've done it my whole life."

"I promise there will be no drama," he says. "But I can't guarantee it won't be awkward for a while."

I stand frozen looking outside. Everything looks different now.

"Let's go rip the Band-Aid off," he continues. "Together."

"I think I'll take a rain check," I say. "And I also think I need a drink."

I grab the bottle of champagne and pop the cork.

"Do you at least want to hear some good news?" Leo asks.

I lift the bottle to my mouth and take a hearty sip.

"Shoot," I say.

"Neither of my parents can drink grapefruit juice," Leo says with a smile. "They're both on statins."

"You must be having such a great time on your winter break," I say to Ava. "Now we get to talk about all the things young girls love to discuss on vacation: incontinence and erectile dysfunction."

Ava doesn't look up from texting. "Those would actually be less triggering topics for most teenage girls than what we actually discuss. And they sound like Taylor Swift songs," she deadpans.

"You mean Cardi B songs?"

She lifts a brow and smiles. "You are learning at the feet of the master. I'm so proud."

Ava returns to her cell.

This tiny speck of molten lava has not only convinced me to see my doctor again, but she has also sacrificed her dwindling pool time to accompany an old man to his doctor's appointment. This young shadow of a woman is my pillar of strength today. She is the only one who knows what I am facing.

Ava has climbed into a visitor's chair in the miniscule exam room in my doctor's office and pretzeled herself into it as if she's lounging in a recliner at home. She is all angles, like a geometry textbook. You could turn me into a Barbie doll and I still couldn't twist my body parts into the ways she has managed to twist hers.

Her fingers move at the speed of light.

"You should be my surgeon," I say, "with nimble hands like that."

"These hands will not be going anywhere near your old ass."

Ava must have been born into my sister's life not simply to drive her insane but also to be a constant reminder of yours truly.

She has inherited what I call the H3 gene in our family directly from me.

I tell her this.

"H3?"

"Humor plus heartbreak equals honesty," I explain.

She finally looks up, tossing her hair over her slim shoulders. "At least as a woman, I can't inherit your T3."

Ava meant this as a joke about my cancer staging, but I can see in her eyes she wants the words back as soon as they leave her mouth.

"It's okay," I say. "You're just being honest."

Sitting here in a drafty gown on an examining table, her joke hits, quite literally, a bit too close to home, especially considering my bare ass is stuck to the flimsy paper.

I wonder how much longer I will have any feeling whatsoever down south if I decide to go through with the surgery, which Ava has already insisted I should have. I walked her through the options the doctor provided as if she were Marcus Welby and not a high school girl with a secret penchant to shop at Claire's Boutique.

Ava actually puts her phone down long enough to look me in the eye.

"Are you scared?"

I nod. "Yes. *Really* scared." I gauge how honest to be with her. "It's just that, for a huge part of my life, my . . . you know . . . little Teddy has defined my life as a gay man."

"You know I'm seventeen, right?"

"Going on forty." I roll my eyes. "Is it okay for me to talk to you like this? The only children I've ever really interacted with are the ones I try to frighten in the grocery store."

"It is. It's actually sorta sweet in a creepy way. Our family sweeps everything under the carpet."

"You still have carpet?" I tsk. "That's just tragic."

Ava laughs. "Grandma hasn't changed it since I was born. Dark brown, baby. Hides all the dirt."

She's funny, but I don't laugh. Ava eyes me closely. "What's on your mind, old man?"

"It's just that . . ." my voice hitches ". . . I actually lost my desire to be intimate with anyone after John died. I don't even see myself having sex with another man again. But this . . ." I gesture at what lies beneath my gown ". . . is all I have that defines me not just as a man but a gay man. Why should I bother to go on if the rest of my life is a never-ending ghost pain?"

"Maybe there is more to life than sex," Ava suggests. "I mean, I can't even imagine my grandmother having had sex."

"That's a great pep talk."

"I'm serious," she says. "You know, most of the time, I just want to talk to Gabe, lie on his chest when we watch TV or listen to him play his guitar. That's sexy to me. Maybe you'll find a man who you enjoy just being with."

"There are no such gay men in existence."

"Your friends," she says. "You're lucky, you know." Ava smiles and continues. "There are treatments to help. I read all the material your doctor gave you, and I've been doing some research on my own."

"I just feel so old, Ava."

She shakes her head. "I know. And after all you've been through, that should be a blessing that makes you want to fight for your life, right?"

"When will I know if someone really loves me again?"

"You'll know," she says. "A reason to fight for the life you have and the love you want will slap you in the face, I guarantee it."

A nurse pokes her head into the room.

"The doctor will be in in a just a moment," she says. She smiles at Ava. "How nice that your granddaughter came to support you."

"I'm his child bride," Ava deadpans.

The nurse's expression turns from sweet to bewildered.

"Oh, my God, I'm so sorry," she says, closing the door quickly behind her.

We giggle in silence until the door pops open a moment later.

"Hello, Mr. Copeland," the doctor says. "It's *very* good to see you."

Doogie Howser shakes my hand. He turns to Ava.

"I'm Dr. Ferguson," he continues, extending his hand to her. "You must be the child bride I've heard so much about?"

Ava's eyes grow large, and she turns to me in slow-motion horror.

Now he's funny?

"You can take the boy out of the country, but you can't take the country out of the boy," I say.

Dr. Ferguson laughs.

I feel the tension in my body momentarily deflate.

Perhaps I have a team working for me and not against me.

"This is my grandniece, Ava," I continue. "She's visiting me for winter break."

"How nice," Dr. Ferguson says. "Where are you visiting from?"

"Ohio," she says with a dramatic sigh. "My father teaches at Ohio State."

"You mean *The* Ohio State!" the doctor exclaims. "I went there for undergrad. Go, Buckeyes!"

"You do know how you get accepted into Ohio State?" Ava asks.

The doctor shoots her a confused look.

"You either have to spell *OSU* or *The* correctly," she continues. "That eliminates roughly half the applicants."

The doctor chuckles.

"Joke I always tell my dad to make him mad."

"Tough, funny girl," I say with a wink. "That's why she's with me today."

"Well," Dr. Ferguson says, "I have to thank you, then, Ava. I'm thrilled Teddy is here today. I wasn't sure I'd see him again." The doctor looks at me. "So? Have we come to any decisions?"

I open my mouth, but Ava interjects.

"He's having a nerve-sparking robotic prostatectomy," Ava says as if she is guest-starring on *Grey's Anatomy.* "There seems to be less reaction to anesthesia, less bleeding from surgery, fewer blood clots, and less damage to surrounding organs or infections at the surgery site."

The doctor's eyes grow bigger with each word. "I'm impressed," he says. "Are you planning to be a doctor?"

"I play one on TV," Ava says.

"Well, Teddy," the doctor says, taking a seat on a stool and opening my chart on the laptop, "you have quite the health advocate."

"I'm so lucky."

"Is there someone more age-appropriate, perhaps, though?" the doctor asks. "I'm not sure we can list her as your emergency contact. How old are you, Ava?"

"Seventeen," she says.

The doctor gives me a concerned look.

"Dude," Ava continues. "He, like, trusts me for some reason. And I trust him for some reason. I got him here, okay? And sober for once! I promise once we get the ball rolling . . ." Ava looks at me. "Sorry for the awful pun."

"It's okay," I say.

"Anyway," she continues, "once we get the ball rolling, I promise his friends will step up. I think he just needs a bit more time to process how he's going to handle telling them, but he needs to get the surgery scheduled ASAP."

The doctor nods and makes a note in his chart.

"You are now his backup emergency contact, behind Ron," Dr. Ferguson says. "Give me your contact information."

Ava does.

She waits until the doctor finishes typing and says, "Thank you. Oh, Teddy told me you went to see his show."

"I did," he says. "As I told him, I was quite moved by it. Have you?"

"Not yet," Ava says. "This weekend. So then you know he has a great set of friends who will do anything and everything to ensure he has the best postoperative care."

"I do."

"My great-uncle is too demure to say this out loud, but he's very concerned about the future state of his penis. He's not sure he'll ever be able use it again, if you know what I mean, but he'd like to know it's on standby and ready to go if he needs it, sort of like a backup generator. Can you assure us that it will work after surgery? Oh, and he is not super excited about smelling like a porta-potty either. What are the options?"

The doctor shakes his head in amazement. "Are you sure you don't want to be a doctor?"

"Thanks," she says. "But I already got my degree from WebMD."

"Great school," the doctor deadpans. "And great questions."

He swivels his stool toward me. "Let me be completely honest about the side effects, Teddy. Urinary incontinence and erectile dysfunction are common after surgery. Roughly eight in ten men experience these symptoms."

"Great odds," I say. "They should have this game at the casino. Call it *Winkle or Tinkle*. You win, and you still lose!"

"Teddy," Dr. Ferguson says, his voice low and serious, "I am a great surgeon. I perform many prostatectomies, and my patients report lower rates of erection problems than the average. Moreover, bladder control usually improves slowly after a few weeks or months. Older men do have more issues, but again, my patients report lower rates of occurrence. Does that mean I can guarantee there won't be any? No. Erections are controlled by two tiny bundles of nerves that run either side of the prostate. You've told me you were able to have erections before surgery, so—as Ava mentioned—I will try a nerve-sparing approach, but if the cancer is growing close to the nerves, I will need to remove them."

I feel as if I've already emerged from surgery: I'm numb. I can't feel anything.

"If this happens," Dr. Ferguson continues, "you won't be able to have spontaneous erections, but you might be able to with medications, aids or pumps."

"Lions and tigers and bears, oh, my!" I sing in my best Judy Garland imitation.

"Again, my hope is we can preserve the nerves."

"When would I know for sure?" I ask.

"Erectile function often returns slowly, from a few months to two years or more."

"Two *years*?" I ask. "So I won't get a boner until I'm in my coffin?"

"Language!" Ava says, wagging a finger at me, mimicking her grandmother.

"Yes, Trudy."

"It's important to regain potency by trying to get an erection once your body has had a chance to heal," the doctor says. "I believe your potency is helped by attaining an erection as soon as possible. It's called penile rehabilitation."

"Is there a nice treatment center on the ocean where I can go for that? With a slew of nurse's aides who all look like Ricky Martin?"

"There are many options for treating ED. Oftentimes, the sensation is there, but . . ." He turns to Ava. "Pardon my language here . . . but your orgasm will be dry."

"Welcome to the desert."

"Much of your recovery will depend on your attitude, treatment plan and care team," the doctor says. "Our ultimate goal is for you to be cancer-free, and to live the rest of your life healthy and happy."

"But not hard."

"Language!" Ava says again.

"Teddy, this surgery will give you a second chance at life."

There is a sudden strobing in my brain. I shut my eyes and see John. John with no second chance.

What is the point? Life ends badly no matter the veneer we place on top of it.

When I open my eyes, Ava is staring at me. She gets up, walks over, leans against me and holds up her cell.

"Selfie," she says. "For Gabe. He wants to see a picture of the new old man in my life."

Ava snaps a photo and shows it to me.

Ava is young. I am old. She is healthy. I am not. Neither of us is smiling in the picture.

It looks as if we are holding one another up, unsure as to who is the child and who is the adult, eyes stunned by the hardship of our histories, both long and short. I know that, taken in context, her life has not been so tough, and much of her problem is just teenage angst. And yet to be a salmon constantly swimming against the current is exhausting and isolating, no matter the age. I look at the photo. And yet—*and yet*—our set chins seem to say, *Be damned, inhumanity of the world, I will fight on if only the slightest bit of hope remains.*

As Ava hits Send, she rubs my back with her free arm and then takes my hand in hers. She nods at me, willing me to try.

And in this child's eyes, I finally see it: a reason to fight.

"Okay," I say to the doctor. "I'll give it a shot."

Our *Golden Gays* performance Saturday night is one of my all-time favorites entitled "Scared Straight."

I asked Barry at the last minute if we could rearrange his carefully preplanned performance to do this particular show, and he was shockingly amenable.

"Just this once. Consider it our finale."

Barry eyed me suspiciously when the word *finale* came out, almost as if he were hiding something, too.

"Consider it done."

"Thank you."

What Barry doesn't know is that I plan to improvise part of our performance when the time comes.

Barry hates when actors improvise his scripts nearly as much as he hates a man on Medicare. I tell him these aren't technically his words—though he does update the old *Golden Girls* episodes to make them even more relevant to today's time—but artists and old men are sensitive. Don't change Barry's words, don't mess up Ron's hair, don't wrinkle Sid's suits and don't mess with my mannequins.

And don't ever rain on a gay man's parade.

This particular episode has deep meaning to me. It was one my mama and I watched together when she was sick. She wept like a baby. I've seen it many times over the years since then.

In the classic *Golden Girls* episode, Blanche's bachelor brother comes to Miami for a visit, and his sister fixes him up on countless blind dates, only to discover her brother is gay and too afraid to tell her. He goes so far as to tell Blanche he is dating Rose, who is keeping his secret.

Many episodes of *The Golden Girls* centered around secret-keeping just as many episodes centered around being gay. In many ways, the show was way ahead of its time with sensitive issues that society was grappling with and wished to ignore. Almost as if the creators were intentionally trying to make up for cutting Coco.

I pull on my tunic and watch my friends get into character with my trademark Dorothy side-eye.

Ron teases his white Rose wig, which does not look that different from his real hair. He picks and sprays, over and over—though a hair on his wig would not move in a Florida hurricane—using a can of old-school Aqua Net, our dressing room turning as foggy as a London winter's night.

I remain incensed at Ron. He is kind to a fault, and I know that will never change, but his acquiescence to Trudy's arrival and kindness to her have flummoxed me. Why is he being so sweet to a woman whose cruelty and rejection not only shaped my existence but nearly ended it? What kind of friend is that?

I watch Sid straighten his gray wig and adjust the collar of his sweater as he transforms into Sophia.

Sid seems distanced lately, and yet he has not disclosed—as he and Sophia would have in the past—exactly what is going on in his life via his typical nonsensical babble. In fact, he has been MIA of late and has already told us he will miss Church of Mary this week to have brunch with Leo. He also told us that Leo wants to speak with us. Is Sid pregnant? I mean, what in the wild, wild world of gay sports is going on there?

Barry adds another layer of lipstick. Blanche has a signature lip: an undercoat of gold glimmer with a bright pop of party red over it.

It always baffled me that Blanche had the most difficulty with her brother, given that she was the character most gay men identified with. She owned her sexuality, slept around without any remorse or regret, and did not let age diminish her fierceness. She dressed provocatively, she flirted and she didn't care what people thought of her.

Barry and I are probably the closest to our counterparts in both look and demeanor. Barry got a firsthand look at the makeup the ladies used and has tried to help us over the years. But has all of this—this show, living with his BFFs—helped him or hindered him? Our Palm Springs man magnet has not only been MIA of late as well, but his late-night boy toy rendezvous have stopped. Is it because we have company? Or does he have a secret, too?

And yet I cannot judge as I may be hiding the biggest secret of all. I've kept it from my friends because I did not want to burden them.

Or is it simply because I'm scared? Teddy? Scared? I never would have pegged myself as a run-away-from-a-fight type of guy, but I'm actually scared.

To die.

For this show to end.

There is a knock on the door.

"Five minutes to curtain!"

The voice of Bette Davis pops into my head, as it does many a gay man my age:

"Fasten your seat belts, fellas, it's going to be a bumpy night!"

I give myself a final once-over and stalk from our dressing room onto the back of the stage.

I peek through the curtain.

Ava and Trudy are seated in the front row. It takes me a second to recognize Trudy. I've been avoiding her, and she has been avoiding me. But her new hairstyle is shockingly youthful. Her outfit is updated. Ron appears backstage.

Someone has been playing Dolly Levi, I see.

I watch Trudy attempt to talk to Ava, who remains glued to her cell. I'm confident Ava will either pass out or storm out when she is informed by the announcer that all cell phones must be silenced and not in use during the performance.

Barry and Sid join us on stage.

The set is divided in two by a wall with a door. It looks exactly like the living room and kitchen of the ladies' home in Miami, down to the bamboo sofa, floral cushions and linoleum.

We move into position. Patty O'Furniture greets the sold-out audience and informs them to silence their phones. I can hear Ava groan.

"Ladies and gentlemen!" Patty says. "*The Golden Gays*!"

The curtains open, and our little show begins.

I glance at Trudy and Ava as the scenes progress. Trudy's face remains stoic. Ava is laser-focused on me for much of the performance. On occasion, she looks over at her grandmother to gauge her reaction.

Finally, it comes time for a scene between me and Sid.

"What's wrong, Ma?" I ask.

"I got three days to live," she says.

"Fine, Ma," I say in a low tone, my voice filled with withering sarcasm. "I'll scratch the Bengay off the grocery list."

I put my hand on Sid's shoulder. I move forward.

He looks at me, confused. This is not part of our blocking.

"And, Ma," I continue. "I might only have a short time to live, too."

I leave my mark and turn to my friends.

I can feel their eyes on me.

"Teddy?" the stage manager says into my ear. "What are you doing?"

I move downstage until I am front and center. I lift my arms to the audience.

"I really might," I repeat. "I have Stage 3 prostate cancer."

The audience gasps and then begins to murmur, wondering if this is real or a part of the show.

"What?" Ron says too loudly into his mic. A loud pop explodes through the theater, and the audience groans. They look around at one another, finally realizing what is happening is completely unrehearsed. Many ignore the rules, grab their cell phones and beginning recording the spectacle.

"I didn't know any other way to break the news to my best friends. My entire life, I've been a fighter. I've always been strong, but I lost the will to live a long time ago when I lost John. I thought cancer would be my way to exit stage right." I turn and face my friends. "I didn't know how to tell any of you. I didn't want to burden you. I didn't want your golden years to be filled with caregiving and medical bills."

I turn and train my eyes on Ava.

"But lately I've found the strength to fight."

"You knew?"

Trudy's voice is audible on stage.

"I paid attention, Grandma," Ava says. "I actually asked how someone else was feeling for once in my life instead of acting as if everything was going to be okay because, guess what, it's not unless you ask."

"Cancer is my secret," I say. "I didn't know any other way to tell my best friends—those I love most in the world—than on this stage. I'm scared. I don't want to be scared any longer, and I didn't want there to be any more secrets in our home. I'm sorry. I hope you can forgive me."

Sid moves downstage with me and takes my hand. I can see the audience collectively sigh and settle back into their seats, thinking the show is back on track and Sophia is going to recite her next zinger.

"I have a secret, too," he says, taking me by surprise. "I'm in love."

A few people in the audience applaud.

"What?" I ask. "With Leo?"

"Yes," he says, pointing into the audience at the handsome man I recognize from Streetbar seated in the front row. Sid stops and looks at the audience, quipping in Sophia's memorable voice, "He's so young, and I'm so old, I just won't buy any ripe bananas."

The crowd roars.

"Are you really in love?" I whisper to him.

"I am." Sid smiles at me. "And—I have one more secret, too."

My eyes widen.

"I was attacked by a woman after my Reading Hour to kids at the library when I was dressed like Sophia."

"What?" I exclaim, as the crowd boos what happened to Sid.

"The police can't identify her, but I am speaking out: Leo is doing a story about the incident on his new news segment." Sid takes my hand. "Let's fight, Teddy. There are so many reasons for us to fight and live."

I feel a body beside me and turn to discover Barry standing next to us.

"Et tu, Brute?" I ask as Dorothy would.

The audience titters.

"I have a big secret, too," he says.

The audience goes, "Woooo!" as if they are on a roller coaster.

"I have been cast as Levi, Billy's long-lost brother in the new *Billy the Hillbilly* movie."

The crowd explodes in applause.

"No!" I exclaim. "Really?"

"Nobody ever believes me when I'm telling the truth. I guess it's the curse of being a devastatingly beautiful woman."

This is a line Blanche has uttered in the show many times before, but it seems to have more nuance when Barry says it tonight.

"Congratulations," I say. "Your dream came true. How? When?"

"That's for after the show," he says.

The crowd expresses their disappointment.

Finally, we all turn to Ron.

"Last but not least," I say. "Let it rip, Ron. The stage is literally all yours."

Ron turns as quiet as the audience. He leans toward me, covers his mic and his mouth and whispers, his voice trembling, "I can't share this secret. That's between you and your sister."

I look into the audience. Ava and Trudy are as bewildered by tonight's show—and secrets—as I am. For once, I have no cutting words, no one-liners, no pithy comeback. I simply stare into the front row, wondering what could possibly top tonight's confessional.

I turn to my friends. We all stare at each other, wondering what to say or do next.

Patty O'Furniture bursts onto the stage sporting a red Reba wig, bejeweled cowboy hat, sequined halter and Daisy Dukes while holding a mic and a bottle of whiskey.

"Leave it to a diva to close a show. Maestro? Hit it!"

Music swells, and Patty croons "Friends in Low Places" as she dances around the four of us.

The curtain closes.

"Honey, that show was so bad," Patty says, taking a healthy slug from the bottle, "it made my tits look good."

A roadrunner inspects the patio outside my bedroom.

Meep meep!

Most people don't know that many famed cartoon characters were inspired by California's landscape. Walt Disney lived in Palm Springs, in a rustic compound of homes known as Smoketree Ranch, and the desert setting inspired some of his most beloved characters. Looney Toons animator Chuck Jones was the mastermind behind Wile E. Coyote and the Road Runner, and the desert scenery in his early cartoons was stunningly realistic.

In person, the fast-running bird is quite handsome—lithe, brownish-black and white-streaked, shaped like a jet fighter—with a thick plume of feathers on the crown of its head. The plume makes the bird appear as if it is sporting a crest when the feathers are raised, a look that is equally regal and comical.

This particular roadrunner is a frequent visitor to Zsa Zsa. I call it Dotty Perkins, after my childhood protector, although I'm not sure if this particular roadrunner is a male or female as both are nearly identical. But this one is so fascinated by watching me work a wig and do my own hair that I knew it had to be Dotty reincarnated.

Right now, Dotty peers inside as I tease, brush and spray, the crest high on its head as if its eponym had just finished backcombing the hell out of its feathers.

"Higher the hair, the closer to God," I swear I can hear the roadrunner say to me in the real Dotty's voice. "And most of us need all the help—and height—we can get."

I look at Teddy and Trudy. I am now hearing voices because they have been engaged in a silent standoff ever since we returned home from the theater. I forced the two into my bedroom to talk.

However, the only noise I've heard in the last twenty minutes has been the hiss of a hairspray can and a short, sharp bark from the roadrunner.

Trudy is wearing a vintage, oversized tunic color-blocked in angled panels of pink and yellow that makes her look significantly thinner. It finally hits me that it's from Teddy's store, and I wonder who gifted it to her to wear tonight. I admire the guts it must have taken for Trudy to wear something like this in public.

The silence buzzes. I could cut the tension with a pair of salon scissors.

Trudy lifts her cell with a shaking hand and aims it at the roadrunner.

"I've never seen one in real life," she whispers, as though it might hear her. "A roadrunner was the one thing I was most excited to see in the desert."

I was not expecting her to speak, and I jump at the sound of her voice, a comb sticking in the back of Rose's wig.

"Gee, thanks," Teddy replies.

I look up as Trudy's face falls.

"That's not what I meant, Teddy."

She snaps a photo.

"Do you remember when we used to watch cartoons on Saturday morning?" Trudy continues, still staring at the roadrunner. "While Mom and Dad slept in?"

"You mean, slept it off," Teddy interrupts.

"We'd grab our cereal—Quisp for you and Cap'n Crunch's Crunch Berries for me—and we'd watch cartoons all morning?"

"Yeah. We've already shared this touching family story, Trudy."

Trudy closes her eyes, and a whisper of a smile appears on her face. She talks as if she is in a trance.

"We'd watch *Land of the Lost*, *H.R. Pufnstuf*, *Pebbles and Bamm-Bamm*, *Scooby-Doo, Where Are You!*," she continues. "But our favorite was *The Bugs Bunny/Road Runner Show*. You loved Bugs Bunny the most."

I swear I can see a tiny smile trace its way across Teddy's face.

"The coyote was always trying to outwit the roadrunner, but it was too smart to get caught," Trudy says. "Remember, Teddy?"

"I do," he says. "Ironically, everybody thinks the roadrunner is the innocent one," Teddy continues, watching it as it watches us. "But they're not like the cartoon character, Trudy, just like life is not a sitcom. Roadrunners are omnivores. They eat and kill just about anything that crosses their paths. Did you know they can kill a rattlesnake? If a pair of roadrunners wants to eat a rattlesnake, they just team up and peck its head until it dies. I've seen it happen. It's horrifying to watch. They will torture anything—birds, frogs, reptiles—just pecking and pecking until it gives up."

Teddy looks at his sister.

"Sound familiar?" he asks.

Trudy's eyes fill with tears.

"Teddy, please!"

I don't mean to say this with so much force, but my words emerge as an angry shout. The comb shakes in my hand.

"Spare me, Ron," Teddy says with so much contempt I can almost feel the venom. "You're the one who caused all of this with your pathetic codependence and unshakeable belief in a God that has never believed in you. You've been alone your whole life and made do with an invisible friend to get you through."

"Teddy, stop it," Trudy now says. "Ron is just trying to help."

"I'll go," I say, "so you two can talk. My presence isn't helping matters."

"No, stay," Trudy says, reaching for me when I stand. "Please."

"Jesus," Teddy exclaims, now standing. "You two deserve each other. Evil twins pretending to be angels."

"I'm evil?" I ask, grabbing Teddy by the arm. "We were living together, and you never said a word about your cancer for how many months now? You were just expecting us to put you in hospice one day, no questions asked? That's a friendship? That's angelic?"

"It's not that hard." Teddy shrugs. "You get a bed and some morphine and count the days until it's over."

"But I love you, Teddy," I say, my voice cracking. "You are my brother and my best friend."

"Well, I've reconsidered death thanks to Ava," Teddy says. "So you'll still get a chance to change my catheter. Lucky us."

Teddy looks at Trudy. He crosses his arms.

"So, what's the big secret?" he asks his sister. "Oh, let me guess. You've decided to give the money from the house to Ron. Or, was that all just a ruse, too?"

A tear trails down Trudy's cheek as she continues to stare out the patio door.

"No, Teddy. There's money for you, but that was just an excuse for why I came."

"Then what?" Teddy asks, exasperated. "What is the real reason? Enlighten me, please."

My cheek trembles, and I look at Teddy, knowing what is coming next.

"I was the prey," Trudy whispers. She suddenly and viciously jabs a finger at the roadrunner and screams, "I was Daddy's prey!"

The roadrunner hightails it toward the mountain.

"I wasn't fast enough or smart enough to outrun my roadrunner," she says, voice low and hoarse, a thunderstorm of tears—a rarity of rain in the desert—drenching her tunic.

I stand and walk unsteadily out of the bedroom. When I am outside, I collapse against the wall, my legs rubber. I slide down the mid-mod wallpaper until I am lying prone on the terrazzo, the tile cool on my hot face.

"When Daddy would drink, he would get . . ." Trudy's voice becomes as quiet as a pin drop. ". . . *friendly*. He would ask me to sit on his lap, or have a daddy–daughter date to get ice cream at the Dairy Queen. He would play with my hair when he was drinking and driving. He would look at me too long. He would . . ." Trudy clears her throat ". . . get excited.

"Mama knew, which I think is why she drank, and why he hit her. She tried to protect me, and I tried to protect you, Teddy, by being Daddy's friend so you wouldn't be around him too much when he was drunk. I knew what he would do to you eventually, and to me, and I couldn't let that happen. I fought him for a long time, Teddy, for such a long time . . . so I met a boy, you never knew him, and got pregnant so Daddy wouldn't try to touch me again. I'd rather he beat me for my sin than . . ." Trudy's voice trails off. The house buzzes in silence. "I finally told him. I thought maybe he would understand why, or forgive me, or kick me out of the house, or I could have a real family, I don't know—but I knew I couldn't be alone with him when he was like that or I would . . ." I can hear Trudy crying now.

After a moment, she gathers herself and continues.

"But one weekend, Daddy got really drunk, threw me into his truck and forced me to have a back-alley abortion." Trudy releases a gasp. "He said God would punish me forever for what I had done—*me!*—and that I could never speak a word of it to anyone, or he wouldn't just kick me out of the house like he did you, he would kill me for humiliating his family worse than you ever did. I wasn't allowed to go out, and he didn't let me watch TV, or listen to music, or have friends. I could only go to church. I lived in hell, Teddy, and I know you did, too, but you were safer on the streets than you were at home. I married Ralph just to get out of the house, and I never told him a thing. I never loved him. I only wanted a home and a family where I felt safe and protected. That's why I sided with Daddy. I didn't want you coming back while he was alive. That's why I couldn't go back again to see Mama. I've been living with this guilt forever. And now that Ralph is dead, I only want to repair all the damage I did to you. No more secrets. They have nearly killed the two of us. *Please* forgive me, Teddy. I don't know if God ever will, but I need my brother to. Please." She sobs. "Please, Teddy!"

I clamp my hands to my ears.

My heartbeat thrums a sad soundtrack, and I shut my eyes.

I hear a loud crash.

I lift my head and peek into the bedroom.

A glass is shattered on the floor.

"Oh, God, no! No no noooo!"

Teddy is standing, but he is bent over, hands on his knees, as though he's about to faint. His body—his entire being—looks broken. He sounds like an animal howling in pain, like the ones I hear late at night, followed by the cackling of coyotes.

"Please tell me that's not true," he finally says. "I can't hear this. I just finally realized I want to live, and now I just want to die. And I just wanted to hate you forever."

"But Teddy, *why*?" Trudy asks.

"Because, if I didn't, then we're equals in this fucked up world."

Teddy straightens up, opens his arms and engulfs her.

"I'm so sorry, Trudy. I'm so, so sorry." He is weeping. I have never seen this man cry, not even at John's funeral. He has always shut off his emotions like a leaky faucet, only Teddy ignored its repair.

"I wasn't there for you," he says. "I didn't know. I swear I didn't know."

Trudy grabs her brother's face.

"Why do you think I was so mean to you?" she asks with an almost wistful smile. "I didn't want you to be around me. I wanted you out of that house. If you hated me and you hated Daddy, you were safe."

Teddy falls to his knees, and Trudy holds him.

I sit up and lean against the wall.

Sid and Barry peek their heads out of their own bedrooms.

"Is everything okay?" Sid whispers.

"I don't know," I whisper back.

"Are we okay?" Barry asks.

I nod.

They come into the hallway, take a seat on the floor beside me and lean their heads on my shoulder.

"I should have told you about Leo," Sid says.

"I should have told you about the role," Barry says. "I'm just going through a lot."

"Me, too," Sid adds. "We love you, Ronny."

"Do you?" I ask.

"More than Barry Manilow," Sid says.

"More than *The Golden Girls*," Barry adds.

"That's a lot," I say. "You know I can't stay mad at my best friends." I remember a favorite Rose line from one of our shows. "After all, we've eaten over five hundred cheesecakes together."

"You mean, drank over five hundred martinis together," Sid corrects me.

"You say toMAYto, I say toMAHto." I smile.

"So, what's going on in there?" Barry asks.

"No more secrets, as I said on stage."

I take a deep breath and tell them why Trudy is actually here.

They sit in stunned silence. Then Barry comes clean about how he got his role and his relationship with Kyle.

"What should I do?" he asks. "I have the role of a lifetime, but at what cost to my integrity? I just feel so gross."

I look at Sid, who looks at me. Our expressions are bemused, to say the least.

"You have integrity?" Sid asks.

"This makes you feel gross?" I ask.

"Not funny," Barry says.

"I'm sorry," I say. "I do have some advice to you, though."

"Yes?"

"You're a writer, Barry. Why don't you write your own rules for once? Write your own story, Barry."

"I'm so angry!" Teddy screams from the bedroom. "I don't know what to do!"

We all stand and peer in the door.

He is holding a mannequin head over his head.

"Not the wigs!" we all cry. "Not the wigs!"

Leo, his parents and I are seated on the patio at Spencer's Restaurant.

This time, I am fully dressed.

This is our rain check, our redo in the desert.

Spencer's is a Palm Springs institution for brunch. Set at the historic Palm Springs Tennis Club, it has been an exclusive gathering place since its inception in the 1930s, hosting celebrities like Katherine Hepburn and Bob Hope. Spencer's sits at the base of the mountain, and tables are perched under a canopy of live trees drenched in lights as if you are living in a dream, the atmosphere matched only by the wonderful food.

"It's beautiful, isn't it?" I ask, babbling as usual like a nervous child, filling the silence since no one is talking. "Have you been here before?"

Miriam and Joseph stare at me, smiles that look as if their family photo is being taken by a trained assassin. They shake their heads no and return to studying their menus in silence.

This brunch was Leo's idea of a do-over after our uncomfortable first encounter. But how many mimosas will it take to erase the image of my nearly nude eighty-one-year-old body from the minds of my boyfriend's parents who are younger than me?

Leo wanted us all to have a chance to really get to know one another. Talk. Laugh. Share.

But we have been politely silent so far.

As if on cue, my cell trills in the pocket of the slacks Esther helped me choose. We spent an entire day at Saks, and Esther had me try on more outfits than a girl going to prom.

"When you die, you will be judged less harshly by God than you will the moment that woman returns to the dressing room," the gay clerk told me when Esther left to retrieve more options.

I surreptitiously pull my phone free and hold it below the edge of the table. But of course: It's a text from Esther.

Do you want me to show up and scare his parents? I'm really good at it. I've had years of experience as an overbearing Jewish great-grandmother.

I look up as I'm trying to decide between the eggs royale with smoked salmon or the banana-stuffed French toast.

I type:

No, but thank you, friend.

You're welcome. PS: Don't talk too much . . . remember suspicious mole? PPS: I hope you don't get Louis as your waiter. He's senile. Way worse than me.

I slide my cell back into my pocket as a waiter appears with menus.

I glance up. It's Louis.

Thank you, Esther. You have eggplant-blouse cursed me once again.

Louis is every bit my age, and has been a server here since—I'm venturing to guess—FDR was president. I pray he doesn't recognize me today. Louis rambles more than I do. He's apt to say anything.

"Welcome to Spencer's!" he says, as another server fills our water glasses. Louis studies my face. "Sid?"

I smile as my stomach drops. "Hi, Louis. How are you?"

"It's good to see you again." He smiles and surveys the table. "And who do we have with us today? Did your family come from Chicago to escape all that snow and visit for winter break?" Louis walks over and places his hands on Leo's shoulders. "What a handsome son you have!"

I want to climb up the tree beside our table and hide in the branches.

"Thank you!" Miriam says, thinking Louis is speaking to her.

Leo shoots me a relieved look just as Louis opens his mouth to say something else. Before he can, I blurt, "Wine! Let's have a bottle of the Russian River Valley Sauvignon Blanc. To start! My treat!"

"Of course," Louis says, catching on.

He hands us our menus. As Louis places a menu in my hands, he leans toward my ear and whispers, "Well done, Sid. Well done."

The four of us chitchat about safe topics like the weather and the recent Super Bowl—*You watch football?* I mouth to Leo—until the wine comes.

The first glass goes down much too quickly.

"So, Sid," Miriam begins in a polished voice, folding her napkin into a lovely diagonal and placing it in her lap. "We didn't have much of a chance to get to know each other the first time we met. Tell us a little bit about yourself. Leo mentioned you were an attorney?"

"That's right," I say.

"Me, too!" Joseph says, sitting up in his chair. "We have that in common!"

Run with this, Sid.

"Actually, I still practice," I say.

"You do?" Joseph asks. "I love that you're still working."

"It keeps me young," I say. "Well, you know, relatively speaking."

They chuckle politely.

I tell them about my work in Chicago and in the desert.

"And you have a family?" Miriam asks when I finish. "In Chicago?"

"I do," I say. "An ex-wife, two children, four grandchildren and three greats."

"How nice," Miriam says. "Do you see them often?"

"As you know, it's never enough."

I wait for a smile, which doesn't come. I forge on.

"But I fly back to see them as much as I can, and I FaceTime with them every few days."

"But it's not the same as seeing them in person, is it?" Miriam asks, reaching over to grab her son's hand.

"Mom," Leo says in a tender but warning tone.

"It's not," I say. I take a sip of wine and shift in my chair. I need to take the focus off me. "Tell me about you? What type of law did you practice, Joseph?"

He spends the next ten minutes telling me about his career as a corporate tax attorney and the firm he started and grew to over a hundred attorneys in Beverly Hills.

I like Joseph. He is sweet, unpretentious, and his stories are not braggadocious but filled with humility and pride.

"And what about you, Miriam?" I ask when Joseph finishes. "Tell me about your life."

"My life was dedicated to my family," she says, eyes lasered on mine. "And it still is."

I do not have the same warm fuzzies for Miriam. She eyes me as suspiciously as she might a Honey Baked Ham at Seder, making subtle digs hidden as compliments.

Our meals come, and Miriam orders a second bottle of wine.

"Leo drove," she says to me. "We're staying with him for a few days. Did you know?"

"That's so nice," I say, not taking the bait. "Isn't it exciting about his new career? Early ratings have been stellar, haven't they, Leo?"

I reach across and touch Leo's arm, and I can see Miriam recoil.

"They have," he says. "Thanks to you, Sid."

"It's such an incredible opportunity," she says, reaching over to grasp his other arm.

"I feel like a wishbone," Leo jokes.

"Make a wish," Miriam says, tugging on his arm.

"I did," Leo says, touching my hand with his. "And it already came true."

"Aww," Joseph says.

Miriam's eyes narrow as Louis brings our meals.

As we eat, a few Palm Springs locals approach our table to say hello to me.

"You know a lot of people in the desert?" Miriam asks, the question coming out as more pointed than casual.

"I've lived in the desert nearly as long as I lived in Chicago," I say.

"Two separate lives," Miriam says. She takes a bite of her chopped salad and studies me. "Have you been in a long-term relationship in Palm Springs?"

"I've actually never really dated anyone before Leo."

Miriam places her knife and fork on her plate and clasps her hands together on the table in front of her.

"And why is that, if you don't mind my asking?"

"You just asked, Mom," Leo says. "You don't have to answer that, Sid. My mother can be very, shall we say, inquisitive."

"That's a polite word for nosy," she says with a wink. Miriam lifts her hands in the air. "You don't have to answer, Sid, of course. Just a curious mom."

I focus on my plate for much too long, cutting my eggs royale into way too many tiny pieces.

"I don't think I ever loved myself enough to love another

person." I force myself to look up from my plate at her. "It's taken a long time. Your son made me see—and love—myself for the first time."

Joseph claps his hands together.

"That is just the most beautiful answer, son," he says to me, though I'm older than he is.

Miriam nods. "Yes, it is. Quite revealing." She smiles at me, but it is more Cheshire cat than mother next door. "You two haven't dated that long, though, correct?"

"New subject!" Leo interjects with an awkward laugh. "I think this will be a great afternoon to lounge by the pool, don't you think?"

When we finish our meals, Louis returns with dessert menus. We order four coffees, the "24 Carrot" cake and a chocolate pot de crème with homemade cookies to share.

"Excuse me," I say. "I need to run to the restroom before dessert."

I stand.

"I need the little girls' room, too," Miriam says. "Mind if I walk with you?"

I wait for her and then hold out my arm for her to take.

"Such a gentleman," she adds, clasping her hands around my arm.

"Smile, you two!"

We turn, and Leo snaps our photo.

"That's a keeper, isn't it, Dad?" he asks, showing his father.

"It is!"

"I can't wait to see it," Miriam says. "Back in a sec!"

I escort her off the patio.

As soon as we round the corner and are out of sight, Miriam jerks her arm away. She grabs me, hard.

"What do you think you are doing?" she asks.

"Going to the bathroom?"

"Did you think I'd just be the compliant mother and simply go along with this?" Miriam hisses, her grip tightening on my arm. People stare. She releases my arm, smooths her hair and composes herself. She leans toward me and whispers, "I do *not* approve of you being in a relationship with my son." She studies my face. "It's just sick."

I feel as though the floor below me has been removed, and I am falling.

"I don't understand," I stammer.

"Don't play me for a fool," Miriam spits. "I will not allow you to take advantage of my son. Is this some sort of fetish? You only like men who could be your son?"

She manages to smile at Louis as he passes with our desserts.

"Leo pursued *me*," I say. "I thought his initial interest was purely professional."

"You're eighty-one, Sid. You know how this is going to end!"

"Excuse me?"

"What does your future together look like?" she asks, shaking her head. "Are you even alive in a decade? If so, what do you envision? Romantic dinners in Paris, a cruise down the Rhine? I bet you don't envision my son feeding you, bathing you, filling prescriptions, wheeling you to doctor's appointments and navigating rather nasty legal decisions with your children, do you?"

The trees whir before me as I think of Teddy's reluctance to tell us of his medical issues.

"He cannot take care of you. He should not *have to* take care of you." Miriam shakes my arm. "He *will not* take care of you, Sid. Leo has his own family to care for already."

"But I think I'm in love with your son," I say, talking slowly to keep my voice from trembling and making me sound like the old man she sees. "And I think he's in love with me."

"How could he love you?" she asks. "What can you possibly offer him?"

Tears well in my eyes. I will them to stop, but I am too weak. "Everything."

A sad, hideous gasp makes its way free.

Miriam pretends to check her manicure as Louis passes again. She waits until he's out of earshot before she speaks again.

"Leo has always been kind to a fault," she says, a genuine smile finally making its way across her face as she talks about her son. "He was always that way as a child. He'd befriend the lonely kid on the playground. He brought home stray dogs. I think it's why he went into journalism. It allowed him to connect with and tell the stories of those he wanted to help." Miriam pats my arm. "I think he sees you as one of those people, Sid. He shared your story about your run-in with that awful woman at the library. I think his heart went out to you. I'm sure he's fond of you, and I'm sure you provide him a sense of safety and security in a new environment, but I believe he's confusing those feelings for something deeper. And I think you're interpreting his kindness for something deeper.

"Joseph and I have been married for sixty years," she continues. "Sixty years, Sid. We have been through everything together. We still hold out hopes for grandchildren one day."

"I have grandchildren," I say.

"Those are your grandchildren, Sid, not ours. Not Leo's. Those are people from a different life," Miriam says. "You have led a different life than Leo. And that life is nearing its finale."

"I've played the cards this life has dealt me as best I can, Miriam. It has not been an easy one."

"I'm sure it hasn't," she says coolly. "But my son has devoted his life to his career, and now he's here in Palm Springs for likely his last chapter in broadcasting but also for his first long-term relationship. This . . . *you!* . . . is not fair to him. It's not normal. It's selfish. He needs a man who is his equal and his age. I'm sure you can see that, can't you?"

I look into the eyes of a woman around my age who should understand the power of love. "But I love him."

"That's not enough," she says. "It will never be enough."

Leo's laughter carries along the wind, through the branches of the trees, and his happiness lights on my shoulder.

I close my eyes and listen, capturing the sound in my brain, hoping that one day—when I am alone and dying and need to remember the happiest time of my life—I will hear his laughter again, and my pain will be quieted. I will fade from this earth hoping and believing—no, knowing—I was loved.

"Please tell Leo I wasn't feeling well," I say.

Miriam nods, and I head to the exit.

The tears don't come again until the valet brings my car, I drive away and Leo's laughter melts away in the warm desert breeze.

The living room slider opens.

Trudy walks out and heads for one of Ron's beloved Knoll patio chairs. Although these mid-century wire frame chairs make designers and MCM lovers swoon at their minimalist beauty, they make the average joe reach for Preparation H when they take a seat on the kitchen grater that calls itself a chair.

I want to save her before it's too late. My sister has endured enough pain in her life. But God, does evil Teddy want to see her take a seat in that chair and then try to extricate herself without Two Men and a Truck.

"Why don't you sit on this chair?" I say, patting the striped cushion. "It's a bit more comfortable."

I've gone soft in my old age.

"Next to you?" she asks.

"I still want the money."

She laughs and takes a seat.

"That's actually why I came out," Trudy says. "My attorney sent the paperwork. It should be in your in-box. You just need to Docusign, and the money will be in your account first of the week after we leave."

"Are you sure?" I ask.

"I'm sure."

"Thank you, Trudy." I reach out and grab her hand. "For saving my life."

Trudy keeps her eyes focused on the mountains in the distance, clouds forming shadows on the peaks, playing leapfrog over the valley like the two of us used to do in our front yard. When she looks at me, I realize she appears entirely different.

The mask is gone.

"Speaking of saving your life, I'm glad Ava convinced you to get the surgery. The world needs you in it, Teddy."

"It does," I say with conviction. "You, too, sis."

"I hope the money will come in handy for medical bills and things like that. I know it must be expensive."

"Thanks, but my friends said they will cover any outstanding expenses," I say. "Barry's loaded now, Ron is rich and Sid is set. I know how to pick 'em."

As I say this, I tighten my grip on her hand and give it a shake.

"What will you use the money for, then, if you don't mind me asking? Travel?"

"I already live in paradise with my best friends," I say. "I was thinking I just might pass the money on to someone."

Trudy turns, her face morphing into confusion.

"You?" she asks.

"We've taught you the art of sarcasm, I see? Don't act so surprised! I'm not that selfish and awful." I wait a beat. "Am I?"

"You wanted me to sit in that wire chair," my sister says. "I know you."

"I do love physical humor," I say. "Actually, I opened a new account. The money is going into a CD. It will make a little interest. I plan to chip in a bit more around here with the house, but if you ever wanted to look at moving out to the desert, or if Ava needed some help with college, let's just say the money would be available for that."

"Teddy." A smile engulfs her face as she shakes her head in amazement at my generous gesture.

"It's hard being so fabulous."

"What are you drinking?"

"Martini," I say. "A Palm Springs classic, as beautiful and dry as those mountains. One is enough, two make me look like Hugh Jackman and three will have you howling naked with the coyotes tonight."

"Why don't I start with one?"

I make our drinks at the cocktail bar on the patio, skewering three blue cheese–stuffed olives and settling them into a martini glass.

"This cocktail is like liquid sunshine," I say, handing it to my sister.

She takes a sip, and her eyes water.

"This cocktail tastes like gasoline!"

"I made it right, then!" I take a seat, grab my martini and hold it out. "Cheers!"

"To a new start!"

We clink glasses.

The edge of the mountain is tinged in light. Candy-color clouds drift among the peaks.

"Remember that oil painting Mama won at a church raffle that hung over the sofa in the living room?" Trudy finally asks. "Light splaying from behind beautiful clouds hugging a mountain, and Mama always said the plume of sun that rose toward the heavens was Jesus lighting our way."

I see it clearly. That painting hung over Daddy every night as he raged, a comical juxtaposition. Mama stared at that cheap stained rendering in a warped frame every night before she fell asleep in her rented hospice bed. I stared at it as a kid praying I could find a place that looked like that. I finally did.

"I remember."

"The sky looks like that tonight," Trudy says.

"It certainly does." I sip my martini. "Your hair looks good, by the way, Trudy."

"Keep drinking," she says with a chuckle. "You're getting nicer."

Ava emerges onto the patio in her swimsuit, headed to the pool once again. She stops when she notices us.

"I'm going to miss this when we leave tomorrow," she says.

"The pool?" I ask. "The weather?"

"No," she says, nodding at me and her grandmother. *"This."*

Ava takes off racing across the patio and yard and leaps into the pool. A resounding splash echoes off Zsa Zsa.

"So, this is happy hour?" Trudy asks. "I like it."

"Are you happy?" I ask.

"I think I finally just might be," she says.

"Me, too."

We clink glasses again, and watch as the sun slips toward slumber.

The sun has yet to rise over Joshua Tree, but Pioneer Town is bright as day.

It's my first day on set.

Lights illuminate the ramshackle bar where—in about an hour—I will shoot my first scene for *Billy's Back*.

"Barry's back!"

I had wanted to take this moment in all by myself, but the director, Mitch Michaels—the Golden Globe winner who has directed the likes of George Clooney, Brad Pitt, Nicole Kidman and Reese Witherspoon—sees me and waves me over from his chair.

"You ready?" he asks.

"Damn straight!"

This ironic turn of phrase does not hit home with macho Mitch.

"You better be! My ass is riding on this! You know Billy Bob Thornton wanted this role."

Mitch is subtly trying to intimidate me. I know because it's happened to me on way too many sets to count. I know what guys like Mitch want to hear because I've used my own macho daddy act to direct the actions of more men than this director ever will.

"Billy Bob *wears* blood," I say. "I *drink* it for breakfast."

Mitch roars with laughter. "See you in an hour!"

I walk toward my trailer and stop cold.

Barry Goggins ☆

My name is centered on the door next to a huge gold star.

After forty years, I'm finally a fucking star!

I cannot help myself: I grab my cell and snap a selfie standing in front of it.

I type a caption so casual and so cool that you'd think I'd been shooting major motion pictures my entire life instead of commercials for local carpet companies.

First day on set! Barry's Back #BillysBack!

I open the door.

This is not like the trailers from my youth, double-wides on concrete blocks with screen doors banging in the wind. This is like a room at the Four Seasons: a beautifully furnished living room, completely decked out kitchen, bedroom in the back.

I run my hand over the lush fabric on the couch and am so taken by its luxe that I do not realize a young woman is sitting in it.

"Hi, I'm Ainsley, your makeup artist." She stands. If she stepped out of her hoodie and into a gown, Ainsley could walk the red carpet without a stitch of makeup like Pamela Anderson. "I'm so sorry for sitting on your couch. It won't happen again."

I extend my hand. "It's nice to meet you, Ainsley. And you can sit on my couch anytime."

I smile, and her face brightens.

"My last gig out here was for a car commercial," I say. "I was paid in fast food."

She giggles and covers her mouth with her hand. "Sorry for laughing."

"I'm sorry for having done it. The things you'll do to make it in show business." There's a knock on the door.

"Yes?" I call.

A young man enters carrying a tray.

"Hi, I'm Zed. I have your oat milk latte with extra foam, a protein smoothie and steel-cut oats with fresh fruit," he says, setting the tray on the counter in the kitchen. "Your refrigerator is filled with ionized water and Oikos Triple Zero yogurt. Let me know if you need anything else or have any questions."

"Just one."

Zed stops, curly hair bobbing into his long lashes. Zed is every bit as pretty as Ainsley.

I gesture at the tray. "What is all this?"

Zed looks at me like I'm crazy.

"Um, it's part of your contract."

"Ah." I nod.

Stu Matthews. My agent is more thrilled than me that I'm back in the game. He's going to squeeze every yogurt he can out of Paramount.

"Thank you," I say.

Zed leaves. Ainsley looks at me and says, "Show business, right?"

I smile—too nervous to eat—but grab my smoothie and coffee, and take a seat at the makeup table that has been set up opposite the couch. Ainsley's equipment is spread out before her. She goes right to work.

"So, how did you get the part?" she asks excitedly. "Everyone says it's a great role. I heard Billy Bob was going to get it."

Hollywood is worse than high school: Rumors fly down hallways, while pretty girls and bad boys get all the attention.

Ainsley applies a liquid foundation to her fingers and taps it onto my face. It is a perfect match to my skin tone, and I see Barry Goggins fade away before my very eyes.

"It's complicated," I say.

"Story of my life," Ainsley says.

I tell her about my career, being cut from *The Golden Girls*—which she had never heard of before—and how Kyle was my first boyfriend in LA.

"We reconnected recently," I say, "and he thought I would be perfect for the role. He introduced me to Mitch, and . . ." I hesitate ". . . it just happened rather quickly after that."

Ainsley stops and pulls her hands away from my face. She scrutinizes her work in the mirror. I expect judgment.

"That's the stuff of Hollywood dreams," she says, starry-eyed. "It's who you know in this town, not what you know."

There could be no bigger understatement.

I nod, close my eyes and run lines in my head as Ainsley works on my face.

"You are a very lucky man," she adds. "And a very lucky actor."

Ainsley says this with great sincerity, although the line strikes me as pure sarcasm.

She does not know the complete backstory of the main character like I do. It is as complicated as my character of Levi.

"It's who you know in this town."

Which is why I'm sitting here right now after forty years of banging my head against a wall.

My character, Levi, is a rarity in film, especially a blockbuster sequel like this, in which fans just want to see Billy and Loretta kill all the bad guys and say their favorite line: *"We is blood relatives."*

That is the fate for Levi in this movie: He, too, will die at the hands of his sister. I will be one and done in this franchise, but reborn again in Hollywood. Stu is already fielding calls and receiving scripts before I've even uttered a line on set. The power of the trades.

As I run lines in my head, the parallels blur between my movie character and the real Kyle: We may seem charming and heroic on screen, but are we good or bad?

Hell, I still don't even know which one I am yet, but—if I were to read my recent receipts—I'd say my finger is leaning heavily on the needle toward bad.

There's another knock on the door. I open my eyes as the door opens.

Zed pops his head in and announces, "You're on in fifteen."

I stare at my reflection. Ainsley has arranged a short gray hairpiece over my too-dark locks, softened my harsh eye lift with makeup and transformed this older gay man into a ruggedly handsome Harrison Ford lookalike.

"You are a magician," I say.

"Thank you." She beams. "But it's all you."

Ainsley places her hands on my shoulders.

"Just look." She points at my reflection. "Your entire demeanor has changed, as if you're carrying the weight of the world on your shoulders. I can see why they chose you."

If you only knew.

"It's just an honor to see an underdog finally come out on top," she says.

She removes the paper apron from around my neck. I head to the bedroom and change into the Western garb that Levi will be wearing. When I step out, Ainsley claps.

"*Hello*, Levi!" she exclaims.

Another knock on the door.

"They're ready for you now, Mr. Goggins," Zed says this time. "A stylist will be on set to tweak your costume."

I take a deep breath.

"Knock 'em dead!" Ainsley says.

As I head down the dusty street toward the bar, I see in the near distance a scurrying mass of people—crew, actors, extras—move in sync like an army of ants.

For the first time, my heart races.

As I get closer, I see a line in the dust—just like the one I made a few days ago here with Kyle—that someone has drawn with the heel of a boot. It is long and deep, almost daring me to cross it. Dust billows in the wind, and I notice in the haze just how clean my new jeans are.

"There he is!" Mitch yells. "First scene. How you feelin'?"

I cross the line.

"Great," I lie.

Mitch stands up from his chair, says something to the cinematographer and hands his script to an assistant. He walks up to me until we are nose to nose. Mitch stares into my eyes.

"I *asked*," he screams in my face, "how *the fuck* are you *feelin'*?"

His breath is all coffee and hypermasculinity.

"Let's do this!" I yell, giving him what he wants.

The crew applauds my crazy act.

Mitch puts his hand on my shoulder.

"This scene sets up the entire fuckin' movie, man. Your character is the reason for this sequel. You, man! *You!*"

Mitch slaps me on the back.

"I want you to walk into the Ozarks bar that Billy and Loretta own like you're a stray fuckin' dog that found its way home after being lost in the woods for years," he says, outlining the scene. "You are broken but you found the strength to crawl back to your family. Loretta will take your order, and when you say 'Missouri Mule,' she'll look up, immediately knowing it's Levi because he was the only man she ever knew who drank that. As her face changes from disbelief to confusion to concern for her and Billy's safety, you will launch into your big speech. As you do, Loretta will slowly dissolve into tears, the camera will close in on her eyes, and there will be a flashback of her remembering when you stopped a bear from attacking her as a girl by being the toughest, most badass brother anyone could ever have. She'll walk around the bar and embrace you, and when you two finally hug—*bam!*—I'll circle the camera from her face to yours, where a tiny smile will cross your lips, and the audience won't know if it's because you're happy to see her or if you're planning your revenge. Got it?"

"More than you will ever know," I say. "This is the role I was meant to play because I want revenge on all those who doubted me."

"Fuck *yeah*!" Mitch yells. "Let's roll. Places, everyone!"

A camera wheels into the bar, and when the saloon doors open, I see what I believe is a fire burning in the back: It is Ida Red reprising her role as Loretta, laughing, drying a beer glass with a towel.

She looks up and sees me. Ida nods and shoots me a wink.

The camera moves toward the bar and then turns to face the doors. As the doors continue to swing, I see Kyle standing at a table off to the side, talking to some extras, his perfect thighs encased in skintight jeans and a flannel shirt open to show his hairy chest and perfect pecs.

He smiles at me just as Mitch yells, "Action!"

I don't even feel myself walking. In fact, I am not of this earth any longer. I am floating somewhere over Joshua Tree, watching this happen, out of body.

I see my wounded dog self push through the swinging doors. I take a seat at the bar. Loretta approaches, cleaning a glass, totally exhausted, not looking up at me.

"Missouri Mule," I say in an Ozarks lilt.

She finally looks. Tears pool in her emoji eyes.

"I tried to help you, sis," I say, my face contorted with emotion. "They threatened to kill me, too, so I had to run and hide. I ended up in the hills of West Virginia where no one would ever find me. I had no one." I hesitate. "Until Mary." I clamp my eyes shut. My chin trembles at the mention of her name. "I married the love of my life, and we had a family—a boy . . ." I stop and pull my cell from my jeans pocket. I show her pictures of my son. "Levi Jr. looked just like his daddy, and little Lori . . ." I show Loretta a photo of my daughter with flame-red hair ". . . well, she looked just like you. She was *named* for you."

I stare at the picture of my little girl, chin now quivering.

"The others found my family and killed them. I came home and discovered them all in bed, as if they were waiting for me to tuck them in and kiss them good-night." A lone tear weaves its way through my stubble. "I'm broken, sis. I have no one. I had nowhere to go." I look up at her. "I need a family." I reach out and take her hand in mine. "I need you." I set my jaw. "I need revenge."

I can see the memory of me protecting her from the bear flashing in her eyes. Loretta weeps. She walks around the bar and whispers the line people have been waiting for her to say. This time, however, it is spoken softly, tinged with love and regret.

"We is blood relatives," she whispers into my ear, holding on to me tightly.

The camera pans around to my face.

Slowly, so very slowly, a smile crosses my face.

"And cut!" Mitch yells.

The crew breaks into thunderous applause.

"Fabulous, Barry! I mean, just fucking fabulous! First take, man, and you nailed it!" he yells. "I see big things coming your way." He walks over and claps me on the back. "The studio can get behind your backstory, too, when we start the press tour. The guy who finally, finally got the break he deserved after all these years."

Mitch turns to the crew.

"Back in five!" he yells. "I want to get some takes of Billy reacting to the scene at the bar."

"Helluva job," Ida Red says, studying me curiously. "Damn shame you gotta die."

I laugh. She doesn't like anyone getting more attention than her.

"Already dead," I say to her with a wink. "So it doesn't hurt as much."

She stares at me as I head out of the bar.

Kyle walks over to me.

"I knew I was right about you," he says. Kyle leans into my ear and whispers, "You are so hot right now."

I laugh as if he's told me the funniest joke in the world and head to my trailer.

"I was watching," Ainsley says when I enter. "Congratulations."

"Thanks. It was a rush."

I grab a bottle of water from the refrigerator and chug it, finally realizing how dry my mouth is, not just from the desert dust but from my nerves.

I take a seat in the chair, and Ainsley touches up my makeup for my next scene.

The trailer door pops open, and Kyle sticks his head in.

"Mr. Moses," Ainsley exclaims nervously.

"Can you excuse us for a moment?" he asks.

"Of course," she says as she exits.

As soon as she is gone, Kyle locks the door, grabs me and kisses me with too much force.

"I made you," he says, grabbing my face, hard. "I made you! Now I want my scene with you." His fingers are pressed into my neck. "You got me so worked up out there. I deserve a reward, cowboy."

Kyle forces me onto the couch.

"I have another scene," I say. "Don't mess up my makeup or clothes."

I am strong, but he is younger, stronger. His hand wraps around my throat. My windpipe constricts. I gasp. We fall to the floor.

"You were so hot today," he whispers. A thread of saliva trickles from the corner of his mouth. "But don't overshadow me or Loretta. I can still fire you. Billy Bob is waiting."

I look up at him. Kyle is no longer present. His face is flushed, his eyes narrowed, his dimples making him look like a sweet man who has lost his mind.

I search his eyes as I gasp for air.

Does he even remember the sweet, innocent kid he was when he first moved to Hollywood?

"You like this, don't you?" he asks, his body, excited, pressed against mine.

This, I realize, is my payback. It is the price I must pay for success. The toll I now owe for taking advantage of so many other men without a single concern for their well-being is finally being exacted.

My arm flails, hitting the small table by the couch.

Yes, Kyle has turned the tables on me from so long ago.

I know I should hit, fight, scream, but I deserve this.

I know when this is over that I should report him to the police, tell my agent and the studio, go to the tabloids with this story, but I won't.

I deserve this.

All of this.

No one would believe me anyway. We think the world changes, but it never really does. The rich and powerful always get their way.

As Kyle chokes me with one hand. His other begins to unzip my pants.

My arm not pinned under my body continues to flail. My fingers touch the script I left on the table. Suddenly, Ron's advice rings in my ears:

You're a writer, Barry. Why don't you write your own rules for once? Write your own story, Barry.

My fingers feel the empty tray Zed left on top of the table.

"I didn't mean to break your heart, Kyle," I squeak.

Kyle's eyes soften for just an instant. His grip eases. I gasp for air.

"Kiss me," he says.

Kyle puts his mouth on mine. He begins to force my jeans off.

I lift the tray and hit him in the head with it.

He falls off of me, screaming, "I'm going to murder you, motherfucker! Your career is over! You are so fucking fired!"

Kyle stands up and kicks me.

I may be on the ground, but I am not defenseless. I refuse to be tossed away and forgotten on the cutting room floor again.

"Kick me again," I say. "And again. You can't hurt me. And

you can't fire me. The studio agreed to a no-termination clause in my contract because I agreed to take less money and made zero demands. And I already told my agent about what happened between us. He's the only person I know who's a bigger dick than you are."

Kyle glares at me.

"You're lying!" he says.

I glare back at him.

"Am I?"

I am. I would never tell my agent what happened with Kyle. I've come too far.

But I've finally realized I'm a much better actor than Kyle Moses will ever be, and I deserve this role. And the next one, and the next one.

"Go on! Use that rage in the movie," I taunt. "I feel sorry for your husband. I made the right decision breaking up with you."

Kyle storms toward the door.

"And if you touch me again, I will have my friends kill you," I say to him. Kyle scoffs. "Mark my words. They will do it. They won't just help me bury your body, they'll take pleasure in dismembering it. That's the beauty of having friends. And there's a reason you don't have any."

He slams the door.

Ainsley comes back in as I'm picking myself up off the floor.

She rushes over to me. "Oh, my God!"

She helps me onto the couch. She looks at me, and then gently lifts my chin.

"Your neck," she says, her eyes wide. "I need to call someone."

"No!" I say. "Please, don't."

Ainsley walks to the kitchen and returns with ice wrapped in a towel. She holds it to my neck.

"Are you sure you're okay?" Her voice is shaky.

"I will be," I say. "The things you'll do to make it in show business."

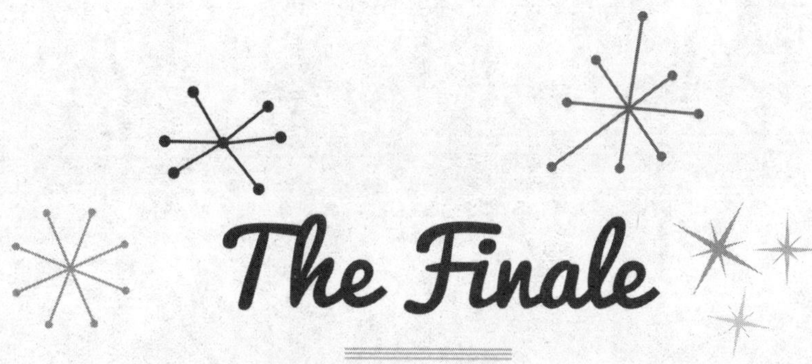

The Finale

A few months later

“On a scale of one to ten, with one representing very mild pain and ten being the most unbearable pain you can experience, where would you rate your pain today?”

“A million!” I yell at Ron. “There is a catheter up my weewee! It feels like I have a U-Haul parked down there, and that parking space is only meant for compact vehicles!”

My shouting does not thwart nursemaid Ron. He props me up even further in bed, and hands me a glass of water, pills for bladder spasms and a stool softener, and a bowl of fresh fruit.

Ron sniffs the air and winces. He yanks down the blanket.

“Not again,” he says.

“Put me out of my misery,” I beg. “Please.”

The incontinence was not supposed to start until my catheter came out, but bladder spasms cause nightly leakage. Even worse, after I put up with being constipated the first few days postsurgery, the water, fruit and stool softeners are kicking in as they are supposed to, but I'm too exhausted and too medicated to realize it and call for help in time. When I finally realize what has occurred, I'm too ashamed, so I sit in my own waste like a baby in his diaper.

“I'll clean you up,” Ron says.

I turn my head away, mortified.

"It's okay," he assures me.

Ron returns wearing gloves and carrying an arsenal of wipes, towels, soap and water. He washes me as I used to bathe my mother when she was dying. The warm washcloth feels good against my skin.

"I should have hired someone to do this," I say. "It's not fair to you."

He gets another washcloth and rubs my legs.

"That's what friends are for," Ron says. He looks at me. "You're my best friend, Teddy, and I love you."

"There are things a child should never see," my mother said to me once as I cleaned her dying body, eyes locked on the portrait hanging on the wall in front of her bed.

"And there are things you should do for those you love," I said.

"You love me?" she asked.

"You shouldn't have to ask," I replied.

"You love me?" I ask Ron.

"You shouldn't have to ask," he says.

"Thank you for being my friend," I say.

His face contorts with emotion. He nods and walks to the bathroom. I hear him washing his hands.

Sid and Barry enter the room. I look at the clock. It is 7:00 a.m. on the dot.

"Your laminated chore chart finally worked," I marvel to Ron when he returns to the bedroom. "After all these years."

"I'm just stunned you didn't have anal cancer because you've been such a raging asshole for so long," Barry deadpans.

We roar in laughter.

"Help me get him up," Ron says. "We need to change these sheets, and you need to stand for a few minutes. You have to start moving around a bit more today, okay?"

"Yes, Nurse Ratched."

Barry and Sid put their arms around me and walk me around

the bedroom, down the hall, through the living room and back again. I am winded easily.

They help me back in bed, and—as my gown goes northward—I pat the drainage bag around my leg.

"I just love you, bladder buddy."

"Good God!" Barry yelps. "No wonder I only date younger men."

"You need some petroleum jelly down there," Ron says, heading into the bathroom. He sets a tube on the tray next to me. "But you're doing that all on your own."

Sid is quiet, but I can tell something is on his mind.

"Just say it, Sid."

"What about . . ." Sid stops, searching for the right word ". . . sex?"

"Jury's still out," I say. "Some flags remain at half-mast forever. But I'm confident I will rise to see another day. Otherwise, what do I have to live for? I do have to try to get an erection once my body has had a chance to heal," I say. "In fact, I will need an erection as soon as possible for my penile rehabilitation. Any takers?"

Barry gags.

"I guess I'll just have to look at old photos of Tom Selleck, then. If it worked when I was young, maybe the magic will work again." I eye Sid and continue. "I suppose you're just asking because your sex life finally got a new lease with Leo."

Sid ducks his head. "That's over."

"What?" I gasp.

"A few too many mommy issues." Sid shrugs.

"Him or you?" I ask.

Sid smiles, but I can tell he is deeply hurt.

"I'm so sorry, my dear," I say. "Is there any chance at all? I know how much you liked him."

Sid looks out the window. "Loved him. I think I loved him."

Suddenly, my heart hurts more than the catheter.

"Want me to be honest?" I ask.

"When are you not?"

"You're already well past the life expectancy of a man in the US."

"Gee, thanks for the pep talk."

"What do you have to lose?" I ask. "I mean, just look at me. My husband killed himself. I am incontinent. My Christian sister got pregnant out of wedlock. Ron is my nursemaid. And I still am fighting for something more in this life. If I can do it, you can, too, Sid. You are the kindest man I know."

"Hey," Ron says, acting wounded.

"You," I point at him, "are the man most likely to get C. diff that I know."

He laughs. "I better go shower. You got this, Barry?"

"I do," he says.

"Sid?" I say.

"What?"

"Look at me."

He does.

"Fight. Let's make this final act the best yet. No regrets."

Sid nods.

"Say it with me. No regrets."

"No regrets."

Sid forces a tiny smile.

"I have to go get ready. It's Reading Hour at the library. I'll be back for the evening shift."

"You mean the evening shit," I say.

He pads out the door in his slippers.

"It's just the two of us," I say to Barry. "Blanche and Dorothy."

"Mind if I sit?"

"Go ahead," I say, gesturing to a chair.

Barry takes a seat on the bed next to me.

"This seems serious," I continue.

Barry looks broken.

"I know you would cry if your eye surgery allowed it," I say, patting the bed. Barry crawls into bed next to me. "Tell mama everything," I whisper.

He tells me about Kyle.

"I'm going to kill that motherfucker!" I yell when he's done.

Barry laughs. "At least I don't have to see him again until the movie premieres," he says. "And he's been treating me like gold, talking me up to producers and directors. His money is on the line with this film, and the last thing he needs is bad press. We all need a blockbuster, and the studio thinks it could set a box office record when it launches."

"I wish I could have come to see you on set," I say. "You've waited for this your whole life."

"Thank you, but I had to do it on my own terms. For once. I just don't know what to do next," he says. "I'm getting all of these scripts for TV and film. I'm getting interest from the hottest directors. It's everything I wanted." Barry sighs. "I'm just not as happy as I thought I'd be for some reason."

"Then be happy! Go back to doing it the way you've always done it. Be in control of your life and work," I say. "You think you only did crappy community theater, but you wrote, acted, directed . . . you did it all, Barry. You changed people's lives with these shows. You changed our lives. And it's been a blast, hasn't it?"

"It has."

"Have you ever considered that your life has worked out exactly the way it was supposed to?" I ask. "Have you ever considered that the three of us were your big break? That maybe being a friend is the role of a lifetime."

He eyes me skeptically. "Who have you become?"

"A eunuch," I say. "It's softened me. And I can sing soprano now."

He laughs.

"You just need to write your happy ending, Barry. What's that fancy word you use for the end of a story, when the strands of the plot are drawn together and everything is resolved?"

"The denouement?" Barry asks.

"That's it. You just need your personal denouement." I nudge his shoulder. "Every great character grows and changes. Perhaps that's what's holding you back right now from taking advantage of your hard-won success. You've grown and changed. I mean, you haven't brought anyone home in ages." I shake my head at how insane that is. "I think you just need to write your own final act."

Barry sits up straight.

"That's it! That's what Ron was trying to tell me, too!"

He leaps off the bed.

"I'll be right back!"

He returns with his laptop, takes a seat in a chair and begins to type furiously. Barry glances at me. "Let me know if you need anything."

"Just keep writing."

A few moments later, my cell rings.

"Hi, sis."

Trudy's face appears on my phone.

"How are you feeling?"

"Like I'm trying to tinkle an ice pick."

"Thank you for the visual," Trudy says. "I sent flowers. Did you get them?"

A gorgeous bouquet sits on a nearby table.

"Yes. Thank you. They're beautiful. How are you feeling?"

"First few weeks of therapy are going well," she says. "And I do have a surprise."

"What now?"

"Ava is looking at the California Institute of the Arts."

"That's amazing! CalArts is incredible."

"And Santa Clarita isn't that far from you," Trudy adds. "Ava says you inspired her. She's interested in studying costume design there."

Barry looks up and applauds.

"You have two very excited gay men here," I say. "It would be great to see her more."

"What about me?"

"I'm seeing you right now."

"What about in person?"

I cock my head at Trudy and position the cell next to my face. "Close enough now?"

"I mean, in person."

I pull the cell away.

"I actually listened to your advice and have been looking at real estate listings in Palm Springs," Trudy says. "I could never have something like you have, but I'd like to live closer to family as well."

I look at Barry, who acts as if he is wiping away a tear. *So sweet*, he mouths.

"What do you think?" Trudy asks. "I would never move if you didn't want me closer to you."

"What about your son?"

"He'll be fine," she says. "They're the ones who ran away from me, and I don't blame them. But they have their own lives. I want to spend the time I have left with my little brother."

"That would be amazing," I say. "You'll be a hit at all the gay bars. Everyone will think you're a lesbian."

"I'm hoping to come out this summer to visit some colleges with Ava. She actually asked me to come with her," Trudy says. "I can look at some homes then and see how hot it gets."

"You'll want to move in October," I say with a smile. "When things stop melting. Just save up for AC."

"I'll give you a call later," Trudy says. "It was good to talk to you."

"Thanks for calling, sis."

I begin to hang up, but Trudy says, "Wait, Teddy?"

"Yeah?"

"I love you."

"I love you, too, sis. Bye."

Just as Trudy hangs up, I see—over her shoulder, hanging on her living room wall—the cheap Biblical oil painting Mama won at the church raffle.

She did go home one last time to say goodbye.

I look out the window.

Candy-color clouds like the ones in the painting, as orange as Mama's Bakelite bracelet, are hugging the mountains at sunrise.

"Haircut?"

I nod to the barber as I enter his shop.

"You're up next."

"Thanks."

I take a seat in Luigi's, an old-school barbershop in downtown Palm Springs that hasn't changed in decades. This is where Elvis, Sinatra and Dean Martin got their hair cut when they played in the desert, and their photos still line the walls.

Luigi's sits in the middle of La Plaza, one of the first shopping centers in Southern California. It opened nearly a century ago and even contained a three-level parking garage. It became a successful model for open-air malls, and though the original tenants are long gone, La Plaza retains its original Spanish architecture and vibe. It is now home to retail shops and great restaurants, from the fabulous Farm to the popular burger joint Tyler's whose scent of french fries wafts through the open door of the barber shop.

I have come here today to have my demons cast out. This is my equivalent of being dunked in the river to be saved.

When I was a boy, my mother so loved my curly blond hair and was so terrified its beauty would be destroyed if I got it cut that she let it grow and grow until people in our little town thought I was a little girl. My father, angry and embarrassed, picked me up from school one day and drove me to the country barbershop to have my golden locks shorn. When the elderly barber lifted the clippers to my head, I shrieked. When he was done, I wept.

"I'm bald!" I cried. "I'm bald!"

My mother yelped when she saw me.

"My baby!" she moaned, which started me weeping anew, until my father slapped me.

"Shut up and be a man!" he said before turning on my mom.

That day, I hid in the root cellar, curling up on the cool floor next to a sack of potatoes, a bin of Vidalia onions and my mother's pickled okra and beets, kicking the walls, damning God, myself and the world, eventually doing the unthinkable: ripping out hunks of what remained of my hair until my scalp bled, hoping the physical pain would remove the emotional hurt. It took the longest time—until the last week, to be honest—to finally understand that it is our addictions—Teddy's drinking, Barry's need to be wanted, Sid's self-flagellation, my desire to please—that slowly kills us.

That is why I am here. To end the insanity.

I have never stepped foot in a barbershop again until today.

I cut my own hair growing up, until I discovered The Curl Up & Dye. I believed that my hair was my superpower, my armor and my protection, like Wonder Woman's lasso.

Unlike Gaspar's, there is no champagne at Luigi's, only talk of sports, a subject I am not fluent in. I stay glued to my cell to avoid the chitchat.

"You're up!"

I nod at the owner of Luigi's, a man with kind eyes.

He holds out his hand before me in a fist. I stare at him blankly.

"Fist bump?" he asks.

I continue to stare.

"It's a way to say hello."

He shows me again, and I hold out a closed fist. He bumps it with his. I will never understand the way straight men think or act.

I take a seat in the same chair that Elvis likely sat in and then take a final glimpse at myself in the mirror, likely feeling as Aaron Presley did when he was drafted into the army and had to get his hair buzzed.

"What can I do for you?" the owner asks.

"New start," I say. "Cut it short."

The barber looks at me. He touches the top of my carefully coiffed curls.

"You sure?"

"I'm sure."

He grabs a spray bottle and wets my hair down. He combs it high and retrieves his clippers.

I jump when they begin to whir.

"You okay, man?" the barber asks, placing a hand on my shoulder.

I nod and focus on the patterns on the cape covering my lap: vintage graphics of shaving creams, brushes, straps and scissors. I do not look up again until he is finished.

"What do you think?"

In my periphery, the barber holds up a mirror. I place my hands over my eyes.

"No," I say. "I don't want to look at myself until I get home."

"Dramatic much?" an elegant elderly man asks, laughing at me.

"Always," I answer. "It's sort of my signature."

I pay the owner, and he gives me another fist bump. I keep my back turned to the mirror. I avoid any reflection on my drive home, my eyes firmly on the road before me. The top is down, and I do not feel my cloud of hair whipping around my head anymore.

I park my convertible and hurry inside, praying no one sees me.

I beeline to my bedroom, turning on all of the bathroom lights, take a deep breath and look into my mirror.

My father is staring back at me.

"Hi, Dad," I say to myself. "There you are, you old son of a bitch. You've been hiding there all these years, haven't you?"

I stare at my reflection. Everything looks different: the shape of my head, my nose, my eyes, the wrinkles, the lack of a chin.

Out of habit, I grab some gel and try to style my hair. It is too short to do anything.

My safety net is gone.

I want to cry, but I laugh instead.

Hair on a head is not like the roof of a house. It is not a simple, shingled layer of protection from rain and sun. No, it is fine design, a thing of precision and beauty, an accoutrement.

I glance up.

Like a vintage Sputnik chandelier.

A home should be a reflection of your soul, who you are, how you live, how you see the world and how you want the world to see you. It should provide you beauty and comfort, but most of all, safety.

I was denied all of this and have spent my whole life trying to create it for others and myself. My life is in this home with my friends. This home is my sanctuary from the cruelty of the world.

I have only wanted to be safe my entire life.

I touch my head.

I think of Dotty so long ago.

"Higher the hair, the closer to God."

I don't know how close or far away I am from God, but I am convinced of one principle: The only thing we can do is continue to spread our wings, be good people and come as close to God as we possibly can through kindness.

I will never be a man of organized religion, but I will always be a child of faith.

I shut my eyes, and I can see my mom brushing my hair as a boy. I am seated in her lap. I am warm. I am safe.

Standing before my mirror, I finally allow myself to bid farewell to her, my childhood, my addiction, my crutch, the one thing that has ruled over me for as long as I can remember.

"It's not your hair that has kept you safe, silly, vain boy," I say to my reflection. "It's you who's kept you safe."

I lean in even closer, and it is then I can see it clearly.

I don't look like my father at all.

No: Smiling, without hair for the first time in my life, I look exactly like my mother.

I turn to leave but glance back at my new image one more time.

"Who am I kidding?" I ask my reflection, rubbing my hand over my hair. "I can't wait until this all grows back again!"

"Thanks, Jeannie!" I call to the library director as we head to our cars after my Reading Hour has ended. "I'll see you next week."

"Sure you don't want to go to lunch?" she calls.

"I need to change. I'm exercising with Esther this afternoon," I say. "And I'm Teddy's nurse tonight."

"Next time!" Jeannie waves as she departs.

I pull my cell from my pocketbook to check missed messages and head across the parking lot.

"Pedophile!"

I jump, dropping my cell.

A foot kicks it away from me.

I look up. The woman who threatened me weeks ago is back, standing in front me with a demented smile covering her face.

She is alone this time.

"You think I'm the one who's wrong?" She laughs. "I saw your disgusting interview. You blame me for being angry? This is *our* time in America, you fucking faggot. We're taking the world back from sickos and Jews like you."

I quickly glance around the parking lot. There's a woman watching us. Her eyes are wide. She grabs her cell.

In the blink of an eye, the disgruntled woman pulls a gun from behind her back.

"We must remove filth like you from the world so it is safe again for our children."

I hear a loud buzzing in my ears.

She points the gun at my head.

"I'd ask you to say a final prayer, but I know the wicked have no faith."

Everything seems to be happening in time lapse: I see each action in slow motion.

Her finger is on the trigger.

The next thing I see is my pocketbook knocking the gun out of her hand. She looks away to see where it has landed. I swing my pocketbook again, and it strikes her once, twice, until she is on the ground. I continue to beat her with my clutch.

The woman grabs me by the collar of my sweater and jostles me back and forth, choking me, until I drop the purse. She slaps at my head, face, chest.

I hear a clink on the asphalt. My grandmother's cameo that I wear as Sophia has toppled free. I grab it, turn it upside down and hold the sharp pin to her eye.

"One more move, and I will blind you, bitch, just like Samson!" I yell.

She stares at me, eyes wide, before squeezing them shut for protection.

I hear sirens approaching.

I hold her to the ground, one hand around her neck, the other holding my vintage cameo above her eye.

I may be eighty-one years old, but it's finally time, I realize, to fight for myself.

"Don't you ever fuck with an old gay man in a dress!"

"May I come in?"

Leo looks at me for a second and then says into the phone he's holding, "Can I call you back?"

He ends the call.

Leo opens the door wide and steps back, and I follow him into his living room.

"I didn't know if I was going to see you again, Sid," Leo says, gesturing for me to take a seat on the couch, but I remain standing.

Leo sits. "You didn't return any of my calls or texts. You ghosted me. At brunch with my parents. I wasn't just humiliated, Sid, I was devastated. I thought everything was going great."

I take a deep breath and then remove my wig. I collapse into a chair next to the sofa.

"I'm sorry," I say.

"Sorry is not enough," Leo says. He begins to text on his cell.

"Leo," I say.

He does not look up.

"Leo."

His eyes finally meet mine.

I tell him about what just occurred in the library parking lot.

"My God! Not again! Are you okay?" he asks. "I'm calling the police."

"I'm fine," I say, truly meaning it. "And they already came and arrested her."

"I'm so sorry, Sid."

"I know."

And then I tell him about the conversation at the restaurant with his mother.

"I'm such an idiot," he says to himself. "I should have known something was up. I cannot and will not make excuses for her."

"She loves you, Leo. She only wants what's best for you. And so did I." I hesitate. "Or I thought I did."

I sit next to him on the couch.

"I was wrong to walk away without talking to you," I continue. "But your mother is right: I am an old man, Leo. You will, hopefully, have many more years on this earth than I will. Should our relationship continue, it won't simply be filled with sunsets, wine and good health, it will have its share of struggles. But I realized today we never know how much time any of us has, and we should fight for each and every second. We should fight for love because it's so rare and so precious."

I take Leo's hand.

"That's all I wanted," he says. "For you to fight for me like I will always fight for you."

"I love you, Leo Levy."

"I love you, Sid Silverstein."

"This sounds like the start of a musical," I joke. "*Very* off-Broadway."

"No, this sounds like the start of a real relationship," Leo says. "This sounds like the start of a new life." He grips my hand. "No matter how long that may be."

He leans toward me. "I cannot believe I am about to kiss Sophia Petrillo on the lips," he says.

"Picture it! Sicily! 1932!" I say.

My cell buzzes.

I glance down. A text from Esther glows in my lap.

> Just saw the news! I'm so proud of you! I knew there was a reason we walk twice a week and do that seated workout class. As Joan Crawford used to say, "Don't fuck with me, fellas!" Sending you a coconut cake from Sherman's for taking that crazy bitch down. Kiss the Hot Jew for me.

I turn to Leo. "Kiss me," I say.

The life of an artist is not that much different than that of a teenage girl: A large portion of our lives are spent staring at the phone waiting for the one we desire to call us.

In my case—and that of most actors, writers, dancers and musicians—the voice of the one we want to hear on the end of the line is our agent's.

I stare at my silent cell as I float in the middle of our pool.

"*A watched pot never boils*," I can hear my mother and Ron say in their Southern twangs.

I turn it upside down and then pick it up again to ensure the ringer is on.

I place it on my stomach, tilt my head back and watch the world slowly spin and sparkle before my eyes.

The desert sun glints off of Zsa Zsa's windows, and I wonder if she ever waited for calls like this from her agent or one of her husbands.

I see Teddy through the window. He is moving around the house more easily now and feeling more like himself every day. He opens his robe and flashes me. I attempt to cover my eyes but am not quick enough.

Teddy flips me the bird at my reaction.

He knows I am nervous and is trying to distract me. That's what a good friend does.

I flip him off. He laughs and walks away.

I spin on my floatie. Teddy returns to the window holding up a bottle of champagne.

He is more optimistic than I am. Where did that newfound optimism come from?

A surly teen along with a big dose of hope.

I shrug my shoulders, nodding at my cell.

Teddy walks away with the bottle.

Teddy is the one who inspired this potential celebration. After talking so openly and honestly with him the other day, he inspired my idea for the project I've been waiting to write my whole life: my own screenplay, an updated version of *The Golden Girls* called—no surprise here—*The Golden Gays.* The sitcom features four best gay friends who are very much like Dorothy, Rose, Blanche and Sophia, except men of a certain age living communally in Palm Springs confronting age, illness, family, secrets and estrangement.

I know the time is right for something like this. I know the world needs to hear our voices at a time like this. I know I should be in control of my own career, not at the beck and call of someone like Kyle ever again.

And there are a lot of Kyles out there.

Mostly, I don't ever want a character like Coco to be cut again.

My cell rings, and I jump out of my skin, nearly fumbling my cell into the pool.

"Hello?"

"Do you have a second to talk?"

The seven words an artist never wants to hear from his agent. It means the agent is calling with bad news. He is buying time. He is trying to soften the blow. Otherwise, he would simply say, "Congratulations!"

"I'm too old for this horseshit, Stu," I say. "Just tell me."

"Netflix is greenlighting your project," Stu says. "There was actually a bidding war between Apple and Netflix, but Netflix came out on top. You're welcome."

For a moment, I am too stunned to speak. My whole career has been one rejection after another until now, when everything is coming up roses. My body has learned to cushion itself for a no as if I am a self-driving car that knows it's going to get into an accident and engages its airbag just before the big blow.

"Did you hear me, Barry? Netflix greenlighted *The Golden Gays*."

I still can't find the words to sum up over forty years of frustration. Instead, a single whooping cry echoes through the quiet canyon. Quail scatter from the surrounding underbrush and scoot across the desert floor.

"Congratulations!" Stu booms.

"Why didn't you just say that in the first place?" I ask. "Why did you ask me if I had a second?"

"I actually *didn't* know if you had a second to talk," Stu says. "You've been doing so much press lately."

"Tell me everything. Don't leave anything out."

For the next half hour, Stu navigates me through the process, who passed, who bid on my project, what studios loved about it and why some were hesitant to bid. He tells me Ian McKellen is interested in seeing the script, and that Neil Patrick Harris—after reading about what happened to me in the press—is interested in recreating the character of Coco.

"You know I admire the hell out of you for doing this," Stu says when he is finished, "but I still think it's a bit of a boneheaded move on your part. You turned down offers for starring roles in sitcoms that you could exec produce, you turned down wonderful supporting roles in feature films that could have made you richer than you ever imagined, and you chose this."

"It's not a vanity project, Stu."

"I know that, Barry, but it is a career-defining project," he says. "If this fails, you might be back at square one. Studios will be wary of hiring you again, and the folks who offered you roles this time might not be so willing to do so next time."

"I hear you loud and clear, but I think my whole life has led me to this," I say. "And if it doesn't work, I'll have fulfilled my dream and will happily go back to doing car commercials."

Stu laughs. "Yeah, right."

"Well, not happily," I amend. "I just want to say thank you, Stu. I know those car commercials didn't make either of us rich, and I damn well know you could have cut me at any time and never thought about me again."

"Do you know why I never did?"

"Why?"

"You refused to give up, Barry. I'll take you as a client over some of my biggest clients any day. They whine and complain because they didn't have the right Smartwater in their trailers, or only got paid two million dollars for an eighteen-minute speaking role in a film. They have zero idea how to survive when the tough times come to call, and believe me, they will come. That phone will stop ringing, and they will wither. You, my friend, are now poised to change the world because of everything you and your friends have endured. You are a survivor."

Stu whispers something to an assistant and continues.

"Run with this break, Barry. You finally you got one forty years after you became an overnight success. Control your own destiny and don't ever look back. I want to call you in a decade and tell you that the studio has renewed the show for another year. I want to call you and tell you that you've been nominated for Emmys and Golden Globes. I want the next chapter of your life to be the best because you never, ever gave up."

"Thank you, Stu."

"Don't thank me, thank yourself."

Stu's voice actually breaks a little bit.

"Are you getting emotional?" I tease.

"I'm an agent," he says, clearing his throat. "I have no

emotion. My blood runs cold and deep. I eat studio executives raw for lunch. Now go celebrate. I'll get the contract over to you ASAP. Start pulling together your writing team, because you know the studio will want to push their folks on you."

"I will."

"Bye, Barry. I love you, buddy."

My heart leaps into my throat.

"I love you, too, Stu."

I paddle to the edge of the pool, set my phone down and climb out of the water. I dry off, grab my cell and race inside to the living room. Teddy is seated in a chair watching, of course, an old episode of *The Golden Girls*. He is still holding the bottle of champagne.

I throw my arms up in victory. "Netflix!" I yell.

Nonemotional Teddy bursts into tears.

"I'm not crying, you're crying." He laughs. "Congratulations!"

Teddy pops the champagne.

We don't have glasses. Old friends don't need glasses. Teddy holds out the bottle, and I take a big swig and hand it back. He puts it to his mouth and drinks.

And drinks. And drinks.

"Leave a little for me," I say, grabbing the bottle.

"I'm rich!" Teddy yells.

I laugh and take a seat in the chair next to him.

We sit in silence for a moment, watching *The Golden Girls.*

I know this episode by heart: It's the series finale in which Blanche's uncle falls in love with Dorothy and proposes. She accepts and tries to convince her mother to move with her to Atlanta, but Sophia realizes Dorothy is finally strong enough to be on her own, and Dorothy says goodbye to the girls for the last time.

"It's okay," Teddy says.

I pivot in the chair to face him.

"I know you'll have to go," he continues. "I'm okay. We'll all be okay."

"I don't want to go," I say.

"I know, my friend. But I want you to go without any guilt. Go only with joy. Go knowing we are all still here because of one another. We will always be here." He gestures at the TV. "Sound familiar?"

I nod my head, not wanting to cry.

I take another swig of champagne.

"Damn bubbles always make my eyes water," I say.

Teddy winks.

"We have to make room for one more anyway," he says. "I think Leo will be joining us soon. Just know your bedroom will always be here waiting." Teddy smiles. "It will never be the same, but none of us are guaranteed forever. We had a good run, didn't we?"

"We had a *great* run." I lift the bottle. "A toast! To friends!"

I drink and hand the champagne to Teddy.

"To friends!" he says.

My cell rings.

"I really have to take this," I say.

"I know."

I answer.

"Oh, my gosh, what an honor to speak to you, Sir Ian! Thank you for calling."

As I walk away, Teddy calls, "Hey, movie star!"

I turn.

"You still owe me twenty bucks. Remember? You stole it from my wallet to buy Starbucks when you were poor?"

"Can you hold on for just one second?" I say into the phone.

I walk down the hall, into my bedroom, and return with thirty dollars.

"Plus interest," I say.

As I slip the bill into Teddy's hand, he grabs mine and squeezes it with all his might.

The Closing Credits

"Hi, John. It's nice to finally meet you. I'm sorry it took so long."

Trudy and I are standing in a cemetery that sits at the base of the mountain. John's grave is situated at the far end of the cemetery in the full sun.

"He always hated to be cold," I explain.

"You'll keep him warm one day," she says, nodding at the plot of earth beside John.

"I will," I say. "With my fiery charm and wit."

"These are for you, John," Trudy says. She places a bouquet of yellow roses against his granite headstone. "I hope you will forgive me."

"He already has. John was kinder than me."

"A charging bull is kinder than you."

"I've taught you well," I say.

Our eyes meet.

"I brought you a gift, too," we say at the same time, before laughing.

"You first," I say.

From the pocket of her jacket, Trudy produces a quart-sized Ziploc bag.

"Is that weed?" I ask. "You *are* becoming a Californian."

"No, it's some of Mama's ashes," she says. "I never knew exactly what to do with them." She smiles. "I do now."

"So you just kept them in a Ziploc all these years?"

"No, Teddy, I had them in a pretty jar on a shelf on the fireplace mantel in my basement," Trudy says. "Mama would've hated to have her ashes scattered in Ohio. You know how Michigan feels about Ohio." Trudy looks at the bag. "I just thought she might like to be here now . . . with us . . . forever."

"I like that, Trudy," I say. "I think she would, too."

"She deserves a little peace."

"We all deserve a little peace."

Trudy and I walk toward the base of the mountain. Trudy opens the bag, and we each grab a handful of ashes. Trudy says a prayer.

"Would you like to add something, Teddy?" Trudy asks when she finishes.

"Yes."

Trudy bows her head in prayer.

"Thank you, God, for granting me a spontaneous erection last night," I say. "Teddy's back in the game!"

"You know how to ruin a moment, don't you?"

"It's a gift," I say. "Love you, Mama."

Just as we toss her ashes into the sky, a gust of wind catches them and blows them back into our faces.

"I just ate Mama," Trudy says, coughing and spitting.

"She always had a wicked sense of humor."

We return to John's grave. I pull a box from the pocket of my jacket.

"My turn," I say. "This is for you."

She opens the box, and her eyes grow wide.

"This was Mama's Bakelite," she gushes. "Where did you get it?"

"It's the only thing I took from the house," I say.

"But why are you giving it to me?" she asks.

"Oh, I no longer wear costume jewelry," I say dramatically. "Only diamonds and pearls when you reach this age, my dear."

I help Trudy place the bracelet on her wrist.

"Look!" I say, as soon as I finish, pointing toward the mountain.

I hold Trudy's arm against the sky, the colors of the sunset matching her bracelet just like the first night I arrived back in Palm Springs after Mama died.

"Excuse me, *please*!"

I snap my fingers to stop the clamor at the Church of Mary. The crowd quiets. I adjust my patriotic bonnet and continue.

"I understand that Barry is now a star . . ." I stop to audibly gag when I say that final word. "I know that everyone is excited to see Ava and Trudy again, and you all are ready to eat, but Ron's dishes won't be getting cold in this hundred-degree heat, and there is no Church of Mary without *my* dish, so may I proceed? Thank you!"

I clear my throat.

"Well, Patty O'Furniture took me to Ride A Cowboy, that new gay country and western bar downtown, and I ended up two-stepping with some military boys from Twentynine Palms who were, let's just say, curious about our lovely town."

Barry salutes me.

"And one of our nation's fine soldiers asked me who was singing the tune we were dancing to, and since my Cher debacle—and thanks to Ava's help—I've brushed up on my pop music and knew instantly it was Sabrina Carpenter."

Ava applauds.

"Thank you. I deserve those accolades after my Chappell Roan debacle this winter," I say. "Any-hoo, this adorable young man—who I believe was hiding a rifle in his jeans—thought I said the Carpenters. I didn't have the heart to correct this man of service, he had zero interest in pop culture, it was the sweetest moment, and—long story long—I think I've fallen in love with a military man."

"Uh-huh. What was his name?" Ron asks. "John Wayne?"

"Actually, it was."

The table explodes into laughter, and it dawns on me that I was duped in the name of lust.

"Hope you enjoyed your dance," Sid says, "but I think the love of your life was just a closeted one-night stand."

"At least my gun finally discharged," I say.

"Language!" Ava yells at me with a laugh.

"Alexa," I call to our outdoor speaker, "play 'We've Only Just Begun.'"

Church of Mary groans.

I reach for the food, but Ron slaps my hand.

"Not until we pray," he scolds me. "Everyone, hold hands and bow your heads."

We do as instructed.

"Thank you, Lord, for allowing us all to be together at the Church of Mary on this beautiful summer Sunday."

"It's going to be a hundred and fifteen degrees today," I say. "Move the prayer along, Ron, before someone melts or dies."

"After that long-winded tall tale of yours!" Trudy says to me. "Ron, take as much time as you want."

"Thank you. Lord, as I was saying before I was so rudely interrupted . . ."

"Amen!" the table yells, at once shutting him down.

Ron sighs dramatically and tips his Uncle Sam hat toward heaven. Per our church's dress code, we are all wearing red, white and blue bonnets. I am sporting a vintage white felt bonnet trimmed with red lace—an American flag in the shape of a heart on the back—that Betsy Ross herself might have made and worn.

Especially if she were going to brunch with a gaggle of gays.

"Amen," Trudy adds, giving Ron a wink.

"Thank you, Trudy," he says.

"Pass the pancakes!" Barry yells.

It is the Fourth of July in the desert, which means it's hotter than a firecracker even in the shade at nine in the morning. Ron has created a red, white and blue brunch bonanza: blueberry pancakes topped with fresh strawberries and powdered sugar, a towering trifle of fresh berries between layers of homemade whipped cream, and patriotic cocktails including a strawberry frosé, a blackberry bramble and a red, white and blue(berry) margarita.

Ron brings me a margarita.

"None for me," I say.

"A sign of the apocalypse," Ava says.

"I haven't had a drink since Barry's celebratory champagne," I say, eyeing Barry. "I'm trying to go a day at a time. It's better for my health right now. And I feel better. I like waking up each morning feeling . . . happy again. Although it is not easy to walk into a gay bar sober."

"Well, I'm so psyched to stay a week out here to go on college visits and house hunt for Grandma," Ava says.

"Pool at sunset only, or you will scorch in this heat," I say. "And I want you in the shop with me learning more tricks of the trade when we're not spending your grandma's money."

"Does everyone have a tux for the TV premiere in September?" Barry asks. From underneath the table, he produces a copy of *Variety* and proudly displays it with a huge smile like a ring girl does in a wrestling match when she shows the sign displaying the number of the next round. There is a huge article about all the buzz surrounding *The Golden Gays*. "It was fast-tracked due to all the positive reviews."

"And the fact that all the stars are old," I say. "By the by, I'm wearing a vintage strapless gown." I look around the table. "I'm not joking. Have you seen the new *Queer Eye*, guys? It's very in right now. I have one from my shop. I thought the attention would be good for my business."

"I have my tux," Ron says seriously. "Custom-made Mr Turk, of course."

"We do, too," Sid says, grabbing Leo's hand. "Matching."

Everyone, even Trudy, groans audibly. I am so proud. We have taught her well.

As Barry and I predicted, Leo has moved into Zsa Zsa with Sid. Miriam and Sid made amends after she got to know him better and his fight at the library made national news and him a local hero (a surprise visit to Miriam from Esther didn't hurt either, I was told), and Leo's parents took on his lease and plan to stay in the desert through the winter to spend time with him and Sid.

Barry clears his throat to get the attention of the table again. He points to the headline of another *Variety* article, this one just below the piece on his new show.

Kyle Moses's Maybach Vandalized in Palm Springs

"I take it everyone has alibis?" Barry asks.

Everyone's heads swivel toward me as one.

"Hey, don't look at me!" I say. "I've been infirmed. I wouldn't have the energy to do something like that. I could barely two-step without assistance."

I glance at Sid and Ron.

"This old broad won her fight," Sid says.

"And I have a reputation to uphold," Ron adds.

Trudy holds up a hand. She has a sheepish expression.

"Guilty," she says.

The table howls.

"Grandma!" Ava yells.

"I followed him to Counter Reformation and pretended to be a valet," she says much too casually. "I might have had three martinis. I should have listened to you, Teddy, and stopped at one."

"Who have you turned into?" I ask.

"One of you," she says. "A friend does anything for her friends, right?"

Barry covers his ears. "I don't want to know." He looks at Trudy. "But thank you."

We eat, play croquet and take naps in the AC until dusk. Then we head to the pool and swim in water that feels like a warm bath. We position ourselves on the patio for the Fourth of July fireworks, and watch them light up the mountains from our perfect perch overlooking downtown.

When they're over, I hand out sparklers to everyone just like my mama used to do in Michigan on the nation's birthday.

We light them and dance around the yard, four old men giggling.

I stand to the side and watch my friends and family dance.

My life flashes before my eyes in blurs of light like the sparklers.

Life is pretty damn simple when you get down to it: We need friends who not only love and accept us but love and accept us just as we are.

We need friends who allow us to shine brightly in the world so our light can be seen.

When it does, we can be our true selves. We can show our faces without shame, without bruises, without masks.

Here is the thing about those of us who are different in this world: You can hate us, beat us, spit on us, laugh at us, demean us, take our rights away, but we will never disappear. Our light is too bright to diminish. We are—just like these sparklers, just like these old, dancing men—what the world needs to be just a bit more interesting.

Life is not a sitcom, but it's pretty damn close—three acts and a finale—so let me impart this last piece of advice, my dears, while I'm still around and in a giving mood:

You better learn to laugh at yourself early in life; you better learn to forgive yourself midlife; and you better have friends late in life, or you will not survive.

And I want you to survive. We *need* you to make this dramedy called life a spectacular one.

I light another sparkler and spin around in the yard until it goes dark and I grow dizzy. Then I fall onto the cool grass and watch my friends dance around the yard and laugh with unbridled joy like the children they were never allowed to be but rediscovered as old men.

We all deserve such a finale in our lives, which brings me to my last piece of advice:

It's a gift to grow old.

★★★★★

A Personal Letter to Readers

Dear Reader,

I was in college when *The Golden Girls* first premiered on TV in 1985.

That show was not meant for a nineteen-year-old frat boy.

I mean, four old women living together in a pink house in Florida? C'mon.

I was—on the surface—your stereotypical '80s frat boy: I could chug a keg beer with the best of them, I was addicted to MTV, I feathered my hair, I pulled all-nighters, I ate Domino's Pizza at midnight.

But I was also hiding a big secret: I was gay.

And I hated myself for that.

So much so that I adopted a secret persona in college that made me the life of the party. I buried my secret, much like I had buried my older brother, Todd, who had died a few years earlier in a tragic accident. I believed God had made a mistake when He took my brother; He should have taken my life instead. I believed my brother—a true country boy—would have given my parents what I believed they wanted: a family, a daughter-in-law, grandchildren.

I believed the rest of my life should be dedicated to not creating another moment of pain for my parents. They did not deserve that.

And so I lived a lie to make others happy.

And I died a little every single day until I tried to end my life and failed.

I had not wanted to go to college and leave my mother and grandmother alone. I was their best friend, and they were mine, but they both pushed me out of the nest and our small town, telling me a bigger world was waiting for me and my gifts.

"We can only go on if you do," my mom told me as she drove me to college. "Live. Dream. Love. Big!"

The only time I saw my mother cry during this time was when I watched her car pull away from my window after I moved into the freshman dorm. She thought she was out of eyesight, stopped the car, put her head on the steering wheel and wept.

My mother and grandmother used to write me letters (remember those?) every month. I would talk to them every Sunday at dinner on the pay phone (remember those?) at the end of the dorm hallway.

One of the ways I also bonded with my mother and grandmother in college was by watching—as I write about in *That's What Friends Are For*—*The Golden Girls* long-distance with them. I remember some sorority friends and little sisters in my fraternity talking about the show, and one Sunday I asked my mother and grandmother if they were watching it. They were. Of course. So, on Saturday evenings before the fraternity parties started, I'd stretch that cord of the rotary phone (remember those?) on the wall in the fraternity house until it snaked into my room and watch the show with the two women I loved most in the world, our laughter crossing the miles.

That show also—I didn't realize at the time—bridged a cavernous divide between generations. It allowed me to see my mother and grandmother in a new light. It allowed them—eventually—to understand and accept me.

What was it about *The Golden Girls*? I mean, what could four old women say that would resonate with a nineteen-year-old boy struggling to find his place in the world?

Plenty, it turns out.

Because we were the same in so many ways.

Ostracized and overlooked.

Diminished by society.

Our voices and worth dismissed.

Unlovable . . . due to age, shame, sexuality.

And yet, somehow, we found our friends and community, we bonded together, and our individual strengths made each other stronger.

Old women and the gay community, it turned out, were exactly the same.

That's What Friends Are For is all about community, be it the family you're born into or the one you create. It's about friends you've known for a lifetime and those you meet who feel as if you've known them forever.

One of the first times I went to a gay bar, it shut down its music promptly at 8:00 p.m. to play *The Golden Girls.* When the show was over at eight thirty, the music came back on.

Community.

This novel is about what I call "living in drag." We all don masks to present a certain image to society and those we love: Perhaps it is to play the perfect mom or dad, the child who doesn't want to disappoint, the spouse who puts on a smile every day despite being deeply unhappy. We do this to play a role we believe we are expected to play, and yet that is not truly who we are.

Age, life, loss, hate, honesty allow us to rip those masks off and be ourselves. But it takes a lot to overcome the fear that holds us hostage and keeps us playing pretend to the world.

Our elders and the gay community have gone through so much, and they no longer have time to play any games. And that transparency—be it Pamela Anderson without makeup or a drag queen in lots of it—is shocking to a large part of the population that has never been able to be honest with itself.

This book is painfully funny: It's about how humor connects us, knocks down walls of hatred, brings people closer or keeps them at a comfortable distance. My elders were some of the funniest people I've ever known—we grow grand oral storytellers in the Ozarks—and so is the gay community, who has overcome hatred of society and self, as well as isolation, to find our friends, and use our voices—and humor—to change the world. Why are gay men funny? The same reason *The Golden Girls* was. We've been hurt, over and over and over again, and yet we refuse to give in to that pain. We reclaim our voices through humor. It gives us strength. We understand that our commonality is found via laughter.

The Golden Girls tackled huge issues during its time on air—aging, family dynamics, friendships, LGBTQ+ issues, the search for meaning after marriage and children, mortality, fidelity, racism, depression, the HIV-AIDS crisis—and it did it all with humor. It's what I've done my entire existence in life and writing: lessen the pain with laughter. Teach and break down walls with humor.

The Golden Girls is still considered by many to be one of the most progressive shows ever to air on television, even some forty years later, and it enjoyed an epic rebound—ironically—during COVID, when so many younger people discovered the show as a way to understand what their isolated elders—many of whom would sadly die—were going through. They watched it together, as I did some forty years earlier with my mom and grandma.

In fact, my mother referenced an episode of *The Golden Girls* after I came out. That particular show—which I mention in the novel—centers on a friend of Dorothy's who reveals that she is gay. Dorothy, wrestling with that news and unable to sleep, wakes up her mother, Sophia.

Dorothy: "How would you react if you were told one of your kids were gay?"

Sophia: "I'll tell you the truth, Dorothy. If one of my kids were gay, I wouldn't love him one bit less. I would wish him all the happiness in the world."

And perhaps that episode, in some small way, paved the way to understanding not only for me but also for the acceptance of gay people when we needed it the most.

TV connects us. I grew up sitting in front of the television on Saturday mornings watching cartoons with my brother. I would race home from school, do my homework and then watch my favorite afternoon shows before my dad got home from work: *The Brady Bunch*, *The Andy Griffith Show*, *Gilligan's Island*, *Batman*, *The Partridge Family*, *The Munsters*, *Dark Shadows*, *I Love Lucy*.

But there were few characters I could relate to growing up: perfect Marcia Brady? David Partridge? Nah. Perhaps Eddie Munster. I mean, this was back in the day when my father thought Liberace was simply "a showman."

Which is why I delve into the character of Coco in *The Golden Girls*. Never heard of him? You're not alone. In the pilot episode of *The Golden Girls*, there was a lead character named Coco, who was the women's gay housekeeper and cook. He was cut from the show to make room for Sophia, who got an incredible response from early viewers. Sophia got the full-time role, and Coco got replaced. Some involved with the show blamed the kitchen: It was too small to have five people constantly featured in it. But I ask in the book: Were audiences ready for a character like Coco? So I fictionalize the life of this actor who had the role of a lifetime ripped away from him and share the struggle of a man trying to get that back his entire career. What must it have been like to be an out gay actor in a time when Hollywood was still so closeted?

Coco was played by the actor Charles Levin, who had a remarkable life and acting career, including *Alice*, *Seinfeld* and *Hill Street Blues*. My character of Barry has nothing to do with the real actor, save for the fact that both are actors and both fought—as any actor, writer, dancer, singer does—rejection and the heartbreak of Hollywood because they are driven by their craft and a dream. In writing Barry, I wanted to reimagine an actor and man who becomes so traumatized by losing out on the role of a lifetime—due to no fault of his own—that it takes an enormous toll on his personal and professional life from that point on. If anything, I hope this note encourages you to look at the brilliant work Mr. Levin did in his career. He passed away in 2019, and my heartfelt condolences are extended to his family and friends.

This novel is a HUGE departure for me in my career—my first novel under my own name—and I wrote this story not knowing what the hell was going to happen with it. Truly! This was a—*gasp?*—Viola Shipman novel?! Would I have to return the money in my contract? Would they reject the manuscript?

No and no.

My longtime editor, Susan Swinwood, reached out to me immediately. She believed this was the book I was *meant* to write. Morever—upon turning in the manuscript—she told me that the reaction to the novel from the entire publishing team was HUGE! I can never thank her enough for pushing me to follow my heart.

I've learned that sometimes the greatest moments in our lives happen when we are most terrified, as writers and souls, and that if we can just corral that fear and walk through the fire to emerge on the other side—heart racing, a bit scorched—what we dreamed of and fought so hard to achieve has the chance to change the world. I truly believe this book can change lives and even the world.

Thanks to my forever agent, Wendy Sherman, who has navigated my roller-coaster ride of a career from memoir to fiction, pen name to real name, hardcover to paperback to hardcover, champagne moment to heartbreak, without ever wavering in her belief in me as an author.

To my publicist, Kathleen Carter, who fights for me every day and every book with such grace and intelligence.

To my entire publishing team: publicists Heather Connor and Leah Morse, senior marketing managers Ashley MacDonald and Diane Lavoie, marketing manager and social media whiz Lindsey Reeder, the entire sales team and so many other people who work tirelessly behind the scenes.

I must also thank Jodi Picoult, #1 *New York Times* bestselling author and one of my all-time favorite novelists, who provided the cover endorsement for this novel. I was reaching for the moon when I asked her to blurb *That's What Friends Are For*, and I was blown out of the water when she said she would love to read it and then again when her endorsement came just a few weeks later in the middle of a Labor Day party. My sudden scream of joy brought the festivities to a halt and then made the wine flow even faster. I can never thank her enough for her support and kindness.

This novel is also dedicated to Palm Springs, which has a long and celebrated history as a haven for the gay community (as well as Hollywood stars). My husband, Gary, first went to Palm Springs on a business trip. He'd won an award for his floral, holiday and interior landscape design, and the ceremony was in the desert. He called me (I was ensconced in a Michigan blizzard at the time) as soon as he arrived. "I feel like I'm in another world," he said. Gary told me the temperature was in the seventies, and it was wall-to-wall sunshine and smelled like orange blossoms. While he was there, he booked a two-week rental for us the next winter, although we couldn't afford it. I was hooked when I stepped off the plane. There is no place like Palm Springs. It's tucked dramatically into the mountains, which change personality throughout the day. The mid-century architecture makes your eyeballs pop, but you understand when you are there how the homes fit into the landscape, a perfect duality of indoor–outdoor living. The town is old-school but also hip, modern and vibe-y.

The last night of our first winter escape to Palm Springs, Gary and I went to dinner. We followed an older couple into Melvyn's, a quintessential Palm Springs restaurant where you feel as if Sinatra might be sipping a martini at the table next to you. The older couple was holding hands. When they were seated at their table, they kissed. "We get old?" I asked Gary, half joking, half serious, not realizing that gay folks aged like the rest of the population. "We get old," Gary confirmed. "So let's get old here," I said, "where we can kiss and hold hands and never have to hide our love for one another." He cried, I cried and we ended up talking to the couple at the next table. I began to save my money to buy a home in the desert. We have wintered in Palm Springs the last twenty years. We own a home that sits tucked into the ridge of a mountain for the last decade. We have never been happier.

And if you would like to donate to a wonderful nonprofit, please check out the LGBTQ Community Center of the Desert, which I reference in the novel, at www.thecentercv.org.

Which leads me to an eternal thank-you to my husband, Gary, who has not only been my spouse but also my support system, BFF, cheerleader, chauffeur, sounding board, shoulder to cry on, coffee companion, gardener, home decorator . . . well, *everything* . . . the last thirty years. I would not be where or who I am without him. I certainly would not be an author without his unwavering support and belief.

The publication of *That's What Friends Are For* marks my twentieth year as an author. So much has changed in my life and publishing over the last two decades: I've lost my mom and dad, my mother- and father-in-law, three beloved dogs, dear friends. But I've gained a community of readers who have become like family. You share—and give—me so much joy and happiness. As I always say at every event, and am saying to you now, I know that your time and money are valuable. I know you could be anywhere else, doing anything else with your time, and for you to be here, right now, supporting me, reading me, means the world, and I will be eternally grateful for that and promise to never take it for granted. THANK YOU, FRIEND!

I'll see you next year with a new Viola holiday novel and then later with a new Wade Rouse novel. XOXO!

Wade

Discussion Guide

1. Did you watch *The Golden Girls*? What memories do you have of the show? Did you watch it with your mom or grandma? What memories do you have of watching it with them, or your family and friends?

2. Did you (re)watch *The Golden Girls* during COVID? Who did you watch it with? What did it mean to you?

3. What are your favorite TV shows? Why? What made you connect with them? Do you think TV has gotten better or worse over time?

4. So much of this novel centers around safety and community, so let's start with the safety and community of friendship: Who are your best friends? When did you meet? What do they mean to you? Why do you love them? How do they make you a better person?

5. I also explore being overlooked as a friend. Has this ever happened to you? How did you address it with your friend(s)?

6. Now let's focus on acceptance: This story centers around four gay men. Do you have gay friends, or a family member who is gay? What discrimination have they faced in their lives? How did you or your family help or hinder them? How did you handle their coming out? Do you know any gay people who have been abandoned by their families?

7. Next, age: This novel is also about four friends who are in their mid-sixties to early eighties. How does American society treat our elders today? Versus other countries? How has that changed over your lifetime, if at all? What do we need to do better for our aging populace?

8. Aging in America presents innumerable familial, ethical and financial issues and concerns. Do you have plans to live in a retirement community? Have you made plans to be cared for at home when the time comes? What did you learn from caring for your parents or grandparents? Have you, or are you, facing any medical issues? How are you and your family dealing with those?

9. Now, love: Have you ever tried to date in your later years? If so, how did you do it (friends, church, dating app)? What was that experience like? How did you feel dating as a more mature adult?

10. Staying on love: Are you close with any gay couples? What has their relationship taught you? How has their marriage changed you? (My mother once said that Gary and I had to fight harder than anyone she's ever known to find true love, and that fight led us not to settle for anything less in life or love.)

11. Let's move to community: Palm Springs has long been a haven for the gay community, an accepting, loving safe

spot in a world that has often shown us rejection and hatred. Do you have a community that is fully accepting of YOU? Where is that? What does it mean to you?

12. Part of community is home: For many gay men and women, home was not a safe, welcoming, accepting environment. As I write in this novel, I had countless friends who were kicked out of their homes, or faced verbal and physical abuse, at an early age and struggled to find love, acceptance and—specifically—home. What was your childhood like? Do you have fond memories of it and your childhood home? Why? Why not? Did you seek a home and a place that reminded you of your childhood and family, or did you choose a place that reminded you nothing of your past? Discuss this happiness, and this trauma.

13. Let's directly discuss safety in America: For many in the LGBTQ+ community, as well as for many women, America is a more unsafe, unwelcoming and unaccepting place to live than it was even a few years ago. Why do you think it's more unsafe? What can we do to ensure the protections and happiness for our most vulnerable communities?

14. I also broach the topic of sex in this novel, especially how it's "used" in today's society. For instance, Barry used sex for revenge and money, and then found himself being exploited. Talk about power and sex in relationships and society.

15. I also broach sex in the gay community and how difficult it is to be considered attractive or sexy in a social media–and app-obsessed world that values physical perfection and casts disdain on aging faces and bodies. For instance, Sid, at eighty-one, has never truly been in love, never experienced sex when in love and feels as if he is not attractive in

the gay community. Do you consider yourself to be unattractive or unsexy, and if so, why? Are you uncomfortable being intimate? How do we find beauty in our aging faces and bodies? How do we tune out the media's constant focus on younger, hotter, prettier, to reveal our own beauty?

16. Finally, I look at community and safety through rituals and practices. For instance, drag queens and drag shows have long been a proud and celebrated part of the gay community. The reasons are long and storied, but it's a way to celebrate our "fabulousness," "fierceness" and style. Ironically, there has been pushback in society that DQs (as we call them) are harmful to children and morals, despite the fact that over-the-top role models have long been a part of our children's education (TV, movies, etc.) and that drag shows are now among the most popular destinations for bachelorette parties. First, discuss the rituals in your life and community that not only provide safety but also are a testament to your history and life. Now discuss why there is such pushback today against things like drag shows and drag queen reading hours for children. Are we truly worried about our children, or are we simply uncomfortable with ourselves?

17. Discuss (as I do in the book) how to stand up against bullies. Discuss (as I do in the book) how to combat book banning in the US.

18. What are you doing to make the world a better, safer place?

Thank You for Being *My* Friend!